WILD HONEY

Carolyn Lampman

RED CANYON PRESS

WILD HONEY

Formatting: Wild Seas Formatting
(http://www.WildSeasFormatting.com)

Published by
RED CANYON PRESS
4530 W. Mountain View Dr.
Riverton, WY 82501

Dedication

To Bethany and Russell who are the light of my life. My children are truly my gift from God.

At first we live in fantasy
The future pure and open wide,
A journey just begun you see,
Nothing there to hide.

The burden of truth sneaks in
With silly facts and such,
But things will never be the same,
Suddenly, it seems,
You just know too much.

Louis R. Lampman 12/16/17

CHAPTER ONE

"**A**re you sure the satchel's up here, Papa?" Alaina's voice drifted down from the loft.

The blacksmith looked up and grinned. "*Ja*, I'm pretty sure it is. I remember your mama putting it up there when Grandpa still owned the shop. Nobody's used it since."

"That's because nobody in this town ever goes anywhere." There was a grunt, then the sound of crates sliding along the wooden floor. Garrick Ellinson watched the dust drift down from the ceiling for a moment, then shook his head and went back to work.

"I'll bet there isn't a satchel or a valise to be found in this whole blasted town," Alaina grumbled.

"Better not let Mama hear you talking like that. She'll wash your mouth out."

"I know, I'm sorry. It's just so frustrating. Nobody ever wonders what the rest of the world is like."

"That's because this is their world. Just about everybody in Nerstrand was born here," Garrick pointed out.

"Everybody but me."

"*Ja*, except you and your mama."

"But Mama's happy here, and I'm...Aha!" There was a sudden triumphant cry from above. "Here it is."

A worn satchel came sailing out of the loft and landed on the floor with a dull thud and a cloud of dust.

Garrick winced. "Be careful, Alaina. That satchel is older than you are."

A moment later, his daughter's grinning countenance appeared at the top of the ladder. "I know, and the last time it was used was to transport my baby clothes from South Pass City to Nerstrand. I was just testing it, Papa. If it can't take a fall like that it will never survive the trip to Wyoming." She tucked her skirt between her legs, grabbed a rope that hung from the center beam, and slid down it to the floor below with the ease of long practice.

Garrick hid a grin as he stuck the piece of iron he'd been working back into the forge. "A young lady would use the ladder," he said with mock severity.

"And she'd still be coming down that ladder instead of standing here talking to you." Alaina stripped off the leather work gloves and tucked them into a cubby-hole on the wall. "The rope is much faster. Besides, Mama wasn't here to see, and you don't care." She picked up the satchel and looked it over, testing the seams and the handles to make sure all was secure. "There, you see, everything is fine other than the clasp sticks a little."

"I promised Jan Andersen I'd have his plow shares for him by closing time, but this is the last one. I can probably fix your clasp as soon as I finish."

"That's what I figured. You can fix anything, Papa." She pursed her lips as she gave the satchel a speculative look. It might even be presentable if I get some of that dirt off. Where's the saddle soap?"

"Over by the harnesses," Garrick said. "I thought we were discussing you acting like a lady."

"Oh, but Papa," Alaina said, batting her eyes at him, "I can be as much a lady as any of them if I choose." With her right hand on her hip and her left held delicately aloft, she sashayed across the room with an exaggerated sway of her hips.

Garrick watched her with a fond smile. Even in the dim light of the smithy, with dirt streaked across one cheek and the carefully constructed hair knot listing to one side, his Alaina was a beauty. And that, of course, was the problem. She had grown up in a town where everyone knew her; a place where she took safety and security for granted. Tomorrow she was going out into the real world, and she had no idea of the dangers that lurked there, especially for a girl...no... a woman who looked like Alaina.

"You won't tell Mama about me sliding down the rope, will you, Papa? She'll just use it for another excuse not to let me go."

"Mama's worried about you. This trip has her all tied up in knots."

"But, Papa, I'm going to see Angel. Besides being my Godmother, she's Mama's very best friend in the whole world!"

"It's not Angel Mama is worried about, it's the big cities you'll be going through and all that time on the train. Wyoming is a long way from Minnesota."

"I know, but it's not like I'm going by myself," she reminded him. Then she made a face. "I still can't believe Angel is sending her brother Jared here to get me," she said. "The last time I saw him, he was a little weasel."

Garrick chuckled as he took the plowshare out and laid it on his anvil again. "That was thirteen years ago, Alaina. He was just a boy; now he's a full-grown man."

"All right, so he's probably a full-grown weasel."

"I hope you didn't tell Mama that."

Alaina bit her lip. "I may have complained about the time he tied my braids to the doorknob."

"What did she say?"

"She laughed and reminded me that he came back and let me go right away. Then she gave me a long lecture on how lucky I was that he was on his way home from New York and was willing to go so far out of his way to pick me up and escort me to Laramie. If I couldn't be properly grateful, then maybe I'd better not go at all." She sat down on a sawhorse with a thump. "Papa, what is she afraid of?"

Garrick smiled and pounded the edge of the hot iron. "That her little girl is growing up and won't need her anymore."

"I'm eighteen. I haven't been a little girl for a long time. Besides, she'll be so distracted, she'll hardly know I'm gone."

"Oh? What do you think is going to distract her that much?"

"Let's see, there's Patrick, Knute, Lars, Jan, Garth," Alaina said ticking her siblings off on her fingers, "and of course baby Mary, who's a full-time job all by herself."

"*Ja*, and Mama won't have you around to help with them. She says you're the best helper a mother ever had, and so do all the other women in this town."

Alaina shrugged. "I like children, especially babies." The only sound in the smithy was the ring of Garrick's hammer and the soft scratch of cloth against leather. This was Alaina's favorite place in the whole world. She loved everything about it; the cinders on the floor, hot metal hissing in the slag trough, the acrid smell of sulfur, and the loft with all its mysterious treasures. Most of all, she loved the sound of the hammer against the anvil, and the man who made it. No matter how upset or angry she was, the sound of Papa's hammer and his deep unruffled voice would soothe her jangled nerves. Yet today, even that failed to calm her.

"Papa, is where I'm going part of the reason Mama is so edgy about this trip?

Garrick held up the piece of metal and studied it. "I think that's part of it. Wyoming wasn't a very happy place for your mama."

"But that's where she met you, and where I was born."

He flashed his daughter a grin and thrust the metal back into the fire. "*Ja*, maybe that's the problem. Maybe she thinks some big Norwegian is going to sweep you off your feet."

Alaina gave a very unladylike snort. "If that were going to happen, it would have by now. Big Norwegians are a dime a dozen around here. Besides, nothing would make her happier than if I married one of them and settled down in Nerstrand."

"Maybe so, but she knows it wouldn't make you happy, and that's what's most important to her."

"It would kill me!" Alaina said. "I crave adventure. I want to see the world." She gave a dramatic shudder. "I'll suffocate if I have to stay here."

"I know." He pulled the share out of the fire. "And that's why Mama will let you go, even though she'd rather keep you here safe and sound."

Alaina looked surprised. "I didn't think Mama understood. She's perfectly content right here with you and the boys."

"She doesn't understand- not really- but she knows you are different and accepts that."

"Sure she does. That's why she worries more about me than the rest." Alaina removed the top of the saddle soap can with an angry twist. "If it were Patrick or Knute going, she wouldn't give it a second thought."

He tapped on the edge of the share, putting in just the right curve. "Boys are different than girls. She'll be the same when Mary is your age."

"No, it's because I'm just plain different." Alaina scrubbed the leather of the satchel fiercely. "I'm not like anybody else in
Nerstrand."

"You don't have an enemy in this town."

"No, but I know what they say behind my back." Alaina put her hand to her chest in mock horror. "Did you hear what Alaina Ellinson pulled this time?" she said in a scandalized falsetto. "Why, I can hardly believe she's Garrick and Becky's daughter."

Garrick chuckled. "I didn't know you could imitate your Aunt Kirsten so well." He smoothed the final edge, held it up for inspection, then plunged it into the trough of cold water. "You're full of high spirits, and not a soul holds it against you. Even Kirsten is proud of the way you stand up for yourself." Garrick rose to his feet, and crossed the room to open the shutters.

"But Mama worries about it, I can tell, almost like she afraid I'll do something really stupid or hurtful." Alaina frowned down at the leather. "It has something to do with the reason she hates Wyoming, doesn't it?"

Bright sunlight flooded the normally dim interior of the smithy, but he seemed oblivious to it as he stared unseeing at the street outside. He was silent so long Alaina didn't think he was going to answer. "*Ja*," he said finally. "It does."

"Then tell me what the big secret is. If it has something to do with me, and it obviously does, I have the right to know."

Garrick gave a heavy sigh and turned away from the window. "I think so too, but it's not mine to tell."

"Who will tell me, then? Mama?"

Garrick nodded as he took the satchel from her hands and inspected the catch. "When she is ready, she will."

"How do you know she will?"

"She has promised me. Mama has never broken a promise to me yet." He sat down next to her and worked the catch. "Go get me that penknife from the workbench."

Alaina was incredulous. "You've discussed this with her?"

He nodded, took the knife from her hand and gently inserted the blade into the catch. "But she is stubborn like her daughter. I have learned not to push either one of you when you get like that." He grinned up at her. "I think you are both part mule."

"So, I'm supposed to just sit and wait until she's ready to tell me?"

"If you're smart, you will. Maybe when you come back from this trip, and she sees how grown up you are, she will realize it's time."

"And in the meantime?"

"In the meantime, you'll have your adventure."

"What if I went home right now and asked her?"

"I think you'd be very sorry. You don't want to upset Mama any more than she already is. It's going to be hard enough for her to let you go without bringing up things she wants left buried."

"Are you sure that's for the best?"

Garrick gave an emphatic nod of his head. "Positive. Do you know how I have managed to live with your mother for nineteen years and survive? By knowing when to keep my mouth shut and not bring her wrath down on my head!"

Alaina gave a gurgle of laughter. Stubbornness aside, there was no one sweeter or more biddable than Becky Ellinson. "I'm going to tell her you said that."

"And she will tell you it's true. There," he said, flipping the catch several times then handing her the satchel. "Get some lard from Mama to grease that down a little and it will be good as new."

Alaina held it up and admired the finished product. "It doesn't look too bad, does it?"

"Like you just bought it," he assured her.

"Garrick," called a voice from the doorway. "Thought I'd stop by and see if you've got the plow shares for me."

"Just finished the last one."

Jan Anderson smiled when he saw the blacksmith was not alone. "Well, hello, Alaina. I didn't see you there."

"Good afternoon, Mr. Andersen. How is Mrs. Andersen?"

"Baking cookies when I left home. She said if I saw you to send you on by."

"Tell her I'd love to, but I have to go home and pack. I'm leaving for Wyoming tomorrow."

"Well, well, all the way to Wyoming! Looks like you're finally going to get your great adventure."

"*Ja*, if she doesn't have second thought and decide to stay home."

"Fat chance!" Alaina said scooting toward the door. "Give my love to your wife, Mr. Andersen, and tell her I'll take her up on those cookies when I get back. Papa, when shall I tell Mama you'll be home?"

"Oh, half an hour or so."

"All right. Bye now." She blew her father a kiss and gave Mr. Andersen a cheery wave.

Late spring was usually her favorite time of the year, but Alaina was barely aware of the beautiful afternoon and the scent of lilacs as she considered the odd conversation she'd had with her father. What great secret could her mother be keeping from her? She pondered the possibilities for a few minutes then gave a prosaic shrug. Papa was right; Mama would tell her when she was good and ready. She'd lived eighteen years without knowing it; another couple of months wouldn't make that much difference.

Always able to put unpleasant thoughts out of her mind, she pushed the mystery aside and turned her attention to the upcoming trip. As long as she could remember she'd dreamed of leaving, and now it was really going to happen. She gave a little skip of joy then hurried toward home, her step light, and her heart full of anticipation.

Alaina was nearly skipping by the time she reached home and rushed into the big airy kitchen. "I'm back, Mama."

"Did you find that old satchel?" Her mother's voice came from the sitting room at the front of the house.

"Yes, it was right where Papa said it was. He fixed the catch, and I cleaned it up with saddle soap."

"Are you all set to go otherwise?"

"I think so." She walked into the front room and

held up the satchel for inspection. "Papa says it looks brand new."

Becky smiled. "Other than being a few decades out of date, it does."

Alaina cocked her head and listened intently. "Sounds like baby Mary is awake and hungry. She probably needs to be changed, too. I'll go get her for you."

Alaina walked into the bedroom she shared with her baby sister and tossed the satchel on the bed. "Hello, sweetie." She bent over the cradle. "I'm going to miss you most of all," she admitted, and then made a face. "But I won't miss your diapers."

With the efficiency of much practice, Alaina changed Mary's diaper and dressed her in a fresh gown. She was rewarded with a toothless grin and a string of baby gibberish. Alaina laughed and tweaked one of Mary's dark curls.

"You look just like Mama when you do that." She smiled down at the miniature version of her mother. Mary was the only one of the children who had taken after Becky. All five boys were the spitting image of their father with their strapping bodies and white blond hair. Alaina didn't look like either of them, but the old folks said she'd probably inherited her honey-colored hair and willowy build from her Irish grandmother's side of the family.

Alaina picked Mary up with a hug and a kiss. She walked back into the front room still cuddling her sister. "How come babies are so soft, Mama?"

Smiling, Becky set her mending aside and began to unbutton her blouse. "I don't know for sure, but it's one of the best things about this age." She took Mary and settled the baby against her breast.

Alaina draped the blanket over them with a soft smile. Sometimes she could hardly wait for one of her own. Most girls her age were already married, but she knew that way lay the destruction of her dreams. Babies could wait. "Papa said he'd be home in half an hour. I'll go start supper before I pack."

"May as well go do your packing now," Becky said with a resigned sigh. "The boys all went fishing so there's no reason to start supper for a while yet. They won't be able to tear themselves away until dark."

With her earlier excitement surging through her, Alaina returned to her bedroom and pulled her extra underwear out of the bureau she shared with baby Mary. This time tomorrow she'd be on her way to Wyoming...the Wild West...it just didn't get any more exciting than that!

It took little time to gather her belongings, and she soon turned her attention to the satchel. She opened the clasp and eyed the inside with satisfaction. There was plenty of room. She would travel in her best dress and carry her coat. Everything else would fit into the satchel easily. There would even be room for her everyday dress and nightgown in the morning before she left For once, she was glad her mother hadn't let her buy a fashionable bustle. It would never have fit.

As she looked down into the satchel, she noticed a piece of heavy paper protruding from the bottom as though the lining had popped loose. She bit her lip. Maybe tossing it down from the loft hadn't been such a great idea after all.

Alaina looked up when she heard the front door and smiled at the sound of her father's voice. Half an hour on the dot. Good, now that he was home, he'd help Mama with baby Mary. She had plenty of time to stitch up the tear. It only took a moment to retrieve a needle and thread from her sewing kit and settle herself on the bed.

When Alaina reached down into the satchel, she discovered what she thought was the underlining was actually a piece of heavy paper. It took a little wriggling, but she finally managed to pull it loose. As she lifted it to the light, she was surprised to see it was an envelope. Curiously, she opened it and pulled out an old photograph.

A quiver of shocked recognition skittered through her as she stared at the handsome young man in the army uniform. He might have been Alaina's twin brother. The blond hair, the light-colored eyes, even the shape of his face was the same as hers. Who was he? An uncle perhaps, or her grandfather?

There was only one way to find out for sure. Alaina set the satchel aside and walked to the kitchen where she could hear her parents talking. Garrick sat with his chair against the wall bouncing a giggling baby Mary on his knee as Becky put a pan of rolls in the oven. They both looked up when Alaina came in.

"Finished packing already?" Garrick asked.

"Almost. You were right about me not tossing that satchel. The lining ripped a little." She glanced at the picture in her hand. "I found this photograph in the bottom. Who is it?"

Becky reached for it. "Let's see." At the first glance, the color drained from her face, and she gave a sharp cry of dismay.

"What is it, Becky?" Garrick asked, shifting baby

Mary more securely onto his lap.

"C...Cameron," she whispered staring at the picture as if it were a poisonous snake.

"Oh, Lord." Garrick exhaled as though the weight of the world rested on his shoulders. "It's time, Becky."

"No!" She raised her stricken gaze to his. "Oh no, Garrick, I'm not ready."

"It's too late for that now. She knew something was up the minute she saw that picture."

Alaina looked back and forth between them, and her uneasiness grew. "Does this have anything to do with Mama's Wyoming secret?"

Becky gasped and cast her husband a disbelieving look. "You told her?"

"No, but it's way past time that she knew. I promised I would let you be the one, but if you don't tell her, I will."

Becky sank down onto a chair with a strangled sob and covered her face with her hands. "I can't."

Garrick closed his eyes, the muscles working in his jaw as though he were in great pain.

"Papa?" Alaina asked in a frightened voice. She'd never seen her parents like this.

Garrick opened his eyes, and looked at her as though memorizing her face. "The man in the picture is Cameron Price," he said finally. His Norwegian accent was noticeably thicker than usual, the way it always was when he got upset. "He's your father."

Alaina wondered for a moment if she was going to be sick as the earth rocked beneath her feet. Her brain seemed frozen. "You're not?"

He shook his head regretfully. "No, Alaina, I'm not."

"Yes, you are!" Becky cried, dropping her hands and

glaring at him. "Cameron may have fathered her but he is *not* her father. A father stays around and takes care of his children. They don't leave without a word in the middle of the night."

"Mama was married before?" Alaina could barely force the words past her lips."

"No, he never married me. He just left me there to face it all alone."

"Cameron was in the army," Garrick explained. "He didn't know your mother was pregnant when he was reassigned."

"Didn't care, you mean," Becky said with bitter reproach.

Alaina gasped. "Then I'm a b—"

"No!" The word was explosive and came from both parents at once.

"Don't even say the word, Alaina. Mama and I were married a good six months before you were born. You're as legitimate as any of the rest."

Alaina's head swam alarmingly, and she sat down across from her mother with a thump. "Why did you lie to me? Why did you make up that stupid story about me being born in a blizzard, and Papa having to deliver me?"

"Oh, no, Sweetheart." Becky reached across the table to touch her daughter's fingers. "That was all true, every word, I swear." Hurt filled her eyes when Alaina pulled her hand away and her voice hardened. "Garrick became your father when he brought you into the world. I told him that on the day you were born and haven't changed my mind since. He's your father as surely as he is baby Mary's."

"Alaina has a right to know about her *real* father,"

Garrick said gently.

"You *are* her real father, Garrick. If you hadn't rescued me, she would never have lived. What did Cameron ever do for her other than leave?"

"He didn't even know she existed until she was eight months old," Garrick said. "And then she fascinated him."

"Only because she looked like him. He didn't care a fig for her otherwise. Besides, I wouldn't be surprised if he became an outlaw or something."

"I doubt it," Garrick said. "He probably stayed in the army where he could be sure of finding lots of action. I imagine he's made General by now."

"Cameron Price was an irresponsible adventurer," Becky insisted. "I can't think he's much different now than he ever was. Maybe he got himself killed in the Indian Wars out West."

Completely bewildered, Alaina grasped onto the one comprehensible fact in a sea of confusion. "You mean he may still be alive?"

Garrick nodded slowly. "As far as we know he is, though Mama's right about the Indian Wars. Knowing Cameron, he was in the thick of things."

Alaina was stunned. "You knew him too?"

"Everybody in South Pass knew him. He was a bone fide Civil War hero."

"I...I don't understand," Alaina said. "What happened to him? Where is he now?"

Becky frowned. "I don't know where he is, and I don't care. Cameron Price is ancient history."

"But, he's my father," Alaina said, in a dazed voice.

"Oh, for...Garrick Ellinson is ten times the father Cameron Price would have been. You should be thanking your lucky stars he was there when Cameron walked out on us without a backward glance."

Alaina hardly heard her mother as she picked up the photograph and gazed at it in sudden sick comprehension. "That's why I'm different; why I never really fit in here."

"Balderdash, you're no different than you were half an hour ago! It's that treacherous man and this detestable picture that's turned your head." Furious now, Becky grabbed the photograph and tore it in half as she stood up. "I don't know why I didn't do that eighteen years ago when he gave it to me," she said, as she lifted the stove lid and threw it inside. "As far as I'm concerned the subject of Cameron Price is closed."

With an inarticulate cry, Alaina jumped to her feet and ran out of the house.

"Oh, little one, I wish you hadn't done that," Garrick said, as the sound of Alaina's running footsteps faded. "That picture was all she had of her real father."

Becky made a rude noise. "A father she didn't even know existed fifteen minutes ago."

Garrick sighed. "Just because she didn't know about him doesn't make him any less important to her. All you accomplished was to set up her hackles and send her off in one of her snits."

Becky raised her fingers to her lips in dismay. "Oh, Garrick. Jared Brady will be here to pick her up in the morning. What are we going to do?"

"We're going to let her go to Wyoming."

Becky stared at her husband. "We can't let her leave when she's so upset."

"I don't think we could stop her. You know how she is once she sets her mind to something."

"What if she runs into Cameron?"

"I doubt that she will. The West is a big place. Anyway, I have always said she has the right to know her real father," he repeated stubbornly.

"Garrick, he left me alone and pregnant. If it hadn't been for you, I'd have died long before she was even born. Have you forgotten that?"

"No, but it won't matter to Alaina. She'll want to know the other half of what she is."

"I'll tell her exactly what Cameron is," Becky said angrily.

"And she'll decide you're lying. Alaina has to find out for herself."

"You're just going to let her leave?"

"Yes, and she'll come back."

"What if she doesn't?"

"Then I'll be very surprised. Part of Alaina is Cameron, but mostly she's like you. She'll see that soon enough."

"Are you sure? If she finds Cameron, he'll turn on that silver-tongued charm of his and fill her head full of all sorts of nonsense."

"Which she'll see through just like you did. Don't you see, Becky? We have no choice. If we force her to stay, she'll only resent us all the more. This way, at least we leave the door open for her to come back."

"What I see is that damnable Norwegian logic of yours is going to let our daughter walk straight out of our lives," Becky snapped. "I suppose the next thing you'll tell me is I should help her pack."

"It might not be a bad idea."

"Oooo." With a final glare, Becky spun on her heel and left.

With a deep sigh, Garrick gazed down at his infant daughter and rubbed his thumb gently across the tiny hand that gripped his finger. Then he leaned his head back against the wall, closed his eyes, and swallowed against the hard knot in his throat.

CHAPTER TWO

Alaina rushed blindly from the house and the truth that twisted her heart. The entire fabric of her life was a lie. Garrick Ellinson, the man she had loved her whole life, was no part of her. The blood of a complete stranger flowed in her veins. No wonder she didn't look or act much like anyone in her family.

She slowed suddenly as she realized where she was heading. Unerringly, her steps had taken her toward the blacksmith shop. The smithy meant her father, solid and sensible; the one who always helped her sort through the confusion in her life. Only this time, he was part of the confusion.

With a whimper, she spun on her heel and changed her direction toward the woods at the edge of town. The forest soon closed over her in soothing welcome. She could hear splashing in the pond just beyond the trees and the sound of male laughter. Apparently, the fishing trip had turned into a skinny-dipping party.

A deeper voice caught her attention. Sven was there too? She swerved toward the sound. Sven was more than her cousin; he was her best friend.

"Sven?" she called.

Through the trees, she could see flashes of skin as the few brothers and cousins who had been sunning themselves on the bank made a mad dash for the water to join the rest. Served them right for going swimming so early in the year.

"Don't come over here, Laine." Sven's voice sounded panic stricken.

"Can I talk to you?"

There was a moment of silence. "All right, give me a minute."

Alaina turned her back to give him privacy as he scrambled into his clothes. They had swum together when they were children, as naked as the day they were born. But that ended several years ago when they suddenly became self-conscious around each other. Though there were some things they didn't share anymore, their friendship had continued unabated. If anybody could help her sort things out, it was Sven.

It wasn't long before he appeared, tucking his shirt into his pants. "Is something wrong?"

As Alaina gazed up at him she felt a lump in her throat. Of all her cousins, Sven was the only one who matched Garrick for size and bore more than a passing resemblance to his uncle. For the first time, it occurred to her she'd lost more than the man she had always thought was her father; she had lost Garrick's entire family. Sven was no more her cousin than Jared Brady. Against her will, she felt her eyes fill with tears.

"Laine, what's the matter?" Sven asked with growing concern when he saw the moisture in her eyes. "What's happened?"

"I...I found a picture and...and..." To Alaina's horror, the tears overflowed, and her voice quavered pathetically. She closed her eyes and tried valiantly to stop the tears from falling. Her uncontrollable habit of bawling like a baby at the slightest provocation was the one trait she hated above all others.

After a moment, Sven put his arms around her and

patted her back clumsily. "It's all right, Laine. Ma says it's good for a girl to cry if she needs to."

His sympathy was all she needed. The dam broke and a torrent of emotion poured forth as she sobbed the story out against Sven's broad chest. Somewhere along the way she stopped crying, but even telling her best friend didn't lessen her anguish.

When she finished at last, Sven stood still for a long time staring at the air over her head. Finally, he looked down at her. "Are you all right now?"

"I think so."

He released her and sat on a nearby boulder. "It doesn't sound like Uncle Garrick and Aunt Becky. There must be more to the story than they told you."

"Probably, but Mama refuses to talk about it and Papa... Garrick says it's her story to tell."

"Where's the picture?"

"Mama tore it up and threw it in the fire."

"I would like to have seen it." He glanced up at her with a slight smile. "I can't imagine a man who looks like you."

"I'll never forgive Mama for throwing it away," Alaina said dramatically. "I hardly got to look at my father before it was gone."

"I suppose you're planning to look for your real father while you're in Wyoming, then?"

Alaina stared at him in astonishment. "How did you know that?"

"Because I know you," he said with a grin. "Remember the time you decided to build a lean-to and live outside all winter because your mother said it was high time you started acting like a girl?"

"She said it was time I realized I couldn't be a boy,"

Alaina corrected him. "I was going to prove I could do anything a boy could."

"And now you're going to find your real father and prove she was wrong about that too."

"I suppose you think it's a crazy idea."

Sven raised an eyebrow. "Would it matter if I did?"

"No."

He chuckled. "I didn't think so. Anyway, Wyoming seems like a good place to start. If he's in the army, he might even still be there."

"I'll bet my godmother knows him too," Alaina said, much struck by the idea. "She was in South Pass City when I was born."

"If nothing else, you may be able to find out where he went after he left."

"And Angel probably knows the whole story and will tell me what happened! Oh, Sven you are the best of cousins," she cried giving him a big hug.

He reached out and touched her cheek. "Except I'm not your cousin am I, Laine?"

Her face fell. "No, I guess not."

They stared at each other for a long moment; then he gave her a crooked grin. "You know, I think I might like that," he said pensively.

Alaina blinked. "You don't want to be my cousin?"

"As cousins we can't ever be more than friends. This way who knows what might develop? Maybe we'll even fall in love."

"Fall in love?" Alaina was flabbergasted. The idea of being in love with Sven had never even crossed her mind. "Do you think we might?"

He shrugged. "Who knows? We've done everything else together. Can't you imagine us married?"

Alaina tried to conjure the image in her mind. "No, not really," she said slowly.

"Neither can I."

Startled, she glanced at him and caught the telltale gleam in his eyes. "You were teasing me!" she said, smacking his shoulder.

"Well, maybe a little." He grinned. "I don't have any trouble imagining you telling me what to do."

She giggled. "Or chasing you around with a rolling pin."

"*Ja*, that too."

Suddenly they were both laughing and Alaina felt her mood lighten for the first time since her world crumbled around her. "Oh, Sven, you always make me feel better."

"Do you want me to come with you?"

"You mean to Wyoming?" she asked in surprise.

"You'll need help if you're going to look for your real father."

"What about your job with the stage company?"

He shrugged. "I could find another when we got back."

Alaina felt a stab of guilt. Sven loved his job with the stage company. He had already moved up from stableman to ticket seller and there was every indication that he would make station master eventually. Yet here he was offering to give it all up for her. "I'll be fine. Jared Brady will escort me out safely enough, and Angel can probably help me locate Cameron Price once I get there."

"Last week you were spitting fire because you had to travel with Jared Brady."

"I'm only going to be with him a few days before we get to Laramie, and it's not like we're going to be alone."

"You're not?"

"He's taking a friend's daughter and her maid back to Wyoming, too. Angel said we could all chaperone each other."

"Well then I guess you don't need me," Sven said with a relieved sigh. "But if you change your mind..."

"I know, Sven, and I appreciate it." Alaina smiled a little sadly. Sven had no taste for adventure; it was the one thing they had never agreed on. He was willing to stay right here in their hometown forever just like everyone else.

Alaina crossed her arms over her chest and rubbed her arms as she thought of the incriminating photograph that had shattered her image of herself. She had always wondered why she was so different from the rest of her family; now she knew.

Alaina stayed away until after dark and then went straight to her room without talking to either of her parents. After tossing and turning all night, she was no closer to understanding or acceptance than she had been the night before. What would everyone in town think if they knew the truth? Sven would never tell, of course. Still, dark secrets like hers tended to creep out into the light of day when you least expected them to. Somewhere in the hours before dawn, a new worry surfaced. What if everyone in town already knew? Had they been talking behind her back and secretly laughing at her all along?

She awakened to the sound of her mother puttering around in the kitchen at dawn. Any other morning, she'd have risen and gone to help put breakfast on the table for the hungry Ellinson brood. This morning she lacked the courage to face her mother. She finished her last-minute packing, then changed and dressed baby Mary for the day.

By the time the two sisters entered the kitchen, Garrick was already gone and Becky was occupied cooking pancake after pancake for her lively sons. Neither woman spoke as Alaina prepared baby Mary's breakfast and sat down to feed her. Alaina and her mother usually jabbered back and forth like a couple of magpies, but today the silence hung over them like a giant black cloud. A lump formed in Alaina's throat, but she didn't know the words that would mend the breach between them. She was feeding baby Mary her last spoonful when she heard Garrick talking to someone outside.

"Sounds like Jared's here," Becky observed with a sigh. "I'll finish with baby Mary. You'd better get your things. I'm sure he won't want to be kept waiting."

"No, I don't guess he will." Alaina stopped for a moment in the doorway of the room she shared with baby Mary. Suddenly it seemed wrong to leave her parents this way with so much hurt between them. "Mama?" she said.

"Yes?" Becky paused in the middle of wiping baby Mary's face to look up at her eldest child.

"I...I..." The words she wanted to say seemed to stick in her throat like the nettles of a thistle and the sting of tears burned her eyes.

"What is it, Alaina?" Becky asked softly.

"Nothing really. I just forgot to tell you I didn't get the butter churned yet this morning."

Becky's face fell and she turned back to the baby. "That's all right. I'll get one of the boys to do it."

Alaina nodded then turned and walked into her

bedroom for the last time. As she shoved her nightgown into the battered satchel, she heard Jared come into the kitchen. He sounded nothing like the scornful youth she remembered as he chatted comfortably with her mother and cheerfully answered her brothers' questions. Of course, thirteen years ago he'd classified her as a baby right along with his sister Betsy who was nearly the same age she was.

A fleeting smile crossed Alaina's face as she picked up her satchel. Come to think of it, she'd changed a trifle herself. She'd been missing most of her front teeth and was covered with freckles. The gaps and freckles had long ago disappeared, left behind with dolls and the other trappings of childhood. Jared would have a hard time finding the little girl who'd tagged along behind, asking incessant questions and irritating the devil out of him.

Pasting a welcoming smile on her face, she stepped out into the kitchen. "Hello, Jared. It's been a long time..." The words froze on her lips as she looked past their guest straight into the aquamarine eyes of Garrick Ellinson. She dropped her gaze, unable to bear the pain she saw reflected there. Unbidden, she focused on the huge callused hands that hung forlornly at his sides.

A dozen images of those hands tumbled through her mind. As a tot, she'd squealed with delight when they swung her high up on his shoulders. When she was six, they taught her to fish, patiently untangling her line a dozen times a day. They fashioned her first pair of skis and lovingly built the beautiful maple hope chest she was leaving behind with all her treasures inside. More than any other feature, his hands personified the man; strong enough to bend an iron bar, yet gentle enough to dry the tears of a child or cradle an injured bird.

And there were scars, dozens of them, some put there by the hot metal from his forge, others by the sharp blades of his wood-working tools. With a sudden twist of anguish, Alaina realized none of them had hurt him as badly as the unresolved questions that lay between them now. If only she knew the right words to say, to make him understand she still loved him, to fix it.

For the first time her resolution wavered. Then her gaze skittered to baby Mary who lay gurgling happily in her mother's arms. Garrick had another daughter now, one who was his own flesh and blood. Suddenly, Alaina felt like an intruder.

"Where is the rest of it?" Jared Brady asked, taking the satchel from her hand.

"The rest?" Through a veil of pain, Alaina tried to focus on Jared.

"The rest of your luggage. Is it outside?"

"No. I mean, that's all there is."

Jared glanced back down at the satchel with a look of surprise. "Oh... Well then, I guess if you're ready, we'd best be on our way."

Alaina flashed Jared an artificially bright smile. "I'm as ready as I'll ever be." She had a momentary impression of dark hair and sympathetic brown eyes before she turned and walked out the door.

"Give Angel and Ox my love," Becky said, stepping out onto the porch as Jared helped Alaina into the waiting buggy.

"I will."

"I....*we* love you, Alaina," Becky quavered, tears streaming down her face as she clutched baby Mary to her chest.

Alaina nodded. "I know."

Garrick stood behind Becky, his arms protectively around her and the baby, painfully silent and stoic. The five boys surrounded them, noisily admonishing Alaina to watch out for wild Indians, and to catch herself a cowboy husband. She looked away. They were a family, each a part of the other, complete. Only she was different, a changeling, the daughter of another man, an outsider.

Jared slapped the reins against the horse's rump, and the buggy started off with a jingle and a jerk. Suddenly, Alaina imagined herself jumping out of the buggy, and running back to hug her mother and Garrick for all she was worth. Never in her life had she wanted to make amends so badly, to repair what she'd broken. But she didn't know how to make herself feel like part of the family again. In her mind's eye, she could see them all standing on the porch watching until the buggy disappeared around the bend. She forced herself not to look back...not even once.

CHAPTER THREE

"I kind of miss the pigtails," Jared said, glancing at Alaina as he drove toward town.

"What?"

"Your braids. As I remember, when Angel brought us to visit that time, they hung halfway down your back."

"You tied them to a door knob," she reminded him.

"I remember that too. It was the only thing I could think of at the time. You were bound and determined to climb up on the hoosier, and Betsy was headed outside into who knows what kind of mischief. So, I tied you to the door and went after her." He grinned. "It was my punishment, you see. Angel said I had to keep you and Betsy out of trouble."

Alaina looked at him in surprise. "Punishment?"

"That's the problem with having sisters old enough to be your mother. Angel was really good at inventing uncomfortable discipline. Watching you two holy terrors was the worst thing she could come up with."

The tale put his behavior in a different light. Alaina had dealt with ornery younger siblings often enough to admire his tactics. "You were kind of a brat yourself," she said, unwilling to forgive him quite so easily.

"Me?" Jared looked taken aback. "I was far too old to be a brat."

"Then what about the frog that showed up in my mother's bed?"

"That's what I was being punished for," he said with a grin. "Actually, it was a mistake, plain and simple."

"It was meant to be me, wasn't it?"

"I found it out back and figured you'd probably like it. I stuck it in the bed where you took your afternoon nap. How was I supposed to know it was your mother's bed?" He shook his head. "I didn't think she was ever going to stop screaming."

Alaina grinned in spite of herself. If the truth were known she'd probably have made it into a pet if she'd found it instead of her mother. "Mama's a lot better about that sort of thing now-a-days. After dealing with my brothers all these years, it'd take a coiled rattlesnake in her bed to set her off."

"You're lucky to have brothers," Jared said wistfully. "I'd have traded all four of my sisters for them any day."

The thought of her siblings brought the first pangs of homesickness, and Alaina's throat tightened painfully. She hadn't realized she was going to miss them.

"This your first time away from home?" Jared asked sympathetically when she didn't answer.

Alaina nodded, afraid her voice would crack if she tried to say anything.

"The first time is the worst. Don't worry this will pass soon enough. The best cure is not to think about it."

Alaina searched her mind for something to talk about that would take her mind off leaving home. "How's Betsy?"

"Just fine and leading her new husband on a merry chase if I know my baby sister."

"Oh, that's right. I think Angel did tell me she was

getting married. Did she have a nice wedding?"

"You haven't heard about the wedding? It was the social event of the century!" While Jared launched into a humorous account of his sister's wedding, Alaina studied his face for the first time and was astonished by what she saw. She'd been so sunk in misery, she hadn't noticed how much Jared Brady had changed. Only the brown velvet eyes and dark wavy hair remained of the boy she remembered.

His face had matured, the blurred features of youth hardening into the planes and angles of adulthood with devastating effect. From the cleft in the firm chin to finely molded lips and high cheek bones there was a masculine beauty about him that Alaina found incredibly attractive.

But it was the slight crow's feet at the corner of his eyes and the deep tan that intrigued her. Jared Brady spent a great deal of time outside in the elements. It seemed completely out of character for the son of a wealthy businessman, as she knew him to be. So did the frown lines between the flaring dark brows.

Right now, as he told about Betsy's wedding, the creases appeared as foreign to his nature as satin and lace. It wasn't long before Alaina was laughing so hard her stomach hurt.

"Well, here we are," he said, as they pulled up in front of the stage station. "Anything you need before we leave town?"

"No."

"All right then. I'll take your baggage in and be right back." He tied the reins to the brake lever and jumped down. "I have to take this buggy back to the livery and arrange for someone to ride my rented horse back to

Minneapolis."

"You rented a horse?" Alaina asked in surprise as he grabbed her satchel out of the back. "Why didn't you just wait and take the stage this morning?"

"Because I didn't want to waste another day. This way, we'll be in Minneapolis in time to catch the train tonight and be back in Omaha by late tomorrow afternoon."

"Are we in a hurry for some reason?"

"No, but I hate to ask Susan to wait any longer than I have to," he said. "She was unhappy enough about staying in Omaha with only her maid while I came to get you."

"That's right. Angel told me you were bringing someone else back too."

"Actually, Susan is my fiancée. She's been visiting her relatives in the East."

"Oh." Alaina wondered why the news that he had a fiancée came as such a surprise. He was twenty-eight, after all. Most men were married by the time they were his age. "I thought Angel said you were escorting a friend's daughter back."

"In a way. Her father is my commanding officer at Fort Bridger."

"You're in the army?"

"No, I'm a civilian, but I work for the government as a surveyor and was assigned to the fort. I hate to make you walk from the livery stable, but I can't very well leave you here by yourself."

Alaina stood up. "Well, of course you can. My cousin Sven works here."

"I should have guessed," he said, reaching up to help her down. "Angel told me you were related to half the town. The big blond, right?"

"How did you know?"

"Family resemblance. He's nearly as big as your father. That reminds me," he said, reaching into his pocket. "Your father told me to give you this."

Alaina stared down at the coin purse in her hand in mute astonishment. It was heavy and thick. "Papa sent me money?"

"It appears that way. If you're sure you'll be all right here I'll take the buggy back."

Alaina smiled. "I've spent my whole life here, Jared. I'll be fine."

"I guess you will at that. I won't be long."

Alaina watched him until he disappeared into the livery stable down the street before opening the purse. She looked inside and gaped in astonishment. There must be nearly a hundred dollars in the old worn purse; a veritable fortune. A tightly folded note was tucked against one side. Alaina bit her lip as she unfolded the paper, but the note, like everything else that had happened during the last twelve hours was a complete surprise.

Dear Alaina,

When we left South Pass City, Cameron Price tried to give this money to your mother to help take care of you. Mama refused to take it, so he gave it to me. I saved it knowing someday you would want to find him. Whatever happens in Wyoming, remember Mama and I love you.

Papa

How could he be so kind to her when she'd hurt him so badly? A welter of confusing emotions swirled through her as she stood there with the evidence of Garrick's love in her hand. Her eyes burned as she remembered how steadfastly he maintained her right to know about her real father. She blinked away tears and went inside to wait for the stage.

With Sven's cousinly teasing, the time passed quickly. Alaina and Jared were on the stage and rolling out of town almost before she knew it. She experienced another flash of homesickness, but then thrust it all behind her. Today was the beginning of her new life. It was time she stopped looking back and started looking forward.

The trip to Minneapolis was uneventful. Alaina barely had time to draw her breath before Jared whisked her across town to the railroad station where they boarded a train and headed for Omaha.

They hadn't been on the train very long when night fell and the porter converted their seats to a bed. Jared let her have the more spacious bottom bunk while he climbed into the one above that folded down from the wall. The wheels clacking along the track, and the unfamiliar swaying motion of the train kept Alaina awake most of the night. Frequent stops at stations woke her up the few times she did manage to doze off. By morning she was almost relieved to get up so the porter make her bed back into a seat.

There was a long line of women waiting to use the single ladies' dressing room at the back of the car, so Alaina returned to her seat to wait her turn. Jared sat down on the facing seat and handed her a roll he'd bought at one of the innumerable stops the day before. Though it had gotten a little crushed, the roll was surprisingly tasty, and she enjoyed every bite.

As she finished brushing the crumbs away, Alaina glanced up to find Jared staring at her as though he'd never seen her before. Suddenly, she was uncomfortably aware of her rumpled clothes and the hair that hung around her face in chaotic disarray. An attempt to refasten the bun on top of her head failed. She barely managed to keep it from all tumbling down around her shoulders.

The odd look on Jared's face was unnerving. "I never thanked you for coming so far out of your way to get me," she said, searching frantically for something to say.

"Thank Angel. Her telegram more or less insisted. When she feels that strongly about something, you're better off doing what she wants. I'd rather deal with an angry cougar than face my sister when I've disappointed her." Jared gave her a lop-sided grin. "Besides, how could I turn down a damsel in distress?"

Alaina's eyes widened in surprise. "Angel's in trouble?"

"I meant you."

"Me?"

"Angel said it was an emergency of some sort." He frowned. "That's what you told her isn't it?"

"No...well...at least I didn't mean to. She must have misunderstood my last letter. I don't express myself very well in writing." Alaina thought back over the letter she'd written her Godmother last month. She vaguely remembered saying she might do something desperate if her life didn't change soon. Could that be why Angel had sent for her? The invitation had seemed like a godsend at the time.

His eyes narrowed. "Then your trip to Wyoming isn't urgent??"

"No, not exactly."

"Oh, this is just great. Susan's ready to murder me for leaving her in Omaha even for a matter of life and death. Now I find out it's nothing more than a silly whim of a hysterical schoolgirl."

"It's not a silly whim," Alaina said, stung by his tone, "and I'm no schoolgirl. I'll have you know I turned eighteen two months ago."

"A very great age, to be sure," he said sarcastically.

"Most girls my age are married already."

"Oh, so your sudden interest in Wyoming has to do with husband hunting, then?"

"No! I...it's...personal and...and I'd rather not discuss it."

"Oh, Lord," Jared murmured in a shocked voice. "I never thought of that. I'm sorry." He stared at her a moment longer, then appeared to give himself a mental shake. "Don't worry, nobody would ever guess to look at you, and your secret is safe with me."

"What secret?" she asked.

"Hey," he said patting her hand paternally, "everything's going to be fine. You're not the first girl to go to Angel when she found herself in a family way."

Alaina nearly choked on her surprise. "You think I'm pregnant?" she asked in a strangled voice.

"You're not?"

"I most certainly am not!" Alaina retorted.

Jared frowned again. "If you aren't expecting, then what's the problem?"

"That's none of your business. I said it was personal, and it is. That doesn't give you the right to assume the worst."

He sighed and ran his fingers through his hair. "Look, I didn't mean to insult you. It just seemed logical from the way you were acting. My sister has a habit of collecting stray girls in trouble. That's all."

Alaina stiffened angrily. "I'm not a stray; I'm her goddaughter! Now if you'll excuse me, I see the lady's dressing room is finally empty. I think I'll go freshen up."

He'd certainly handled that well, Jared thought as he watched her stalk down the aisle to the dressing room. So much for the timid little country bumpkin. Until now he'd been pleasantly surprised by her sweet uncomplaining attitude, especially since he'd expected a spoiled imp like his sister Betsy. Alaina might have been raised in the country, but there was nothing the least bit timid about her. She had obviously perfected the womanly art of turning the tables on unwary men.

Women! He'd spent his life surrounded by them, and they were all completely incomprehensible. He'd gone out of his way to help her, at great inconvenience to himself, and now he was the villain. Typical female logic. It made no sense at all.

Jared sighed and looked out the window, trying hard to hold on to his anger. But all he could think of were Alaina's incredible blue eyes. Even at five years old, her eyes had reminded him of sunbeams and stardust. They were no less beautiful now. A pale robin egg blue, flecked with darker blue and ringed with indigo, they were the kind of eyes that haunted a man's sleep and twisted his guts in the strangest way. The kind of eyes that were going to send Susan into a jealous frenzy.

Jared closed his eyes and pinched the bridge of his nose. Why couldn't Alaina be the freckle-faced, gangly adolescent he'd expected? It would have made life so much simpler. With hair the color of wild honey and eyes so blue a man could drown in them, Alaina would turn male heads everywhere she went. Susan wasn't going to like that one bit. Nor was Alaina likely to be awed by the slightly older, more sophisticated Susan.

Putting the two of them together was going to be like pouring kerosene on a forest fire. "Oh, Angel," he murmured. "What have you done to me?"

CHAPTER FOUR

"Wake up, Alaina, we're here."

Alaina started and sat up rubbing her eyes. "Where?"

"Omaha," Jared said, as she eagerly looked out the window. "I'm sorry we don't have time to spend sightseeing."

"That's all right. I'm sure I'll see plenty of interesting things before we get to Laramie City." She picked up her satchel and threw her coat over her arm. "Do we have another train to catch today?"

Jared resisted the urge to reach over and straighten her bonnet. "No, we'll be staying the night. Susan and her maid are waiting for us at the Victorian. I'll get you a room as soon as we get there."

"I've never stayed in a real hotel before."

"Well, you will tonight." He took the satchel from her hand and headed toward the street. "Come on, let's see if we can find a carriage."

Alaina tried not to gawk at all the amazing sights while he arranged their transport. Once inside the coach, however, she could hardly contain herself as she gazed avidly through the dingy glass window at the throngs of people in the street. Cowboys in dusty boots and sweat-stained hats rubbed shoulders with businessmen in suits. "The Wild West!" she breathed.

"Not quite," Jared said in amusement. "Omaha is almost civilized. You'll see the difference soon enough."

"I can't wait!" Alaina was vaguely aware of Jared watching her with amused tolerance, but she didn't care a snap of her fingers what he thought. All the sights outside the dirty glass were new and exciting. Other than a few trips to Minneapolis where they stayed with family, most of her eighteen years had been spent in her tiny hometown.

Her awe increased by leaps and bounds when they arrived at the Victorian. A huge chandelier hung in crystalline splendor from the vaulted ceiling of the lobby. The late afternoon sunlight glinted off the crystals and threw sparks of light on the intricate paintings that ran along the top of the walls. Naked cherubs danced gaily around the room, darting in and out among flowers and vines. Alaina wondered how long it had taken the artist to create it as she gazed around in open-mouthed wonder. Jared's angry voice called her attention away with a jerk.

"What do you mean you don't have any rooms?" he demanded.

"Just what I said," the clerk murmured apologetically. "All of our rooms are full."

"When I asked you day before yesterday, you said getting another room today wouldn't be a problem."

"That was day before yesterday. You should have made a reservation."

"I tried, but you said I didn't need one."

"I didn't know we were going to fill up. Perhaps another hotel..."

"I don't have time to run around Omaha looking for another room. You promised me—"

"Jared!"

The cultured voice stopped Jared in mid-tirade and

drew a long-suffering grimace from the clerk. Alaina glanced toward the curved marble staircase and caught her breath in surprise. The beautiful woman who walked down the last few steps with a graceful air, was just the sort of woman she'd expect Jared to marry. From the tips of her satin slippers to the top of her perfectly coiffed auburn hair, she was the epitome of wealthy elegance. Alaina suddenly felt horribly awkward and immature in her simple country dress and sturdy shoes.

"I didn't expect you back until after dark," Susan said, moving gracefully to the desk and turning her cheek up to Jared.

Jared dutifully dropped a kiss on it. "We caught the early train."

"I'm glad. It's been so dull without you."

"I missed you, too, Susan," he said with a fond smile.

Susan rewarded him with a brilliant smile of her own then turned her attention to Alaina. "And this must be Elaine."

"It's Alaina," Alaina said, wondering why Susan's smile seemed completely different when it was focused on her instead of Jared. "It's nice to meet you."

"Why, Jared," Susan said, as though Alaina hadn't spoken, "You led me to believe your sister's goddaughter was a child. She's almost a young woman."

Though Susan was obviously not much older than she, Alaina suddenly felt about six years old.

"Now that you're here, I won't have to have dinner sent up to my room," Susan was saying. "You will take me to the dining room, won't you?"

He made a face. "I can't, I'm afraid. There's been some kind of mix-up. The clerk says there aren't any more rooms. It looks like I'll have to give Alaina mine and go find another place to stay." He sighed. "It's really going to make things difficult, since our train leaves at nine o'clock."

"Nine o'clock!" Susan looked revolted. "What an ungodly hour. Do you realize how early we'll have to get up?"

"Yes, and it will be that much worse because I won't be here to help. God knows how far I'll have to go to find a room."

"You know, there is a much simpler solution," Susan said. "Elaine can share my room."

Jared looked doubtful. "I hate to inconvenience you."

"Don't be silly. It won't be any trouble at all, there's plenty of room. Besides, she looks about done in."

"It was a fast trip," Jared agreed.

"Poor girl," Susan repeated sympathetically. "I'll take her up and get her settled. We'll meet for dinner in say, twenty minutes?"

"All right." He flashed his fiancée a grateful smile. "I should have known I could count on you, Susan."

"Yes, you should have. A wife's job is to take care of annoying little details for her husband. Come along, dear, I'll take you up and get you settled."

An annoying little detail, was she? Alaina had to bite her tongue as she followed the other woman across the lobby and up the stairs. She wondered how Susan would deal with an annoying little detail like a swift kick in the backside. A moment later Alaina took herself to task for such an uncharitable attitude. In spite of what Susan had said to Jared, it was bound to be vexing to have a stranger in her room. The other woman really was being very kind under the circumstances.

"You must be exhausted," Susan said, as she reached the top of the stairs. "Men don't understand how tiring traveling can be for a woman. I'll have a tray sent up so you can eat in your room."

"I'm not all that tired, and it will only take me a minute to freshen up. I can easily come downstairs."

Susan unlocked a door and stepped aside so Alaina could enter. "Nonsense. I wouldn't hear of it. You need your rest."

Alaina entered the room and looked around in surprise. After the opulence downstairs in the lobby she had expected something far more extravagant. Though she had no idea what a hotel room should look like, she wasn't prepared for a room smaller than the one she shared with baby Mary at home.

She was setting her satchel on the bed when a door on the far side of the room opened and a harried-looking woman looked in.

"Was you needing me for anything, Miss Prescott?"

Susan shook her head. "No, Phoebe, I just brought Miss Ellinson up. She'll be sharing your room tonight."

Phoebe raised her brows. "Mr. Jared's friend?"

"His sister's godchild," Susan said with a frown. "She's nothing to Jared."

"Course not. Will you be wanting your usual cup of chocolate at bedtime tonight?"

"No, and don't wait up for me. I'll likely be late."

"Not if Mr. Jared has a lick of sense," Phoebe muttered as the door slammed behind her mistress. Her frown relaxed as she turned to Alaina. "I'm Phoebe Lane," she said with a smile, "Miss Prescott's maid."

"It's nice to meet you. I'm Alaina Ellinson."

"I know, Mr. Jared's friend." Phoebe grinned. "I'll bet her royal highness about burst a stay when she saw you. She was expecting someone in braids and short skirts."

"Miss Prescott has been very kind."

"Sure she has. That's why you're sharing a room with me instead of having one of your own like you should."

"There weren't any more so she said I could stay with her."

Phoebe nodded knowingly. "Then shunted you off into her maid's room just like she intended to all along. I'll wager she came out smelling like a rose with Mr. Jared too. She's a sly one, she is."

Through the open door, Alaina could see Susan's room. It was fully as luxurious as Phoebe's was plain. She blinked as she realized how skillfully Susan had manipulated the situation. She'd disposed of an unwanted extra for dinner and earned Jared's gratitude in the process with absolutely no inconvenience to herself.

"Have you been her maid long?" Alaina asked curiously.

"She hired me in Denver just before she left for the East when her other maid ran off to get married. I thought it would be a good experience with the travelin' and all." Phoebe grimaced. "It's been an experience all right. It's no wonder she has a hard time keeping maids. I never saw anybody so persnickety in my life. If Mr. Jared ever saw that side of her, she'd never have finagled that marriage proposal out of him."

"Maybe he will."

Phoebe made a rude noise. "Not a chance, at least

not while he can still wiggle out of it. The betrothal won't be official until her parents announce it after we get back to Fort Bridger. She'll be nice as pie around him till then, even when she's being a witch to the rest of us."

"You mean they just got betrothed on this trip?" Alaina asked in surprise.

"I think she's been trying for a while, but Mr. Jared never got around to popping the question."

"She must have been pleased when he finally did."

"Relieved more like. Miss High and Mighty was getting a little panicky. She just turned twenty-two you know. Folks were starting to whisper about her being an old maid. I'm not sure how she managed to convince him, but she finally did and never misses a chance to tighten her claim. I'll bet she's downstairs right now basking in his gratitude because she took such good care of you."

"You make her sound horribly self-centered and selfish."

"No worse than she is. Speaking of which, I guess I'd better get back to work. I swear she tried on six gowns before she found one she wanted to wear tonight. It will take me half the night just to pick up her mess before I do her packing. "Make yourself at home," Phoebe said over her shoulder. "I'll be right next door if you need anything."

"Would you mind some company while you work?" Alaina asked.

Phoebe flashed her a big smile. "Wouldn't mind at all, in fact I'd be glad of it."

The evening passed surprisingly fast as Phoebe regaled Alaina with stories of growing up in the West. Phoebe reminded Alaina of a little brown sparrow. She was slight with nondescript brown hair, a smattering of freckles across her nose, and an open friendly smile. By the time they finished their rather plain supper, they were vastly pleased with each other and well on the way to becoming friends.

Exhausted by her sleepless night, and unfamiliar routine of traveling, Alaina went to bed shortly after dark and was soon sound asleep. She started awake a short time later as Phoebe jumped up from the bed.

"What's the matter?" Alaina asked in alarm.

"Her highness is back," Phoebe said, hurriedly stuffing her feet into her shoes. "She'll have my head if she catches me napping."

For the first time Alaina realized she could hear Jared and Susan talking through the door. "But she told you not to wait up for her."

"Won't matter. Especially since Mr. Jared doesn't seem to be falling in with her plans. She'll likely be in the devil's own temper." Phoebe grinned as she straightened her dress. "Does my heart good to see her not get her way for once." The door in the other room opened and Phoebe winked at Alaina before schooling her features into a subservient expression and hurrying into Susan's room.

"Goodnight, Sweetheart," Susan said in a soft throaty voice. "Think of me in your dreams." The door shut with a gentle click. There was a soft sigh, then, "Well, what are you standing there for, Phoebe? Help me get ready for bed."

As Alaina listened to Susan's sharp orders, she didn't know whom she felt the sorriest for, Phoebe who had to put up with it now or Jared who was walking into a lifetime of it.

"Wake up, Alaina," Phoebe whispered shaking her shoulder hours later. "It's morning."

"What time is it?"

"A little after seven. Mr. Jared says we have to be downstairs and ready to go in a little less than an hour. I let you sleep as late as I dared. Your breakfast is on the bureau."

"Oh!" Alaina scrambled out of bed. "I didn't realize it was so late."

Susan's petulant voice came through the door. "Phoebe, have you found my green ribbon yet?"

"Sorry I can't help you pack," Phoebe whispered.

"Phoebe, what's keeping you?"

"Be right there, Miss Prescott." With a wink at Alaina, Phoebe whisked herself through the door into the other room.

Alaina dressed, packed her things, ate breakfast and still arrived in the lobby long before Susan and Phoebe. Jared was already there pacing the marble floor in obvious agitation. He came to an abrupt halt when he saw her.

She smiled. "Good morning."

"Good morning." He glanced up the stairs. "Dare I hope that Susan is right behind you?"

"Phoebe was still packing when I left."

"Damnation!" he said under his breath as he looked at his watch again. "We're going to miss our train if she doesn't hurry up."

"Maybe she doesn't realize how late it is," Alaina suggested.

"Good point." Jared glanced up the stairs again. "I guess it wouldn't hurt to go tell her to hurry some."

"That's all he knows about it," the desk clerk muttered as

Jared bounded up the stairs. "A grizzly would think twice about telling that woman to hurry."

Alaina bit the inside of her lip and pretended not to hear as she walked across the lobby and sat down to wait. It might be interesting to see what kind of reaction Jared got from his fiancée.

She didn't have long to wait. Less than five minutes later,

Jared and Susan appeared arm in arm. As they descended the curving staircase, Alaina couldn't help thinking they looked like the king and queen making an entrance. Though they seemed totally absorbed in their conversation, there was little doubt that Susan knew every eye in the room below was turned toward her.

"I know," she was saying, "but I just can't be ready at the snap of a finger like some people. I refuse to appear in public unless I'm properly groomed."

"And you look stunning as usual," Jared said soothingly. "I merely mentioned that we're going to have to hurry to catch our train."

Susan bit her lip and looked up at him apologetically. "Oh dear, that *is* my fault. If I hadn't told Phoebe to pack for Elaine, we'd have been down long ago."

"That was very generous of you," Jared said patting her hand where it lay on his arm, "but probably unnecessary. Alaina is used to taking care of herself. I'm sure she wouldn't have minded packing her own bag."

"Yes, she does seem rather..." Susan paused delicately, "countrified doesn't she?"

The corner of Jared's mouth quirked upward. "She's

as countrified as fresh air and sunshine."

Alaina stiffened in indignation. How dare he make fun of her? She might not be particularly sophisticated, but at least she didn't lie and blame other people for her shortcomings like his precious fiancée. She turned away in disgust. Maybe he deserved Susan after all.

CHAPTER FIVE

"Is that where we're supposed to sleep?"

Jared heard Susan the minute he entered the train car. He swallowed a sigh. In the few minutes it had taken him to find the dining car and check on supper, the porter must have come to convert the seats into beds. He'd hoped to get his fiancée into the dining car before that happened.

"Yes, ma'am," the porter was saying. "Our Silver Palace Sleepers were designed with the passenger's comfort in mind."

"Your idea of comfort and mine differ greatly." Susan's sniffed. "I'll take a private Pullman any day."

"They aren't available on the Central Pacific Railroad," Jared reminded her, rejoining the party. "They're serving dinner in the dining car. I've reserved a place for us."

"I certainly hope the food is better than the sleeping arrangements."

The porter bristled defensively. "Our chef is world renowned."

"I'm sure we'll find his efforts quite satisfactory," Jared said with a placating smile.

"Well, I'm certainly not going to sleep in one of those top berths and neither is Phoebe," Susan snapped. "I'm afraid of heights."

Phoebe looked surprised. "I don't mind, Miss Prescott."

"I may need you during the night," Susan said with a toss of her head. "I don't want to have to climb a ladder to get to you."

"I'll be happy to take a top berth," Alaina said quietly.

Susan gave her a cool nod. "Why thank you, Elaine. I'm sure you'll be perfectly comfortable there."

Jared frowned. Alaina's expression reminded him more of a storm cloud than sunshine. So far there hadn't been any open hostility between the two women, but he wasn't taking any chances.

He tucked Susan's hand through the crook of his arm and tried to ignore the feeling of impending doom. "We'd best head back to the dining car," he said. "They're holding a table for us."

The train's sway along the track made walking awkward. Phoebe and Alaina tried to hold each other steady, but were soon giggling merrily as the train's undulations made them stagger back and forth. Determined to move with her usual grace, Susan held Jared's arm in a death grip. He found himself wishing she'd relax a little and have some fun.

Though the food was excellent, dinner was not a rousing success. Since Susan ignored both Alaina and Phoebe, conversation was desultory. Somewhere between the soup and the pheasant under glass, Jared became aware of an undercurrent between Phoebe and Alaina.

Every so often, when they knew Susan wasn't looking, they'd grin at each other or wink conspiratorially. They reminded him of two schoolgirls making faces behind the teacher's back. Though it had been years since he indulged in such childish behavior, he found himself wishing Phoebe and Alaina would let him in on their private joke.

When dinner was over, Jared escorted the three women back to the now converted sleeping car, then took himself off to give them some privacy to prepare for bed.

Susan laid claim to the women's dressing room at the end of the car, so Alaina took off her shoes and climbed into the tiny upper berth. She had to sit cross-legged with her head nearly touching the polished ceiling of the car to remove her dress. It was difficult and uncomfortable, but she was determined not to appear rumpled the next morning. All day Susan had been making snide comments about Alaina's appearance, like her quaint hairstyle, or the cute little dress that was just like the one Susan had worn before she was old enough to let her skirts down.

As if things weren't bad enough, the curtains around her berth didn't quite close at the bottom. Afraid someone would pass by and look in, Alaina hurried as fast as she could. Even so, it took several minutes of concentrated struggle to take off her dress, hang it on the strap looped there for her convenience, remove all but one of her petticoats and to loosen her corset. Maneuvering herself around so she could crawl under the covers was another ordeal. When she snuggled down into her berth at last, she discovered it was rather like sleeping on a board.

Even so, it wasn't long before the day caught up with her, and she began to drift off. Just as the first tendrils of sleep curled through her mind, the train went around a particularly sharp curve and lurched violently. Alaina's relaxed body pitched over the edge of the berth.

She smacked into an unsuspecting fellow passenger who was walking down the aisle.

"This is an unexpected surprise," said an amused masculine voice as strong arms steadied her.

Alaina looked past the blue uniform of a soldier up into the brilliant green eyes of a total stranger. "Oh!" She felt the heat climb her face as she stared up at him in horrified embarrassment. "I...I'm so sorry. The train—"

"No need to apologize," he said setting her back on her feet. "I've been thrown out of these train berths myself."

"What the hell is going on here?" said a familiar menacing voice.

Alaina winced. What a rotten time for Jared to come back. He stood there glaring at her benefactor as though he'd just as soon take the man apart as listen to an explanation. "I fell out of bed," Alaina said wishing she could sink through the floor and disappear. "He broke my fall."

She might as well have not spoken for all the attention Jared paid her. "I think you'd better explain yourself, Lieutenant," he growled.

"It was just as she said," the stranger said releasing her. "The train went around a sharp curve and threw your wife out of bed. I happened to be walking by and caught her. It happens all the time."

"Oh, but we're not..." Jared's frown stopped her in mid-sentence. Alaina felt like an idiot. Other passengers were already sticking their heads out of their berths to see what was going on. Lord, could it get any worse?

"Elaine, what on earth?" As if on cue, Susan emerged from the women's dressing room modestly wrapped in her traveling cloak. The other woman's look of shocked dismay made Alaina suddenly aware that she was standing there in front of a dozen people wearing only her shift and a petticoat. She closed her eyes in mortification. Was it possible for a person to die of embarrassment?

"Jared, she's practically naked," Susan whispered in horrified accents.

"Damn," Jared said, as though he'd just noticed. "Phoebe, hand me that gown will you?"

Alaina opened her eyes just in time to see Phoebe give Jared Susan's blue satin dressing gown. "This will solve the problem nicely," he said, stepping forward and placing it around her shoulders.

"Thank you," Alaina murmured gratefully, slipping her arms into the sleeves and pulling it closed with the long satin belt. Unfortunately, the garment looked like it had been created more for seduction than modesty. The way it clung to her curves and dipped enticing between her breasts made Alaina feel nearly as exposed as before.

If looks had the power to kill, Susan's would have dropped Alaina on the spot. With sudden clarity, she realized Susan had intended to appear in the frothy creation of satin and lace herself. The other woman must have been waiting for Jared to return before making her entrance. She'd obviously changed her mind when the intended audience of one turned into a crowd.

Alaina couldn't fault her for that. All she wanted to do herself was hide. She turned toward her berth. "I think I'll go back to bed," she whispered in a choked voice as she prepared to climb to her berth. "Good night."

Strong hands grasped her around the waist and boosted her up. Alaina didn't know if it was Jared or the stranger and at that point, didn't much care. All she could think of was getting out of sight before she died of humiliation. She scrambled inside and let the curtains fall closed behind her. Alaina sighed in relief as the stranger bid her companions good night and took his leave. With any kind of luck, she'd never see him again.

"It's a good thing he was a gentleman," Susan told Jared accusingly. "What do you suppose she was thinking of?"

"Probably wishing us all at the devil, and I can't say that I blame her."

"I've never been so embarrassed," Susan said in mortified accents.

"What did you have to be embarrassed about? Alaina was the one who got thrown out of bed in her underwear."

"I meant for her, of course," Susan amended. "You know how my delicate sensibilities are affected by others' pain."

Alaina thought she heard a derisive snort, but she couldn't tell if it came from Jared or Phoebe. With a shake of her head, she removed the borrowed dressing gown and crawled under the covers again. The loop that she'd hung her dress on suddenly caught her eye. Had she misunderstood its purpose? After a moment, she pulled the dress free and grabbed the strap. Securely anchored to her bed, the embarrassment faded and she was soon fast asleep.

The first rays of sunlight were creeping in through the windows when Alaina next awakened. She felt hot and sticky, and vastly uncomfortable. Not only did her berth feel like the inside of an oven, the mattress hadn't softened one bit during the night. She turned stiffly from her side to her back, wincing as her muscles protested the movement.

A moment later, she forgot all about her discomfort as she gazed at the ceiling above her in amazement. The early morning sunlight reflected an image of the next berth in the highly-polished wood of the ceiling. Jared slept on his back, naked from the waist up. One arm was flung carelessly over the side of the bunk and his long legs were bent to fit in the cramped space. Even in the imperfect reflection, she could see the well-developed chest and arms, and a thin line of hair that ran down his belly and disappeared enticingly beneath the blanket.

As Alaina's gaze followed the smooth masculine contours of his body, she felt an odd twist in her middle. Jared Brady could make her angry faster than anyone she knew, but she found herself wondering what it would be like to touch him, to trace the strong column of his neck or the firm muscles of his chest.

With a sudden violent movement, he lifted his hand to brush away a fly that landed on his cheek. As he shifted on his berth, it occurred to Alaina that he could wake up any minute and catch her watching him sleep. She'd had enough humiliation the night before to last her for a while. There was no way she was going to set herself up for another embarrassing episode. Regretfully, she pulled her gaze away and sat up.

Deciding she'd rather face an angry Susan than take a chance on Jared waking up while she was dressing, Alaina put on the blue dressing gown and gathered her things. She cautiously peered out through her curtains then slipped out of bed and hurried down the aisle to the women's dressing room.

By the time Alaina had finished dressing and

combing her hair, the conductor was moving through the car waking the passengers. Alaina met Phoebe just outside the door of the dressing room. "I suppose you're after this," she said, holding up the dressing gown.

"Nope, but I'm sure glad to see you're already up," Phoebe said with a relieved smile. "Can you disappear for a while?"

Alaina blinked. "What?"

Phoebe glanced over her shoulder and lowered her voice to a whisper. "Her royal highness is not in the best of moods this morning, and I think you're the cause."

"But why? I didn't do anything."

Phoebe grinned wickedly. "Of course, you did. Look at all the attention you got last night and in the expensive peignoir she's been saving to impress Mr. Jared with to boot. You even had the gall to look better in it than she does."

"Oh, surely not," Alaina protested.

"Yup, I've seen her in it, and it looks a whole lot better on you. Neither the lieutenant nor Mr. Jared could take his eyes off you, and that didn't set too well. She'll need some time to cool off before she sees you."

Alaina bit her lip. "Oh, dear. I guess I could go to the dining car."

"Phoebe!" They both winced at the sound of Susan's voice.

Phoebe rolled her eyes. "I have to go."

"Wait, don't forget this," Alaina said, thrusting the dressing gown into Phoebe's hands. "I'll see you at breakfast."

With a grateful wave, Phoebe hurried back to Susan's berth.

Alaina sighed as she watched her friend go. Poor

Phoebe. She'd probably wind up getting the brunt of Susan's displeasure though she had nothing to do with the cause. Inadvertently, Alaina's gaze strayed to the curtains surrounding Jared's berth. The image of how he'd appeared in the first rays of the morning sun came to mind, and she swallowed hard. She wondered if she'd ever be able to look at him without thinking about the body that lay beneath his clothes. With a wry smile, Alaina turned away. Of course, the minute he opened his mouth, the urge to kick him would probably drive any such improper thoughts right out of her head.

She soon forgot all about Jared as she threaded her way through the other cars, dodging fellow passengers in various stages of dress and irritation. It was obvious she wasn't the only one who had problems with the berths. One woman seemed particularly exasperated as she complained loudly to anyone who would listen. Alaina narrowly missed being struck by an especially wild gesture as she squeezed around the woman's considerable bulk. The woman stopped long enough to glare at her.

"I'm terribly sorry," Alaina murmured backing away. "I didn't mean to...oof." She stumbled slightly as she collided with a solid wall of flesh behind her.

"Well, good morning," said a vaguely familiar masculine voice, as strong hands steadied her.

Startled, she turned and immediately recognized the young lieutenant from the night before. "Oh, my." Alaina could feel heat creeping up her neck and imagined her face turning bright red.

He smiled disarmingly. "We do seem to have a habit of running into each other, don't we?"

"I'm sorry...I didn't...I mean, I wasn't..."

"Don't think anything of it. On a crowded train like this, it's impossible not to bump into people now and then. Actually, I'm rather glad this happened."

"You are?"

He nodded. "In all the ruckus last night, I never apologized for embarrassing you."

"That wasn't your fault." Alaina dropped her gaze to her tightly clasped hands. "I never got the chance to thank you for catching me."

"Glad I was there to do it." He smiled again. "We didn't get around to introducing ourselves, either. Lieutenant Sean Kirkpatrick at your service."

"I'm Alaina Ellinson."

"I was on my way to the dining car. Perhaps you and your husband could join me for breakfast."

"Oh, I don't think—"

Suddenly Jared was there beside her. "We have other plans, thank you. Come along dear." He gave the young Lieutenant a tight smile as he took Alaina's elbow in a firm grip and propelled her along through the crowd.

"That was rude!" Alaina exclaimed.

"And what you were doing was foolhardy."

"Foolhardy! All I was doing was talking to him."

"That's how it starts. You aren't in your one-horse hometown anymore. Out here in the real world, men like the lieutenant are just waiting to take advantage of sweet little innocents like you."

"Oh, for pity's sake." She pulled her elbow out of his grasp with an indignant yank. "You sound just like my mother. Even if every man in the world were out to seduce me, I have enough sense not to let them succeed."

Jared raised a brow. "If you keep getting the same

advice from people around you, perhaps you should listen. It's just possible they might know what they're talking about." He took her elbow again. "Come on. I don't have all day to stand around explaining what should be obvious. We need to get a table in the dining car. Susan will have a fit if she has to wait for her breakfast."

"And we certainly wouldn't want to upset dear Susan, would we?" Alaina snapped jerking her arm free for the second time.

"I'll pretend I didn't hear that."

"Suit yourself," she said. With a final glare, she turned and marched toward the back of the car.

Jared gritted his teeth. Contrary little hornet! Alaina Ellinson might have the face of an angel, but she was as irritating as a burr under the saddle.

CHAPTER SIX

"That nice young Lieutenant is looking over here again," Phoebe whispered to Alaina. "I think he's interested in you. He's hardly been out of sight since we met him and that was three nights ago."

"He probably feels sorry for me," Alaina whispered back. "He thinks I'm married to Jared."

"Where on Earth did he get that idea?"

"From Jared, that's where. I'm sure Lieutenant Kirkpatrick thinks I'm the unluckiest woman he's ever met."

Phoebe frowned. "I don't see why. Any woman would be thrilled to be married to Mr. Jared. He's the kindest man I've ever known."

"That's because he likes you," Alaina muttered glowering at Jared who sat on the opposite seat. As far as Phoebe was concerned, he walked on water. She couldn't see the autocratic bully behind the handsome face. Of course, he hadn't been treating Phoebe like a ten-year old that couldn't be trusted out of his sight for five minutes either.

Any softening in Alaina's attitude toward Jared had evaporated when he took it upon himself to be her self-appointed watchdog. If a stranger so much as glanced her way, Jared was between them bristling like a porcupine. She couldn't even strike up an innocent conversation without him butting in and dragging her away.

All in all, the trip hadn't been nearly as exciting as she had hoped. Garrick Ellinson and Cameron Price were never far from her mind. More than once she had slipped off into a pensive silence, though no one seemed to notice. She longed to share her secret with someone, but Phoebe had enough on her hands just dealing with Susan. The farther they traveled, the more irritating Susan became. At least being mad at Susan kept Alaina from thinking too deeply.

"There's Laramie City," Phoebe cried pressing her nose to the window. "I can see the water tower."

Glad to be distracted from her irritation with Jared, Alaina looked over Phoebe's shoulder. A handful of bleak clapboard houses huddled next to the track, their dingy paint cracked and peeling. "It isn't much to look at is it?" A loud whistle from the locomotive cut off her words. The screech of metal on metal replaced the rhythmic clack of wheels as the train slowed.

"There's nothing here but the railroad and the Territorial Prison," Susan said with a shudder of disgust.

Jared frowned. "My sister and her husband don't feel that way. They based their business empire here."

"Business is another matter entirely," Susan said, dismissing the subject as though it were of little importance. "Is that your sister?"

Jared looked out the window. "It sure is. Looks like she brought the children along too."

"She brings her children out in public with her?"

"Angel and Ox waited a long time for babies. They take their children just about everywhere with them," Jared said, as the train came to a stop in front of the depot. "Make sure we have everything."

It only took Alaina a few moments to collect her

satchel, but she knew better than to try and leave the train before Susan. The last thing she wanted was to be the cause of a scene, especially in front of her godmother. This way, Susan was too busy making sure Phoebe and Jared had all her bags to pay Alaina any mind.

As she stood patiently waiting, several other passengers moved past her on their way out. She stepped aside when one stopped next to her.

"I guess this is where we say good-bye."

Startled, Alaina looked up and encountered Lieutenant Kirkpatrick's rueful smile. "I guess so," she said.

"Do you and your husband live in Laramie City?"

"No, I'm just visiting." Alaina caught sight of Jared's disapproving frown, and her jaw tightened. "And I'm not married. Jared is my...uncle."

"Your uncle?" The Lieutenant glanced at Jared and Susan. "Then she's your aunt," he said, as though he'd just figured out a difficult puzzle. "I wondered."

Alaina bit back a smile. Wouldn't Susan love that? "I'm only traveling as far as Laramie City with them."

"Ah, I see. Will you be staying long?"

"Well, I'm not exactly sure—"

"Good morning, Lieutenant. This is where we get off," Jared broke in. "I'm sure you'll understand if we don't stop to chat."

"Of course. I was just telling your niece good-bye."

"Good-bye, Lieutenant," Alaina said quickly. "Have a good trip."

"Thank you." The Lieutenant gave her a warm smile. "And good luck to you."

"Thanks. I may need it."

"Susan and Phoebe are already on their way out,"

Jared said taking Alaina's arm and propelling her toward the door. "What was that all about anyway?"

"Just what he said. He stopped to say good-bye."

"How did I suddenly become your uncle?"

"I didn't want to leave him with the impression that we were married." Alaina glared at him. "I can't think of a worse fate."

"Neither can I," Jared said with feeling.

Susan was standing impatiently by the door. "Jared, hurry. Your sister is waiting."

"I'm coming." He glanced down at Alaina with a forbidding frown. "Please try to remember this isn't the safe little town where you grew up. The people here aren't what you're used to. It's dangerous to talk to men you don't know."

"Thank you for that little piece of wisdom. I think I can manage to stay out of trouble now," she said sarcastically. "You'd better run along. We wouldn't want to keep Susan waiting."

The muscles in his jaw bunched into a hard knot. "No, I wouldn't. I've waited a long time to introduce her to my family. Now if you'll excuse me..."

Alaina bit her lip as she watched him walk away. She really couldn't blame him for being angry, but he had a way of bringing out the worst in her. Uncertain what to do, she stood back and watched as Jared presented his fiancée to his sister. Suddenly, Alaina realized she was intruding on a family gathering. Maybe that's why Susan was so hostile.

Alaina turned to watch new passengers board the train, and focused on the hiss of steam rather than the cozy family group on the platform. She felt very alone. It wasn't long, however, until Angel extricated herself and hurried over. Alaina could see a few streaks of silver in the red hair that hadn't been there before and a few extra lines in her face, but otherwise she was unchanged.

"Alaina!" Angel cried over the hiss of the engine. She enveloped her goddaughter in a rose-scented hug. "I'm so glad you came. I can't tell you how much I've been looking forward to your visit. My heavens, what happened to the little girl I used to dandle on my knee?"

Alaina smiled and hugged her back with deep affection. "I grew up."

"You certainly have. Goodness, you must be a head taller than I am." Angel gazed at her fondly for a moment then took her arm and led her back to the others as the locomotive picked up steam and chugged out of the station." How are your parents?"

"Mama's fine."

"Just Mama? What about Papa?"

"Garrick's fine too," Alaina said, dropping her gaze.

Angel looked surprised. "We're going to have to have a long chat, aren't we?"

Alaina twisted her fingers together. "Yes, we are."

"Don't worry, we'll have plenty of time for that," Angel said, giving her another hug. "Let's go home so you can rest before lunch. I'll bet you're all exhausted."

As it turned out, it was late afternoon before Alaina and Angel got their chance to talk. The houses farther from the tracks were more to Susan's taste, particularly the one belonging to Ox and Angel Treenery. It was an imposing three-story structure with twin towers on either side of the entryway, a curved oak staircase, several stained-glass windows, and a large formal garden. There was a steady stream of visitors from the moment they arrived home. It seemed as if all of Laramie

City had turned out to see Jared.

Susan dominated every conversation, unobtrusively of course, and with proper deference to her hostess. She was in her element, but Alaina had never felt more out of place. Her small-town upbringing had not prepared her for making pointless polite conversation. Worst of all, she was uncomfortably aware of Susan watching her like a hawk, waiting for her to commit an unforgivable social faux pas. She was even denied Phoebe's company since the other woman was busy unpacking her mistress's clothing, not that Susan would allow a mere servant to come to tea anyway.

About the only time Alaina felt at ease was when Angel allowed her daughters to join the grownups for tea. The oldest was twelve, the youngest six, and Alaina was more than happy to entertain them with a game of charades. The lively threesome reminded her of her brothers and helped keep the loneliness at bay. They were still playing when the last of the guests departed. It wasn't long before their squeals of delight brought Susan's disapproval down upon all of them.

"Do you think it's a good idea to have the children here?" she asked. "I'm sure some of your visitors thought it most peculiar."

Angel smiled benignly. "My friends are quite used to my children. They always come to tea."

Jared grinned. "My mother started it, and my older sisters continued the tradition. Betsy, Shannon and I always came to tea too, whether we wanted to or not."

"For you and Shannon it was just another opportunity for mischief," Angel said, sipping her tea. "My children come for the cookies and milk."

"How fortunate that Elaine is with us then," Susan

said with thinly veiled distaste. "I know I wouldn't have the slightest idea how to entertain children."

Jared gave Susan an amused glance. "It's just a matter of understanding what children like to do, which Alaina obviously does."

Angel smiled. "It's no surprise to me that Alaina's a wonder with children. She's Garrick's daughter after all. I never saw anybody better with little ones."

Alaina ducked her head. Her response brought a puzzled frown to Angel's face. "Jared," she said. "Ox is coming in on the four o'clock train. Why don't you take the children down to the station and meet him?"

"Sure," he said cheerfully. "What do you say, Susan, do you want to come along?"

"Oh, yes," Susan gushed. "I can't tell you how much I've looked forward to meeting your brother-in-law."

"Come on, Uncle Jared," the girls cried pulling him to his feet. "Let's go meet Daddy."

Susan glanced at the watch pinned to her bodice. "Goodness, I need to freshen up."

In a matter of minutes Angel and Alaina were alone. Angel's smile was complacent. "I had a feeling Susan wouldn't be able to resist the chance to meet the rich and powerful James Oxford Bruton Treenery III as though she were part of the family already."

Alaina gave her a confused look. "Who?"

"Ox. Only people like Susan ever use his full name. Anyway, now we can chat."

"Won't Ox wonder why you didn't come down to meet him?" Alaina asked.

Angel shrugged. "Not when I tell him I haven't had a chance yet to visit with our favorite goddaughter. Now then, are you going to tell me what's wrong?"

Alaina dropped her gaze to her lap. Now that the time had come to ask about Cameron Price, she found it unexpectedly difficult to put her question into words. "It's my father."

"I suspected as much, but I can't for the life of me think of anything Garrick could have done to upset you so. God never made a gentler soul."

"He's not my father," Alaina whispered.

"What?"

"Cameron Price is my father, not Garrick Ellinson."

"Oh, Lord."

Alaina glanced away. "Mama told me she wasn't married when she …she…"

"When she knew Cameron," Angel said gently.

Alaina looked at her godmother. "You knew, didn't you?"

"I knew," Angel admitted, "but I hoped you'd never find out."

"Why?"

"There was no reason for you to know."

"No reason!" Alaina was incredulous. "Cameron Price is my father."

"Not really. Well, technically, he is I guess, but he's never acted the part. Garrick and your mother were married long before you were born."

"Pa… Garrick said Cameron didn't know Mama was pregnant. I'm sure he would have married her if he'd known."

"Perhaps," Angel didn't sound totally convinced. "The point is, he wasn't there, and your mother was alone and starving. Garrick married her and saved you both."

"Cameron left money for Mama to take care of me."

Angel looked surprised. "He did?"

"Yes, he did, almost a hundred dollars. Papa… I mean Garrick gave it to me just before I left home." Alaina jumped to her feet and took a turn around the room. "It's all so confusing to me. Can you tell me what happened?"

Angel sighed. "It's a long story, and not really mine to tell. Your mother is the one—"

"Mama said the subject was closed."

"What did Garrick say?"

"That I had the right to know about my real father."

"He would," Angel muttered.

"Garrick said Cameron didn't even know about me until I was eight months old, and then he was fascinated with me."

"In his own way he was, I suppose, but—"

"Don't you see, Angel, Cameron Price never had the chance to be a father to me. My mother and Garrick robbed him of that when they got married and took me away. It was wrong."

"Wrong? Alaina, I've never seen two people more in love than your mother and Garrick!"

"What about me?"

"What about you? Garrick couldn't have loved you more if you'd been his own flesh and blood. From the moment you were born, that man doted on you. He's been a father to you in every way that matters."

"Except that he isn't really my father." Alaina looked down at her hands. "I want you to help me."

Angel raised her brows. "Help you what?"

"Find Cameron Price."

"Find… Alaina, I haven't seen him since you were a baby. I wouldn't have the slightest idea where to start looking."

"Oh," Alaina frowned in disappointment. "I thought you might know where he is."

"No, I really didn't know him all that well. He left South Pass City about the same time your mother and Garrick did. I haven't heard anything about him since. I'm afraid I can't be of much help."

"Well, someone must know where Cameron Price is."

At that precise moment, the door swung open and Susan swept in. "I seemed to have misplaced my gloves..." she began but broke off when she heard Alaina's words. "Cameron Price!" she said in astonishment. "What earthly business would you have with him?"

Alaina's eyes widened. "You know Cameron Price?"

"Of course, I do. Captain Price is one of my father's senior officers at Fort Bridger."

"Did you hear that?" Alaina turned shining eyes to Angel. "He's at Fort Bridger. When does the next train leave?"

"Hold on now, you can't just jump on a train and take off for Fort Bridger by yourself," Angel said in alarm. "It isn't safe."

"What isn't?" Jared asked, walking in.

"Nothing for you to worry about," Alaina said, brushing past him to get out the door. "I suppose I can wait and go to Fort Bridger with you and Susan."

"That's a much better idea," Angel called after her approvingly. "We haven't had nearly enough time together."

"She wants to go to Fort Bridger!" Jared stared at

Angel in dismay. "Why?"

"To see Cameron Price. Susan told her he was there."

"Cameron Price! He's there all right, but why does Alaina want to see him?"

Angel glanced at Susan then looked down at her nails. "It's personal."

"Personal...Angel, I wouldn't let any goddaughter of mine within ten miles of him!"

Angel frowned. "Still a lady's man I take it?"

"Captain Price is a true gentleman," Susan said indignantly. "My father says he's one of his best men."

"He's a brilliant strategist and a damn good army man," Jared agreed. "But he's held the same rank since the War between the States. Word has it, he's been busted five times for sleeping with the wives of his superior officers."

"That's not true! It was all because of one general's wife who used him to make her husband jealous. Her plan worked so well the general destroyed any chance Captain Price had of ever getting another promotion," Susan said indignantly. "You'll pardon me if I don't stay to chat. I seem to have left my gloves in my bedroom."

"I see Cameron hasn't changed much," Angel observed, as the sound of Susan's angry footsteps receded down the hall. "He always did have the ability to turn a woman's head." She rose to her feet and paced to the window. "I need more time with Alaina before she sees him. Can you and Susan delay your trip to Fort Bridger for a few days?"

"What difference will that make?"

"Isn't it obvious? The longer she's here, the better chance I have of changing her mind."

"If you're worried about me taking her to Fort Bridger, you can relax."

"Why is that?"

Jared gave a short laugh. "Are you kidding? I wouldn't escort her to the corner to buy a newspaper. Five days of traveling with Alaina Ellinson was enough to last me a lifetime."

Angel looked surprised. "Why? She's an absolute sweetheart."

"That's what I thought at first, too. But then she showed her true colors. That girl has no respect for authority."

"Authority? Oh, Jared, what did you do?"

"Nothing but try to keep her out of harm's way. Alaina's spent her life in a small town surrounded by a family of men nobody would even dream of tangling with. It's given her a false sense of security that's going to get her in trouble. I merely pointed that out to her several times."

"Please tell me you didn't call her a flirt."

"No. To be honest, I don't think she does it on purpose," he admitted. "She attracts men without even trying. They swarm around her like bees around a flower. I couldn't let her out of my sight on that train without some would-be Romeo cozying up to her."

"You sound jealous."

"Jealous! She irritates the hell out of me."

"And Susan doesn't?"

"Of course not. She's a true lady; not only beautiful, but predictable as well."

Angel raised an eyebrow. "Predictable?"

"If you leave her somewhere, she'll be there when you get back."

"A most useful trait, to be sure," Angel murmured.

"You won't find Susan dashing off to explore all the cars on the train or striking up a conversation with a total stranger. Her manners are impeccable."

"Just the sort of woman Father always wanted you to marry."

"I never really thought of it that way, but I guess she is." Jared glanced at the clock on the mantel. "I'd better get moving if we're going to get to the station before Ox." He walked out of the room completely unaware of the speculative look on his sister's face.

CHAPTER SEVEN

"**W**hen does the next train leave for Fort Bridger?" Alaina asked the man behind the ticket counter.

"The train don't stop at Fort Bridger. It goes right on by the fort and stops at Evanston, but there's stage service from there out to the fort." He pulled out his pocket watch. "The next train is due in any minute."

Alaina glanced around nervously. It was the same train that Ox would be on. She needed to get out of sight before Jared and the rest arrived. "How much is a ticket?"

"Let's see." The clerk opened the ticket drawer. "You'll have to change trains at Granger and—"

"Never mind. She won't be needing a ticket." Jared's voice broke over her like a shower of ice.

And who might you be?" asked the clerk.

"Nobody important," Alaina said. "Now about my ticket-"

"The name's Jared Brady, Angel Treenery's brother and this is our niece."

The clerk peered at him with a nearsighted squint for a minute then broke into a huge grin. "Why sure, Jared. I remember you now. You've grown a might since I saw you last. This is your niece, you say?"

"That's right." Jared leaned forward confidentially. "Her parents sent her out here so Angel could keep an eye on her. She's a little uncontrollable."

"That's not true!" Alaina glared at Jared. "He's lying

through his teeth."

Jared shrugged. "You see how she is."

The clerk nodded. "Used to have one just like her at home. Put the missus and me at wit's end, she did." He gave Alaina a severe look as he closed the ticket drawer. "Reckon you won't be needing a ticket after all. Best go with your uncle now like a good girl."

"You can't refuse to sell me a ticket on his say so," Alaina said indignantly.

Jared smiled complacently. "He won't have to. Ox will be here any minute to back me up."

"Ox will know the right way to handle her," the clerk said approvingly. "You tell Angel not to worry about this one buying a ticket out of town. Nobody here will sell her one."

"Thank you. I'm sure Ox and Angel will appreciate it," Jared said taking Alaina's arm.

"You're despicable," Alaina hissed as he led her outside the depot to the platform.

"And you're a spoiled brat. It's a good thing I happened to see you in time to stop this nonsense. Were you just going to sneak off without telling Angel where you'd gone?"

"I left a note in my room. She knows why I have to get to Fort Bridger even if she doesn't agree."

"The fact that she doesn't approve should tell you something."

"You know nothing about it."

"I know you have no business going off on your own like this. You wouldn't last ten minutes before some charlatan had robbed you of every cent you had. You may as well put going to Fort Bridger out of your mind."

"Who died and left you king? I don't have to do

what you say."

"Maybe not, but I'm not taking you to Fort Bridger. Without access to the railroad you can't get there on your own." He smiled smugly. "I'd say I won this round. Here are the others. You'd best put a smile on your face or the children will be asking all sorts of questions you don't want to answer."

Alaina gritted her teeth. Someday she was going to stuff that arrogant, self-assured attitude right down his throat. A moment later, happy, excited children surrounded her. Their pleased welcome and Susan's obvious displeasure at their exuberance went a long way toward improving her mood. By the time the train pulled into the station, Alaina was able to greet her godfather with a warm hug and a happy smile.

From the corner of her eye, she saw Jared relax his stance. Suddenly Garrick's voice came back to her with an oft-repeated piece of advice. "Patience, *min datter*. Solutions for even the most difficult problems will come to you in time." As a rule, that particular bit of logic irritated the devil out of her for patience was not one of her virtues. Still, it might just be a matter of biding her time until she could give her self-appointed jailer the slip. With that thought in mind, she went out of her way to appear resigned to her fate.

By that evening, Jared seemed to take for granted that he had successfully foiled her escape. It was obvious he hadn't mentioned it to anyone as the family sat down to dinner.

"If what I hear is true, the army will be putting you back to work any day, Jared," Ox said, helping himself to the potatoes.

"Oh?"

"The pass over the Snowy Range is open already. Isn't that where you were surveying last fall?"

Jared looked surprised. "Yes, but we weren't expecting the pass to clear until July."

"It was an open winter, and there wasn't much snow in the high country," Ox pointed out. "I don't know as I'd get too excited just yet, though. We could still have a spring storm or two up there."

"I'll send a telegram to Fort Bridger tomorrow," Jared said. "They may decide to send the survey crew out early this summer."

"If not, maybe you and Susan could go back to Fort Bridger by going over the pass and down into Saratoga," Angel said with a twinkle in her eye. "Ox took me that way shortly after we were married. I'd never been camping before."

"Camping?" Susan looked horrified.

"Only for three or four nights," Angel assured her. "Once you reach Saratoga, it's only a day and a half trip north to the railroad at Hannah. The scenery is breathtaking. If you're lucky you may even get to see a bear or a moose."

"A bear?" Susan said faintly.

Angel nodded. "Jared loves the mountains, you know. He's gone to the Snowys every summer since he was little. I'm sure you'll soon learn to enjoy it as much as he does."

"Relax, Susan." Jared said. "Angel's teasing you."

She stiffened indignantly. "I see."

"Don't take it personally," Ox said with a grin. "Angel and I have a few scores to settle with Jared from our courting days."

"Like the time Jared and my sister Shannon locked

us in the barn together," Angel added.

Jared laughed. "You should be thanking me for that. If it hadn't been for Shannon and me, you two would have never gotten married."

"Ha! Ox was lucky to survive you two and your shenanigans at all."

Ox raised a brow. "You know, Susan, you might want to reconsider marrying this fiancé of yours. He was quite a terror as a boy. His children will likely be the same way. One time he...."

Normally Alaina would have enjoyed listening to the tales of Jared's misspent youth almost as much as watching Susan's growing consternation. But tonight she could barely concentrate on what the others were saying. All she could think about was the pass over the mountain and the escape route it represented.

By the time everyone said their goodnights and headed for bed, Alaina had come up with a plan that would get her to Fort Bridger despite Jared Brady. Though she'd never actually been in the mountains, she'd grown up going on overnight trips in the woods with her father and brothers. Best of all Jared couldn't stop her from buying a train ticket once she got to Hannah.

In the privacy of her room, Alaina dug out the battered purse Garrick had given her. Since Jared had insisted on paying for everything on their trip, she had spent very little of her money. There was plenty to rent a horse and buy supplies. The horse would be no problem; she'd passed the livery stable on her way from the train station. Supplies would be a little more difficult, but surely, she'd find some place to buy them between Laramie City and the mountain.

She settled down into bed with a smile on her face. The thought of thwarting Jared Brady was almost as intoxicating as the promise of adventure. As she drifted off, she wondered what it would be like to have him actually approve of something she did. Though it wasn't likely to happen, the novel thought was nearly as intriguing as the idea of besting him.

The first rays of the sun were just peeking up over the horizon when Alaina awakened Phoebe pretending to have a headache. Phoebe was most sympathetic and promised to make sure no one woke Alaina once she got back to sleep.

When Phoebe quietly closed the door and returned to her own bed, Alaina put pillows under her blankets to look like she was still asleep. Then she dressed and crept out of the house. With any kind of luck, they wouldn't realize she was gone until early afternoon. By then she'd be well on her way.

The sleepy boy at the livery stable was less than enthusiastic about renting her a horse until she mentioned her relationship to Ox and Angel Treenery. The boy's unwillingness disappeared in an instant and he became most obliging. She was secretly glad when he told her he didn't have a sidesaddle and that she'd have to settle for a regular saddle instead. It would make crossing the mountains much easier. With a final reminder to deliver the note she left in his keeping, Alaina climbed into the saddle and turned her horse west toward the mountains.

Though Alaina hadn't ridden astride much in the last few years, and her skirts made it a bit more cumbersome, she had little difficulty controlling her mount. When she stopped in the tiny town of Centennial to buy supplies, she was rewarded with the information that the pass was indeed open. The talkative storekeeper told her it would take several days of hard riding to get to Saratoga, so she bought enough food to last ten days to be safe. Jerky, and a small sack each of beans, flour and cornmeal and a few odds and ends made up her purchases.

It would be so much easier if she could have carried more canned goods, then she wouldn't have to stop so early every night to camp. Unfortunately, she only had so much room on her horse. She bought an empty flour sack to carry it all in and two blankets to keep her warm. Then, as a treat to herself for outsmarting Jared Brady, she added a loaf of fresh bread and a small wheel of cheese for her lunch.

By early afternoon she was well into the foothills and had started to climb. Angel hadn't exaggerated a bit when she called the scenery breath taking. Alaina stopped by a sparkling clear stream to eat and gazed about in wonder. Bright yellow wild flowers poked through the tender green grass, while ground squirrels chattered at her from a nearby boulder. Across the meadow, she could see the faint outline of a doe and her fawn watching her from the trees. No wonder Jared loved these mountains.

It was surprisingly chilly, so she put on her coat. For once she was glad she didn't have a more stylish pelisse. The coat, though definitely what Susan would call countrified, would at least keep her arms warm while she was riding. A pleased smile crossed her face when she found her woolen mittens in the pockets. Now she was ready for anything!

As she packed up the remains of her meal, Alaina

found herself thinking about Jared. Though it was possible she might reach the Fort ahead of Susan and him, it was doubtful. She was still wondering how she was going to get around him, when the first drops of moisture hit her face. Startled, she looked up at the rapidly darkening sky. Huge fluffy snowflakes drifted lazily down from heavy gray clouds. At first there were only a few, but before long they began to cover the trail. Alaina shivered as a slight breeze tugged at her cloak. Suddenly, the mountains seemed anything but friendly.

"I'm sorry to disturb you, Mrs. Treenery," Phoebe said apologetically from the sitting room door, "But there's a stable boy out front who says he has a message for you."

Angel looked surprised as she rose to her feet. "How strange. I wonder who it's from."

"Something terrible must have happened," Susan observed as Angel left the room. "I knew it was a mistake for your brother-in-law to take the children on such a dangerous outing."

Jared folded the newspaper he'd been reading. "They went fishing, for heaven's sake. The worst that could happen is someone falling in and getting wet."

"One of the children could have drowned."

"Highly unlikely. The creek they went to is barely knee deep."

"When did she give you this note?" Angel asked, coming back into the room with the boy from the livery.

"'Bout dawn. She rented a horse and headed out to meet the folks she was traveling with." The boy from the livery watched as Angel put on her glasses and read the slightly grubby paper in her hand. "Said not to give it to you till noon, but Mr. Peebles sent me home early so I thought I'd stop on my way."

"You did just right," Angel said folding the note. "Did she say anything else?"

"Just that she had to hurry, or they were going to leave without her and that you'd understand."

"Thank you, Johnny," Angel said pressing a coin into his hand. "I appreciate you taking the time to drop this by."

"Sure thing Mrs. Treenery." With a grin and a wave, the boy left.

Jared studied his sister's frown. "What's wrong, Angel?"

"Alaina left for Fort Bridger early this morning. According to the note, she went with a family who were headed that way."

Jared tossed the newspaper aside. "Damn, I should have known better than to believe she'd give up that easily."

"What are you talking about?"

"She tried to buy a train ticket to Fort Bridger yesterday, but I stopped her. I convinced the clerk she was running away, and he promised not to sell her one."

Angel groaned. "Oh, Jared, you didn't."

"I thought you didn't want her going to Fort Bridger."

"I don't, but that's not the way to stop her. You made her feel trapped and desperate. Where do you suppose she met this family?"

"There is no family." Jared rose to his feet and paced to the window. "I was with her every minute until we walked back into this house. There was nobody around but us."

"I always did think she was too headstrong for her own good," Susan said with a sniff. "She pays back your kindness by sending a note with a stable hand, of all things. The very idea."

Angel ignored Susan as she studied the note. "I wonder why she rented a horse. Outside of taking a train, there's really no way to get to Fort Bridger this time of the year unless you head back to Cheyenne or north to the stage stop at Medicine Bow, and she wouldn't know about that."

"The mountains," Jared said suddenly. "Hell and damnation, she's headed for the pass!"

"Oh, no." Angel closed her eyes. "We made it sound like an outing in the park. She has no idea how dangerous the Snowy Range can be."

"Damn it to hell anyway. That girl is going to be the death of me yet," Jared muttered, stalking to the door.

Susan rose to her feet in dismay. "Jared, where are you going?"

"To bring back one spoiled, willful little brat before she gets herself hurt."

"Don't you want me to send for Ox to go with you?" Angel asked, following him into the hall.

"No time. She's got several hours start on me as it is. Don't worry, Sis, I'll bring her back in one piece." He grabbed his hat from the hall tree and jammed it on his head. "Of course, I won't promise not to paddle her backside when I find her."

"Don't do anything stupid," Angel warned. "She's not your ten-year old niece."

"I'm well aware of that. My nieces are all better behaved than she is. Throw some supplies together for me, will you? I'm going to see what your husband has in the way of good horseflesh."

Less than forty-five minutes later Jared was ready to go. He'd chosen a big raw-boned gelding and a showy long-legged mare for the trip. Both were built for speed and endurance.

"Why are you taking so much?" Susan asked, watching him tighten the pack on the mare's back. "I thought you were coming back tonight."

"Just in case. You never know what you're going to run into in the high country. Those clouds look like they might even turn into snow."

Angel handed him a canteen and a cloth sack. "Here's your water and a bite to eat so you don't have to stop."

"Thanks." He stowed them and swung up into the saddle. "We may wind up going to Fox Park or Woods Landing if the storm breaks so don't panic if we don't make it home right away. We could be stuck there a week or more if the pass closes again."

"Hurry back," Susan said plaintively. "I'll miss you."

"I'll miss you too, sweetheart. Take care of her, Angel," he picked up his lead rope and rode out of the yard without a backward glance.

By pushing his horses to the limit, Jared reached Centennial by early afternoon. A short stop at the mercantile gave him the first hope of the day. A young woman had stopped for supplies a mere three hours before. As he stepped outside the store, he frowned. He didn't like the look of the sky nor the chill in the air.

Unless he missed his guess, they were in for some nasty weather.

Jared pulled up the collar of his coat and urged his mount forward. Alaina was only a few hours ahead of him and not pushing her horse. With any kind of luck, he'd catch up with her before the storm broke, and they'd be able to make it back to Centennial before dark.

Twenty minutes later the first snowflakes began to fall. Within the hour, drifts were beginning to pile up around him, and the trail underfoot became treacherous. The sharp air stung his nose and ears. *Only a fool would continue on in this weather,* Jared thought to himself as he huddled deeper into his coat. Even as he cursed Alaina for her blatant stupidity, worry curled around the edges of his irritation. With the tent he'd brought along they could survive the storm, but would he reach her in time?

Except for the cold, it was like riding into a world made of white cotton. The falling snow deadened all sound, even the creak of the trees. A slight movement in a tree ahead of them suddenly caught his attention, just a tiny flicker of black moving back and forth. Squinting into the storm, Jared could see the vague outline of a mountain lion crouched low along a branch that hung out over the trail ahead of them. Jared swore under his breath as he pulled his glove off with his teeth and reached for his six-gun.

His finger had barely touched the trigger when the horses caught the big cat's scent and reared in fright. The gun went off and flew out of his hand as Jared was thrown from the saddle. He landed in the snow with a bone-jarring thump, then rolled out of the way just as the packhorse galloped by, her sharp hooves missing him by inches. Stunned, he watched in helpless dismay as the terrified mare disappeared up the trail and the mountain lion melted into the storm after her. Ignoring the pain in his side, Jared struggled to his feet and lunged for the gelding's trailing reins.

Already skittish, the frightened animal reared again, and Jared felt the icy reins slipping through his frozen fingers. Desperately, he wound the reins around his hand, wincing as the leather bit cruelly into his wrist. Praying the sound of his voice would calm the frightened animal, he started talking.

"Whoa, there, boy," he said in a soothing tone. "That old cougar wasn't after us. He's probably as scared right now as you are." As he continued talking, the horse began to quiet. It took several minutes for Jared to locate his glove in the snow, but he knew he risked frostbite without its protection. Of the six-gun there was no sign. Because it was heavier than the glove, it was most likely buried in the snow. After a futile search, Jared gave it up as a lost cause. By the time he was able to remount, He was shaking with cold and reaction. He knew he was dangerously close to the end of his endurance, and that his only chance for survival lay in returning to Centennial.

He didn't even glance back the way he'd come as he guided the gelding back onto the trail and headed up the mountain. All he could think of was Alaina wandering helplessly in the blizzard until she dropped from exhaustion or the cougar got her. Without the tent and his supplies, he had little chance of helping her even if he could find her. Still, there was no way he could turn away and leave her to her fate.

The cold penetrated his trousers as though they weren't there. His legs were covered with icy-hot pinpricks of pain. Even his coat did little to stop the shivering. Just when it looked as though things couldn't get much worse, the wind started to blow, and the storm turned into a full-fledged blizzard.

Jared lost all track of time as the horse plodded onward through the snow. His ribs throbbed with pain and his face stung where the wind driven snow hit the exposed skin between his hat and bandanna. He was beginning to lose the feeling in his hands and feet when he caught the smell of smoke. At first he thought he was hallucinating, but it came again, stronger this time.

Someone had found enough shelter from the storm to start a fire. Maybe there was a cave nearby or even a cabin. Suddenly, hope surged within his breast. Alaina might have found her way here too. His eyes searched the gloom trying to locate the source of the smoke.

He almost missed it in the gathering dusk. The wind had piled snow over the structure until it was little more than a hump huddled against a sheer rock wall. If the gelding hadn't whinnied to another horse tethered in the shelter of the trees, Jared would have ridden right by without giving it a second glance.

Praying that whoever had built the lean-to was willing to share it, Jared rode his horse into the trees. He dismounted with difficulty, tied the animal to a bush and made his way through the knee-deep snow to the small shelter. Vermilion spots appeared before his eyes as he lifted the wool blanket that covered the entrance and pitched forward into dark oblivion.

CHAPTER EIGHT

Slowly, awareness came to Jared. His hands and feet felt swollen and his ribs throbbed, but the rest of his body was surprisingly warm. The tantalizing smell of cooking meat teased him into full wakefulness. He opened his eyes and stared at the figure huddled on the far side of the fire.

"Alaina! Thank God you're safe."

Her head jerked up at the sound of his voice, and she smiled at him in the dim light. "You're finally awake."

"How long was I out?"

"I don't know for sure, but I think it's before noon. The wind stopped about an hour ago."

He struggled to sit up. "My horse—"

"Don't worry, I took care of him right after you got here. He wasn't in much better shape than you were, but he recovered faster. Both horses seemed all right last time I checked them. Would you like some soup?"

"I sure would. It smells delicious."

"It smells better than it tastes, I'm afraid," she said, scooping it out of the small pot with a tin cup. "I boiled some of the jerky I bought in Centennial yesterday. We'll have to share the cup. It's the only one I have."

The broth was thin and watery, but the salty brew seemed to be exactly what his body craved.

"What are you doing up here, Jared?" Alaina asked.

Jared stared at her in astonishment. "What do you think I'm doing up here? I came looking for you!"

She sighed. "That's what I figured. I guess I should have known you would."

"Damn right you should have, but then I don't suppose you stopped to think at all, did you?"

Alaina gazed at him for a moment then looked away. "No, I guess I didn't. Mama says it's my worst fault."

"If you'd taken two seconds to consider anybody but yourself, we'd both be sitting in Angel's parlor sipping tea now instead of in this mess. I damn near died out there."

"I'm sorry."

"Sorry doesn't do much good, does it? Didn't your father ever tell you not to venture into country you don't know by yourself?"

"Yes, but you all said was that the pass was open."

"Only an idiot would try to cross the Snowy Mountains alone, especially this time of year. If I hadn't promised Angel, I'd give you the spanking you deserve."

Alaina thrust out her jaw. "I'd like to see you try."

They glared at each other for a long moment. Jared was the first to drop his gaze. "Look," he said, running his hand through his hair, "It's all water under the bridge now. We're obviously stuck here for a while and I really don't want to fight with you," he said. "What do you say we call a truce?"

"I will if you will," Alaina said warily.

"I promise to be on my best behavior."

She gave him a wry smile. "I guess that means I'll have to be, too. Friends?"

He grinned and toasted her with the cup. "Friends."

"Where's our host?" Jared asked as he finished the

soup and handed the cup back to her.

"Who?"

"The man who built this shelter. Surely he didn't leave in this storm."

Alaina's smiled deepened as she dipped another cupful of soup out of the pot. "No, the person who put the lean-to together didn't leave."

"Then where is he?"

"You're looking at him."

Jared stared at her. "You?"

"Of course." She took a sip from the cup in her hand. "You forget I was raised by a Norwegian in Minnesota. We had to prove we could build a lean-to and get a fire going before we could go skiing by ourselves."

"I'll be damned." From the rock wall at the back of the shelter to the smoke hole in the center of the intertwined branches over his head, the lean-to showed the hand of an expert. "This is pretty amazing."

She shrugged. "I started building it as soon as the snow began to fall. P… uh… Garrick would say I didn't make it tight enough. It was pretty drafty until the drifts plugged all my holes."

"I don't know more than half a dozen men who could have done as well," he said admiringly. "It looks like you could survive half the winter in here."

"It's just a matter of being prepared. You could do a little better at that yourself. All I found on your saddle was a bedroll and a half-full canteen. You should always have food for at least a day."

"I left Laramie City with enough food for a week as well as a tent and grain for the horses."

"Where is it?"

"A mountain lion spooked my horses, and I got

bucked off. The last I saw of my packhorse, she was headed toward the high country at a dead run. She didn't bother to leave my supplies behind."

"You're lucky you found me when you did. Though I have to admit, you scared me half to death when you came in through that door."

"No worse than you scared me by running off that way. All I could think of was you freezing to death in a snow drift somewhere."

"I can take care of myself!"

"Sure you can. That's why we're trapped in a blizzard on the side of a mountain."

"Look Mr. High and Mighty, nobody asked you to..." Alaina stopped and gave him a rueful smile. "We're doing it again aren't we?"

He looked surprised for a moment then nodded reluctantly. "Yes, and I guess I started it this time. Sorry."

"I didn't have to rise to the bait," Alaina admitted. "So what do you want to talk about?"

He blinked. "I don't know."

Alaina's lips twitched. "Not being able to fight does kind of limit us, doesn't it? Hmm, how about where did you get the rope burn on your wrist?"

Jared glanced down at his right hand. Abrasions dotted with a few small scabs encircled his wrist. "I got that when I caught my saddle horse. My ribs hurt so much worse, I hadn't even noticed."

"What's wrong with your ribs?"

"I think I may have broken a couple when I got bucked off. I seemed to have bruised my shoulder too."

"Want me to take a look?"

"I suppose you're going to tell me your father taught

you how to deal with injuries too?"

Alaina grinned. "No, his mother. Granny Ellinson is known for miles around for her healing skills. Folks send for her before they send for the doctor."

"So you're following in her footsteps?"

"Hardly, but I do know a broken bone when I see one. My brothers have had several over the years."

He gazed at her for several long moments before he finally shrugged. "I guess it wouldn't hurt."

"Here," she said, "let me help you with your coat." It took both of them working together several minutes to remove the heavy sheepskin coat.

Jared winced and sucked air in through his teeth as they worked the sleeve off his bad shoulder.

"Damn," he said. "It's worse than I thought."

Alaina draped the coat across his back. "Here, relax and lean back against the wall. I think I have something here that will help."

"I sure hope so," he muttered as he settled back against the cliff wall. "Felt like you were sticking hot pokers into me."

Alaina crawled over to the far side of the lean-to and studied the wall. "Here it is," she said, pulling out a long stick.

"What's that?"

"A willow switch I cut down by the creek. The bark makes a soothing tea." It only took a few minutes to strip the bark and set it in a pan of water on the fire. "It should be ready pretty soon. In the meantime, I'd better check that arm."

"All right," he said closing his eyes. "Have at it."

Determining the extent of Jared's injuries was Alaina's only concern until she had undone his shirt and was reaching for the buttons at the top of his long johns. Unbidden, the image of him asleep in his train berth popped into her mind. Her fingers suddenly faltered as she remembered in vivid detail what lay beneath.

Jared opened his eyes and gazed up at her. "What's wrong?"

"I...I'm afraid I'll hurt you," she stammered.

He smiled slightly and closed his eyes again. "I'll try not to scream too loudly. We wouldn't want any starving grizzlies coming to investigate."

"Grizzlies?" Alaina bit her lip and slid the first button through the hole.

"Mmm. They come out of hibernation about this time of year, lean, mean and hungry as hell."

"I'd just as soon not meet one then," she murmured. The trail of open buttons reached all the way down to his navel, exposing a deep V of muscle and smooth skin. Alaina took a deep breath and slipped her hand underneath the fabric at the top of his chest. Ever so gently, she slid her fingers along the warm slope of his shoulder. The flickering fire bathed his skin with golden light as she pushed the red flannel down over his arm. Alaina licked suddenly dry lips and glanced back at his face to see if he was in pain. With a start, she realized his eyes were open and watching her.

"Did I hurt you?"

"No." His voice had a funny husky sound to it that sent her heart skittering against her ribs.

She swallowed hard. "I'll try to be gentle."

There was a deep purple bruise across two of his ribs and the upper part of his arm was red. Alaina grimaced against the pain she knew she caused him as she probed the injuries, feeling for broken bones or twisted muscles.

"I think your shoulder was wrenched," she said at last. "With any kind of luck, it should only be sore for a day or two. I can't tell for sure about your ribs so I'll bind them to be safe. It might not be a bad idea to make a sling for your arm."

He released his breath in a whoosh, and leaned his head back against the cliff. "Whatever you say, Doctor, just don't torture me anymore." Even in the dim light, his face looked pale.

"I think the tea's ready." She poured a cup and blew across the top to cool it. "Careful, it's hot," she said, handing him the cup.

Jared took a sip and made a face. "Yuck. I think I liked the jerky soup better."

"It'll help the pain. Drink."

"You're sure getting bossy." Jared took another sip of the tea and set it down. "Now what?"

"Close your eyes."

"What?"

"I said close your eyes. I'm going to take off one of my petticoats, and I'd rather you didn't watch."

"I see," he said, obediently closing his eyes. "You'll have to excuse me. My mind's a little muzzy. I can't for the life of me figure out why you picked this particular time to get undressed."

"There's a good ten yards of material in each of my petticoats."

He smiled. "Well that explains it."

It took several long minutes of concentrated effort in the cramped confines of the lean-to, but eventually she managed to struggle out of the petticoat. "There. Hand me that knife, will you?"

Jared watched in surprise as she methodically cut

the petticoat into long strips. "What the heck are you doing?"

"Making bandages. There, that ought to be enough. I'm going to need some help with this, but first you need to finish that tea."

"At your service, ma'am." He took a deep breath then drained the cup and made a face. "Boy that's nasty stuff. I assume you know what you're doing?"

"Not really, but I think we'll be able to muddle through. I helped Granny last year when my cousin broke his ribs. I'm going to rig some support for your shoulder so that you don't strain it any worse."

"Are you sure one petticoat will be enough?"

"If not there's plenty more were that came from. Here, lean forward so I can get this around you." Alaina soon discovered helping her grandmother with a younger cousin was very different from working on Jared. Before, worry had been her predominant emotion. It was there now too, but was overshadowed by stronger, less familiar feelings.

Her senses seemed more fine-tuned than ever before. The strong muscles of his chest beneath her fingers, the whisper of his breath across her cheek, the faint smell of leather and horses, all hit her with the subtly of an earthquake. Her stomach twisted in the oddest way, and the air suddenly became difficult to breathe. It was all she could do to keep her hands steady as she wrapped the strips of cloth around his chest to bind his ribs. When she finished, she found herself curiously reluctant to stop. With gentle hands, she followed the contours of his chest, softly smoothing the bandage, making sure it was firmly in place but not too tight. "There," she said at last. "How does that feel?"

"Incredible." The husky sound was back in his voice. It was like a soft caress against her ear.

Startled, she glanced up and found herself only inches from his face. He had the most beautiful eyes, she thought, staring into them. Like soft brown velvet, deep and sensual. "You mean it doesn't hurt any more?" she asked.

"Hardly at all." His voice was a deep sexy rumble as he cupped the side of her face with his good hand. "Can I ask you a personal question, Alaina?"

She gazed up at him. He had such a nice mouth. "I guess so."

"Have you ever been kissed?"

"No," she said in a breathless whisper.

"Don't be frightened," he murmured against her lips. "I won't hurt you."

An assurance that she wasn't frightened flashed across her mind then disappeared in a swirl of sweet sensation as Jared's mouth caressed hers with gentle persuasion. It was magical, like a single fragile snowflake, delicate and exquisitely beautiful. He broke it off slowly, feathering soft kisses against her lips as though he couldn't quite bring himself to break contact.

"I think that tea of yours has an unusual side effect," he said in a slightly shaky voice. "That wasn't what I intended to do at all."

Alaina stared up at him in bemused wonder. "That's all right. I didn't mind."

"I only wanted to say thank you."

"I'll consider myself thanked, then," she said with a smile. "Here, I'll help you put your shirt back on."

"Don't bother, I can manage," he said a trifle curtly.

"Are you sure?"

"Positive."

Stung by his rejection, Alaina pulled back and started digging through her supplies. She studiously ignored Jared's struggles to get dressed. It was nothing to her if he hurt himself.

In a surprisingly short time, he was dressed and shrugging into his coat. "I think I'll go check the horses."

She didn't bother to look up. "Would you mind taking your canteen and getting some water? We're almost out."

"Will do."

Jared breathed a sigh of relief as the blanket fell shut behind him. He leaned on a huge boulder that formed a partial windbreak for the lean-to and took in great draughts of the frosty air. It was a welcome change from the sultry heat inside the lean-to. From the minute Alaina reached inside his clothing to check his injuries, he knew he was in trouble. It was obvious her grandmother hadn't taught her to be brisk and matter of fact when she examined a patient. Alaina clearly didn't realize the effect her tentative touch could have on a man.

The pain had been an almost welcome diversion, but the willow bark tea had successfully reduced it to a dull ache. He still might have been all right except for Alaina running her hands all over his body to check the bandage. No man could resist sensual torture like that. The kiss had been a mistake, a loss of control he'd regretted almost as soon as it was over. A mistake he'd repeat in a heartbeat if he dared.

Thank God he could still use his arm. Allowing her to help him dress would have been a disaster. Heaven knew where that would have wound up. And so he'd escaped. His buttons were awry, but at least he couldn't give in to temptation again.

Jared looked up at the sky and smiled. Patches of bright blue showed through ragged tears in the clouds. Good, they'd be able to head down the mountain in a matter of hours. The sooner he delivered Alaina back into his sister's capable hands, the better.

Jared took his time getting water and checking the horses. He was surprised to find Alaina had had enough presence of mind to hang the saddles in a tree and drape the horse blankets over the leather to keep them dry. She never ceased to amaze him.

Still not ready to return to the warm, sensual interior of the lean-to, Jared reconnoitered to see if there was any sign of the cougar. By the time he returned to the lean-to, he was completely cooled down. If he hadn't quite forgotten the kiss, he at least had control of himself.

"I was about to come looking for you," Alaina said, as he ducked through the doorway. "I thought maybe you got lost or fell into the creek or something."

"Nope, just checking the trail. It would be just my luck if that cougar decided to come back to this one looking for game," he said, pulling off his gloves. "The snow is melting already. We'll be able to leave in time to get back to Centennial this afternoon."

Alaina sighed as she handed him the sling she'd fashioned for his arm. "I can give you some of my jerky, I guess. I'm not sure how much this snow is going to slow me down so I don't dare part with any more of my supplies."

"What are you talking about?"

"You're going back to Laramie City today aren't you?"

"Yes."

Alaina dropped her gaze. "I'm not going with you."

CHAPTER NINE

"Not going with me!" Jared stared at her in astonishment. "You can't seriously be thinking of going on."

"Thanks to your interference, this is the only way I can get to Fort Bridger."

"My interference! I was just trying to keep you from committing a terrible mistake."

"You know nothing about it."

"I know you're bound on a fool's errand," he said scornfully. "Angel told me you were going to see Cameron Price and asked me to stop you."

Alaina looked stricken. "She did?"

"Angel doesn't want you to get hurt. Cameron Price is way out of your league. He'd laugh you right out of the fort."

"What makes you such an expert on Cameron Price?"

"I've known him for two years. Do you think you're the first woman to go chasing after him?"

"This is different."

"That's what they all think. He'd have you for breakfast and be on to someone new by lunch."

"It's not like that. Our relationship is...unusual"

"Cameron makes all women feel that way." Jared took off his hat and tossed it in the corner. "He was probably seducing innocents like you before you were born, and he's never asked a one of them to marry him."

Alaina flushed. "That's not true."

"Come on, Alaina, use your head. He's old enough to be your father."

"That's how I know you're wrong," Alaina said angrily. "Cameron Price *is* my father."

There was a minute of stunned silence then Jared laughed. "Cameron Price has a long-lost daughter does he? Funny I never heard anything about it."

"I don't know why he'd tell you since you're obviously not a friend of his."

"Oh, come on, Alaina you really don't expect me to believe that, do you?"

"I don't care if you believe it or not, it's true."

"Does Angel realize you think he's your father?"

"She knows he is. You forget, she was there when I was born. Besides, I've seen a picture, and I look like him."

Jared stared intently into her face. After a moment, his eyes widened slightly. "Good Lord," he murmured. "You do."

"So, you understand why I have to go to Fort Bridger?"

"Revenge?"

Alaina gave him a blank look. "Why would I want revenge?"

"For what he did to your mother, obviously."

"For what he did to her! What about what she did to him? She turned her back on the father of her child and married another man."

"Knowing Cameron Price, it was probably the other way around."

"That's where you're wrong. He loved my mother, but Mama had fallen in love with Papa. I think she broke his heart."

Jared made a rude noise. "Price doesn't have a heart to break."

"Maybe that's why. He probably never got over my mother's rejection."

"You're deluding yourself, Alaina. If he remembers your mother at all, it's because she was the only woman to ever refuse him anything."

"That's all you know about it. He left money for me." She touched her satchel. I have the note here to prove it."

"Of all the idiotic..." Jared sighed in defeat. "We could spend the rest of the day arguing and you'd never change your mind about him, would you?"

"No." Alaina glowered at him defiantly. "I'm going to Fort Bridger and you can't stop me."

"I won't have to. The snow's going to do that for me."

"You said it was melting."

"Here it is. It won't be in the high country. You're still quite a way from the summit."

Alaina shrugged. "I'll take my chances."

"Oh, no you won't. I'll carry you off this mountain if I have to."

"You might try." Alaina glared at him. "Frankly, I don't think you're man enough to do it."

Jared laughed outright at that. "I suppose you're going to stop me."

"You wouldn't stand a chance. I've spent my whole life wrestling with my brothers and cousins. They taught me a trick or two."

The stubborn set of her jaw made Jared pause. If he tried to use physical force, she might well turn it into a wrestling match. Rolling around on the floor of the lean-to with her was the last thing Jared wanted. It might start as a simple contest of wills, but it almost certainly wouldn't end that way. If an innocent touch could result in a kiss that damn near set his boots on fire, God help him if he suddenly found himself in an intimate position like that.

"Look, Alaina, this mountain is nothing to mess with," he said in a more reasonable tone. "I just don't want you to get into trouble up here."

"It seems to me like you're the one who got into trouble. If you hadn't found my lean-to when you did, you'd have frozen to death."

"Which proves my point. I know these mountains, and I still nearly died."

"I, on the other hand, took precautions," Alaina reminded him. "I was safe because I used my head. I'll be fine."

"I can't let you go by yourself."

"If you feel that strongly, you're welcome to join me, but I'm going on, with or without you."

Jared frowned. There had to be some way to convince her how foolhardy her plan was. "How much food do you have?"

"For the two of us? I'd say enough for four or five days, a little more if I go alone."

"It would take at least that to get to Saratoga. We'd have to leave tomorrow morning to be safe."

Alaina frowned. "I guess so."

"I'll make you a deal, then," Jared said. "If we can safely travel up the mountain tomorrow, we will."

Her eyes narrowed. "What if we can't?"

"If that pass isn't clear enough to travel by tomorrow

there's no way we can make it to Saratoga before our supplies run out."

"You're saying if the snow is still too bad we might as well head back down to Centennial, right?"

Jared shrugged. "Either that or we sit here until we run out of food and then go back." He watched the expressions chase their way across Alaina's face. She didn't like his solution but couldn't argue his logic.

"All right," she said finally. "But you have to shake hands on it."

As she gripped his hand, Jared found himself curiously touched by her naive trust in the simple gesture. He vowed he wouldn't be the one to teach her that a handshake didn't necessarily ensure honesty.

"I suppose there isn't much chance of it melting by morning is there?" she asked.

"No."

"I figured as much when you gave in so easily." She gave him a baleful glance. "But don't think that means I'll consider leaving here this afternoon. You promised we'd wait until morning, and I'm going to hold you to that."

Jared smiled slightly. "Then I suppose it's useless to point out we could sleep in nice warm beds in Centennial tonight."

"Worse than useless," Alaina said digging into her bag. "It would probably make me angry, and I have better things to do than fight with you."

Jared raised an eyebrow. "Such as?"

"Beating the pants off you for a start." She held up a deck of cards. "I always take them with me in case I get stuck somewhere with nothing to do."

"Sorry, I don't know how to play any ladies' card

games."

Alaina grinned. "Neither do I. How about blackjack?"

"Fine with me," Jared said. "But I think I should warn you I'm pretty good at it."

"We'll see," she said with an enigmatic smile.

Jared soon discovered Alaina's skill was nothing short of amazing. By late afternoon, he'd lost far more consistently than he'd won. "Remind me never to play anything but penny-ante poker with you," he said, idly flipping through the deck. "Are you sure these things aren't marked?"

"I don't need to mark them. It's a matter of knowing when to fold and when to bet. I remember what's been played and then figure the odds. It's as simple as that."

"It is, is it? And who taught you this *simple* system."

"My fa...." A look of consternation crossed her face, and she cleared her throat. "Uh...Garrick did. Mama says he's one of the best."

"He must be. It's a good thing I didn't bet Ox's horse. I'd have a hard time explaining how I'd lost one to a mountain lion and the other to a slip of a girl."

"Garrick says you should never bet more than you can afford to lose. Let's see now," she said, tallying up her winnings. "You owe me your saddle, rifle, bedroll, coat, and all your supplies if we ever find them." She gave him a speculative glance. "I guess you can keep your boots. It's too cold to run around barefoot."

"That's big of you. If I'd known you were going to be so easy-going, I'd have bet my shirt and pants," he said sarcastically. "Maybe my luck would have changed."

"Garrick says your luck never changes if you're

losing." She grinned. "You'd be pretty embarrassed if you were sitting here in your underwear right now."

"How am I supposed to get my gear back?"

"Hmm." Alaina looked thoughtful. Suddenly her face brightened. "I know, if you fix supper, we'll call it even. How's that?"

"Suits me fine." His eyes twinkled merrily. "Best darn wages I'll ever earn for cooking. I'm not known for my culinary talents."

"If you're that bad, maybe I should reconsider."

"Nope, a deal's a deal. Point me toward the food."

They had just finished their supper of canned beans when the wind started to blow. It was all Jared could do to keep a smile of smug satisfaction off his face. If another storm moved in, even Alaina would have to admit defeat and head back down the mountain with him. In the meantime, they were safe and snug in the lean-to with enough food to last out the most severe spring storm.

It was obvious Alaina knew what the wind meant too. She said little and there was a pathetic droop to her mouth as she prepared for bed. Jared almost felt sorry for her. It was for her own good, he reminded himself. The trip over the mountain was far too dangerous for a woman. Even so, he was aware of an odd little sting of guilt as he settled down on his side of the fire and closed his eyes to sleep.

At first, Alaina wasn't sure what woke her. Something wasn't right, but her sleep-befuddled mind couldn't identify the problem. Then she heard it. A tiny whisper of sound so normal she hadn't noticed it at first.

Normal, but out of place here. Above the howl of the wind she could swear she heard water dripping. It didn't make sense.

As she sat up and listened intently trying to identify the source, Jared suddenly jerked upright on the other side of the lean-to. "What the hell...?"

"You hear water dripping too?" Alaina asked.

"I don't just hear it, I feel it. It's practically raining over here."

Alaina glanced toward the fire pit. "It can't be the fire. There's nothing left but embers."

"I'll go look around." Jared said, crawling out of his bedroll. Only a few minutes passed before he was back. "Better get your gear packed. It's a Chinook."

"What in the world is that?"

"A warm wind blowing down from the top of the mountain. The snow's melting. Look, there's already a stream of water running across the floor."

Alaina scrambled out of bed. "Oh dear, we could be right in the path of a flood."

"My thoughts exactly. We ought to be safe enough on top of that boulder outside."

"What about the horses?"

"They're up on a bank. Plenty high enough to be safe."

It took little time to vacate the lean-to, but climbing to safety on the rock proved to be more difficult than either of them anticipated. Alaina was surprisingly agile even in her long skirts and bulky coat. She had no trouble clambering to the top of the boulder, but Jared was another matter. With the limited use of his left arm and his sore ribs, he couldn't get enough purchase on the boulder to pull himself up.

Finally, in spite of Jared's protests, Alaina slid down the rock and gave him a boost from behind. Then she climbed back up. "How long do we have until dawn?" she asked, settling herself next to him.

Jared pulled out his pocket watch and squinted down at it in the dim light of the moon. "About three and a half hours."

Alaina sighed. "It will probably seem like a lot more. Want to share my blanket?"

"Pardon me?"

"I assume yours is wet since the roof was dripping on you," she said, unfolding her blanket.

"I'll be fine."

"Don't be ridiculous. It's going to get pretty chilly before morning." She scooted closer to him and threw the blanket around both of them. "Anyway, with the wind blowing the way it is, I'll be too cold to sleep otherwise."

Jared glanced down at her in surprise. "You're planning to go back to sleep?"

"I didn't get much rest last night. I was too worried about you."

"But we're sitting on a rock."

"I know. I can go to sleep just about anywhere. Papa says it's my Viking heritage. Mama's people were Danish, you know, and Papa's were..." she trailed off as she realized it didn't matter what Garrick's family was. They were no part of her.

"My ancestors were English," Jared told her. "They liked their beds soft and warm."

"That's probably why the Vikings sent them running for cover. They were too dependent on their comforts," Alaina said drowsily.

"You're serious about going to sleep aren't you?"

"Mmmhuh."

The top of Alaina's head was already nodding against his uninjured shoulder. With a resigned sigh, Jared put his arm around her. "Sweet dreams," he murmured, pulling the blanket around them both.

Alaina smiled and snuggled closer into his warmth.

The bright sun shining on her face woke Alaina several hours later. She lay within the circle of Jared's arms, her head resting against the curve of his neck. It was surprisingly comfortable, so comfortable, in fact, that she didn't want to move. She tilted her head slightly to look up at Jared's face. In spite of his misgivings, he had fallen asleep where the boulder leaned against the cliff. As though he felt her gaze upon him, he opened his eyes.

"Good morning," she said cheerfully. "Did you sleep well?"

"Not particularly. How about you?"

She sat up and stretched. "I don't think I stirred all night."

Jared grinned. "You weren't kidding about being able to sleep anywhere."

"No, I...Oh Jared, look," she cried. "The Chinook melted all the snow!"

Jared stared around in amazement. Every speck of snow was gone. Only a few mud puddles and a couple of deep channels where the water had run down the mountain remained to show that it had ever been there.

"Let's get going," she said, sliding down off the boulder. "I'll fix breakfast."

"The trail is probably still blocked on top."

"We won't know until we get there, will we? Come

on, Jared, you promised."

"Oh, all right," he grumbled. "But don't be surprised if we have to turn around and come back."

Half expecting him to change his mind now that the snow had melted, Alaina hurried through the breakfast preparations and helped him saddle the horses. In less than half an hour they were on the trail. Alaina breathed a silent sigh of relief as she followed Jared upward toward the summit. Though he didn't like the turn of events, he wouldn't go back on his word.

They began to see the remnants of snow banks as they climbed, but the trail remained clear. The higher they went, the blacker Jared's mood became, but Alaina paid little attention as she feasted her eyes on the beautiful scenery. The scent of pine was heavy in the air as the trail wound up through the virgin evergreen forest. With surprising frequency, the trees gave way to sun-kissed meadows, crystalline mountain lakes and breath-taking vistas where the trees were replaced with huge granite cliffs that fell away into nothing.

"Well, I'll be." Jared said. "There she is just waiting for us to come along."

Alaina brought her horse to a stop behind Jared's and peered back into the trees. "Who?"

"My packhorse."

"Are your supplies still on her?"

"Looks like it, why?"

Alaina smiled brightly. "Then we'll have no problem getting to Saratoga."

"Don't get your hopes up," Jared said with a disapproving frown. "It's hard to say what shape they're in."

Alaina wiped the smile off her face as she followed

him back into the trees. No sense in ruffling his fur any worse than it already was. Jared looked anything but happy as he dismounted and surveyed the damage. Alaina couldn't see what he was doing in the deep shadows of the trees, but she could hear. The sound of breaking branches punctuated with a string of curses soon filled the air.

After several minutes Alaina cleared her throat. "Are you all right?"

"You've got my arm so bound up it's damn near useless." With a muttered curse, he pulled the sling over his head and flung it to the side.

"I think it's probably all right to take it off now," she said lamely. "Uh...is there anything I can do to help?"

"As a matter of fact, I could use a hand here."

"Is the horse all right?" Alaina asked, as she dismounted.

"She seems to be, but she's got herself stuck pretty tight."

When her eyes adjusted to the dim light, Alaina saw what he was talking about. Branches and twigs from five different trees penetrated deep into various parts of the pack effectively immobilizing the mare without harming her. Even with the two of them working at it, extricating the mare proved to be an onerous task.

They were finally starting to make progress when Jared lifted his head and stared off toward the top of the mountain. "Do you hear that?" he asked urgently.

Alaina stopped her struggle with a particularly stubborn branch to listen. Far off in the distance she could hear a strange popping noise. "What is it?"

"Rifle fire."

"Good heavens, it sounds like a war. What do you

suppose is going on?"

"I don't know," he said solemnly, "but I think we'd better be prepared for the worst."

A shiver of apprehension ran down Alaina's back, and she redoubled her efforts to free the mare. She had just pulled out the last branch when Jared suddenly grabbed her and shoved her behind a clump of underbrush.

"What do you think you're doing...." she began indignantly, but he put his finger to his lips warningly and nodded toward the trail. Motioning for her to stay put, he quickly untied both of their horses, picked up the lead rope of the packhorse, and led all three deeper into the trees.

Perplexed, Alaina listened intently for a moment. At first, she couldn't identify the sound that had galvanized Jared into action, but as it drew nearer, she suddenly understood. Though she'd never actually heard them before, the bloodcurdling war whoops were unmistakable. Long before the horsemen thundered into view, Alaina knew who they were and shrank back deeper into the protective shadows. A band of marauding Indians was one part of the Wild West she had no desire to experience first-hand.

CHAPTER TEN

Alaina shuddered as the last of the Indians disappeared around a bend in the trail. If one of them had glanced to the left as they rode past...

Suddenly Jared was beside her. "That was a little too close for comfort."

"I've never actually seen wild Indians before."

Jared made a derisive sound. "You still haven't. Other than a few renegade half-breeds, they weren't any more Indian than I am."

Alaina glanced up at him in astonishment. "Are you sure? I mean they looked like Indians to me."

"A few feathers, some buckskins and a dash of paint here and there will fool most people. Did you notice their saddles?"

"They looked like ordinary saddles to me."

"Exactly. Indians don't ride saddles, at least not the kind you're used to. They don't make that much noise either unless they're attacking."

"If they aren't Indians, who are they and what are they doing here?"

"I don't know, but I sure don't intend to stick around and find out. Come on, let's get going before they come back looking for us."

"They don't even know we're here," Alaina said in surprise.

"They will when they find your lean-to."

"Oh, I hadn't thought of that." Alaina's stomach

jumped nervously as she followed him back to the horses. "Where do you think they were headed?"

"It's hard to say. There were enough of them to attack Centennial of they wanted to. From the look of them, I don't think they were planning on paying a friendly call wherever they were going. Come on, let's move."

Alaina looked over her shoulder. For the first time, the mountain became a place of danger and her trip a foolhardy undertaking. With a shudder, she turned and hurried after Jared.

Within moments they were mounted and headed up the mountain again. A new sense of urgency pushed them onward toward the summit where there was more protection and less chance of being seen. They were nearly there when Jared stopped suddenly and sniffed the air.

"What is it?" Alaina asked fearfully.

"Smoke. There, above the trees, see it? We'd better check it out. Someone may need help."

With a sense of foreboding, they approached the column of smoke. They could hear the crackling roar of the fire long before they saw the cabin, or what was left of it.

Only one wall remained standing. The rest of the log structure was little more than a smoldering ruin, destroyed by the fire that raged through the underbrush in the forest beyond.

"Stay here," Jared said. "I'm going to take a look around."

Time passed slowly as Alaina waited for Jared to return. He seemed to be taking an awfully long time. As she sat there wondering if he could be in trouble, she gradually became aware of a strange mewling sound, almost like a whimper. She cocked her head and listened intently. There it was again, and it seemed to be coming from the trees on the opposite side of the clearing from the fire. With her usual disregard for Jared's commands, she climbed down from her horse and went to investigate.

Cautiously, she entered the deep shadows of the trees. The sound came again, louder now. It seemed to be coming from a pile of pine needles and sticks at the base of a large pine. Alaina knelt next to the tree and brushed away the debris to uncover a brightly colored blanket beneath. Frowning, she gently pulled back the blanket and found herself staring down into a pair of bright hazel eyes. "A baby!" she said, rocking back on her heels.

The baby didn't make a sound as she pulled the blanket away dumping the pine needles and sticks on the forest floor. "What in the world?" she exclaimed as the blanket fell away. The baby was wrapped in brightly beaded leather that was laced down the front and secured to a board.

"I wonder who left you here," she murmured, touching the baby's downy cheek. "I'd better take you to Jared."

It only took a moment to brush away the rest of the forest debris and pick up the baby, strange contraption, and all. As she cautiously approached the shell of the cabin, an odd sound came from the edge of the woods. Mystified, Alaina stopped and listened intently for several seconds. It sounded for all the world as if someone were vomiting. "Jared?" she called quietly. "Jared, can you hear me?"

"Jesus, Alaina, don't come over here!" he said urgently.

Alaina frowned. "Are you all right?"

"I'll be there in a minute."

"Look, Jared, if someone's sick I might be able to..."

"No, damn it. Just do as I say for once and stay where you are!"

"All right." She was still trying to decide whether to stay where she was or ignore Jared's orders when he came staggering around the corner of the cabin. His face was pale, his expression haunted.

"Come on," he said urgently. "Let's get the hell out of here."

"Jared, what's wrong?"

"Damn it, Alaina, we don't have time for this."

"Quiet, Jared, you'll scare him."

"What?" For the first time Jared looked down at the bundle in her arms. "Good, Lord!"

"He was hidden under a pile of trash, and strapped to this thing, whatever it is."

"It's a cradleboard. Indian women use them to carry their babies." Jared glanced back over his shoulder. "His mother probably put him in it today to keep him safe."

"Are you sure he's an Indian? He has auburn hair and hazel eyes for heaven's sake."

"He's Indian all right. His daddy had bright red hair, but his mama was a full-blooded Bannock. I met them last fall."

"Was?" Alaina gave him a horrified look. "They're both...?"

"Dead," he said in a flat voice as he reached out a shaking hand to touch the baby. "I'm surprised you found him. Indian babies are taught not to cry when they're in their cradleboards."

"He didn't really cry. It was more of a whimper. He's kind of a cute little—"

"Look, Alaina, we don't have time for this now," Jared interrupted. "I want to be as far away from here as possible in case those renegades come looking for us when they find the lean-to."

"What about the baby's parents?"

"There's nothing more anybody can do for them."

Alaina was appalled. "Aren't you going to bury them?"

"It would take me most of the afternoon to bury them, even if I had a shovel, which I don't. That time would be far better spent putting distance between those renegades and us. My other concern is that fire over there. As wet as everything is from the snow, it shouldn't be a problem. On the other hand, I want to tangle with a forest fire even less than the renegades."

"I guess you're right." Alaina couldn't quite keep the doubt out of her voice.

"Look," he said, "I don't like it any better than you do, but I don't see that we've got much choice."

"No, I guess we don't." Alaina looked down at the cradleboard. "What are we going to do with him?"

"I don't know. Zeke didn't have any relatives that I know of, not that they'd want this baby anyway."

"How could they not?" Alaina protested.

"As a rule, whites aren't too wild about Indians, even ones this size."

"But he's half white!"

"Most folks wouldn't see it that way. Half-breed is a dirty word around here."

"Maybe his mother's people..."

"Even if I knew where to find them, the chances are they couldn't take him. Most tribes have too many mouths to feed as it is."

"Oh, Jared, we have to do something."

"I know." Jared traced the baby's downy cheek with his knuckle. "Don't worry, we'll think of something. In the meantime, we better get going."

"All right, but first I need to fix him up a sugar-teat to keep him happy. Here," she said, handing the baby to Jared, "Hold him so I can get the sugar and a clean handkerchief out of my saddle bag."

It only took a few minutes for her to make a small bag from the handkerchief, fill it with sugar and tie it off, but Jared's impatience nearly drove her crazy. He scanned the area constantly, jumping at the slightest noise, and peering into the shadows of the trees.

"Those renegades have surely found our lean-to by now," he said pacing across the clearing and back.

"I never even thought about taking it apart. If I had, there wouldn't be anything to find."

"There was no reason to think we needed to."

Alaina stuck the sugar-teat into the baby's mouth, and smiled as he started to suck on it. "There you go, sweetheart, that should keep you happy for a while. Jared, will you hand him up to me as soon as I get on my horse?"

"The cradleboard is made to carry on your back," he pointed out as she mounted her horse.

"I know, but I won't be able to look at him. It's the only way I'll know for sure if he's sick or not."

Jared glanced at the baby before handing him up to her. "He seems content enough now."

"It's the sugar-teat. They settle the fussiest baby."

"I hope so. We've got a long day ahead of us."

Alaina looked at the smoldering cabin as Jared swung up into the saddle. "I won't hold you to your promise anymore."

He glanced back in surprise. "What promise?"

"We don't have to go on to Saratoga. In fact, it would probably be best if we went back to Laramie City."

"It's a little late for that now," he said, turning away in disgust. "In case you missed it, there are a dozen or so cold-blooded killers between us and Laramie City. Believe me, if there were any way to get us off this mountain right now, I'd do it."

Alaina bit her lip and followed him out of the clearing feeling small and selfish. If it hadn't been for her they wouldn't even be here. A small noise drew her attention to the baby in her arms. On the other hand, if they hadn't come along, he'd have starved to death. "Lucky for you I'm so stubborn," she murmured.

They traveled fast and hard, trying to put as much distance between them and the renegades as possible. It was long after noon when they stopped for a quick lunch. By then, Alaina's arms and shoulders were so tight from the strain of holding the cradleboard and guiding the horse that she was unable to dismount by herself.

Jared frowned as he took the baby from her and helped her down. "Why didn't you say something?"

"There wasn't anything you could have done if I had," she said with a shrug. "Right now, we'd better feed our friend here. I imagine he's pretty hungry."

Jared gave the baby a baffled look. "What does he eat?"

"Pretty much the same things we do as long as it's

fairly soft He only has a few teeth."

"Well then, I guess jerky's out of the question then," Jared said. "I'll go see what I can find."

The baby whimpered and Alaina nodded knowingly. "I'll bet you need to be changed too."

Jared frowned. "I hadn't thought of that either. What are you going to use for diapers?"

"The rest of the petticoat that I used to bind your ribs. I'll just tear it up into squares as I need them."

"What if you run out? We may be up here for a while."

"Don't worry. I have four more."

He stared at her in disbelief. "You're wearing five petticoats?"

"Don't look so surprised. Some women wear even more. I have a friend that never has less than seven on at a time." She cocked her head to the side. "You expect me to believe you didn't know that when you have four sisters?"

"We never discussed it," he said. "I'll leave you to it then. I'm going to see what I can find to eat."

She grinned as he walked away. Poor old Jared was in for a shock when he married Susan. He was going to discover all sorts of feminine fripperies he didn't know existed.

When she was sure Jared was busy, she flipped up her skirt and tore a square of material off her petticoat. "All right," she said to the baby. "Let's see if we can get you out of this thing."

By the time Alaina had unlaced the leather front of the cradleboard, Jared had returned with lunch. "Here's some bread and butter that Angel sent with me yesterday," he said. "It isn't much, but it's all I could find."

"That's fine. It will hold him until we stop for the night. I'll cook him some cornmeal mush for supper. How strange," she said, parting the front of the cradleboard. "He isn't wearing a diaper. This thing seems to be filled with some kind of fuzz."

"It looks like cattail fluff," Jared said in surprise. "Maybe that's what Indians use instead."

"Oh, my!"

"What's wrong?" Jared asked in alarm.

"Nothing really. It's just that he's a girl instead of a boy."

"A girl?"

"Yes, definitely a girl," Alaina said, as she lifted the baby out of the cradleboard. "A diaper may not be what you're used to, Bright Eyes, but at least you'll be clean and dry."

"Bright Eyes?" Jared said in amusement.

"It fits doesn't it?"

Jared glanced down at the baby who lay on Alaina's coat kicking and squirming joyfully. The hazel eyes staring up at them were bright with curiosity. "I guess it does, at that."

"It will work until someone gives her a real name. Have you thought of what to do with her?"

"No, but I did think of someone who might be able to help, Whiskey Jug Johnson. He's lived in these mountains since he wasn't much older than our friend here."

"I wouldn't think anyone with a name like Whiskey Jug Johnson would have the slightest idea what to do with a baby."

"You might be right, but maybe he'll know of a

family that has room for a baby. I was thinking of swinging by his cabin anyway. If nothing else, Whiskey Jug will know where the renegades are camped. He'll be able to tell us whether we need to go on to Saratoga or how to get around them on our way back to Centennial."

Alaina ignored another slight sting of guilt as she washed her hands in the creek. "How far is his cabin?"

"If we push it, we should get there tomorrow sometime. We'd better eat so we can get going again."

By tacit agreement, Alaina and Jared both ate jerky and left the softer, more easily chewed bread and butter for the baby. Within half an hour they were on the trail again. Though Alaina protested, Jared carried the baby on his back, insisting his arm was much better and that he was better able to handle the added weight. When Alaina realized she could still keep an eye on her charge, she relaxed, secretly relieved to give up the added burden.

It was late afternoon when they finally stopped in a protected clearing alongside the trail. Jared would just as soon continue on until dark, but the baby was fussing and Alaina was drooping in the saddle. Bright Eyes quieted as soon as she was fed and had a fresh diaper. Alaina cooked supper while Jared set up the tent for the night.

As Jared finished his meal, Alaina went through his pack selecting some articles and putting others back in the pannier. He watched in amusement as she tucked a bag of cornmeal, a spoon, a pan and her woolen shawl into the empty flour sack she'd carried her supplies in.

"I assume you have a good excuse for stealing me blind."

"I'm not stealing anything," she said indignantly.

"These are all things the baby needs. I'm just making them easier to get to. My mother always called it her necessity sack."

"There's probably a good reason for wrapping up all the left-over cornmeal mush, too," he said with a grin. "I suppose it's for lunch tomorrow."

"In a way. That's what Bright Eyes is going to eat on the trail. I made extra on purpose."

"That makes sense." Jared tossed the dregs of his coffee into the fire. "Well, I think I'll take a look around. It will be dark soon. Why don't you and Bright Eyes go to bed?"

Alaina glanced up with a worried frown. "Do you think those renegades will still be looking for us?"

"If they were going to find us, they would have already done it. They probably figured we headed down the mountain ahead of the storm."

"Wouldn't they see our tracks and realize we went up instead of down?"

"Their horses would have obliterated any track we left when we headed up the mountain. Anyway, they had some destination in mind when we met them. I doubt they'd give it up without pretty good cause."

"If you're so sure there's no danger, why are you going to check things out?"

Jared shrugged. "Better safe than sorry. Besides, I thought you might need some privacy to get ready for bed."

"Oh." Alaina blushed. "I...I won't be long."

"Take your time."

"All right." She smiled shyly. "Thank you, Jared."

"Don't mention it." He picked up the canteen and his rifle and strode out of camp without a backward glance.

Alaina shook her head as she picked up the baby and went into the tent. Just when she decided it was high time she put Jared Brady in his place and gave him a piece of her mind, he turned around and did something nice. He was far too attractive for his own good, anyway. When he was thoughtful like that, he was darn near irresistible. She almost liked it better when he was highhanded and arrogant. At least then she wasn't dreaming about kissing him again. The man was going to drive her crazy.

"He's right," she told Bright Eyes. "The sooner we get off this mountain and back to civilization the better off we'll all be."

Alaina barely had time to lay out the bedrolls before Jared threw the canvas door of the tent wide and grabbed the cradleboard. "Come on!" he said urgently, as he thrust his arms through the straps on the back. "The renegades will be here any minute."

Alaina stared at him in shock. "I thought you said they weren't looking for us."

"They aren't. We just happen to have the incredibly bad luck to be camped right square in their trail. They don't know we're here yet, but they will soon enough."

"Can we out run them on the horses?"

"We couldn't even get a horse saddled. Damn it, Alaina, we don't have time for this. Hurry up!"

With the image of a fire-gutted cabin in her mind's eye, Alaina grabbed her shawl and necessity sack, scooped up the two blankets, and ran for the door.

CHAPTER ELEVEN

At first Alaina couldn't locate Jared. Afraid the renegades would hear her if she called out to him, she scanned the camp frantically. Panic was clawing at her throat by the time she saw him untying the horses on the other side of the clearing. She wasted no time hurrying over.

"Did you change your mind about the horses?" she asked hopefully. "Can we out run them if we ride bareback?"

"Not without a pretty good head start. But our only hope lies in convincing them that's exactly what we did."

"What are you going to do?"

"No time to explain. Head for the trees, I'll catch up with you."

Without another word, Alaina turned and ran as fast as she could toward the forest where the trees were the thickest. She was almost there when their three horses nearly ran her down. Frozen with shock, she was still staring after them when Jared seized her arm and dragged her back into the trees. They were barely out of sight before their camp was suddenly filled with men on horseback.

"Get down!" Jared said and pulled her to the forest floor.

Frantic to escape the renegades, Alaina struggled to get away, wiggling and twisting until Jared finally had to lie on top of her and pull her hands above her head. "Damn it, Alaina, they're going to hear you," he whispered in her ear.

The words seemed to have no meaning for her, as she stared up at him with huge frightened eyes. The muscles in her throat worked convulsively as she sucked air in through her mouth in a whistling gasp. Jared could almost see the scream building and knew if he didn't do something fast she'd bring the men down on them like ants on a peppermint stick. If only he could keep her distracted long enough for the hysteria to pass. In desperation, he did the only thing he could think of. He kissed her.

She tasted like sunshine and clean mountain air, fresh and intoxicating. As he felt the tension go out of her body, Jared realized he could easily forget the men in camp if he wasn't careful.

Reluctantly he pulled his mouth away. "Don't make a sound," he breathed in her ear. "They won't even think of looking for us here until they catch up with the horses and find out we aren't on them. We're safe here for a little while." He felt her nod and lifted his head slightly to look back at their camp through the trees. While Jared watched, a man came out of the tent waving Alaina's extra dress.

"Hot, damn there's a woman with them," he shouted excitedly. "This is our lucky day."

"Only if we catch them," said another, as he rose from the ground where he had been studying the hoof prints that led out of camp. "Looks like they saw us coming and decided not to wait around for company. Should be able to catch them, though. They can't be that far ahead. You five stay here in case they double back on us. The rest of us will track them down." He remounted his horse and headed out of camp with most of his men following right behind.

"That's our signal to leave," Jared whispered in Alaina's ear. "Be as quiet as you can." He rose silently to his feet, and reached down to help her up. Praying the men wouldn't start searching the woods for them until dusk, he re-scattered the pine needles, destroying the evidence that they'd been there. But when he pointed to the west, she stopped him with a hand on his arm. It wasn't until she moved around behind him that Jared remembered the precious cargo he carried on his back. A moment later she was back, indicating that Little Bright Eyes was sleeping peacefully.

Jared motioned for Alaina to follow him and headed toward the sinking sun. A short distance away from camp, they came to the rocky outcropping that Jared had seen earlier. "If we walk along the top of the rock they won't be able to figure out which way we went," he whispered.

Alaina nodded and started the difficult climb. Jared felt a flash of admiration as he took her hand to help her over the worst of it. Most women he knew would have succumbed to the hysterics that had threatened earlier, but Alaina had miraculously pulled herself back together. Even now she tackled the rugged outcropping without complaining.

Once they reached the top, Jared stopped to take his bearings, then headed north. The sun dropped below the horizon and twilight enveloped them in its welcome shadow. Jared breathed a sigh of relief. The renegades wouldn't be able to track them until morning now.

His relief was short-lived. They had traveled less

than half an hour before full darkness made walking treacherous. Snow and ice still covered the uneven rock in places. One misstep could easily result in a serious injury. Jared took Alaina's hand to guide her, but after the fourth time he stumbled, she pulled free from his grip.

"You can't see where we're going can you?"

He glanced over his shoulder at her. "That's a pretty stupid question."

"Not really. Some people can see in the dark, and others can't. I take it you're one who can't."

"I suppose you can."

"Yes, as a matter of fact. Why don't you let me lead the way?'

Jared frowned. "You don't know where we're going."

"Do you?"

"To Whiskey Jug's. You won't have any idea where we need to take off across country."

"And you'll lead us off a cliff long before we get there because you can't tell where you're going. Seems to me, we can sit down and wait until morning, or you can let me lead the way."

Jared glared at her in the darkness. "All right," he said grudgingly, as he moved aside and let her take the lead. "Just watch out for holes and ice-covered rocks."

"Don't worry. I have no desire to break a leg up here. How will I know when we get there?"

"I think there's a small spring along here somewhere. That's where we turn."

"You think?" she asked in surprise. "I thought you said you knew where we're going."

"I do, I'm just not real sure how to get there."

"That makes a lot of sense," she said sarcastically.

He looked up at the stars. "I know where we are, and I know where we want to go. It's just a matter of putting the two together."

"Have you ever been here before?" she asked suspiciously.

"Not precisely here, but I'm pretty sure we surveyed the other end of this outcropping last summer."

"You're sure it's the same one?"

"I've been all over these mountains and others like them and never seen another formation quite like this one. As far as I know, it's unique."

"But there could be another like it?"

"It's possible. Still, if we head north, we're bound to hit an area I'm familiar with sooner or later."

"And you won't recognize it when we do because you're blind as a bat in the dark."

"Do you have a better solution?" Jared asked irritably.

She stared at him for a moment, then turned and began picking her way through the rocks. "Be careful, there's a hole just to the left of us."

Other than an occasional warning of dangers on the trail, they trudged along in near silence for what seemed like hours. At last, Alaina came to a stop and pointed to her left. "Is that the spring?"

Jared peered into the darkness. "I can't tell. Do you see it?"

"Not really, but I can hear it. I think it comes out of the hill just down from us."

"It seems to be about where I expected it," Jared said glancing around. "As I remember, there's a ledge right here somewhere. We can rest there. "

Alaina switched around and looked at him in surprise. "What for?"

"You won't be able to lead us across country because you don't know the way," he pointed out. "The moon will be up in a few hours. We might as well get some sleep in the meantime."

"But why up here? Surely it would be more comfortable down below where we'd have a nice soft mat of pine needles."

"The whole point of walking along this hunk of rock is to hide our tracks. The renegades will be sure to suspect we came this way, but they'll have no way of knowing where we leave it or what direction we're traveling. Everything we've done will be useless if they can tell where we came down off the outcropping."

"And lying on the ground would leave plenty of evidence, wouldn't it?"

"A blind man couldn't miss it."

Alaina sighed. "Well, I guess we'd better find that ledge, then. Any idea where it is?"

"As I remember it was slightly to the left of the spring. Our best bet is to head toward the sound of running water." Jared listened intently for a moment, then shrugged the cradleboard off his shoulders and handed it to her. "You and Bright Eyes wait here. I'll go see if I can find it."

"Be careful," Alaina said, as she watched him pick his way carefully down the side of the rock.

"Ouch, damn it..." The clatter of falling gravel punctuated by a string of curses floated up through the night air.

"Jared?" Alaina looked over the side uncertainly. "Are you all right?"

130

"Hell no, I'm not all right. I just slid halfway to Colorado."

"Did you find the ledge?"

"I found a ledge of some kind, but it's too blasted dark to tell if it's the right one."

"Do you want us to come down?"

"Might as well. It will serve our purpose until the moon comes up, and I can see if we're where I think we are."

Alaina knelt and contemplated the steep rocky slope below her. "I can just barely see you. Do you think you could reach the baby if I lower her down to you?"

"If we both stretch I might."

Alaina lay down on the ground and carefully slid the cradleboard over the jagged rocks and loose gravel into Jared's outstretched hands. "Have you got her?"

"Yes. Give me a minute to get her situated, and I'll be back to help you."

"Don't worry about it. I can see a safe way down," Alaina said and was over the edge before he could stop her.

Jared watched her descent with a jaundiced eye. His skin still smarted from scraping over the same rocks she so easily found finger and toeholds in. Then she was standing next to him wiping her hands on her skirt.

"There, that wasn't so bad," she said with satisfaction.

"That's easy for you to say. You don't have broken ribs to contend with."

Alaina bit her lip. "Do you want me to take a look at them?"

"Maybe later," he said gruffly. Having those hands of hers all over his naked skin under the concealing blanket of darkness was definitely not a good idea. "Did I see you stick a tin cup in your possibles bag?"

"It's a necessity bag, and yes, as a matter of fact, I did. Why?"

"If you'll dig it out, I'll get you a drink. I imagine you're rather thirsty."

"That's a pretty mild description for the way my mouth and throat feel right now. Where's Bright Eyes?"

"Over there where the ledge is wider." He could hear Alaina moving along the ledge behind him as he made his way to the spring and dipped out a cup of water.

"Oh look, Jared. There's a hollow almost like a cave over here. We'll actually be able to lie down and go to sleep."

"If we're lucky, we may even be able to find a couple of boulders to use for pillows," he said sarcastically.

Alaina's grin flashed in the dark as he handed her the cup. "There's less of the soft Englishman in you than I thought." She took a drink from the cup. "Oh, my that's cold, but delicious."

"Fresh mountain spring water is the best in the world if you ask me. Want some more?" he asked as she drained the cup.

"No, thanks. I'll have some more later. I think I'll take Bright Eyes out of the cradleboard for a while. She can sleep with me until we head out again."

"Are you sure that's a good idea?"

"Positive. She needs a chance to move her arms and legs. Think how you'd feel if you were in the same position all day."

"How are you going to keep her warm?" he asked as she lifted the baby out of the cradleboard.

"I'll wrap her in my shawl." She glanced up at the stars. "I don't suppose we dare chance a fire."

"Not unless we want unwelcome visitors."

She sighed as she pulled off the blankets she had wrapped around her shoulders and dropped them to the ground, before laying Bright Eyes on them. "It's a good thing I managed to grab these. Could be pretty chilly without them."

"Nights are cold up here even in the middle of summer. We're going to have to share the blankets if you don't want to freeze."

"Freezing isn't high on my list of things I enjoy." She leaned a hand on the rock face and eased herself down to sitting position. "What a day."

"I've had better myself. You act like you're in pain."

"I have sore muscles I didn't even know existed. I hate to admit it, but you were right about carrying the cradleboard in my arms."

Jared sat down next to her and began to massage her shoulders. "Your muscles are pretty tight. Maybe this will help."

"Mmmm. That feels good. I haven't hurt like this since the last time I wrestled with my cousin Sven."

Jared's eyes widened. "The young giant I met at the stage station?"

Alaina nodded. "We were twelve. He's several months younger than I am, and I'd always managed to beat him before. Mama wasn't even sympathetic. She said if I'd been acting like a young lady, it wouldn't have happened. Ladies don't knock their cousins down and sit on them."

Jared chuckled. "I know a lady who would have."

"Not Susan?"

"No, of course not," Jared said. The idea was ludicrous. "I was referring to my sister Shannon. She knocked me down more than once."

"I've never met Shannon."

"No, my mother sent her to live with my aunt in England years ago. Said my aunt could turn her into a lady if anyone could."

"And did she?" Alaina murmured drowsily.

"Maybe not in the way she intended to, but Shannon married a peer of the realm. Her name is Lady Roxham now."

"No wonder Susan wants to marry you."

He stopped rubbing her shoulders abruptly. "What's that supposed to mean?"

Startled, Alaina looked back at him. "I'm sorry," she mumbled. "I was thinking out loud."

"And just what is it you think my sister's marriage has to do with my betrothal to Susan?" he demanded.

Alaina shifted uncomfortably. "Only that Susan is probably thrilled with the idea of being related to a real English Lord."

Since Susan had repeatedly insisted they spend part of their honeymoon in England with Shannon and her husband, Alaina's gibe struck a nerve. "I guess it shouldn't surprise me to hear you malign her that way even after she's been so good to you."

"I've had enemies who treated me better than Susan," Alaina snapped. "And I wasn't maligning her."

"You said Susan is marrying me for my family connections," he said acidly.

"That's not what I said, though it wouldn't surprise me if that were part of the reason. Anyway, I think you underrate yourself. I'm sure she's just as impressed by your handsome face and all that lovely Brady money as she is by the prospect of being related to an English aristocrat. Now that," she said, picking up one of the blankets, "was maligning your fiancée. I think it's time we tried to get some sleep, don't you?" With that she spread one of the blankets on the ground, placed the baby on it, then lay down on it herself and covered them both with the other blanket.

There was an empty space for him on the other side of the baby, but Jared was determined not to use it. He sat down on the hard ledge and wrapped his coat around himself with angry defiance. *Let her freeze, damn it!*

Jared's anger slowly trickled away in the cold night air. He gradually came to realize he'd over-reacted to her statements about Susan. Alaina really hadn't said anything particularly derogatory until he goaded her into it. He tried to ignore the unwelcome thought that some of his own doubts about Susan might have been responsible for his reaction.

With a deep sigh, he rose to his feet and walked the few steps to the blankets. Stripping off his heavy winter coat, he tenderly laid it over Alaina and the baby before climbing between the blankets and cuddling into the warmth of the other two. It was surprisingly warm and comfortable in the makeshift bed. He was just beginning to drift off when Alaina spoke.

"Jared, why did you kiss me?"

His eyes popped open in surprise. She was less than a foot away from him, all wide-eyed and kissable. Jared swallowed hard. "You were going to scream. I couldn't think of any other way to stop you."

"Oh."

The slight inflection of confusion and disappointment in her voice caused an odd constriction in his chest. "I'm sorry. It was the only way."

"I just wondered, that's all. Good night."

"Good-night." As she closed her eyes, Jared had the irrational desire to pull her into his arms. Thank God Bright Eyes lay between them, he thought. There was only so much temptation a man could resist.

CHAPTER TWELVE

"Alaina, wake up."

Alaina blinked and stared groggily up at Jared. It felt like she'd only been asleep a few minutes. "What's the matter?"

"Nothing. The moon just came up. We need to put as much distance between us and the renegades as we can before morning."

"Oh." She sat up and rubbed the sleep from her eyes. "Are we where you thought we were?"

"More or less. This is the right spring, but it's slightly farther north than I remembered."

"How do you know that?"

"The stars. Anyway, that puts us considerably closer to Whiskey Jug's than I thought. If luck is with us, we should be there sometime tomorrow. I brought you a drink of water from the spring. The canteen is full, but it's hard to say when we'll come across another stream."

"Thanks." Alaina watched Jared as he gathered their meager possessions. At least he didn't seem to be holding a grudge for her outburst. He had a way of bringing out the worst in her. With a sigh, she drank part of the water then held the cup to the baby's mouth. She smiled as Bright Eyes drank greedily. Not all babies were trained to drink from a cup at this age.

"How's Bright Eyes?" Jared asked as she laced up the front of the cradleboard.

"Falling asleep again. I swear, this is the easiest baby

I ever had anything to do with."

Jared smiled. "You seem to know quite a lot about them."

"My sister is almost the same age as Bright Eyes. Besides, I've been helping my mother and all my aunts with their babies for as long as I can remember. Papa says I'll probably have a whole house full of them some day," she said, handing him the cradleboard.

"Are you sure Bright Eyes is all right?"

"Positive," she said, helping him put his arms through the cradleboard straps. "She's just a sound sleeper."

"Probably part Viking."

Alaina grinned. "I wouldn't be surprised."

"Do you want me to carry the blankets?"

"No," Alaina said, throwing them around her shoulders. "I can use the extra warmth. I'm half frozen!" She glanced up at him. "Can you see the way down from this ledge or do you want me to lead again?"

"My eyes are working just fine now that the moon's up. Besides," he said turning away, "there's a game trail from the spring down that any fool could follow."

Alaina couldn't help wondering if the fool he referred to was himself. It was difficult to understand why it bothered him to have to admit a weakness. Most people couldn't see in the dark, for heaven's sake. Male pride was unfathomable at times. With a shrug, she wrapped the blankets tighter around her, and fell into step behind him as he led the way down off the outcropping.

"Won't the renegades suspect we went this way?" she asked as they reached the bottom.

"Probably, but then there are any number of spots

WILD HONEY

that were just as likely between here and our camp. I'm hoping they will have taken the time to check out enough of them that they'll just give this one a once over and move on. As soon as we get to the timber, I'll come back and cover our tracks."

Twenty minutes later, the last vestige of their passing had been obliterated to Jared's satisfaction, and they were on their way again. Alaina couldn't help being impressed. Not only had he outwitted the renegades, he appeared to know exactly where they were, and how to get where they were going. So much for the pampered rich boy she vaguely remembered from her childhood. Even Susan's irritatingly arrogant fiancé was gone. This Jared was every inch the competent frontiersman and ever so much more appealing.

As they threaded their way through the sparse timber, she had little to do but follow along and contemplate the man in front of her. It was pleasant to watch his long-legged stride as he moved effortlessly down the game trail, skirting the remnants of snow banks where they'd leave telltale footprints. She knew from experience that the cradleboard was anything but light. Yet, despite his bruised shoulder and injured ribs, he showed little sign of fatigue. Finally she understood the heavily muscled body she'd glimpsed that morning on the train. It came from spending the better part of every year in the wilderness. This was his element. The untamed land was as much a part of him as the rifle he carried in his hand.

When Susan wasn't around, and Jared wasn't trying to run her life, Alaina had to admit she really didn't mind him so much. In fact, if the truth was known, there were times when she found herself actually liking him.

139

As she followed him through the forest, she couldn't help wondering if he'd find a reason to kiss her again.

Alaina was drooping with fatigue by the time the first fingers of dawn kissed the sky. It was hard to believe Jared was still striding along as though he were out for a pleasant stroll. With no more sleep than he'd gotten in the last two days, he had to be exhausted. She found herself vaguely irritated that he could keep going when she was about to drop.

"Damn," Jared said. "I was hoping it would still be dark by the time we got here."

Alaina peered around him. A grassy hillside stretched before them rolling downward toward a thick growth of willows at the bottom and the trees beyond. "Where are we?"

"This is the last open area where the renegades will be able to see us before we get to Whiskey Jug's place. We can either take a chance and cross it now or wait until tonight. In the meantime they might catch up with us from this side."

"We don't have much choice, do we?"

"Not that I can see."

Alaina sighed wearily. "Well, I guess we may as well get a move on then."

"Tired?"

"Heaven's no. I'm fresh as a daisy."

"Me too." He smiled down at her. "Don't worry, those willows are over my head. Once we get to them we'll be able to find a place to hole up for as long as we want."

"I could sleep for a week," she warned as Jared

stepped out of the protective shadow of the trees and set off down the hill. She felt a strange prickling sensation between her shoulder blades. What if the renegades had somehow beat them there and were watching from the forest? Halfway expecting to feel the sharp pain of a bullet in her back any second, it was all she could do not to run down the unprotected hillside.

A short time later Jared pushed through a thick wall of willows. "Watch yourself," he said over his shoulder. "These things will hit you in the face if you aren't careful."

"Thanks for the warning," she said sarcastically as the branches snapped back narrowly missing her cheek.

Moments later he stopped so abruptly she nearly crashed into his back. "This should do nicely," he said, looking around with satisfaction.

They stood inside a fifteen-foot circle surrounded by willows. It looked for all the world like an open-air room. "How did you know this was here?" she asked in amazement.

"I didn't, but there are almost always places like this in a willow thicket. This is even better than I hoped for. A whole crowd could walk by and never see us. You want to give me a hand with this?" he asked, shrugging out of the straps on the cradleboard.

Alaina reached out to take the cradleboard. "Well, well," she said. "Look who's finally awake. That figures, she wakes up just as we're ready to sleep."

"Maybe if we change her diaper and feed her, she'll doze off again."

"It's possible." Alaina sat down and began loosening the leather ties. "At any rate, I bet she'll be glad to get out of this contraption again. It must be rather like wearing a straitjacket."

"I know just how she feels," Jared said ruefully as he rubbed his chest.

Alaina frowned. "Are your ribs bothering you again?"

"Not really. The binding is kind of getting to me, though. I feel like I can't breathe."

"I can take it off as soon as I see to Bright Eyes."

"All right. I'll set up camp."

By the time Alaina had used the last of her petticoat to diaper Bright Eyes, Jared had their meager breakfast ready. "It's a good thing you thought to make extra cornmeal mush last night."

Alaina made a face. "It won't last very long with all three of us eating it. Let's hope we make it to your friend's place today."

"We should. If memory serves me correctly, we're only two or three miles away. It should be a fairly easy walk. What are you doing?" he asked in alarm as she started to unbutton his shirt.

She looked up in surprise. "Getting ready to take your bandage off. Then we can eat and go to sleep."

Jared eyed her warily. "All right, but I can take my own shirt off."

"Oh, I don't mind..."

"Look, I'm not some little brother you need to take care of. I can undress myself without your help!" Jared said irritably.

"Fine. You can take off your own bandage too."

They glared mulishly at each other for several long minutes then Jared sighed and ran a hand through his hair. "This is a stupid argument."

After a moment, Alaina nodded ruefully. "It is, isn't

it? I guess we're both just tired."

"I thought Vikings never got tired."

"I'm only part."

Jared chuckled. "And I suppose it's the other part that's tired." He finished undoing his buttons and shrugged out of his shirt. "All right do your worst. I'll try not to get too embarrassed."

Alaina frowned as she unwound the bandage. Embarrassed? Since when was Jared Brady shy? She glanced up at his face, and was surprised to find his full concentration centered on the baby. Maybe it was just as well. This way he couldn't tell how hard her heart was beating or know of the strange gyrations her stomach was going through.

At last the strips of cloth lay in a heap on the ground, and Alaina gave Jared's injury a quick examination. The swelling had completely disappeared and the deep purple bruise had already faded some. "It looks a lot better," she said cautiously. "How does it feel?"

Jared gingerly took a breath. "Still hurts some, but it's better than it was."

"Good. That probably means they aren't broken. I'll bind them up again when you wake up and... Oh, Jared," she gasped as she caught sight of his back. Long painful looking scratches and abrasions covered much of the broad expanse. "What in the world happened?"

"That's where I slid down the side of the outcropping last night," he muttered as he put his shirt back on. "It hurt like the devil when it happened, but it's all right now."

"A scrape like that can be extremely dangerous. I'd better wash it off. I wish I had some of Granny Ellinson's salve to put on it."

"It's fine."

"If it gets infected..."

"I said it was all right!" he said. "Don't you get it? I don't want you fussing over me like some old mother hen. Save it for Bright Eyes."

Stung, Alaina pulled back. "All right, I will." You'd think she'd done something to offend him instead of offer to tend his wound. The man was impossible! She left him to finish dressing and went to feed Bright Eyes. Though the congealed cornmeal mush was anything but tasty, the baby ate her portion eagerly and drank nearly a whole cup of water. Alaina worried that the mush and water wouldn't be enough for her to survive on for long, but for now, at least, she seemed content to settle down on the blanket with the sugar-teat.

Alaina studiously ignored Jared as she ate her own scant meal and lay down next to Bright Eyes. She glanced his way only once as she pulled the blanket over herself and the baby. He watched her with dark inscrutable eyes and an unreadable expression. It was impossible to tell what he was thinking. For some reason that irritated her more than all the rest. With one last angry glare she snuggled down next to the baby and closed her eyes. She was sound asleep long before Jared joined them in the makeshift bed.

Alaina drifted along in a dream world surrounded by sweet, blissful warmth and a delicious feeling of well-being. Another body, strong and masculine, stretched the length of hers, and muscular arms held her close. With sudden clarity, she knew she lay in safety of a lover's embrace, with her head pillowed on his chest and her leg thrown possessively over his. Jared. His hands skimmed her naked body, lighting fires and stirring passions that left her aching with an unfamiliar yearning.

Alaina awoke slowly; her sleep befuddled mind trying to sort reality from illusion. Gradually she realized some of her dream was real. In their sleep she and Jared had drifted together, each seeking the warmth of the other's body. That was where the similarity to the dream ended. His embrace was loose and impersonal. The stubble of a two-day beard scratched her skin where her forehead rested against his chin, and his shoulder was hard and unyielding under her cheek. It felt wonderful.

Alaina smiled and cuddled closer. There was something very nice about waking up this way even if it wasn't particularly comfortable. Last night on the ledge, the cradleboard had kept them apart, but—

Her eyes suddenly popped open in alarm and she tried to wiggle out of Jared's embrace.

"Huh? Wha..." Jared jerked awake and looked around in confusion.

"Bright Eyes," Alaina said, pushing against his shoulder. "She's gone!"

Jared was instantly awake. "What?"

Alaina struggled to sit up. "I don't know where she could be. She's too little to crawl away, but...Oh!" Bright Eyes lay in the crook of Jared's other arm, happily sucking on the sugar-teat. "How in the world did you get over there?" she asked reaching over to pick the baby up.

"She was fussing earlier, and I didn't want to wake you."

Alaina collapsed back onto the blanket with Bright Eyes nestled in her arms. "I was scared half to death when I woke up and found her gone. My heart's still pounding."

"I know," Jared said softly. "I can feel it."

Startled, Alaina looked into his eyes. For an instant, there was a sensual glow within their velvety depth, as though his dreams had matched hers. Then, the light was gone, leaving her to wonder if she'd imagined it.

With a mighty stretch, Jared sat up and rubbed his hand over his face. "Boy, did I sleep hard."

"Me too. What time do you suppose it is?"

He pulled out his watch. "Nearly eleven o'clock. We'd better get a move on if we're going to make Whiskey Jug Johnson's this afternoon."

Alaina nodded and reluctantly moved away. "You know, Jared," she said, as she finished diapering the baby. "I've been thinking about Bright Eyes. I think I know what to do with her."

"Oh?"

"I'm going to keep her."

"What? You're not even married. How in the hell are you going to raise a baby by yourself?"

"You don't have to get so upset," she said irritably. "I didn't actually mean I was going keep to her all by myself. I'll take her home to Mama and Papa. They won't care that she's part Indian."

"Are you sure about that?"

"Positive. Besides, this way baby Mary will have somebody to play with. The rest of us are all too old." She tucked the baby into the cradleboard. "Mama and Papa will probably even be pleased."

"No doubt they've been sitting around wishing they

had another mouth to feed ever since you left home," Jared said sardonically.

"I wouldn't be a bit surprised." She picked up the cradleboard and gave Jared a blinding smile. "They both love children, you know."

"What are you going to do with her in the meantime?"

Alaina bit her lip. "Obviously I'll have to postpone my trip to Fort Bridger and head straight back to Minnesota."

"Good plan," Jared said approvingly. "Now all we have to do is get off this mountain and back to civilization."

"Would you deliver a letter to my...to Cameron Price for me?"

"I'll put it in his hands personally."

"I...thank you."

"Think nothing of it."

"Are you ready to have me bind your ribs again?"

For a moment, Jared toyed with the idea of telling her no. She nearly drove him crazy every time she touched him. It wasn't getting any better with practice either. On the other hand, the binding did keep his ribs from hurting. Thank God they'd get to Whiskey Jug's today. "All right, but be quick about it."

"I don't know what you're so grumpy about," she grumbled as he unbuttoned his shirt. "You won this round. I'm going back to Laramie City without a fight."

"I'm sorry. I guess I'm just not a very good patient." Jared tried to ignore the guilty jab from his conscience that reminded him how disappointed she must be. It wasn't like it was his fault. She was doing this because she wanted to, not because of anything he'd done. Even so, his exultation dimmed a bit.

"This won't take long," she said, taking the first wrap around his chest.

Jared sucked in his breath. Those fingers of hers wandering across his body were torture, sheer heavenly torture. They couldn't get to Whiskey Jug's too soon.

Though both Jared and Alaina had slept soundly, fatigue dogged their steps as they wound their way through the heavy timber. It was mid-afternoon when Jared finally stopped.

"Damn," he said, staring across a small clearing. "I never even thought of that."

Alaina looked over his shoulder curiously. There was little to see except a few charred logs among the tender young shoots of grass. "Are we getting close to Whiskey Jug's?"

Jared sighed in defeat. "You might say that. Those logs are what's left of his cabin."

CHAPTER THIRTEEN

Alaina looked around in dismay. "This is where Whiskey Jug Johnson lives?"

"Lived," Jared corrected her. "He obviously isn't here anymore."

"They burned his cabin, too?"

"It looks that way." Jared wearily rubbed his face. "Damn, Whiskey Jug was a good friend."

Alaina touched his arm sympathetically. "I'm sorry."

"So am I. He deserved a better end."

"What do we do now?"

"That's a good question. Unfortunately, I'm fresh out of answers."

"Maybe we should head back to Centennial?" Alaina said cautiously.

"It's too late for that. Even if we didn't have to worry about the renegades, Centennial is clear over on the other side of the mountain from us now. We'll be better off heading for Saratoga."

"How far is that?"

Jared glared at her. "A good thirty miles."

"Thirty miles! Are you sure?"

"Not precisely. It could be anywhere from twenty-five to forty." Jared said sarcastically. "What difference does it make? It might as well be a hundred. Thanks to your idiotic decision to go over the mountain we're stuck here in the middle of nowhere on foot."

"Now wait a minute," Alaina protested indignantly. "This isn't all my fault. You're the one who forced me to come this way. I would have taken the train if it hadn't been for your interference. In fact, if it hadn't been for you, I'd be with my father right now."

Jared made a rude noise. "Your father. Frankly, I think you're safer up here dodging renegade outlaws with me than you would be at the Fort with Cameron Price."

"You've never seen what he'd be like as a father."

"Neither have you. Face it, Alaina, there are some men who shouldn't be parents."

"And I suppose you're an expert on who should and who shouldn't?"

"No, but I do know Ox Treenery was ten times the father my own—" Jared suddenly broke off what he was saying and listened intently. "Uh oh," he muttered.

"What is it?"

"Horses, lots of them, and they're coming this way."

"Do you think it's the renegades?" she asked fearfully.

"I don't know, but I don't want to stick around and find out."

"Neither do I."

They were well back in the trees when the riders came into sight. With little more than a few cursory glances at the surrounding forest, the small band rode across the clearing, and down the trail on the other side.

"Running into them this way is becoming a rather nasty habit," Alaina whispered as they disappeared over the brow of the hill.

"It was the same bunch that attacked Zeke and his wife." Jared rose to his feet and peered after them. "But

I don't think they were the ones that raided our camp yesterday."

"How do you know all that?"

"They didn't have our horses with them, for one thing, and they're dressed as Indians."

"But how do you know they were the ones who attacked Bright Eyes' parents?"

"You really don't want to know."

"Of course, I do," Alaina said angrily. "Stop treating me like a child."

He gave her a long look, then sighed regretfully. "The third one from the front was a real Indian."

"So?"

"He had a fresh scalp hanging from his lance. It was Zeke's."

"Oh." Alaina thought she might be sick. Jared was right; she really didn't want to know.

"You stay here," he said, shrugging out of the cradleboard straps. "I want to see where they're going."

Alaina stared at him in shock. "You're going to follow them? Are you crazy?"

"Only a little way. Whiskey Jug built his cabin here for a reason. You can see the whole valley from this hilltop."

"And the whole valley can see you."

"Not if I'm careful."

And he calls me idiotic, she thought as he crouched down and made his way across the clearing to the top of the hill. When he was nearly there, he dropped to his stomach and crawled the last ten feet.

Jared lay peering over the edge for so long, Alaina began to get antsy. She glanced down at Bright Eyes and was unsurprised to find her sound asleep. An eternity passed, and still Jared hadn't moved. Alaina fidgeted with a button on her coat. What in the world was so interesting? Finally, she could stand it no longer. With a final glance at Bright Eyes, she crept forward on her hands and knees to where Jared lay.

"Don't you ever stay put when you're told to?" he asked sharply.

"Not very often. Anyway, I wanted to see what was going on."

"It looks like we may have stumbled on to something the army will be very interested in," he said, looking out across the valley again. "What do you think of that?"

Alaina followed his gaze and caught her breath in surprise. Not one, but two valleys were spread out below her, intersecting at right angles to each other. The pale green of grass broken by darker strips of mature pine flowed together in a textured carpet that covered the floor of two valleys and flowed up the opposite mountain to a sheer rim rock of forbidding cliffs at the top.

"It's beautiful," she breathed.

Jared looked momentarily surprised. "No, not that," he said irritably. "Look over there."

Alaina obediently looked to the north. A huge village of tents spread across the floor of the valley. "Oh, my," she said. "An army camp."

"But not any army Uncle Sam knows anything about. That explains why we can't move without stumbling over them."

"It does?"

"We've been running into hunting parties. There are a lot of mouths to feed down there."

"What are they doing here?"

"I don't know, but I'd venture to guess they're up to no good. We need to get to a telegraph as soon as possible so we can let the army know they're here."

"How do you propose to do that?"

"By following that creek down there." He pointed to a strip of medium green that wound its way down through the smaller valley. "That's the quickest way out of these mountains."

"Isn't that where they'll be looking for us?"

"If they decide we're worth hunting down, it won't matter where we go. They'll have enough men to find us no matter where we hide. We're just going to have to hope they have bigger fish to fry." Jared sighed as he backed away from the brow of the hill. "Our biggest problem is going to be finding food."

"I thought a government surveyor would know how to live off the land." Alaina said with a blank look. "There is all kinds of game in these mountains."

"Right," he said sarcastically. "When I can't shoot my rifle without worrying about half the riffraff in Wyoming Territory coming after my scalp."

"What about fish? There must be some in that creek down there."

"I'm sure there are. We might even manage to catch one or two. The question is, are you willing to eat them raw? A fire would bring the renegades down on us even faster than the rifle."

"Nuts and berries?"

"Way too early in the season. Two weeks ago this whole area was buried under snow. Nothing's had time to bloom much less produce fruit." He sighed. "You and I could survive on raw fish or even insects if we had to, but Bright Eyes can't."

Alaina frowned. "We've got to be missing something. I guess I'll have to keep my eyes open."

"You do that," Jared said. He didn't even bother to look at her as he went back to pick up the cradleboard and set out down the hill opposite the trail the renegades had taken.

Alaina glared at his back. *Jared Brady's insufferable side had a really bad habit of popping up. To hear him talk you'd think this was all her fault! With his background, he should have some manners. Despite all his money and important family connections, he wasn't half the gentleman her cousin Sven was.*

They were almost clear to the bottom when a flash of white caught her eye in the grassy meadow to the right of their trail. At first glimpse, it looked like a pile of huge snowballs, but a second later she felt the shock of recognition. *Giant puffballs!*

"Jared," she whispered. "Look what I found." But he was too far ahead to hear her. Alaina bit her lip indecisively. With the renegades so close by, she didn't dare raise her voice. On the other hand, she couldn't pass up the mushrooms. These shouldn't be here this early in the season; there might not be any more to find.

Without taking time to think about it, she darted out into the open meadow. Her fingers trembled with fear and haste as she picked the large white spheres and stuffed them in her sack. Every second she spent in the open increased her chances of being discovered, but she was reluctant to leave any behind.

She had just put the last one in her bag, when she was suddenly jerked to her feet. "What the hell do you think you're doing?" Jared hissed as he dragged her out of the meadow and back into the protection of the trees. "We're not playing games here. Can't you get that through that thick head of yours? What if those men had seen you?"

Alaina snatched her arm out of his grip. "Then they'd have seen me. I had to take the chance." She reached into her bag and pulled out one of the puffballs. "Look what I found."

"You risked your life for a mushroom?"

She stamped her foot. "Not just any mushrooms, you idiot. Giant puffballs. We can eat them."

He looked doubtful. "I thought mushrooms were poisonous."

"Not these. In fact, they're a great delicacy. There's nothing else that looks anything like them, so I know they're safe."

That's more than I can say for you," he growled. "You scared me half to death."

"Nobody asked you to worry about me," Alaina spat back at him.

"You could have gotten us all killed. If you don't have enough sense to protect your own hide, at least have some consideration for Bright Eyes and me."

Alaina glared at him for a moment longer then dropped her gaze. "You're right." she whispered. "I'm sorry."

Jared didn't answer as he stalked off down the hill again. He felt as though he'd been punched in the stomach. Worried about her? How about frantic? He'd died a thousand deaths when he saw her out in the open like that. Now he was suffering the pangs of a guilty conscience. If he hadn't had such a fit about food, she wouldn't have endangered herself that way.

Half an hour later Bright Eyes started to whimper and Jared called a halt to eat. He sliced two of the puffballs while Alaina attended to the baby. A dry diaper and some cornmeal mush helped, but Bright Eyes was still fussy. Alaina held the little one in her arms and rocked her back and forth. "You miss your mama don't you, sweetheart," she crooned. The baby stopped crying and gazed up at her. Alaina chucked her under the chin and began singing a soft lullaby.

A curious warmth flowed through Jared's veins as he watched the domestic scene. An image of Alaina surrounded by a bevy of children with honey colored hair and beautiful blue eyes, flashed through his mind. The picture was an appealing one, and he found himself slightly envious of her future husband.

As he took another bite of the surprisingly tasty puffball, his gaze idly flicked to the empty cradleboard. Attracted by the bright beads, several hungry honey bees swarmed around it looking for nectar. He wondered how long it would take them to realize it wasn't a flower and move on. Abruptly he sat up and stared at the insects.

"Alaina, where's the sugar-teat you made for Bright Eyes?"

She broke off her song and stared at him. "The sugar-teat?"

"Exactly."

"It's right here," she said, handing it to him. "What do you want it for?"

"I'm going to do a little tracking." He opened the cloth that made up the sugar-teat and laid it down next to the cradleboard. Within seconds the bees were crawling all over the sweet, sticky mass. "Good, now hand me your bag of dry cornmeal."

Alaina looked at him as though he'd lost his mind, especially when he ran a finger along the bottom of the sack where the fine powder had sifted through. When it was liberally coated, he carefully daubed it on the back of a bee.

"Jared, what in heaven's name are you doing?" she demanded.

"Marking him so I can see him even from a distance. Look, there he goes." Jared rose to his feet. "Now all we have to do is follow him home."

The journey was a short one. Jared followed the bee across a small clearing to an old dead tree. He looked the tree over carefully then returned with a big grin on his face. "Tonight we dine in style," he said, dropping down next to Alaina and the baby.

"What on earth are you talking about?"

"Our little friend just showed me where his hive is, and where there's a hive—"

"There's honey! Oh, Jared, you're so clever. Can we go get it now?"

"Not unless you want to get stung. We'll wait until after dark when it gets cold. They'll be too sluggish to bother us then. In the meantime," he said, settling down on the blanket and putting his hat over his face. "We sleep."

Hunger and the intense cold woke Jared hours later. Alaina had covered him with the other blanket, and lay next to him with Bright Eyes wrapped in the shawl and nestled in her arms. She slept with a slight frown on her lips, as though her dreams were less than pleasant. He couldn't resist reaching over and smoothing the hair back from her face.

Alaina's eyes fluttered and opened. "Hello," she said softly.

Jared's voice stuck in his throat as she gazed at him in the bright light of the rising moon. Even after the disastrous last two days, she was beautiful. He'd never wanted to kiss anybody so badly in his life. With infinite tenderness, he traced the curve of her face with his hand and leaned forward.

"Nuh!" Bright Eyes squawked, voicing her displeasure at being squashed between the two adults.

"What's the matter little lady?" Jared asked, propping himself on one elbow, and tickling the baby with his free hand. "Not enough attention?" He was rewarded by a giggle from Bright Eyes and a smile from Alaina.

"She really is a sweetheart of a baby," she said, putting her finger in Bright Eyes' hand.

Jared felt a warm glow as he watched the baby's fingers curl around Alaina's. Suddenly, he couldn't wait until he had children of his own. He tried to imagine lying in bed like this with Susan, their baby between them, basking in the warmth of their love. For some reason, the picture eluded him.

"Did you sleep well?" he asked.

"Not especially. I had to wake up every few minutes and break the icicles off my nose. How about you?"

He rolled over and got up. "I think I finally got so tired I could sleep through anything. Well, what do you say? Are you ready to tackle a bee tree?"

"I'm hungry enough to tackle one of those grizzlies you told me about the other day."

Jared chuckled. "Let's hope the bees are easier to deal with."

While Alaina changed Bright Eyes and wrapped her in the shawl again, Jared found a good stout stick and made his way across the clearing to the bee tree. After a few experimental tries he found a split in the old bark and began applying pressure.

"Looks like we're just in time, Bright Eyes," Alaina said. Moments later one whole side gave way with a splintering crack. She stood there expectantly, with Bright Eyes on her hip and the pan she'd brought along to cook cornmeal mush in her other hand.

"Easy as taking eggs from a hen," Jared said triumphantly.

Alaina frowned. "What about all those bees?"

"Don't worry, you aren't the only one with icicles on your nose," he said, carefully brushing the insects away from the comb. "With bees the colder they get, the slower they move. These little fellows won't give us any trouble."

"Papa says you always have to leave some of the honey for the bees so they don't starve."

"Don't worry. They won't even miss what we take. Honey's a good high energy food source, but we won't be able to eat a lot of it at one sitting."

"Want to bet?"

Jared grinned. "Hungry?"

"No, of course not," Alaina said sarcastically. "I enjoy starving. It saves me having to let my corset out a notch."

"I don't think you'll have to worry about that as long as we're up here. With this and the mushrooms, we should be all right for several days. Here."

Alaina stared at the large chunk of honeycomb he dropped in the pan. "How do you eat it?"

"You've never had wild honey before?"

"Yes, but my mother always cut the end off the comb and let the honey drain out."

"It's kind of like eating candy." Jared broke off a small piece and stuck it in her mouth. "Here, try it."

Alaina cautiously bit into the waxy structure. "Mmm, this is delicious! It tastes different than the honey at home."

"Probably because of the different flowers here. "Be sure to check for bees," he said, as Alaina refilled the sugar-teat with honeycomb. "I might have missed some."

"Let the bees watch out for themselves. I'm going to have a tough enough time trying to figure out how to eat this." She gave the sugar teat to Bright Eyes. "Where's the creek anyway?"

"Just beyond those willows."

Alaina broke off a chunk of honeycomb and held it by her fingertips. "It's a good thing, because I have the feeling things are going to get a little sticky before we're finished."

"And a nice cold bath will be as pleasant as the rest of this trip has been," Jared said with a grin.

"What do you do with the wax when the honey's gone?"

"Spit it out. You might want to save a piece when you're finished, though. You can chew it all night if you want to."

"Just like a cow chewing her cud. What a delightful picture," Alaina said, licking the honey from her fingers. "You know, the inside of a puffball kind of looks like a loaf of bread. I wonder how this honey would taste on one."

But Jared didn't answer. He couldn't. The sight of Alaina's tongue traveling the length of her long graceful fingers was turning him inside out. It was all he could do not to grab her hand and finish the job himself. He'd take her fingers into his mouth one at a time, sucking the sticky sweetness from each of them with slow deliberation. Slowly, erotically, he'd move to the tiny folds of skin between her fingers and beyond. Jared could almost feel the rasp of his tongue against the contour of her palm, her wrist, the inside of her elbow, the tip of her breast.

With an inarticulate cry, he surged to his feet.

"What's the matter?" Alaina asked in alarm.

"Nothing," he growled. "I just need to get a drink. We'll be leaving in five minutes so be ready to travel when I get back."

"But you've hardly eaten anything. You must be starving."

"I'll live," he said, stalking off toward the creek. He was starving all right, but it wasn't the kind of hunger mere food would take care of. If he had any brains at all he'd douse himself in the frigid creek until the fever in his blood cooled. His body seemed to forget what a young innocent Alaina was, and that he had a fiancée waiting for him in Laramie City.

CHAPTER FOURTEEN

"**I** quit," Alaina muttered as she plopped wearily down on a rock. "You may have the stamina of a bull moose, Jared Brady, but I've gone far enough. Send a horse back for me when you get there," she called after him.

Jared glanced back over his shoulder in surprise. "What's wrong?"

"What do you think is wrong? I expected to walk all night, but the sun has been up for hours. I'm worn to a frazzle."

Jared felt a surge of guilt. "I'm sorry. I never thought..."

"Well you should have," Alaina snapped waspishly. "I'll bet you wouldn't expect Susan to keep up such a grueling pace."

"No, but I can't imagine Susan in a situation like this."

"Neither can I. You'd never force her to take off into the wilderness on her own."

"Susan isn't impetuous, if that's what you mean."

"No, I'd say calculating is probably a better description than impetuous," Alaina muttered.

"That was uncalled for."

"I suppose it was," Alaina said, spreading the blanket out on the ground. "But you know, I don't feel the least bit guilty. You can do what you want, but I'm going to get some sleep."

"Fine." He took the cradleboard off his back and set

it down next to her. "I'm going to go scout around."

"Suit yourself."

Jared gritted his teeth. She sounded so childishly petulant that for an instant he had the urge to take her over his knee and paddle her. "For once, stay put until I get back."

"Don't worry, I'm too tired to go another inch."

"Well, that's a relief," he muttered as he dropped the canteen next to her. "I'll leave this here in case you get thirsty."

Alaina glanced up at him in surprise. "You aren't going to take it with you?"

"You and Bright Eyes might need it." He shrugged. "I can always find the creek."

"I...thanks."

"Sure." He bent over to pick up his rifle. "I think you're safe enough here in the trees. I should be back in half an hour or so."

"Jared?" Alaina said hesitantly. "I'm sorry I'm such a grouch. Mama always said she'd rather twist a mountain lion's tail than put up with me when I'm tired. "

"Smart lady," he murmured.

"Are you sure you don't want to sleep for a while? You didn't get much more than I did."

She looked so delectable lying there that for one insane instant he was tempted. But then his better sense intruded. If he lay down next to her right now, there probably wouldn't be much sleeping for either of them. "Maybe later. I want to make sure we don't get any company." With a regretful glance, he shouldered his rifle and walked away.

Maybe if he got clear away from her for a little while

he'd be able to get himself back under control. The erotic fantasy he'd woven in his mind wouldn't leave him alone. Over and over he imagined licking the honey from her fingers then moving on to other equally delightful activities

He tried to substitute Susan for Alaina in his mind, but somehow, he couldn't picture his oh so proper fiancée with honey all over her hands. Nor could he imagine licking it off. She'd probably throw a fit and call him a disgusting cretin. The mental picture brought a smile to his lips, but at least his blood wasn't boiling any more.

Jared topped a small rise and looked around with dawning recognition. Last year's base camp lay hidden in the cliff just beyond that small stand of trees. How could he have forgotten? Not only was it a safe secure place to sleep for a few hours, the surveying crew had left a cache of supplies buried there under a pile of rocks when they'd pulled out in the fall.

Alaina and Bright Eyes would almost certainly be safer there as long as the renegades hadn't found it. He glanced indecisively back over his shoulder. On the other hand, Alaina wouldn't appreciate him waking her up right now especially if they couldn't use the old camp after all. What a crab! A rueful smile tugged at Jared's mouth as he started toward the trees. He'd rather play hide-and-seek with an entire army of renegades than face Alaina while she was still tired.

A short time later, he slipped through a narrow crack in the fifty-foot granite cliff and looked around in satisfaction. The place was undisturbed. Either the outlaws hadn't discovered its existence, or they had no use for it. Whichever the case, it was a safe haven.

Opening the cache was a simple matter. The crew hadn't bothered to secure the site. They'd only wanted to stash the unused supplies and get out of the mountains before the first snowfall hit. Nobody really cared if someone else found it before they returned. He grinned to himself as he lifted the rocks off the oilskin they'd used as a protective cover. Who would have thought he'd be this glad to see canned beans and hardtack?

A little less than an hour had passed by the time Jared topped the small rise again and scanned the area anxiously. He'd been gone longer than he intended, but all seemed quiet. The sigh of relief had barely cleared his lips when a band of horsemen suddenly appeared on the brow of a hill a mile away. A knot of ice formed in the pit of his stomach as they turned and headed straight toward the clump of trees where he'd left Alaina and Bright Eyes.

For an endless moment, Jared stood there frozen in one spot, staring in disbelief. Then he was running like he'd never run before, jumping logs and pushing through the underbrush with great ground-eating strides that matched the terror in his heart. He barely noticed when his ribs began to ache from his labored breathing. It would take a miracle to escape this time, especially since Alaina was sure to be sound asleep.

But Alaina was wide-awake and Bright Eyes was screaming at the top of her lungs when Jared finally got there. He took in the scene in an instant and wondered if this were all just an incredibly bad dream. Instead of the miracle he'd been hoping for, a huge grizzly stood on its hind legs, looming over the cradleboard like some dark angel of death.

"Pick on somebody your own size, you big bully," Alaina yelled, as she chucked a rock at the beast. The animal just stood there on its hind legs staring at her as the missile hit his head with a solid thwack. In fact, it wasn't until the next rock bounced off his ear and another smacked him on the nose, that the bear reacted. With a low growl, he dropped to all fours and started toward Alaina.

Jared didn't even hesitate. With one smooth motion, he swung his rifle to his shoulder and pulled the trigger. The bear jerked but kept going as Jared desperately ejected the shell, slammed another into place and fired. This time the bullet dropped the bear almost at Alaina's feet. Without even taking time to draw a breath, Jared scooped up the cradleboard and ran to her.

It was almost as if she didn't know he was there. She stood rooted to the spot staring down at the bear, as though it might rise up on its hind feet and come after her again.

"It's all right, Alaina, he's dead. The bear is the least of our worries right now. There are half a dozen renegades just beyond the trees and headed this way. Those rifle shots are going to bring them down on us like buzzards on a corpse." He thrust the rifle into her lax hold just long enough to transfer the cradleboard to his back. Then he grabbed the rifle with one hand and Alaina's arm with the other. "Come on."

"I only left for a second," she wailed. "But when I came back the bear was there, and..."

"Alaina," he said urgently. "We don't have time for this. I know it's asking a lot, but you've got to pull yourself together. If we don't run we're going to die."

"Bright Eyes..."

"Was just scared. She stopped crying as soon as I picked her up. She's fine, but I can't save her by myself. We've got to get her out of here."

Concern for the baby finally broke through her paralysis. With a bewildered nod, she lifted her skirts and started moving. Moments later she'd caught Jared's urgency and was running with him as fast as she could.

The cliff seemed impossibly far away and the distance between filled with too many open spots. Already Jared's ribs felt as if they were on fire. They had barely reached the top of the small rise when Alaina stumbled and nearly pulled them both down. As Jared tried to catch his balance, the rifle went spinning out of his hand and slid back down the hill the way they had come. He only paused an instant, then headed for the relative safety of the trees ahead. Going back for the rifle might mean the difference between making it to the cliff in time and not.

Evergreen branches and underbrush tore at their clothes as they ran through the trees. Though the going was easier, the open areas were almost worse, for Jared expected to hear a shout of discovery behind them or feel a bullet slam into his body. They were both at the end of their endurance when they broke through the last stand of trees, and the cliff loomed in front of them. Jared didn't think he'd ever been gladder to see any place in his life.

Alaina suddenly pulled back on his hand. "No," she panted. "Can't."

The stitch in Jared's side felt more like a knife than a pain from overexertion. Though she hadn't run as far as he had, Alaina must hurt just as bad for she had shorter legs and had to run in a heavy skirt. He tugged on her hand. "Almost there."

She shook her head emphatically and pointed to the sheer rock wall ahead of them. "They'll...catch...us."

All at once he understood her panic. She thought they were going to be caught against the cliff like rats in a trap. He didn't have the time or the breath to explain about the hidden crevice in the cliff wall. "Trust me," he gasped, his face contorting with the painful effort.

Their gazes met and held for a heartbeat, then Alaina nodded, and Jared urged her forward again. They had just reached the cliff when the sound of horses crashing through the trees behind them lent speed to their feet.

Alaina gripped his hand in pure terror, then they were inside, the sheer rock walls towering over them like protective sentinels as they ran down the natural corridor. A moment later, the narrow passageway opened up into the wide grassy area and they stopped at last.

Jared pulled Alaina into the safety of his arms and just held her as they leaned against each other, their breath coming in painful gasps.

Alaina grabbed the open edges of Jared's coat and pressed the side of her face against his chest as her breathing gradually slowed. There was nothing lover-like in the way he held her, but she felt safe and secure in his strong arms. It was the first time she'd felt that way since she returned from answering the call of nature and saw the bear going after Bright Eyes.

Suddenly she was struggling in Jared's arms. "Bright Eyes!" she babbled. "Oh, Jared, the bear was licking her face. Is she all right?"

"I don't know. She stopped crying when I picked her

up." Jared released her to shrug the cradleboard off his shoulders. But Alaina didn't wait. She was there peering into the baby's face before Jared could get his arms free.

"She isn't moving!" she wailed. "Oh, Jared, how could I have forgotten her even for a moment?"

"We had a few distractions." Jared carefully set the cradleboard on the ground and touched the baby with gentle fingers. "I don't see any sign of teeth marks."

Alaina frowned. "Are you sure? She was screaming at the top of her lungs and I could swear I saw that bear lick her. That's why I started throwing rocks."

Suddenly, Jared started to smile. "Of course. I should have realized. The bear was after the honey! Bright Eyes had it all over her face from the sugar teat." He rubbed a soft cheek with his knuckle. "This little lady wasn't hurt. She was just complaining about having her face washed. She must have fallen asleep while we were running from the renegades."

Alaina looked at Jared in astonishment. "She almost got eaten by a bear, and five minutes later she was asleep?"

"It looks that way." Jared grinned. "I think she could sleep through about anything. Tornado, earthquake, buffalo stampede, you name it."

"How about hunger?" Alaina asked woefully. "All our food is back there with the bear and our blankets."

"Not all of it." If possible, Jared's grin got even bigger. "That's what took me so long to get back. I wanted to surprise you. Turn around."

Alaina turned and gaped in astonishment. There, on the ground, was a small pile of food rations and two bedrolls spread out next to each other. "What is this place?"

"Last year's final base camp for the surveying crew. We pulled out last fall just ahead of a blizzard. To move faster, we left most of our supplies here. I'd forgotten about it until I saw the cliff. Some of the supplies had been ruined by weather and rust, but we've got several cans of beans and some hardtack. "

"Do the renegades know about this place?"

"I doubt it. If Whiskey Jug hadn't brought us here, we'd never have found it. The only way they could know where we are is if they came out of the trees in time to see us disappear into the cliff. If they had, they'd be here already."

"Did you hear something?" Alaina asked suddenly.

Both listened intently for several seconds. Then it came again, the sound of dislodged pebbles clattering against the rocky floor of the passageway.

"They found us!" Alaina whispered.

Jared glanced around the enclosure frantically as an odd scraping noise moved down the rock passageway toward them. There wasn't so much as a stick to defend them. Without his rifle, they didn't stand a chance in Hell.

"Jared?" she quavered uncertainly. "What are we going to do?"

"The only weapon we have is surprise. If there's only one I may be able to overpower him." He strode over to the entrance, picked up a large rock, and flattened himself against the cliff wall.

Alaina glanced from the peacefully sleeping Bright Eyes to Jared waiting next to the entrance. Bright Eyes didn't need her, but Jared might. She wasn't strong enough to overpower a man, but with a rock she might be able to knock one down. Without another thought, she hurried over to the entrance and picked up a rock.

Jared flashed her an encouraging smile as she took up a position opposite of him behind a large boulder. The scraping continued toward them with nerve-wracking slowness. An odd snuffling snort sounded from the corridor, then a long moment of silence. Alaina frowned. What sort of man would make a sound like that?

Then the scraping started again, much closer this time. Whoever was coming down the corridor was almost upon them. Alaina and Jared looked at each other. As their gazes met, Alaina realized with a sudden jolt that Jared had come to mean a great deal to her. Hard on the heels of her astonishing discovery came the certain knowledge that they could both die in the next few minutes. For a terrified instant she wanted to run to the other side of the enclosure and hide. Telling herself not to be such a coward, Alaina swallowed hard and lifted her rock.

CHAPTER FIFTEEN

Alaina stared unblinkingly at what she could see of the entrance to the rocky corridor. What if she fell apart when Jared needed her the most? She tensed as the scraping came again, much closer this time. Her panic rose in a tide. Tightening her grip on the rock nervously, she kept her gaze glued to the opening where the men would come through.

Suddenly, unbelievably, Jared laughed. "Well, I'll be," he said softly. "I think the current resident just came home. Look."

Perplexed, Alaina looked over her boulder and blinked in surprise. Instead of an invading army of riffraff she found herself being regarded by a disgruntled porcupine. It stared at the two humans for a long moment, then turned and lumbered toward a large pine tree growing by the back wall, its quills scraping against the cliff as it went.

Alaina's rock fell from nerveless fingers. "I nearly died of fright because of a stupid porcupine?"

"It looks that way." Jared grinned as she stepped out from behind her rock. "Don't worry, he won't bother us unless you have a wooden leg you haven't told me about."

"No, but with our luck, he'll probably decide he has a taste for cradle boards."

"Even a porcupine gnawing on her bed wouldn't wake Bright Eyes."

Alaina started to giggle. It came from deep inside and rose on a wave of hysteria that suddenly turned to tears. One minute she was laughing, the next she was crying, deep, wrenching sobs fed by days of uncertainty, fear and exhaustion. She was hardly aware when Jared pulled her into his embrace.

"Shhh, it's all right." He rubbed her back comfortingly and murmured soft words of encouragement until the storm finally subsided.

Reluctant to step away, she stayed within the shelter of his arms, nervously twisting a button on his shirt. "I made it through the bear and the outlaws, then cried over a stupid porcupine. You must think I'm the biggest idiot in the world."

"Hey, I was just as scared as you were."

"You couldn't have been."

"Want to bet? My heart's still pounding like a Gatling gun."

She blinked away the last of her tears and focused on his face. It was covered with the stubbly beginnings of a beard, there were dark circles under his eyes, and his shirt was torn in several places. Alaina thought he was beautiful. She lifted a finger to trace an evil looking scratch that followed the contour of one eyebrow. "How did that happen?"

"I don't know. It's been a rough five days." His voice was soft and husky, and it sent a shiver of pure delight coursing through her.

"Doesn't it hurt?"

"Not much." The words were murmured against her mouth and Alaina forgot everything else in a deluge of sensation. He nibbled at her lips until she opened them in shy acquiescence and his tongue swept in to gently explore the inside of her mouth.

Alaina slipped her hands inside his coat and circled his waist with her arms. Jared's kiss was warm and wonderful, like the essence of a pleasant dream. The warmth expanded and grew until it felt as though her heart was pumping molten heat through her body. When he cupped her breast, teasing the tip of it through the fabric of her dress, the warmth exploded into white-hot flames.

Suddenly Alaina wanted to give him a taste of the same pleasure he was giving her. Intent on her task, she pulled his shirttail and undershirt free of his pants and ran her hands up his back underneath. His skin was smooth and vibrant as she stroked the hard muscles with wonder and delight. Never would she have believed touching another's body could create such delicious sensations in her own.

Abruptly, he tore his mouth away and leaned his forehead against hers, breathing nearly as hard as when they'd arrived at the cliff. "This is insanity, Alaina."

"Is it?" Alaina gazed up at him. "It's the first time in five days I haven't been scared half to death."

"Oh, sweetheart, you have no idea what you're playing with."

"Yes, I do. My mother made very sure I didn't grow up ignorant of what goes on between men and women. I know exactly where it will end if we continue."

"Then you know why we have to stop."

Alaina gave him a sad little smile. "The renegades know we're around here somewhere, your rifle is gone, we only have enough food for a couple of days, and we're both nearly at the end of our strength. What do you honestly think our chances are of making it out of these mountains alive?"

"Honestly?" Jared gave a defeated sigh. "Slim and none."

"That's kind of what I figured too." She reached up and traced his cheek with her hand. "I don't want to think about death, Jared. Make me forget that it lurks right outside, just waiting for us to leave."

"But—"

She silenced him with a kiss, one he didn't even try to resist. His small moan, as her tongue sought tentative entrance to his mouth, gave her an odd little thrill. Emboldened by her success, she undid the buttons that ran down his chest. But when she pushed his shirt open and lifted the bottom of his undershirt, he caught her hand.

"This is ridiculous. We're both still wearing our coats, for God's sake."

Alaina felt herself coloring clear to the roots of her hair and dropped her head in embarrassment. What he must think of her!

A moment later she realized she had completely misunderstood as he swept her up in his arms and carried her the short distance to the blankets. He set her back on her feet and gazed tenderly down into her eyes.

"If we're going to do this, sweetheart, let's do it right." His voice was a husky caress as he pushed her coat down over her arms and dropped it to the ground.

Alaina closed her eyes when he tipped her head back to trail kisses down the sensitive cord of her neck. She savored the jolt of awareness that spread through her entire body as he undid her buttons one by one. His hands and mouth touched the warm flesh with fire as he removed her dress and one remaining petticoat. The air still had a slight chill but Alaina was so focused on the incredible things Jared was doing to her, that she hardly noticed.

His coat came off next, and then his boots. Alaina watched, mesmerized, until he reached for his shirt. "No," she whispered, "I started it. I want to finish the job."

Jared didn't say a word. He just let his hands dangle at his side while she slid his shirt down over the thick muscles of his arms. It fell to the ground in a heap at last, and she started to tug his undershirt upward. She had it pushed all the way up to his chest when he muttered a curse and grabbed the bottom of it. He jerked it over his head and impatiently tossed it to the side.

Alaina caught her breath in wonder. With all of her brothers and cousins, she'd seen her share of naked male chests, but never one that made her feel this way. Maybe it was because he was a full-grown man or because of all they'd been through together. Whatever the reason, her heart was pounding, and the air becoming increasingly more difficult to breathe as her palms traced a path over the strong muscles of his chest and continued upward to the broad shoulders. It was even more incredible than she had anticipated. She swallowed hard as she ran her hands slowly along the top of his shoulders.

Alaina would have been quite content to continue her explorations a bit longer, but Jared had other ideas. One minute she was standing there fondling his body, and the next she was on one of the blankets underneath him. She didn't precisely know how it happened and didn't especially care when Jared's mouth found hers again.

Jared was in the grip of passion like none he'd ever

experienced before. It was as though their close brush with death had opened the door to a wildly primitive side he hadn't even known existed. His body was bathed in heat, stoked by the wanton mating of their tongues and the feel of Alaina's hands on his naked skin. The blood surged through his veins hot and thick, a tide of lust so overpowering he was helpless against it. The urge to take her right then was nearly irresistible, but a spark of sanity remained. He had to get this under control, to slow himself down until Alaina was as ready as he was.

With that goal in mind, Jared left her lips to explore other delights. Every part of her, from the tip of her nose to the arch of her foot, received his undivided attention. It was immensely satisfying, and Alaina's moaning response was all he could wish. Unfortunately, it did little to cool his ardor. He wanted to remove the last of Alaina's clothing slowly, to fan the flames of her desire to a fever pitch. Instead, he dispatched of them with hasty efficiency and rolled to one side to get rid of his own.

Alaina's body ached with unfulfilled desire, but her whimper of protest had barely cleared her lips before he was beside her again. He leaned on one elbow and gazed down at her tenderly as he arranged one of the blankets from the other bedroll over them. The hair-roughened texture of his leg against hers startled Alaina, and she felt a momentary flash of embarrassment because they were both naked.

Then she looked up into his eyes, and it didn't matter anymore. The heat she saw in the depths matched the fire he'd kindled within her. She rolled to her side so that her body was pressed against the hard length of his. His skin against hers sent shock waves of pleasure through her.

Jared tenderly traced the curve of her cheek with the backs of his fingers. "Are you sure you want to do this, sweetheart?" His voice was rough and ragged as though he was in the grip of some violent inner turmoil.

"Oh, yes," she whispered, putting her hand against his heart. "I don't think I've ever been more sure of anything in my life."

"Good," he murmured against her lips. "I'm not sure I could have stopped anyway."

But Alaina knew he would have if she'd asked, that he was sincere in giving her a chance to back out. With sudden insight, she knew Jared Brady was a man of integrity, a man like Garrick Ellinson who never willingly hurt another person no matter what the cost to himself. In that one stark moment, a startling truth burned across her heart. She was in love with Jared Brady.

The next instant she forgot everything except what Jared's hands and mouth were doing to her. It wasn't long before he had pushed them both to their limits and rolled her beneath him with a single fluid movement.

Alaina cried out in surprise as a deep burning pain suddenly ripped through her, but she only had a moment to wonder what it meant. The discomfort faded rapidly as Jared swept her into a maelstrom of sensuality that completely overshadowed all that had come before. Higher and higher they rose, twisting and spinning together in a kaleidoscope of sensation until they shattered into a thousand brightly colored pieces and drifted gently back to earth.

Afterward Jared held her close, his fingers tracing small circles on her shoulder as their hearts slowed and their breaths mingled sweetly.

"Never in my wildest dreams did I imagine making love would be like that," Alaina said with awe. "It's no wonder people make such fools of themselves over it."

Jared chuckled. "I assume that means you enjoyed it."

"You could say that." Alaina yawned and snuggled closer. "We may have to try it again later just to make sure."

Jared smiled and closed his eyes as he nestled her head against his shoulder. "We might at that."

Jared awoke with a jerk as a long shadow fell across his face. A man stood over them, his face obscured by his hat and his huge body outlined by the sun. Jared tightened one arm protectively around Alaina while the other hand groped for the rifle he'd forgotten wasn't there.

Alaina blinked sleepily and peered up at the intruder. "Papa?"

Deep rumbling laugher broke over them as the giant sat on the other bedroll. "Not hardly, honey. It's a good thing, too. I reckon Jared would have some mighty tough explaining to do if your papa were standin' in my shoes right now."

"Whiskey Jug!" Jared cried with real pleasure. He released Alaina and sat up to grip the other man's hand in welcome. "Damn but you're a sight for sore eyes. Hardly recognized you without your beard."

Whiskey Jug rubbed his clean-shaven jaw self-consciously. "Hardly recognize myself without it." He grinned as he glanced at the clothes strewn around haphazardly. "Looks like I could have picked a better time to come visiting."

"It could have been a whole lot worse too." Jared ignored Alaina's mortified gasp. "When we found what was left of your cabin, I thought you were dead."

Whiskey Jug grimaced. "That was sort of a little misunderstanding between me and the misses."

"You're married?" Jared asked in surprise.

"In a manner of speaking. Brandy sorta dropped into my lap, you might say. Anyhow back when we were just gettin' acquainted, she took offense at something I said and tried to set fire to my britches. Wound up burnin' down my cabin."

Jared raised an eyebrow. "That must have been some insult."

"You know how women are," he said with a shrug. "Never know for sure what will get them riled up."

"That comes with experience. It won't be long before you'll know just how to handle her."

Whiskey Jug rubbed the side of his nose. "I don't know as that will ever happen. Brandy ain't like most women."

"How did you know we were here?"

"Didn't. Ducked in here to hide from some renegades. Stumbling onto a love nest was about the last thing I expected. Anyhow, I reckon it's time you and me went for a walk, Jared," Whiskey Jug said cheerfully, as he got to his feet.

Jared reached for his pants. "Why? Do you think you were followed in here?"

"Nope." Whiskey Jug grinned. "But it appears like your woman ain't feelin' real friendly toward either one of us right now."

Jared glanced over his shoulder at Alaina. There was little of her to see for she was huddled under the blanket in acute embarrassment, but the anger flashing in her eyes was unmistakable. "What's wrong?" he asked in surprise.

"What do you think is wrong?" she hissed. "I'm not wearing a stitch of clothes."

"Oh." Jared hadn't even thought about it. Everything had gone clear out of his mind when he saw Whiskey Jug alive. He glanced around the glade in consternation. There was no private place for Alaina to get dressed. "We'd best go check the entrance just to make sure you weren't followed, Whiskey Jug," he said. He flashed Alaina a hopeful look but only got a glower in return. A spark of resentment began to grow in him. After all, it wasn't like he knew Whiskey Jug was going to show up.

Jared never looked back as he dressed, or when he walked away with Whiskey Jug Johnson, but he could swear he felt Alaina's glare between his shoulder blades all the way to the passageway. "What do you know about those renegades out there?" he asked, determined not to think about Alaina and her unreasonable attitude.

"Not much, other than most of them ain't any more Indian than I am."

"I know. I recognized several army deserters among them, and I suspect more than a few are on wanted posters somewhere. What do you think they're up to?"

"Don't know. There was quite a bunch of them prowling around out there just now. Haven't given me any trouble yet, but that's mostly cause they don't know I'm around."

"It's probably best if they don't find out either. They

murdered Zeke and his wife three days ago." Jared felt the familiar roiling in his gut as he recalled the grisly scene. "Zeke was still alive when I got there, but just barely. He died in my arms before I could do anything for him. He said they'd tied him to a tree and made him watch while they took turns with her. From the look of her bruises, they weren't what you'd call gentle. Scalped them both to make it look like Indians."

"Jesus! Zeke was a good man and his wife was a sweet little thing. Neither of them ever did the least harm to anyone." Whiskey Jug ran a hand roughly through his hair. "My wife's going to take this real hard. Brandy was some sort of cousin to Zeke. She was real fond of him and his wife."

"Then she'll know what to do with the baby."

"Baby?" Whiskey Jug said in surprise.

Jared nodded toward the cradleboard, which lay almost out of sight behind a rock. "Alaina found her in the cradleboard hidden in the woods right next to Zeke's cabin."

"Damn savages."

"My sentiments exactly. We've spent the last few days trying to avoid them, but they seem to be all over this mountain."

"What are you doing up here without an army escort anyway?"

Jared grimaced. "We're not exactly on army business."

"I heard you were gettin' married, but I didn't figure on you spending your honeymoon in the mountains. Specially not this time of the year."

"We're not married."

"You're not..." Whiskey Jug began in surprise, then

he grinned. "No wonder she was so squeamish. Don't reckon you're the first to jump the gun a bit."

"It seemed like a good idea at the time."

Whiskey Jug chuckled. "It usually does. I hope that papa she was talking about is an understanding fellow."

"Me too," Jared said absently. "He's the only man I ever saw that makes you look puny." Whiskey Jug laughed and slapped his friend on the back with enough power to knock the smaller man off his feet, but Jared hardly noticed. The enormity of what he and Alaina had done hit him full force. He was honor bound to marry her, of course. The blood on the blanket was proof of that, even if he hadn't felt the barrier of her innocence give way.

The life he had planned with Susan, all his dreams for the future, everything he'd worked so hard for, lay in ashes around his feet, destroyed by a single act of lust. He felt many things--resentful, angry, even a bit foolish. But the most incredible emotion of all was an overwhelming surge of profound relief.

CHAPTER SIXTEEN

"**W**ell, here we are," Whiskey Jug said, as they came out into a clearing.

At first, Alaina couldn't see anything except more forest. Then, as she looked closer, she noticed a small cabin hidden back in the trees. She blinked and looked again. It only appeared to be about four feet high. "That's where you live?" she asked in surprise.

"Home sweet home." Whiskey Jug glanced uneasily toward the cabin. "Uh...I'll just go let Brandy know we have company."

"Can't wait to meet this dragon," Jared murmured as Whiskey Jug hurried away. "He almost seems afraid of her."

Alaina smiled slightly. "What do you expect? She burned down his cabin over a misunderstanding. Imagine what she'll do when he brings home uninvited guests."

Silence settled between them. It had been an uneasy hour and a half since Whiskey Jug found them naked and asleep in each other's arms. There was much that needed said, but neither knew how to broach the subject. Long minutes passed as embarrassment hung in the air like a dark cloud.

"We must look a sight," Alaina said, finally. She nervously smoothed back the tangled mass of hair, but it made little difference.

Jared almost smiled at the useless gesture but

thought better of it. "Maybe that's why Whiskey Jug was afraid to bring us home." He glanced at the afternoon sun. "At least we'll have a safe place to sleep tonight."

"If she doesn't send us packing. Do you think Whiskey Jug would still take us down the mountain to Saratoga?"

"Don't be silly. She's not going to—" Jared broke off in startled surprise as a loud crash sounded from the cabin. They were still staring at each other in wide-eyed consternation when a small figure came hurtling out of the door toward them.

Though the clothing matched Whiskey Jug's, the loose leather shirt and pants couldn't hide the very feminine figure beneath. Shoulder length brown hair surrounded her head like a halo, but her most noticeable attribute, as she ran across the clearing, was her diminutive size. It was doubtful if the top of her head would reach Whiskey Jug's shoulder.

"A miniature dragon," Jared murmured.

"Where is she?" Brandy cried when she reached them. "Where's Erika?"

"E...Erika?" Alaina stammered in confusion.

"Zeke and Sunshine's baby."

"Oh," said Alaina, "you mean Bright Eyes. Jared has her safe and sound."

"See, Alaina, I told you she was part Viking," Jared said, pulling the cradleboard off one shoulder and swinging Bright Eyes around the front as Whiskey Jug joined them. "Erika, meet your cousin Brandy."

Bright Eyes and Brandy stared at each other from identical hazel eyes for a long moment, then Brandy reached out and touched the tiny cheek reverently. "Oh, Adam, can you believe how beautiful she is? Just look at her."

"I reckon so," Whiskey Jug said, squinting at the baby doubtfully.

Brandy took the cradleboard from Jared and smiled at Alaina. "I can't thank you enough for taking care of her the way you have."

Alaina returned her smile. "Oh, it's no bother. Not much anyway," she amended as Jared made a choking noise behind her. "About the only real difficulty we have is feeding her. She isn't really old enough to be without milk."

"Reckon we have the solution to that problem," Whiskey Jug said, scratching his head.

Brandy gave a satisfied nod. "That's right. Adam bought me a goat last time he went to Saratoga." She stopped suddenly and sniffed the air. "Oh dear, my stew will be burnt to a crisp if we aren't careful. Why don't you come in a rest a bit before we eat? You look about done in."

"I am pretty tired," Alaina admitted.

"Gentlemen, I suggest you go down to the creek and get washed up. Supper will be on the table in ten minutes." Brandy said over her shoulder as the two women headed back toward the cabin. Then she turned back to Alaina. "Hope you like venison stew. It's a little early for vegetables but..."

Whiskey Jug heaved a sigh of relief. "Guess we'd best go get washed up like she says.

Jared quirked an eyebrow. "Adam?"

"It's my given name," Whiskey Jug said, blushing deeply. "Brandy nagged at me until I told her what it was. Now she never calls me anything else."

Jared chuckled. "Brandy isn't exactly what I

expected. I can't believe she actually talked you into buying a goat."

"The goat's the least of it. She insisted on a privy out back, and a place for bathing down in the creek."

Jared laughed outright at that. "Better watch out, Whiskey Jug. She'll civilize you if you aren't careful."

Whiskey Jug rubbed a hand across his clean-shaven chin. "She might at that," he said with a soft smile. "She might at that."

Alaina followed Brandy down into the cabin and gazed around in astonishment. No wonder it looked like it was four feet high; the rest of it was underground. "I've never seen a house like this," she said.

"Neither had I, but the cabin burned so late in the fall this was the only kind Adam had time to build before winter set in. Somebody else dug the hole years ago, so all we had to do was reshape it a little and put up the walls." Brandy shrugged. "It isn't what you'd call beautiful, but the wind doesn't affect it much, and it kept us warm all winter."

"After the last few days, it looks like a palace to me."

Brandy pulled a homemade broom out of the corner and proceeded to sweep up a pile of broken crockery. "This is all that's left of my favorite bowl," she said with a sigh. "I wouldn't have dropped it if Adam had just come out and told me what was going on instead of dithering around like an idiot."

"The crash we heard," Alaina said with dawning comprehension.

"He had me so shook up I lost my grip."

Alaina gave her a sympathetic look. "I'm sorry

about your cousin and his wife."

"They were good people," Brandy said sadly, "and they came to such an awful end." Her lip trembled as she blinked away sudden tears.

Alaina touched her arm gently. "My Grandmother always said the best way to get through grief is by concentrating on the living."

"You're right." Brandy took Bright Eyes from Alaina and hugged her tightly. "At least Erika's safe."

"Yes, and she's such a good baby." Alaina sniffed appreciatively. "It smells wonderful in here. We haven't had much to eat over the last few days."

As though she understood Alaina's words, Bright Eyes woke with a whimper.

"Sounds like this one's hungry too," Brandy said. "Guess we'd better feed her." It took a few minutes for the two women to rig a bottle and fill it with goat milk, but soon Bright Eyes lay in Alaina's arms greedily nursing while Brandy put supper on the table.

"I've never seen a baby sleep as much as this one does," Alaina said.

"From what Adam said, it sounded like you've been on the move almost constantly the last few days. She's probably as exhausted as the two of you."

"I suppose she is at that. If she runs true to form, she'll be asleep as soon as she finishes this bottle and I change her. Of course, I'll have to admit, I'm looking forward to a good night's sleep myself."

Brandy gave her a speculative glance. "I'll bet you'd love a bath, too wouldn't you?"

"Wouldn't I just. I feel like I'm packing half the mountain around on my skin."

"Well, it just so happens Adam and I have our own

private bathing facility. One of the reasons there was a cabin here in the first place is that there's a hot springs back in the woods. It's a good thing it gets dark late this time of year. You'll have plenty of time for a bath before bedtime."

The anticipation of being clean again was nearly as overwhelming as the thought of eating her fill. The savory smell of the cooking stew gave a sharp edge to her hunger that couldn't be ignored. By the time Whiskey Jug and Jared came in, Bright Eyes was sleeping comfortably in her cradleboard, and Alaina felt like she was in imminent danger of starving.

The stew and large slices of homemade bread were sheer ambrosia. Alaina ate until she could eat no more. The men disappeared when the meal was over, shooed outside by Brandy's threat to let them wash dishes if they didn't have anything better to do. Her conspiratorial wink let Alaina know the results were exactly what she wanted.

"Can't do a thing with them under foot," she said with satisfaction. "Now, for your bath. Let's see, you'll need soap and towels." Brandy dug the requisite items out of a chest and piled them in Alaina's arms. "I'm sorry it's lye soap. Adam promised to get me some gentler soap when he was in town, but there wasn't any."

Alaina smiled. "I'm used to lye soap. Besides, I need it to wash my dress."

"Then we'll have to find you something to wear while it dries." Brandy tapped her finger against her upper lip as she gazed at Alaina's tall slender figure. "None of my clothes will even come close to fitting. About the only thing I have that will work is an old nightgown that belonged to Adam's mother, but it's not exactly appropriate for day wear."

"That should be fine. It's not like I'm going to be wearing it to town or anything."

"No, I guess not." Brandy retrieved the nightgown and added it to the pile in Alaina's arms. "There, now all you have to do is follow the trail down to the creek. The hot springs is right next to the waterfall. This time of year, so much water comes over the falls that the spring is hidden, but if you wade through the pool at the bottom you'll find it."

"You're not coming with me?"

Brandy shook her head. "Not just yet. I need to get some kind of a bed set up for Erika. Don't worry. If you stay on the trail, you can't get lost."

"All right." Alaina glanced at Bright Eyes, but the baby was sound asleep in the cradleboard. With a shake of her head, she left the cabin and made her way down the path toward the distant roar of a waterfall. Brandy was right; there was no way she could get lost.

Within a few minutes the waterfall came into sight, an impressive tumbling cascade of water that frothed down over hidden boulders to a good-sized pool below. She stared at it appreciatively for a few minutes, noting the slight yellow undertones of the spring run-off beneath the foaming white. Even though it was high water, the pool looked safe enough. The hot springs must be just beyond the curve of the bank, concealed by the waterfall.

Alaina set the towel and soap on a large flat rock and sat down to take off her shoes. Pleasant anticipation surged through her as she unbuttoned her dress and the water bubbled invitingly near her bare feet. *First things first,* she thought, stepping out of her dress and loosening the drawstring on her remaining petticoat.

She knelt and dunked her dress into the water. Pulling the garment back up onto a flat rock that had obviously been used for a scrub board before, she frowned. With numerous small tears and several missing buttons, it was ready for the ragbag. As she scrubbed out the worst of the dirt, she wondered how much longer it would have to serve her. The money Garrick had given her had been left behind in the tent with everything else. Without it, there was little chance of getting a new dress.

When her clothes were as clean as she could get them, she hung them over a willow, grabbed her soap, and turned back to the creek. The water was breathtakingly cold as she gingerly stepped into it, and didn't get any warmer as she waded in deeper. Carefully picking her way across the moss-covered rocks beneath her feet, Alaina headed for the far side where she knew the hot springs lay. Just as she reached the deepest part of the pool, her foot slipped off a slick rock, and she fell backwards into the frigid water.

It was like being dipped into an icy snow bank. After what seemed like an eternity of numbing cold, Alaina came up coughing, sputtering and gasping for breath. She would have yelled if she could have gotten enough air into her lungs to do so, but the ability to breathe seemed to have deserted her. Long icy ropes of wet hair straggled down over her shoulders and back as she tried to hurry toward the warmer water she knew lay just around the bend.

When Alaina finally reached the far edge of the waterfall, she could see her goal through a curtain of falling water. A small pool lay beyond, nestled among luxuriant greenery. Steam curled invitingly into the air, promising warmth and a chance to take a long relaxing bath.

A ledge skirted the edge of the pool about three feet under the surface of the water. Alaina scrambled up on the smooth rocky surface and carefully made her way along its length. Her shift and drawers clung to her like an icy second skin, and gooseflesh rose all over her body. Currents of mixed warm and cold swirled around her thighs as she walked through the curtain of water at the edge of the falls and stepped down off the ledge.

Blessed warmth flowed around her, and she closed her eyes in real pleasure.

"I guess I should have figured Brandy would send you down," said a familiar masculine voice.

Alaina gave a startled squeak and whirled around. "Jared!" she cried. "What are you doing here?"

"The same thing you are; taking a bath."

"Oh." It was completely inane but Alaina couldn't think of anything else to say. All she could do was stare. Jared stood waist deep in the pool, and if he was wearing a stitch of clothes, she couldn't see it. He'd shaved off the unsightly stubble on his chin and washed his hair, but the return of his good looks was the least of it. Water droplets glistened enticingly across the broad shoulders and down the seductive curve of his muscular chest. The sight of all that wet skin was doing funny things to her insides.

As she gazed at him in mute appreciation, a sudden image of what she must look like popped into her head, and she glanced down. Sure enough, her shift was all but transparent as it clung to her breasts. Thankfully, her hips were under water, though he must have gotten a full frontal view as she came through the waterfall.

Embarrassment colored her face as she looked up at him, but the hot gaze she encountered burned the self-consciousness away and kindled an answering flame within her. Heat flowed through her veins like sun-warmed honey as sudden memories of their morning interlude flooded her mind. What would it be like to make love in the sensual warmth of the hot springs?

"Alaina," Jared whispered, though it sounded more like a moan. He took a step toward her, then another.

Alaina wasn't even aware of moving through the water until they met in the middle of the pool.

Jared raised both hands to cup her face. "This is crazy," he murmured, tenderly tracing the curve of her mouth with the pad of his thumb.

Alaina's lips parted slightly. "I know."

Slowly, as if in a dream, Jared lowered his head toward hers. Their lips were a hair's-breadth apart when Whiskey Jug's voice broke over them with chilling force.

"You best hurry up, Jared," he yelled from the other side of the waterfall. "Brandy's on her way down here with the baby."

"Damn," Jared muttered, lifting his head and glancing back over his shoulder toward the sound. "All right. I'll be out in a minute," he called back. He dropped his hands to Alaina's shoulders and smiled ruefully down at her. "I guess we should be grateful to Whiskey Jug for warning us. Think how embarrassing to be caught in a compromising position twice in one day."

Alaina felt her face go hot. "Oh, Jared, I—"

"Shhh," he said, leaning forward and dropping a kiss on her forehead. "It was more my fault than yours. Besides, nothing happened. Why don't you take your bath? Brandy will be here soon and you can forget all about this."

"Forget it. Why?"

"Because..." He stared down at her blankly for a moment then the corner of his mouth quirked upward. "Oh hell, remember it then, and this too." He pulled her tight against him and bent to kiss her.

Alaina's mouth opened beneath his as her arms circled his naked, waist and a multitude of sensual delights crashed in upon her. The heat of the water swirled around them as his hands caressed the sensitive skin of her back, and his tongue explored the inside of her mouth with silken strokes. It was a magical moment suspended in time, erotically tender and all too brief. Long before she was ready, Jared broke it off and stepped back with a stunned look on his face.

"Kiss me like that much longer and even a long swim in the cold water won't make me presentable" he said cryptically. "I'll see you back at the cabin."

Alaina watched as he dove under the water. He surfaced when he reached the waterfall and turned back for a last look. Their gazes met and held for a long intense moment, then he disappeared through the curtain of water.

Alaina was still standing there like a moonstruck debutante when Brandy and Bright Eyes arrived.

CHAPTER SEVENTEEN

"Oh, sweetheart, I'm going to miss you so," Alaina whispered as she hugged Bright Eyes. She kissed the downy head and handed the baby to Brandy. In the rays of the rising sun, the baby's hair looked almost red. Alaina bit her lip and looked away.

"She's going to miss you, too." Brandy said. "Don't worry, I'll tell Erika all about you when she's old enough. Her children and grandchildren will grow up hearing stories of how you and Jared saved her."

"Take..." Alaina took a deep breath to keep her voice steady. It wasn't easy when she was so close to tears. "Take good care of her. And thanks for everything." She wondered for the dozenth time how she could have been so incredibly stupid. It hadn't even occurred to her that Brandy and Whiskey Jug were planning to keep Bright Eyes until this morning.

She should have figured it out when Brandy brought Bright Eyes to the hot springs the night before so Alaina could show her how to give the baby a bath. Or when Brandy chattered happily about how much she had to learn about taking care of babies. She and Brandy had talked a long time. Alaina had even gone so far as to tell her new friend the real reason she was going to Fort Bridger, but the topic of leaving Bright Eyes behind never came up.

It was all Jared Brady's fault. If it hadn't been for their encounter in the hot springs, she would have realized what was going on. As it was, Jared and his kiss were all she could think of during the long evening and into the night when Brandy put pallets on either side of the fireplace for them. Even her dreams were filled with erotic images of him. It wasn't until this morning when Jared commented on how well she was taking the idea of leaving Bright Eyes behind, that she realized what was going on. The worst of it was that she couldn't even argue, for it made perfect sense. Brandy was Erika's family.

"Are you ready?" Jared asked.

When Alaina nodded, he mounted Whiskey Jug's extra horse in a single fluid motion and reached down for her. Swallowing against the knot in her throat, she grabbed his arm at the elbow, put her left foot into the stirrup and swung up behind the saddle. Brandy handed up the small bundle of provisions she'd put together, and they were ready to leave.

With a final wave, Whiskey Jug and Jared turned their horses toward the trail and headed out of the clearing. Alaina looked back over her shoulder until Brandy and Bright Eyes were out of sight.

"You all right?" Jared asked over his shoulder.

"Fine. I'm just a little tired."

"Me too, but then I guess that's to be expected after the last few days. Why don't you try to relax and get some rest?"

"Oh, right, as though a person can rest on the back of a horse going down a mountain."

"I thought you could sleep anywhere."

"Even Vikings have their limits."

"At least put your arms around my waist so you don't have to work so hard at staying on."

She could almost hear the smile in his voice. "I'm not a baby, Jared. I've been riding double with my brothers and cousins for most of my life."

"I'm not your brother or your cousin, and I won't make fun of you for hanging on," Jared said sharply. "Besides, we need you to watch our backs to make sure the renegades don't sneak up on us. You can't do that if all your concentration is going into staying on the horse!"

Alaina hesitated a moment, then gave in to the temptation of being close. If Jared didn't know she'd be just as secure holding onto the cantle with her hands as she would with her arms around his waist, she certainly wasn't going to enlighten him. Even the high cantle occasionally jabbing into her stomach wasn't as much of a deterrent as it should have been. The feel of Jared in her arms more than compensated for any discomfort. Maybe the twenty-mile trip into Saratoga wouldn't be so bad after all.

Jared knew the minute Alaina fell asleep. They'd been traveling steadily for several hours by then, and the mid-morning sun was warm against their backs when he felt her sag against him. He smiled softly as he tucked her clasped hands under his free arm so she wouldn't fall off even if she relaxed her hold on him. Leaving Bright Eyes had been hard on her. She hadn't made a whimper of protest, but her restless movements all night proved how little she'd slept.

His rest had been disturbed too, but it wasn't the baby that kept him awake. It was the memory of Alaina in the hot springs that tortured him. He'd finished out the scene in his mind in a dozen different ways, each of them more erotic than the last. She swept away his better sense, but making love to Alaina was as close to heaven as he'd ever been. Even now, her breasts pressed against his back reminded him of how they looked beneath her wet, clinging shift and the way she responded to his kiss. At least he had something in this forced marriage to look forward to. His smile widened at the thought.

Whiskey Jug chose trails the renegades weren't likely to know about. He took a round-about route, but the trip down the mountain was uneventful. It was late afternoon when they finally reached the town of Saratoga.

"Reckon old Sam Twitchel over at the mercantile will give you the best price for your watch," Whiskey Jug said, stopping in front of the biggest store on the single main street. "Wish I had some cash to lend you."

"It doesn't matter. I should be able to get enough for a couple of hotel rooms and horses to take us on down to the railroad at Hannah."

"Too bad there isn't a telegraph any closer. The sooner you let the army know about those renegades the better off we'll all be."

"With any kind of luck, we should be there by tomorrow or the day after. You sure you won't change your mind about spending the night?"

"Nope." Whiskey Jug swung down from his horse and reached up to help Alaina. "Hate to leave Brandy alone any longer than I have to. I can get part way home before dark," he said, as he set Alaina on the ground.

"Can't say I blame you. We sure appreciate all you've done for us. I doubt we'd have made it out alive by ourselves."

"I expect we're about even then. Brandy's mighty pleased with that young'un you brought us." He grinned. "Course, I expect we'll get around to making one of our own soon enough."

Jared laughed as he dismounted. "And the practice is half the fun."

"No doubt about that." Whiskey Jug glanced at Alaina's red face. "Uh... sorry ma'am. Reckon I best get a lead rope on my extra horse and head on back up the mountain."

"I'll give you a hand," Jared said. In very little time, he'd switched the bridle for a halter and Whiskey Jug gave them a final wave as he rode out of town.

"I hope he makes it home all right," Alaina said, biting her lip.

"Don't worry, it'll take more than a bunch of outlaws to get Whiskey Jug. He's forgotten more about the Snowy Range Mountains than those renegades will ever know. Come on, let's see if we can get a couple of rooms and a good meal before dark."

Sam Twitchel's store was so dark after the bright sunlight outside, that Jared had trouble finding the proprietor behind the counter. He finally located the man up on a ladder apparently stocking shelves. With buckteeth, a wide, slightly flattened nose and thick spectacles, he reminded Jared of a rabbit.

"Something I can help you folks with?" he asked in a soft nasal voice.

"Whiskey Jug Johnson said you might be interested in buying my gold watch."

"I do buy things like that on occasion." He came down the ladder and reached under his counter for his magnifying glass. "Let's have a look at it."

Jared inwardly winced as he passed the watch across the counter. It had belonged to his grandfather and had come down to him through his mother on his eighteenth birthday. It felt as if he was selling part of his soul, but there was no help for it. Unable to watch, he idly scanned the shelves behind Twitchel's head. A dress of bright blue calico caught his eye. He could almost see Alaina wearing it. Maybe there'd be enough extra from the sale of the watch to buy it for her.

"Very nice," Twitchel said, as he examined the intricately scrolled design on the outside of the watchcase. He opened the front and peered down at the tiny rubies that marked the minutes between the gold numbers. "Very nice indeed. What did you say your name was, young fella?"

"Jared Brady." Jared tried not to stare at the hairs that grew out of Twitchel's rather pointed ears. He almost expected the man to start twitching his nose.

"Brady...hmm...interesting," he muttered, flipping open the back of the watch and gazing at the smoothly working gears inside.

Jared couldn't help wondering which he found interesting, the inner workings of the watch or the name Brady. "It was made in Switzerland," he said helpfully.

"I'm not surprised. The Swiss have a way with watches. Yes indeed, this is quite a beautiful piece." Twitchel snapped the back shut. "I'll give you eight dollars for it."

"Eight dollars! The case is worth more than that. It's fourteen carat gold."

"That may well be, but I'll likely have a hard time selling it."

"Why? It keeps perfect time."

"It also has the initials HRL on the back cover. Not many people want a watch with someone else's initials on it." Twitchel peered over his glasses. "Besides, that ain't you."

"It was my grandfather!"

He shrugged. "So you say. Could also be you stole it, and I don't deal in stolen goods."

Jared straightened angrily. "Then why did you offer me anything at all?"

"Because your wife looks about done in." Twitchel frowned. "Reckon I'd have a hard time sleeping tonight if I turned her out in the street. Eight dollars is the best I can give you under the circumstances. Take it or leave it."

Jared's jaw muscles clenched, and his hands knotted into fists. It would be so satisfying the shove Twitchel's rabbit-teeth down his miserable little throat. "I'll take it."

"Oh, Jared, no," Alaina murmured, laying her hand on his arm. "We'll figure out something else."

"This has nothing to do with you," he growled shaking off her hand. "I'll be back to get my watch, Twitchel. You can count on it."

"And I'll be happy to sell it back." Twitchel finished counting out the money. "With a modest profit, of course."

"Of course," Jared gritted out as he scooped the money off the counter and stalked out of the store. He didn't slow even when he reached the street, though he knew Alaina had to run to catch up with him.

"You didn't have to sell your grandfather's watch," she began. "I could have—"

"I don't want to hear about your cock-eyed scheme whatever it was," he snarled. "I did what I had to do and if you have a lick of sense, which I doubt, you won't bring it up again."

Miraculously, she shut her mouth and kept it closed all the way down the street to the one hotel in town. The bored looking young clerk was swatting flies with a rolled-up paper of some sort when they walked in. His expression brightened at the sight of them but dimmed dramatically as he took in their disreputable condition. "Is there something I can do for you?" he asked cautiously.

"We'd like a couple of rooms."

"I'm sorry, sir. We're full up. All we have left is the bridal suite." He eyed the rip in Jared's shirt. "And that's four dollars a night. Bath water is four bits, unless you want it hot, and then it's six bits. "

"Four dollars a night! I've stayed in fancy European hotels for less than that."

"I'm sure you have," he said, with more than a touch of disbelief. "However, our bridal suite is especially nice. It's the only room in the hotel with its own stove."

"It's almost the middle of June. What would I need a stove for?"

"I was merely pointing out how luxurious our bridal suite is. Why the governor himself stayed in it just last fall."

"On his wedding trip, no doubt," Jared said sarcastically.

"No, I believe he came to Saratoga to do some hunting. He found the accommodations quite satisfactory. We do everything we can to ensure our important guests are comfortable." The clerk flicked an imaginary speck off the sleeve of his jacket. "I'm terribly sorry we couldn't help you folks. Perhaps the saloon down the street. They sometimes rent out rooms to..."

"We'll take it," Jared snapped.

"But..."

"I said we'll take it!"

"It's all right, Jared," Alaina murmured. "I don't mind staying at the saloon."

"Well, I do. We're staying here and that's final!"

"That will be four dollars...," the clerk paused significantly, "...in advance."

"Of course. I wouldn't have expected anything else in this backwater." Jared slapped the money on the counter.

"And your baggage?"

Jared pulled himself to his full height and glared down at the young clerk with all the pomp of his aristocratic British relatives and the arrogance of his wealthy American upbringing. "Our baggage went the way of our carriage, horses and servants. If you had eyes in your head you'd realize we've had a run-in with some of your local outlaws."

"Outlaws?"

"Highwaymen, bandits, road agents, whatever you call them in this God forsaken country. I hate to think what would have happened if Whiskey Jug Johnson hadn't come along when he did. He rescued us and brought us here."

"We might still be where he found us," Alaina added. "It all happened so fast, we were lucky to escape with the clothes we had on."

"And you can see what kind of shape they're in after our ordeal." Jared fought to keep a straight face by fingering a three-corner tear in his shirt. If they were still wearing what Whiskey Jug had found them in, the clerk wouldn't have given them a room for a thousand dollars. "I don't suppose you have valet service."

The young clerk looked a little uncertain as though it had finally occurred to him he might have made a mistake. "V…valet service?"

Jared sighed in disgust. "Never mind. Just see that a pallet and extra blankets are in our room by the time we return from dinner. I assume you can handle that?"

"A pallet sir?"

He fixed the clerk with an icy stare that was worthy of his aristocratic great-grandfather in the midst of a London season. "Yes, a pallet. My wife snores, which is why we wanted two rooms in the first place. I seem to remember you saying the exorbitant rate you're charging me would ensure we would have everything we needed. Perhaps you should speak to your superior and get this straightened out."

The young clerk visibly wilted. "That won't be necessary. I'll take the pallet up myself. Whiskey Jug Johnson is a friend of the owner. I'm sure she'd want me to give you the best."

"Fine." Jared slid some coins across the desk. "This should take care of any extras we might require."

"Yes, sir. Very good, sir. If you just sign here." The clerk pointed to the register and turned to pull the key out of its cubby hole while Jared signed in. "Your room is number 10 at the top of the stairs and about halfway down the hall."

"Thank you. We'll be back after dinner. I trust you'll have fresh water and towels taken to our room along with the pallet."

"I'll see to it personally, Mr...." he looked in the book. "Brady."

"Good." Jared held his elbow out to Alaina. "Come along, dear. We'll want to get supper before the restaurant closes."

Alaina took his arm and they swept regally from the hotel lobby, tattered clothing and all. They were nearly to the door when a noise that sounded suspiciously like a giggle escaped Alaina through her nose.

"God bless you," Jared said, as he whisked her out the door and down the street. Luckily, they were past the windows of the hotel before she could control it no longer and laughed out loud.

"God bless you?" she said between giggles. "Do you really think he believed that was a sneeze?"

"Who knows? He swallowed the story about losing a carriage and all our baggage."

"And servants, don't forget. I never realized you were such an accomplished liar."

"Me? What about you? We were lucky to escape with the clothes we had on," Jared mimicked in a falsetto. "You're lucky I didn't give the whole thing away right then and there. As I remember it, when Whiskey Jug found us, all we were wearing was a blanket."

Alaina blushed slightly. "It sounded good didn't it? What do you suppose won him over, your haughty ways, or the owner's friendship with Whiskey Jug?"

"I don't know, but I'd sure like to meet this friend of his that owns the hotel. Better yet, I'd like to be there when Brandy meets her," Jared said with a grin.

Alaina slapped his hand playfully. "Trouble maker." Then she sobered. "Are you sure spending so much money on a room is a good idea?"

"I don't see that we had much choice. I'm sorry we

couldn't get separate rooms and having to let him think we're married."

"After the last few days separate rooms doesn't seem very important. Besides we couldn't have afforded them anyway. How are we going to get to the railroad?"

Jared shrugged. "Don't worry, I'll find work tomorrow."

"I can help too," Alaina offered.

"That won't be necessary," Jared said firmly. "It won't take me long to earn the rest of what we'll need to rent a couple of horses and buy train tickets in Hannah. Ah, here we are. Let's see if the restaurant people are any more friendly than the rest of the town."

He walked into the restaurant with the relaxed air of someone used to being obeyed without question. If he'd seen Alaina's determined look, he might not have been so complacent.

CHAPTER EIGHTEEN

"I can't believe how expensive everything in this town is," Jared grumbled as he gave the restaurant owner a dollar for their dinner.

The woman shrugged. "It's because we're so far off the beaten path. Costs a lot of money to have supplies freighted in from the railroad, especially in the winter time."

"But the food was wonderful," Alaina said with a smile. "I enjoyed every bite."

"Why thank you. It was a pleasure to serve you."

The woman's emphasis on the last word was so slight Alaina wondered if she imagined it.

The corner of Jared's mouth quirked in response as he took Alaina's arm. "Come on my little peacemaker," he said. "Let's go see if our hotel room is worth the ridiculous price I'm paying for it."

In spite of the further depletion of their meager funds, Jared was in a good mood and had been ever since he'd put the hotel clerk in his place. Alaina had enjoyed the camaraderie, but it was as though the confrontation at the hotel had brought another Jared to the surface.

She glanced up at his profile in the last rays of the sun as they walked down the street together. Dark stubble had sprouted again since he'd shaved at the hot springs and his hair was shaggy and unkempt. He still looked like her Jared, but he had subtly changed somehow. Now he was every inch the son of a wealthy American businessman and an English aristocrat--rich, powerful, and Susan Prescott's fiancé.

As they entered the hotel, Alaina thought wistfully of the Jared she knew. A man who led a woman and child who had no claim on him through the wilderness against impossible odds and put his life on the line for them over and over. The man she'd fallen in love with.

The clerk shifted nervously as Jared approached the front desk. "Good evening Mr. and Mrs. Brady. I trust you had a good dinner."

"Tolerable," Jared said in a condescending voice. "I assume our room is ready?"

"Yes sir. I saw to it personally."

"Good." Jared turned to Alaina and nodded toward the staircase. "After you, my dear."

The steep, narrow stairs led to a long dark hallway at the top. Alaina bit her lip as she stepped out of the way to let Jared by.

"Doesn't look promising, does it?" he said, walking past her and squinting at the numbers on the doors. "Here it is." He fitted the key in the lock, and opened the door. He stepped back as it swung open and gestured for Alaina to enter first.

It was large and surprisingly well lit, with a welcoming glow coming from two beautifully matched hand painted lamps. A huge walnut bedstead covered with a white wedding quilt dominated the room. A matching bureau and dressing table lined one wall while a decorative screen graced the other. "Oh, Jared," she cried as she stepped over the threshold. "It's beautiful!"

"Well, I must admit, I'm pleasantly surprised," he said, as he shut the door behind him. "At least there's space for the pallet. A cheaper room probably wouldn't have that."

"Ah, yes, the infamous pallet, because I snore, if I remember right."

Jared raised an eyebrow. "Would you rather I'd told him we need two beds because we aren't married?"

"Of course not."

"There, you see? Besides," he added with a grin, "you do snore."

"I do not!"

"Oh, yes you do, like a trooper."

"I don't believe you."

Jared chuckled. "Maybe I'll just wake you up next time it happens. Why is it, all you women get so upset when you find out you snore?"

"You've had a lot of experience with women who snore, then?"

Jared shrugged. "Some. But they always deny it."

"A true gentleman would never mention it," Alaina said, with a toss of her head. She glanced at him out of the corner of her eye, knowing she shouldn't ask but unable to stop herself. "Does Susan snore?"

He turned away to hang his coat and hat on the wall pegs. "I have no idea, but I doubt it."

"No, probably not," Alaina muttered under her breath, "not the oh so perfect Susan."

"Did you say something?" he asked, looking over his shoulder.

"No, just thinking out loud." At least Jared had never slept with Susan. The knowledge brought Alaina a spurt of pleasure. "Jared, look at this! They left us a hair brush and shaving supplies."

Jared smiled. "A little extra money does it every

time." He rubbed his face and looked in the mirror. "On the other hand, our friend at the front desk might be trying to give us a subtle hint. We don't exactly fit the dignity of the bridal suite. Hmm, I wonder if I should shave now or wait until morning. Whiskey Jug's hunting knife wasn't the best razor I ever used."

"It will last longer if you do it in the morning." Alaina dipped her finger into the china pitcher. "On the other hand, the water's warm now."

"That settles it. I'll do it now. Never cared much for an ice cold shave and it's hard to say whether we'll get any more warm water tomorrow."

"Good point. I think I'll take a sponge bath."

As Jared sharpened the razor on the strop, Alaina poured some of the water into the bowl and carried it behind the screen, then came back to get one of the lamps.

When the razor was honed to a nice sharp edge, he laid it on the dresser and started to roll up his sleeves. He glanced in the mirror and froze. Alaina's silhouette was clearly outlined behind the screen in the lamplight. While he watched, she stepped out of her dress and threw it over the top of the screen. Her petticoat was next and then her corset. Jared didn't even realize he was holding his breath until his chest started to hurt. He let it go with a soft whoosh. What in the hell was he doing, watching her undress like some randy adolescent peeking through a keyhole at his sister?

Disgusted with himself, he pulled his gaze away and poured water into the bowl of the shaving stand. He managed to ignore the sounds of splashing behind him while he worked up a lather in the shaving cup and spread it across his face. It shouldn't be too tough to remain focused on his own reflection as he shaved. All he had to do was pretend he was alone. The first few swipes down his jaw went normally, and Jared relaxed. He was in control.

"Jared?"

"Hmm?" Jared automatically glanced up at the sound of his name and nearly dropped the razor. Alaina had removed her shift and was washing her upper body. Her head was thrown back for easier access presenting an incredibly erotic profile to his astonished gaze. He was mesmerized as the washcloth slowly glided down the long line of her neck to her generous breasts.

"Ouch!"

The cloth stopped and she turned toward the sound. "What's wrong?"

"I just nicked myself a little. Nothing for you to worry about," Jared said, daubing at the blood welling out of the cut under his nose. "What was it you wanted to know?"

"I was just wondering how much money we're going to need to get down to the railroad at Hanna."

"With the price of things around here, it's hard to say. We'll need horses, of course, and provisions. I figure about twenty dollars to be safe. It may take a few days to make that much money. I was expecting more from my watch." Jared frowned at himself in the mirror. The cut wasn't all that bad, but it wouldn't stop bleeding.

"We could get by with one horse like we did today. That would save some money."

"It would also take us longer to get there. It's about thirty miles from Saratoga to Hanna. We can do that in one day if we both have horses. Otherwise, we'll have to camp somewhere, and that means blankets and more food. In the long run, it'll be cheaper to rent two horses." He glanced at the mirror again in time to see Alaina shake out the nightgown Brandy had sent along and slip it over her head. The erotic show was over. His relief warred with his disappointment.

"There is another way," she said, as she came around the edge of the screen. "I could —"

"How many times do I have to tell you I'm not interested in your scheme?" Jared asked irritably, hoping to make her mad enough so she'd keep her distance. "I said I'd take care of it and I will."

"Oh, dear, you really cut yourself badly," she said, frowning.

"It looks a lot worse than it is. Once I get it to stop bleeding, you won't hardly even be able to see it."

She walked over to the dresser and peered at his wound closely. "I guess you're right," she said doubtfully, as she picked up the hairbrush. "I've never seen a little cut bleed like that."

Jared swallowed a sigh of relief as she moved away. Even swathed in the voluminous nightgown, she was tempting. Her scent stayed with him as she climbed onto the bed and settled herself in the middle. Why she always smelled so damn good to him was a mystery. One that was almost as unexplainable as how she could look so incredibly erotic sitting cross-legged on the bed in a nightgown big enough to fit a woman of twice her girth.

"How did you manage to cut yourself, anyway?" she asked, dropping the brush in her lap and pulling the long braid over her shoulder.

He swallowed against a sudden constriction in his throat as he watched the long, graceful fingers unplait her hair. "Just clumsy I guess." If he weren't careful, he'd whack off part of his lip. Forcing himself to concentrate on his reflection in the mirror, Jared went back to shaving.

For the most part, he was successful until he rinsed his razor in preparation of shaving his neck. His gaze involuntarily strayed to the bed behind him. Alaina sat there surrounded in a cloud of hair that reached nearly to the wedding quilt. "My God," he murmured as she pulled the brush through the golden mass.

Alaina looked up and met his gaze in the mirror. "What?"

"Your hair. I never realized it was so beautiful."

"Thank you," she said, blushing with pleasure. "I've always thought it was kind of a boring color. My mother's is dark, you see, and my fa...I mean...Garrick and my brothers all have hair so blond it's almost white. Mine is just kind of in between."

"It's the color of wild honey," Jared said in a husky voice.

Alaina grinned at him in the mirror. "Let's hope it doesn't attract bears."

Jared returned her smile. "I don't think there's much chance of that here." Not bears perhaps, but everything she did tonight seemed to bring out the animal in him. Jared flexed the muscles in his jaw and resolutely tipped his head back to finish shaving. If she distracted him now, he'd probably wind up cutting his own throat.

Ignoring Alaina as she gave her hair the requisite one hundred strokes, he finished shaving without mishap. "Well, I don't know about you," he said, with an exaggerated stretch. "But I've had about enough fun for one day. I think I'll go to bed." He picked up the pallet and carried it behind the screen. Mindful of Alaina's mistake, he blew out the lamp before stripping down to his drawers. No sense letting her know what a show she'd given him.

"You know, Jared, I should be the one to sleep on the pallet. It was your watch that paid for the bed," she said, as he rolled the pallet out on the floor and spread the blanket over it.

"It paid for the pallet too. Besides, I'd rather sleep on the floor than on a bed that's too soft. Take the bed and enjoy it."

"You're sure?"

"Positive."

"All right," she said, uncertainly. "Good night then."

"Good night." Jared crawled into bed and closed his eyes. He tried to close his mind, too, but it was impossible. The crackle of static as she pulled the brush through her hair painted a vivid picture of her in his imagination. Gradually the image mixed with the memory of her behind the screen. In the semi-dream state of near sleep, he had just created an image of her dressed only in a cloud of hair and a smile when she blew out the lamp. He woke up with a jerk.

Jared listened to the rustle of blankets and imagined her settling into bed. He smiled in the darkness as he heard a very feminine sigh and pictured her relaxing into the soft feather bed. He was nearly asleep when another noise came from the other side of the screen that brought him to full wakefulness. Jared turned his head to catch the sound. He didn't have long to wait. It came again, and this time there was no doubt what it was. A muffled sob.

Jared rolled out of bed, and stepped around the end of the screen. He could see Alaina's huddled form in the dim moonlight. She lay on her side with her face buried in the pillow. Her shoulders shook with the force of the suppressed sobs. The anguished sound tugged at Jared's heartstrings.

Jared made his way around the side of the bed. Alaina wasn't aware of his presence until he knelt beside the bed and put his hand on her shoulder comfortingly. "Alaina," he said softly. "What is it?"

She started violently and blinked up at him with tear-drenched eyes. "I...I'm sorry. I di..didn't mean to wake you."

"You didn't." He reached up and smoothed the hair back from her face. "It's something I did isn't it?"

Her lip quivered and the tears glistened on her cheeks as she shook her head. "N..no, I...I'm j...just being silly."

"For Pete's sake, Alaina, just tell me what's wrong."

She buried her face against his shoulder. "I was thinking about Bright Eyes."

"Bright Eyes!" he said in surprise. "You don't have to worry about her. She's in good hands with Whiskey Jug and Brandy."

"I kn..now but...but, oh, Jared, I miss her so much."

Her grief was nearly a tangible thing as she sobbed against him. The impact of her pain was like a band tightening around Jared's heart. "Oh, sweetheart," he murmured, lying down beside her and pulling her into the shelter of his arms. He didn't know the words to comfort her, so he just held her and let her cry out her anguish against his chest. He stroked the back of her head with a gentle hand until the sobs quieted into small hiccupping gulps of air.

"Better?" he asked softly.

"I...I think so."

"Good." It was time for him to leave, but he couldn't resist leaning forward to kiss her forehead. Softly, naturally, her arms went around him ,and her lips nuzzled his neck. He closed his eyes as she trailed kisses down onto his naked chest. Hot waves of lust licked at his body, igniting a fire in his blood that threatened to consume them both.

It would be so easy to give in, to bury himself in her willing body, driving them both higher and higher until they exploded in mindless ecstasy. But he knew he couldn't; it would be taking gross advantage of...Jared lost his train of thought as her mouth stopped to explore a masculine nipple. No woman had ever touched him there; he hadn't even known how exquisitely sensitive it was. When her tongue flicked against the hard nub, his ability to reason disappeared in a soft moan.

Suddenly, he couldn't remember why he shouldn't make love to her. In fact, he thought distractedly, as her hand wandered down to the hard plane of his stomach, he was going to have to marry her anyway, so they could do anything they wanted.

And oh how he wanted. She caressed him as though she knew exactly where and how to touch him. With a start, Jared realized she was loving him exactly the way he'd loved her. Her lips were a warm invitation he could no longer resist. With a groan, he rolled her beneath him and caught her mouth with his own.

It was wildly exciting, as intoxicating as catching a moonbeam on his tongue and savoring it. He wondered vaguely why he always had such peculiar fantasies when he kissed her. Then he ceased to think at all as her tongue began to dance with his, matching stroke for stroke, answering his aggression with her own.

Then kissing wasn't enough. He wanted more, to touch every part of her, to feel the warm vibrant skin against his own as she responded to his caress. His hand traced the swell of her ribs downward, but was instantly frustrated. She lay beneath the blankets and he lay on top. Irritated, he tugged at the quilt but to no avail. His weight held it securely in place.

With a muttered curse, he rolled from the bed, and threw back the blankets. The sight of her stopped him in his tracks. She hadn't rebraided her hair. It lay around her in the moonlight like a cloud while those incredible eyes of hers stared up at him with a look that would have melted ice. Jared wasn't made of ice. In fact the heat she kindled within him threatened to make his blood boil if he didn't do something about it and fast.

"I don't think we'll need these do you?" he asked, stripping off his drawers.

"Definitely not." She smiled at him as he climbed into bed beside her. "It's a very warm night." With a soft smile she slid her arms around his neck and cuddled up to his naked body. "Mmm this is nice."

His mouth found hers again and Alaina gave herself over to the sensations that washed through her. Her hands roamed freely, delighting in the firmly muscled length of his body, so different from her own.

Jared ended the kiss abruptly, and leaned his forehead against hers for a moment while he caught his breath. "Whew," he said, levering himself up on one elbow. "We'd better slow down a bit."

Alaina traced the contour of his chest with her

finger. "Why?"

He caught her hand as it moved down his stomach. "Because, my little passion flower, I want it to last more than a minute or two, that's why. Where did this god-awful nightgown come from anyway? I can't believe it's Brandy's."

"It isn't. She said it belonged to Whiskey Jug's mother."

"Must have gotten his size from her," he murmured, running his hand from her shoulder to her hip. "It's very much in the way, you know."

"So take it off," she said in a husky voice.

"I thought you'd never ask."

"What are you doing?" Alaina asked in surprise when he moved to the foot of the bed.

"Relax, sweetheart," he said, picking up her foot and massaging the bottom of it with his thumb. "I do things in my own way. I promise you won't mind a bit."

"Oh, my," she said, as he moved to her toes. She sucked in her breath as he leaned forward and kissed her ankle. A moment later his hands moved to her legs and the hem of the offending nightgown. Slowly, erotically he pushed the material up to her knees. With gentle hands and soft kisses, he alternately worked and worshiped the muscles of her calves, gradually making his way back up to the hem of the nightgown.

She nearly lifted off the bed when his tongue flicked the back of her knee. But that sensation was nothing compared to what came after. Alaina lost all sense of time and place as Jared slowly, inexorably pushed the nightgown up. Everything disappeared except his hands and his mouth as they slowly followed the path of the material across her thighs, and up her body. By the time he reached her shoulders Alaina hardly noticed when he drew the garment over her head and tossed it away.

Her breath was ragged as he stretched his long hard body the length of hers and claimed her lips again. He gently nudged her legs apart with his knee and Alaina braced herself for the pain she knew was coming.

Only this time there was no pain. Instead there was a wonderful fullness followed by wave after wave of incredible sensation. She knew she was alternately whimpering and moaning, but she had no power over it as he stoked the fire within her until it raged out of control. Just when she thought she might die of it, they both exploded into a golden shower of light that pulsated and shimmered in glorious fulfillment.

Alaina gradually became aware of Jared's full weight resting upon her. It felt wonderful. She was disappointed when he rolled to the side. The thought barely had time to register before he pulled her into his arms and cradled her head against his shoulder.

"I didn't know it could get better," she said, running her hand across his stomach.

Jared smiled and closed his eyes. "Neither did I."

"It was stupid of me to get so upset about Bright Eyes," she said after a moment. "I know she's where she belongs, and I know Brandy will take good care of her. It's just that I'd kind of gotten used to the idea of raising her. I'd started thinking of her as mine."

Jared hugged her a little tighter. "I know. Don't worry. You'll have little ones of your own soon." *We'll have them together*, he thought with a surge of surprised pleasure. Little girls with honey blond hair and mischievous blue-eyed boys. For the first time in many weeks Jared went to sleep with a smile on his face.

CHAPTER NINTEEN

"Mrs. Brady?"

Alaina woke up to the sound of someone pounding on the door. "Who is it?"

"I have your water."

Alaina sat up in bed and frowned at the door. "What water?"

"Your bath water. Your husband paid for it this morning and said to deliver the water at ten o'clock."

Jared had ordered her a bath? A little thrill of pleasure shot through her even as she felt a stab of guilt for using some of their dwindling cash supply so frivolously. "All right. Just a minute." Where was that nightgown? She hadn't seen it since Jared summarily disposed of it the night before. After several minutes of searching, she gave up and grabbed the quilt off the floor. She wrapped it securely around herself and went to open the door.

Alaina was glad she hadn't found her nightgown when the clerk from the day before and two adolescent boys trooped in with buckets of water. The quilt might look odd, but at least when its bulk covered her she was decent.

She could have sworn the clerk peeked at her out of the corner of his eye as he pulled the pallet out from behind the screen. In fact, all three kept giving her sidelong glances when they didn't think she was watching. Alaina had the uncomfortable feeling they all knew exactly what had gone on in that room the night before. No, that was ridiculous. The clerk had probably regaled the two boys with the story of how she snored. *Funny, Jared hadn't mentioned it again last night,* she thought with a slight smile. Of course, neither of them had gotten enough sleep to know whether she snored or not.

It only took a few minutes to move the large hipbath into place behind the screen and fill it, but it seemed much longer to Alaina who waited in embarrassed silence. At long last, they dumped the final bucket of water and the two boys left. Instead of following, the clerk just stood there staring at her with the most peculiar look on his face.

After several long moments, Alaina raised an eyebrow. "Was there something else?"

"Oh..." He turned dark red then cleared his throat uncomfortably. "Will...uh.... will you and your husband be wanting the room for another night, Mrs. Brady?"

"Another night?" Alaina frowned. "I'm not exactly sure what our plans are yet. Can we let you know?"

"As long as it's by noon."

"Noon...all right. I'm sure we'll have decided by then."

"Good." He gazed at her a moment longer, then seemed to shake himself. "If there's anything else I can do, don't hesitate to ask," he said, with a warm smile as he walked toward the door.

"All right, I will. Thank you." Alaina shut the door behind him and turned the key in the lock. She knew she was being silly, but the look in his eyes made her vaguely uncomfortable. Why was it when Jared looked at her like that she got all soft and mushy inside, but if anyone else did she got nervous? Maybe Jared's lectures back on the train had more effect on her than she realized.

With a shrug, she crossed to the hipbath, shedding her discomfort with the quilt. By the time she settled into the water, the clerk was all but forgotten. Jared filled her thoughts completely. Who would have thought there were so many different ways for two people to enjoy each other? She'd lost count of the times they'd made love; each experience more incredible than the last.

Alaina closed her eyes as aches and pains began to seep out of her bones, tight muscles relaxed, and the healing warmth flowed in through her pores. She drifted along in a pleasant daydream of Jared, reliving their night together, wondering if the next would be as wonderful. Eventually, the water began to cool, and she sat up with a regretful sigh.

As she worked the scented soap into a lather, she suddenly remembered the young clerk's question. Without finding Jared, she had no way of knowing what his plans were other than he wanted to make the trip to Hanna in a single day. It was too late to start today. That meant at least one more night here.

Alaina frowned. Jared didn't know small towns liked she did. The work he was likely to find in a town this size wouldn't pay much; surely not more than a dollar a day if that. He wouldn't even be able to pay for their room, let alone have enough money left over for the trip to Hanna and train tickets from there. She could do it, of course, though it involved some risk. Still, if she was successful...

With her usual impetuousness, she climbed out of the tub and walked across the room oblivious to the trail of water she left on the floor. A concentrated search of the dresser turned up an old sock left behind by a former occupant, but nothing else. The bureau was similarly empty. Alaina bit her lip and looked around the room speculatively. If he'd taken it with him, her plan was doomed. Then her gaze fell on Jared's coat. Of course, the obvious place.

She found what she was looking for in his pocket. Wearing a beatific smile, she pulled out the two dollars that stood between them and total disaster. It wasn't as much as she'd like, but it should be enough.

"Your horses are fed and all the stalls cleaned, Mr. Ferguson," Jared said, leaning the pitchfork up against the wall.

The blacksmith who also owned the livery stable looked up from his forge in surprise. "You're finished already?"

"I used to clean my sister's horse barn for punishment when I was a kid," Jared said with a grin. "I got lots of practice."

"Kind of ornery, eh?"

"My sister thought so anyway. Mind if I wash up in the water trough?"

"Be my guest."

Jared stripped off his shirt "Know anybody else who might need a strong back for the rest of the day?" he asked as he sluiced water up his arms and across his chest.

"Hmm," Jack Ferguson rubbed his jaw thoughtfully. "Can't think of anybody right off hand. Sam Twitchel hires a drifter now and then to help unload supplies, but he just got some a couple of days ago."

Jared dunked his head. "I was afraid you'd say that," he said, when he came up for air. "I hoped to find more work."

Ferguson sighed. "Too bad you ain't one of them bookkeeping fellas."

"You mean an accountant?"

"Yep. Did fine when I just had the smithy, but after I opened the livery stable it got too complicated."

"Sounds like what you need is a new system," Jared said, reaching for his shirt.

"I reckon so, but there ain't anybody around here can set one up for me, and I don't know how."

"I do."

The blacksmith gave him a doubtful look. "You do?"

"My father was a fanatic about keeping accurate business records, and he insisted I learn. I've been doing books since I was fourteen."

Ferguson's eyes narrowed. "You don't look much like a business man to me."

"Tell you what, I'll take a look at your books and see what I can do. For the use of a couple of horses, I'll straighten your books out and set you up with a usable system. If you aren't satisfied when I'm done, you don't have to pay me anything."

"Don't reckon you could mess them up any worse than they already are," Ferguson said with a shrug. "You got yourself a deal."

"Good. Do you suppose I could get your son to run down to the hotel and give my wife a message?"

"Sure thing."

Jared dashed off a note to Alaina telling her the good news, and to stay at the hotel until he got there. Jack

Ferguson's books were in worse shape than Jared had anticipated. Even so, he had everything straightened out with a new system in place by four o'clock, and Ferguson trained to use it by five. Jack Ferguson was so pleased, he added a nice bonus to the money Jared had already earned for feeding and cleaning. He promised two of his best horses for the next day's trip, and even offered them a free place to stay for the night.

Jared whistled as he strode down the street toward the hotel. He had a little over four dollars in his pocket. With the two dollars left over from the sale of his watch, he had enough for supper and one of the cheaper rooms at the hotel. The room would undoubtedly be smaller, but it didn't matter since they wouldn't need the pallet. Funny how he hadn't seriously considered the use of Ferguson's loft. Before he even had a chance to think it through, he found himself explaining that his wife preferred the comfort of the hotel.

His wife. The idea was beginning to grow on him. What Alaina lacked in sophistication she more than made up for in other ways. Last night for instance. Even in retrospect, their lovemaking seemed inspired. He'd never been tempted to experiment that way before, and she'd been game to try even the most outrageous of his ideas. Of course, she was such an innocent, she thought their behavior had been normal. She'd said as much after he'd shocked her awake this morning with an intimate caress and they'd made love in the early light of dawn. Jared felt a slight twinge of guilt for leading her into such decadence, but quieted it with the reminder that he was going to do the honest thing by her.

As he passed Twitchel's store, he suddenly remembered the blue calico dress hanging in the back of the shop. Like Alaina's dress, it was of simple country design with a full skirt rather than the more stylish narrow skirts women were wearing now. On the other hand, it was practical. Alaina could sit on a horse wearing it, and, most importantly she'd love it, even if it was several years out of style. With the prices in Saratoga being what they were, his few extra dollars probably wouldn't be enough. Still, it wouldn't hurt to check. On a whim, he turned back and went in.

Ten minutes later he came out again with a smile on his face and a paper wrapped parcel under his arm. The dress had been surprisingly inexpensive considering the price of everything else in town. But then Sam Twitchel had been downright affable. Jared suspected he might have gotten a good price on his watch if he'd had the money to buy it back. As it was, he didn't even want to mention it. If he showed too much interest now, he risked having Twitchel jack the price up even farther when he came back.

Maybe his luck had changed and there would be enough money left from the room for a bath. Surely he could talk Alaina into sharing it with him even though she'd already had one today. His mood was buoyant as he entered the hotel.

"Good afternoon, Mr. Brady." The same clerk was behind the desk but his attitude was completely different today. It was amazing the difference a little arrogance mixed with money could make. The observation irritated Jared, as it always did. Though he wasn't above using such tactics when necessary, he much preferred the straight forward, man-to-man exchange he'd had with Jack Ferguson or even Sam Twitchel.

"It is indeed," Jared said with a smile. "Have you seen my wife?"

"Yes, sir." He avoided Jared's eye. "This morning when we took her bath up."

Jared frowned. The minute he mentioned Alaina, the man's attitude changed; almost as though he had a guilty conscience. "Have you seen her since?"

"Just when she paid me for another night." He blushed to the roots of his hair. "I'm sorry, but I clean forgot to give her your message."

"She paid for another night?" Jared said in surprise.

"I'm truly sorry, Mr. Brady," the clerk said in a rush. "It's just that she's so dog-gone pretty that I forgot all about the note and —"

"I don't give a damn about the note," Jared snapped.

The clerk's blush deepened as he realized he'd confessed his sins for nothing. Jared hadn't even cared. "She said I was supposed to ask you if you'd be wanting a bath when you came in."

"Where is she now?"

"In your room, I think. What about the bath?" He called as Jared turned and strode purposefully toward the stairs.

"I'll let you know." How did Alaina manage to pay for another night? There was nothing to sell, and there were no respectable jobs for women, not in this town anyway. Even more damning was the young clerk's guilt. Jared could only think of one thing that would cause it. With a feeling of dread, Jared took the stairs two at a time, and found the door to the bridal suite locked against him.

He pounded on the thick wooden panel. "Alaina, let me in."

"Who is it?" Her voice came through the door uncertainly.

"It's Jared. Now open the door."

A moment later he heard the sound of a key grating in the lock, before the door swung inward. "Who were you expecting?" he asked.

"Nobody really. I just felt like locking the door. Oh, Jared I have to tell you—"

"You don't have to hide it from me," Jared said, closing the door behind him. "It was the clerk at the front desk wasn't it?"

"Well, he did make me a little nervous this morning when he delivered my water."

"And when he demanded payment for another night?"

"I don't know as I'd call it demanded really. It was more like—"

"Alaina, just tell me what he did to you."

She gave him a blank look. "Did to me? Nothing. I mean he stared at me in the strangest way, but that was all. When I came back from the saloon, he—"

"The saloon! What the hell were you doing there?"

"That's what I was trying to tell you earlier," Alaina said with exasperation. "If you'd ever let me finish a sentence—"

"That doesn't answer my question. What were you doing at the saloon?"

"Trying to earn enough money to get us to Hanna." She crossed to the dresser and opened one of the drawers. "Look," she said, pulling out a small roll of bills. "There's plenty here for the trip."

Jared's feeling of unease increased tenfold. "How did you earn that kind of money at the saloon?"

"By playing blackjack, of course. I tried to tell you last night, but you wouldn't listen."

"Blackjack!" A strange mixture of relief and fury flashed through him. "What the hell were you thinking?"

"The same thing you were, making money for the trip to Hanna. I knew you'd never be able to earn enough on your own."

"So you took it upon yourself to remedy the situation by going to a saloon and gambling?"

"I knew there was some risk, but—"

"Some risk!" Jared's voice rose angrily. "What you did was downright dangerous. Do you know what men think of women they find in the saloon?"

"That they're *stupid.* That's exactly why I knew my plan would work. Those men were so busy laughing at me, they didn't even know they were in trouble until it was too late."

"You were gambling, for Christ's sake!"

"Yes, but I knew what I was doing. Papa says the most important things to remember are to watch what's been played, and to walk away while you're still winning. The minute I'd won enough money, I left. The hardest part was getting anybody to play with me."

"Probably because they knew damn well you shouldn't be there!" he thundered.

"I don't understand what you're so mad about, Jared. I only took one dollar with me, and if I'd started to lose I would have quit. I knew I was taking a chance, but it was the only way to get the money we needed."

"It may surprise you to know that everything is already arranged for our trip tomorrow without your help," Jared snapped. "In the future I expect you to act a little more circumspect. The last thing I need is a wife who goes off half-cocked on any harebrained scheme that happens to tumble through her mind."

Alaina's jaw muscles tightened. "I'm not your wife," she reminded him caustically. "Nor do I want to be."

"Well, that's just too bad isn't it? You will be my wife and there isn't a damn thing either of us can do about it."

"What are you talking about?"

Jared gave a humorless laugh. "I think it's pretty obvious don't you? To put it bluntly, we have carnal knowledge of each other, which is a pretty mild description for what we did last night."

"That doesn't mean—"

"The hell it doesn't," he snarled. "Any choice either of us had in the matter disappeared when you convinced me to make love to you on that mountain. The minute I took your virginity, our fate was sealed."

Alaina bristled defensively. "You could have refused."

"Oh, right. Just like I could have refused last night when you started in on me."

Alaina gasped at the unfairness of it. "You're the one who came to me not the other way around!"

"I came to comfort you, not get involved in a night-long orgy."

"Why *did* you make love to me then?" she asked in a rigidly controlled voice.

"Christ, Alaina, I'm not made of stone. No man could have resisted." Especially not after three days of almost constant arousal and then watching her in the mirror last night. She was so damnably tempting; a saint couldn't have turned away. Jared had no aspirations to sainthood. "You even had the hotel clerk panting after you, and all he did was bring you a bath."

"I suppose that was my fault too," she said icily.

"I don't know. I wasn't here."

"No, you weren't were you?" she snapped. "And thanks to you, neither was my nightgown! If I had known they were coming I might have found it, or at the very least gotten dressed. As it was, I barely had time to grab the quilt and wrap it around me before I let them in."

The image of Alaina dressed only in the quilt with her hair hanging around her in all its golden splendor hit Jared with the subtly of a cannon shell. No wonder the young clerk had been so smitten he felt the need to apologize to the lady's husband.

Two things occurred to Jared at the same time. It was horribly unfair to take his frustration out on her when none of it was her fault, and he was responsible for the pain in her beautiful blue eyes.

"Oh hell!" he muttered tossing the package he carried onto the bed. "We leave for Hanna at daybreak. I'll be at the livery stable until then." With that he was gone.

"Ooooo!" Alaina grabbed a pillow off the bed and threw it at the door, then angrily dashed away the moisture that threatened in her eyes. She would not cry over the beast no matter how mad he made her. He hadn't even given her a chance to tell him about his stupid watch. It would serve him right if she took it back to Sam Twitchel and got her money back. See if she ever did anything nice for him again!

How dare Jared blame her for everything? It was every bit as much his fault as it was hers, maybe more so. Never seeing him again would suit her just fine, she thought, stalking over to the window and moving the curtain aside so she could see the street. Jared emerged from the front door of the hotel a moment later and headed down the street with a long angry stride. Though she watched him walk all the way to the livery stable, he never once looked back.

Alaina flopped down on the bed and glared into the mirror. It wasn't as if he was the only one trapped by the circumstances. The thought of marriage to a man who didn't want her was repugnant in the extreme. Ruthlessly, she pushed away the enticing image of life as Jared Brady's wife. That silly little fantasy was in the past. What she needed now was a plan for the immediate future. For a moment she entertained the idea of renting a horse and going to Hanna on her own. It would be quite satisfying, but she soon realized the folly of it. That was exactly what had gotten her into trouble in the first place.

The reflection of the innocuous brown paper parcel at the foot of the bed caught her eye in the mirror. Curiously, she turned to look at it. It's bulkiness looked soft and flexible. After a moment, Alaina leaned over to pick it up. Had Jared even realized he left it behind? Well, he couldn't possibly be any angrier with her than he was right now, she thought as she untied the string and folded back the paper. Her eyes widened in startled surprise when she saw what lay inside. He'd bought her a new dress!

Alaina held the garment to her shoulders in front of the mirror. The color was exactly right for her, and so was the style. In fact, it was a dress she might well have chosen for herself. To her horror, her lower lip began to tremble uncontrollably, and her eyes filled with moisture. For the third time in as many days she burst into tears.

CHAPTER TWENTY

"Jared?" Alaina called poking her head inside the building she thought was the livery stable. The familiar odor of charred wood and slag metal flowed over her in a wave of nostalgia. A blacksmith shop. With a sigh, she closed the door and felt her way along the building to the other door. Maybe coming down so early hadn't been such a good idea after all. Still, as angry as Jared was the night before, Alaina didn't want to take a chance on him leaving town without her.

Expecting the inside of the barn to be dark and quiet, Alaina was startled to find several lanterns burning in the interior. Jared, it seemed, was already up and about. She found him saddling a large raw-boned gelding that looked as if he could trot all the way to Hanna and never break a sweat.

As Alaina stood watching Jared tighten the cinch, she suddenly realized she didn't know what to say to him. It wasn't so much their angry words from the night before that held her tongue, as a long night of reflection. In retrospect, she'd realized much of what Jared had said was true, though she refused to accept all the blame for it. Jared's honor dictated that he marry her, regardless of his personal preferences. It wasn't fair, she had no intention of holding him to it, and she was going to tell him so the first chance she got.

Yet, somehow the conversation she'd imagined with cold clear logic the night before seemed impossibly difficult to broach now. She was still trying to come up with an opening when Jared noticed her.

"Well," he said. "I didn't expect to see you here."

"Why not? You said we'd be leaving at daybreak."

"Which is still half an hour away. I planned on picking you up at the hotel on the way out of town."

Alaina shrugged. "I couldn't sleep, so I just decided to come down."

Jared threw a saddle blanket on the second horse. "In that case, we'll get an even earlier start than I expected. We can go as soon as I get this horse saddled if you're all set."

"I'm ready. Jared, I..." Alaina rubbed her toe in the dirt on the floor, suddenly shy and unwilling to start another argument.

"Looks like I got here just in time," Jack Ferguson said, walking through the doorway. "My wife would have never forgiven me if I'd missed you. She sent some food for the trip."

"That was very kind of her," Alaina said, accepting the sack with a smile.

"It was the least we could do after your husband helped us out and all."

Jared glanced over his shoulder. "After that meal your wife fed me last night, I'd say we're even. She's a remarkable cook."

"I'll tell her you said that." The blacksmith gave Alaina a sympathetic look. "It's too bad you weren't able to come to supper last night, Mrs. Brady. My wife wanted to meet you, but she understood when your husband said you weren't feeling well. I hope you're better this morning."

"Oh...yes,...I'm almost fully recovered. It's one of

those ailments that comes and goes." She gave Jared a sidelong glance. So much for giving his watch back as a peace offering. "It's caused by an irritation."

Ferguson clicked his tongue sympathetically. "You sure you should be travelin' already? Could be the trip will make it worse."

"You're probably right about that." She adjusted the cuff of her sleeve. "But I'm hoping to get rid of it for good soon."

Jared gave a snort. "I think it's contagious."

"The disease?" Alaina asked sweetly.

"No, the irritation." He led both horses outside. "I'm beginning to come down with it myself."

Ferguson's eyes widened in alarm. "It's contagious?"

"Only after prolonged exposure," Jared told him reassuringly. "Are you ready to go, Alaina?"

"As ready as I'll ever be." She stepped into Jared's cupped hand and sprang into the saddle. A moment later he'd mounted his horse and was receiving last minute instructions from Ferguson for the return of the horses. A handshake later, Jared and Alaina were riding out of town just as the first fingers of dawn touched the sky over the mountains.

Alaina watched the horizon lighten from purple, to pink, to orange as the sun poked its golden head above the crest of the Snowy Range. It promised to be a gorgeous day. Green rolling hills stretched before them on either side of the well-defined road, and wildflowers of every hue bloomed among the grass. With a sigh of real pleasure, she decided to just sit back and enjoy the scenery. Relief flowed through her as she made the decision. There would be plenty of time to have it out with Jared later.

An hour later Jared finally broke the long silence. "According to Jack Ferguson, I underestimated the distance to Hanna slightly."

"Oh?"

"It's closer to forty miles than thirty. I think we can still make it in a day, but it's going to be tough. I wouldn't even suggest it, except for the renegades on the mountain. The sooner we get to the telegraph and let the army know about them the better."

"I agree."

"Luckily it's all downhill so we should make pretty good time. If we have to, we can camp tonight and make it in early in the morning, but I'd rather not do that."

"It doesn't matter to me. I'll let you be the judge."

He glanced at her serene profile "Well, well, well, I see you've decided to try a new tactic," he said sardonically.

"What?"

"Being agreeable for a change. I've got to admit, it's a distinct improvement."

"I'm always agreeable." She glared fiercely at her horse's ears. "At least to most people."

Jared made a rude noise.

"Are you trying to pick a fight?"

"No, I just wondered if I was going to be given the silent treatment all the way to Hanna."

"I was enjoying the ride. I had no idea you wanted to talk."

"It's going to be a mighty long day if we don't."

"It will seem even longer if we start fighting this early."

He gave her a crooked grin. "Surely there's

something we can talk about that won't cause a fight."

Alaina pursed her lips thoughtfully. "I am curious about one thing," she said after a moment. "What on earth did you do for the Fergusons to earn their undying gratitude that way?"

"I set up a new bookkeeping system for his business."

"Their gratitude seems kind of excessive for that."

"Yes, but in the process of putting everything in order, I found almost a hundred dollars that he didn't know he had."

"Oh." Alaina lapsed back into silence. "By the way," she said, after a long pause. "Thank you for this dress. It's beautiful."

"It looks good on you," he said gruffly. "Besides, the one you had wasn't any more than a rag."

"I know. I threw it away. It wouldn't have mattered though, I like this one much better."

"It matches your eyes," he said. "I thought of you the first time I saw it."

She smiled softly. "And I'll think of you every time I wear it."

The silence stretched between them once more. After several minutes, Jared tried again. "We'll also send a telegram to Angel when we get there. She and Ox will be worried sick about us."

"Not to mention Susan." From the startled flush on Jared's face Alaina had the distinct impression that he'd forgotten he left his fiancée in Laramie with his sister.

"Uh...yes, of course. That goes without saying. I suppose we'd better tell them to expect us tomorrow or the next day sometime," he said. "We'll take the first train we can back to Laramie City."

Alaina sighed. So much for enjoying the ride. "I'm not going to Laramie City," she said quietly.

His brows snapped together in a frown. "What?"

"You heard me. There's no reason for me to go back to Laramie City. My father is at Fort Bridger and that's where I'm going."

"Oh, hell. Are we back to that again? What happened to your plan to go home as soon as we got back to civilization?"

"That was before when I had Bright Eyes to worry about. Without her, there's no reason to go back to Minnesota just yet."

"Don't expect Cameron Price to welcome you with open arms," Jared said scathingly. "I doubt that he even remembers your mother. Even if he does, the reminder that he's old enough to have a full-grown daughter won't go over very well."

Alaina sighed. "If you had never known your father, wouldn't you wonder about him and want to know how you were like him?"

Jared made a derisive sound. "I've spent a good part of my life trying *not* to be like my father. He manipulated people for the sheer joy of it and made money into a God. Luckily, my sisters both married good men who showed me a better way. I spent every second I could with them."

"But you had a choice. I don't even know what my real father is like."

"He's a hard-drinking, womanizing bastard who isn't worth your time!"

Alaina stiffened angrily. "Papa called him a hero, and Susan says he's one of her father's best men."

"That may well be, but he's not a man I want my

future wife associating with, even if he is your natural father."

There it was, Alaina thought with a sinking feeling, the other topic she'd been trying to avoid all morning. If she'd had any doubts about marrying him, she knew better now. No matter how she felt about him, she had to let him go, for both their sakes. "I've decided not to marry you, Jared."

"Is that right?"

"I know it's something you feel honor bound to do, but it really isn't necessary you know."

"Oh, and how do you figure that?"

"No one knows what happened except you and me."

"We signed the register in that hotel as Mr. And Mrs. Brady. We spent the night together in that room, and every employee in that hotel knows it."

"Oh, come on, Jared. They'll be so glad to see us alive, nobody's going to bother to check the hotel register."

"Whiskey Jug knows, and he probably told Brandy."

"They hardly ever come out of the mountains, and they wouldn't tell anyone even if they did," Alaina said in disgust. "You're grasping at straws."

"The fact remains that I ruined you whether anyone knows it or not."

"I don't feel ruined. Besides, as you pointed out last night, I'm the one who started it both times, and since you weren't exactly a willing participant—"

"The hell I wasn't! All right so maybe it isn't what I would have chosen, but I certainly didn't push you away."

"Which is exactly why I've decided you are as much

to blame as I am," she said with a satisfied smile.

"Let me get this straight now. I was supposedly seduced; by an eighteen-year-old virgin, I might add. Of course, I'm as guilty as she is because I didn't put up much of a fight, therefore I needn't marry her." He gave her a disgusted look. "I suppose that somehow makes sense with that twisted logic of yours."

"The point is, we're both the victim of circumstances. Neither of us intended this to happen and shouldn't be punished for it."

Jared frowned. "You consider marriage to me a punishment?"

"Do you expect me to believe you *want* to marry me? Everything I do irritates you."

"It wasn't what I had planned but..."

"I know it wasn't. Besides you already have a fiancée."

"What's that got to do with it?"

"Quite a lot, I'd think. You proposed to her, didn't you?"

"Yes, of course."

"There you see?" she said triumphantly. "You never even asked me. Anyway, Susan is exactly what you want. I have none of the skills she does."

"Which you never miss a chance to make snide remarks about."

"Right, and that proves my point. We'd be miserable with each other."

"We weren't miserable night before last," he pointed out.

"No, but we were *last* night, or at least I was. My mother says you should never base a marriage only on physical attraction, and that's all we have."

"May I ask how you plan to explain your lack of a maidenhead to your future husband?"

"If he loves me, it shouldn't matter."

"No man is *that* understanding."

"Sven is."

Jared raised a brow in surprise. "Your cousin?"

"Not by blood. We discussed marriage as soon as we discovered we weren't related." She told herself it wasn't really a lie. They *had* talked about it. "We're promised to each other."

"I see. You've never mentioned this...engagement before. I wonder why."

"It's a secret betrothal." Alaina said blithely. "We're going to announce it publicly when I get back. Besides, it's really none of your business, is it?"

"What if you discover you're going to have my child? Do you think Sven will be understanding about that as well?"

"Oh..." Alaina was momentarily nonplused. Pregnancy was something she hadn't considered.

Sensing her confusion, Jared ruthlessly pressed home his advantage. "My baby might be growing inside you right now. Would you keep my child from me the way your mother kept you from Cameron Price?"

"N...no."

"Then the way I see it, you're honor bound to marry *me*." Jared tried not to sound smug, but it was a difficult task. He had her, and she knew it.

"But...but what if I'm not? We won't know for a while."

"No, but the longer we delay the more obvious it will be when the baby is born."

"*If* I'm pregnant." Alaina's brow cleared as if she'd

just solved a momentous problem. "If I'm not, there's no reason to get married is there?"

Jared's hands tightened on the reins as a sudden image of Alaina swollen with his child popped into his mind. A wave of longing rocketed through him that had nothing to do with lust. "Alaina, I won't let my child be born out of wedlock, and I won't allow another man to raise him," he warned.

She pursed her lips consideringly. "All right," she said at last. "If I'm pregnant, I'll marry you. In the meantime, we'll go on just like before."

With that he had to be satisfied. She refused to be swayed, no matter what argument he used. Finally, he gave up. His head was beginning to ache, and he lacked the energy to pursue the debate any further.

Alaina was surprised he gave up so easily. As the day wore on, she realized there was something seriously wrong. The farther they went, the more Jared drooped in the saddle. By the time they finally arrived in Hanna shortly after sunset, he was barely able to dismount by himself.

"Jared what's wrong?" she asked in concern.

"Just tired," he mumbled. "Let's go find the telegraph office."

He seemed a little better after they sent their messages and made their way down the street to the hotel. Unlike Saratoga, they were able to get two separate rooms with little difficulty and registered as brother and sister. It wasn't until he let Alaina pay for them out of her blackjack winnings that she realized how sick he was.

"I think I'd better go get the doctor."

"Don't be stupid," he said sharply. "I'll be fine in the

morning. I haven't had much sleep the last few nights."

"Doc's out of town anyway." The old man at the front desk sent a stream of tobacco juice into the spittoon. "Won't be back till day after tomorrow."

Alaina bit her lip worriedly. "Is there anyone else who could take a look at him?'

"Oh, for pity's sake, Alaina. It's just too much sun and not enough sleep. Stop treating me like a child."

"Fine. Then let's go get something to eat," she said peevishly. "I'm starving."

"You go on ahead; I'm not very hungry. I think I'll go to bed."

Alaina resisted the urge to run after him as he trudged toward the stairs. "Leave your door unlocked so I can check on you later," she called. His only response was a slight nod.

Despite her fears to the contrary, the local restaurant was still serving supper. The only other customers were three cowboys who were finishing their own meals. Though they kept glancing her way, she ignored them, and was relieved when they finally left. The lonely walk back to the hotel in the darkness was a little nerve-wracking, but she made it without mishap.

The elderly clerk hailed her when she walked in the front door. "Glad to see you're back, Miss. Telegram came for your brother right after you left."

"Thank you," she said, taking the telegram from his hand. A feeling of intense relief flowed through her as she read the contents. Angel had received Jared's message and someone would arrive in Hanna on the eleven-thirty train in the morning. "Why didn't you deliver this to my brother?"

"Tried but couldn't get him to come to the door."

"He didn't answer?"

"Nope. Knocked loud enough to wake the dead too. Figured he stepped out without me knowing it."

Without another word, Alaina hurried up the stairs to Jared's room. Luckily, the door was unlocked, and she let herself in. She smiled to herself as loud snores filled the tiny room. *Just let him try to tease me about snoring again.* His clothes lay in an untidy heap on the floor and his half naked body was sprawled across the bed as though he'd been too tired to even crawl under the covers. His feet rested on a neatly folded patchwork quilt at the end of the bed.

She crossed the few feet to the bed and pulled the quilt out from under him. With an affectionate smile on her lips, she tenderly covered him with it, then reached down to feel his forehead. It was warm but not dangerously so. Perhaps he was just overly tired as he said.

The moonlight bathed his features in silver, giving him an oddly vulnerable look. Her heart twisted painfully as she gazed down at him. Oh, how she loved him. Had her mother felt this way about Cameron Price? Unable to resist the temptation to touch him, she traced the curve of his cheek with her hand.

"Alaina?" he murmured sleepily.

"I'm sorry," she said softly. "I didn't mean to wake you."

"Coming to bed?"

"I don't think that's a good idea. You need your rest."

"What I need is comforting. I hurt all over," he said plaintively. "If you held me in your arms, I'm sure I'd feel better."

"But you wouldn't get any rest," she said, gently extricating her hand.

"No, I suppose not." His eyes drifted closed. "I still think I'd feel better, though."

"Sleep tight," she whispered pulling the quilt over him again. Impulsively she leaned down and brushed her lips across his forehead. She was nearly to the door when the snoring started again. Grinning to herself, she quietly closed the door and went down the hall to her room.

The next morning, Jared's condition was markedly worse and so was his temper. It was a relief to leave his grumpiness to go meet Angel's train.

Anticipation filled her as it pulled into the station. Angel would know exactly what to do about Jared's illness. She scanned the faces of the passengers as they disembarked, but Angel was not among them. Worried, Alaina made her way to the conductor who was standing by the steps.

"My godmother was supposed to be on this train. Are there any other passengers?"

"Why, Elaine, how nice of you to come meet me." A cultured voice cut in before he had time to answer.

Alaina's stomach tightened in dismay. Oh no; it couldn't be. She whirled around just in time to see Susan Prescott step off the train.

CHAPTER TWENTY-ONE

"Susan!" Alaina watched in astonishment as the other woman descended the train car steps. As usual, it looked as though she had stepped out of a bandbox. From the tips of her kid shoes to the organdy and lace hat perched on shining curls, she was a sight to behold. A matching parasol and kid gloves completed her ensemble. Alaina couldn't help thinking Susan was a bit over-dressed for Hannah, Wyoming. "What are you doing here?" she asked.

"Joining my fiancé, though I hardly think this is the place to discuss it," Susan said, with a meaningful look at the conductor. "Where *is* Jared?"

"Back at the hotel. Isn't Angel with you?"

"No. Mr. Treenery is quite ill, and she felt it necessary to stay with him."

Alaina had a sinking sensation in her middle. "Oh, no, what's wrong with Ox?"

"It appears he contracted something from the children. Of course, I suppose that's to be expected when one allows them to roam all over the house the way they do."

"The children are sick too?"

"Yes, all three of the little beasts, though they're pretty much over it now."

"What's wrong with them all?" Alaina asked in alarm.

"Chickenpox!" Susan said, with barely concealed

disgust. "The doctor said Mr. Treenery's is an especially severe case because he's an adult. He also said Mrs. Treenery and I are immune to the infection since we had it as children."

"Yes, so did I," Alaina said absently, as they started down the street toward the hotel. Chickenpox. Could that be what was wrong with Jared? She frowned thoughtfully as she tried to remember her own bout with the disease and, more recently, her youngest brother's. The most predominant memory was constant itching, sores, and being hot and irritable. Her normally sweet-tempered brother had been downright testy the whole time. Jared was certainly grouchy enough.

"If you've already had them, you should go back to Laramie City and give Mrs. Treenery a hand," Susan said. "She has a lot to cope with."

"Why didn't you stay and give your support?" Alaina couldn't help asking.

"I'm of absolutely no use in the sick room. Besides, someone needed to come salvage your reputation. Since your godmother couldn't be here, I came in her place."

They had been steadily moving away from the station as they talked. Now Alaina stopped in the middle of the street and stared at her companion. Save her reputation? Susan would be more apt to shred it. "Why?"

"What a question!"

"It's a perfectly logical question. We both know you've never had much use for me. Why the sudden concern?"

Susan stiffened. "I don't know what you're talking about."

"Oh, come on, Susan. Let's be honest with each other

for once. If you want to protect my reputation, it's for some reason of your own."

Susan glared at her for a long moment, then started down the street again with an angry swish of her skirt. "All right then, to put it bluntly, I think the way you defied everyone and ran away is utterly reprehensible, and you deserve every black mark the world might put on you. Unfortunately, the man you spent all this time with is *my* fiancé, and I have no desire to see him forced into marriage with you. If your escapade became known, that's exactly what would happen."

For a horrified moment, Alaina thought Susan knew what she and Jared had done on the mountain and again in Saratoga. Then she realized the other woman was only referring to the time they'd spent together. "What's your plan?"

"As far as anyone knows, you never left Laramie City. If we say you've been in bed with the chickenpox, no one will give it a second thought."

No one except for me and maybe Jared, Alaina thought with a pang. With Susan's story, Jared would be free to walk away when she was certain there was no baby. This was exactly what she'd hoped for. "Good, then we don't have to get married. Maybe you'll have better luck convincing Jared than I did."

Susan gave her a startled glance. "You and Jared already discussed it?"

"Yes, and you know how he is when he decides to be bull-headed about something."

"Actually, he always treats me with the greatest respect," Susan said with a hint of superiority.

"Probably because you never cross him." Suddenly Alaina frowned. "Where's Phoebe? Don't tell me she got the chickenpox too."

"The ungrateful wretch quit and went back to Denver just after you left!" Susan gave a disdainful sniff. "She was extremely rude about it too."

Good for her, Alaina thought, biting back a grin. "You and I will have to chaperone each other then?"

"Certainly not! *You* are going back to Laramie City while Jared and I continue on to Fort Bridger. Since we will be there by tonight, there's no need for a chaperone."

"I hate to disillusion you," Alaina said, as they entered the front door of the hotel, "but nobody is going anywhere, at least not today."

"What are you talking about?"

"Jared's too sick to travel."

"What?"

"He went to bed last night with a slight fever and a headache. This morning he was too sick to even get up."

"Oh, no!" Susan cried putting her hand to her throat. "What is it?"

Alaina told herself she was pleased Susan was so concerned. "I don't think it's serious, but I suspect it will be a few days before he'll be well enough to complete the trip." She glanced at Susan's perfectly groomed hair, then looked away and cleared her throat. "I'm sure you'll want to freshen up before you go up to see him. Would you like to use my room?"

"No thank you," said Susan, self-consciously patting her elaborate coiffure. "I'll get one of my own."

"That's probably a good idea," Alaina said, heading for the stairs. "Jared's room is at the end of the hall when you're ready."

Jared was dozing when Alaina let herself into the

room and moved quietly to his bedside. His face and the point of one shoulder were the only parts of him that weren't covered by the quilt. Both were completely clear.

Gently, so as not to wake him, she eased the quilt down lower. Red blisters covered most of his chest and stomach.

"Decide to join me after all?"

Alaina jumped. "You startled me," she said accusingly, as she glared down at him. "I thought you were asleep."

Though his eyes were red-rimmed and glassy, a spark of mischief lurked in the brown depths. "I was until you started undressing me."

"You were already undressed. How do you feel?"

"Like the devil. I don't think there's a part of me that doesn't hurt, and I itch like crazy. If I'm going to die, I wish I'd just do it and get it over with."

"Well, I'm pretty sure I know what's wrong with you, and it isn't fatal." She pointed to the blisters dotting his chest. "See those? You, my friend, have chickenpox."

He looked up at her in disbelief. "Oh, come on, Alaina, kids get chickenpox. I know you learned a lot from your Granny Ellinson, but this time you're dead wrong."

"It's not something I learned from her, though she'd probably have recognized the symptoms immediately. When I found out Ox and the children all have chickenpox, it occurred to me that you might too. The blisters prove it."

"I can't believe—" A sudden knock at the door interrupted him. "Who's that?"

Alaina didn't bother to answer as she stepped across the small patch of floor and opened the door.

"Oh, Jared, darling," Susan cried rushing into the room. Her headlong flight stopped at the foot of the bed, Alaina noted cynically. She apparently didn't want to risk catching whatever her beloved had.

Jared's mouth fell open in shock. "Susan!"

"I've been frantic about you ever since that snowstorm hit the mountain. Ox tried to go after you. He found your lean-to but got sick and had to come home. He said you'd made it through the storm and were probably all right," Susan said tearfully, "but now I find you at death's door."

"He's not dying," Alaina informed her. "He's got chickenpox. It's safe for you to come in. He can't give you anything."

"Is Angel with you?" Jared asked Susan sharply.

"No."

"Damn! Did she send the money I asked for?"

"Yes, but—"

"Alaina, do you know if the man left to take the horses back to Jack Ferguson?"

"He said he wasn't leaving until afternoon."

"Good. If I hurry, you can catch him. Run and get me some paper to write a note."

"What for?"

"I'm going to have Jack buy my watch back from Twitchel."

"Oh, but—"

"Alaina, for once just do as I tell you without arguing with me," he snapped. "It's past noon already."

"Don't disturb yourself, darling," Susan said in a soothing voice. "You need to stay calm if you're going to get well. Alaina, dear, run along and do as he says. We don't want to upset him."

"Heaven forbid that I should do a thing like that," Alaina muttered to herself as she stalked down the hall. If they'd given her a minute to explain, she could have told his royal majesty, his precious watch was safe and sound in her room. Jared's grouchiness was difficult enough to put up with, but Susan's attitude was going to make life intolerable. It was enough to make her turn tail and run.

The thought brought her up short. Why not? In spite of Susan's distaste for the sick room, she was perfectly capable of taking care of Jared. He was going to spend several uncomfortable days, but he wasn't in any real danger.

It only took a moment to find Jared's watch and start back down the hall, but by then the idea of leaving had taken firm root in her mind. Ever since they'd returned to civilization, he'd been steadily changing back into the autocratic tyrant that had irritated her so badly on the trip out. She'd left *her* Jared behind on the mountain.

Susan and Jared belong together, Alaina told herself. *Maybe he'll even be a better patient for Susan. Of course, he could be worse.* That insidious little thought brought a grin to her face.

Susan was sitting on the edge of the bed bathing Jared's forehead with cool water. Alaina's stomach tightened for an instant then she forced herself to relax. Susan and Jared would probably spend hours holding hands and gazing into each other's eyes if she wasn't here to interfere.

Jared struggled to sit up as Alaina entered the room. "Did you bring the paper?"

"No, I brought something better." She grasped his wrist, turned his hand over and dropped the watch into his palm.

"My watch!"

"I bought it back from Twitchel day before yesterday."

"Why didn't you tell me?"

"You didn't give me time to tell you anything. If you'll remember, you left rather abruptly."

"It seemed like the best idea at the time," he said frowning. "Whatever possessed you to get my watch back?"

"I could see it meant a lot to you when you sold it."

"Not as much as a hotel room did at that point. I'd have sold my soul for a warm bed."

Their gazes met for a long, emotion charged moment. The memory of that bed and the passion they'd shared in it seemed to sizzle in the air between them. Jared was the first to glance away.

"I'll pay you back. How much did he cheat you out of?"

"Consider it a gift," she said softly, "like my dress."

"No, your money is —"

"A dress?" Susan broke in sharply. "You bought her a dress?"

"She needed it."

"I hardly think —"

Alaina glared at the other woman. "Don't worry about it, Susan. He bought me a dress so I wouldn't embarrass him any more. The one I was wearing was little more than a rag."

"You should have bought it for yourself," Jared said gruffly, "instead of spending your money on my watch." He stared down at it in bemusement. Twitchel wouldn't have let it go without a tidy profit."

"Pardon me," Alaina said sarcastically. "I'd forgotten how much my *gambling* offends you."

"Gambling!" Susan's voice was little more than a shocked squeak.

Alaina smiled sweetly at her. "That's right, Susan, gambling; blackjack to be precise. What's more, I'm very good at it. Now, if you'll both excuse me, I have some packing to do if I'm going to catch the afternoon train."

Jared's head jerked up. "What are you talking about?"

"With Susan here, you don't need me to take care of you, and I have other commitments."

"You're not going anywhere!"

"Want to bet?"

Jared's face darkened angrily, and he started to get out of bed, but Susan's hands on his chest stopped him. "Jared, don't. With Mr. Treenery and all the children ill, Angel needs her."

Jared gave Alaina a suspicious glance. "You're going to Laramie City?"

Susan didn't give Alaina a chance to answer. "Of course, darling, where else would she go?"

"Where else indeed?" Alaina murmured.

"I don't like the idea of you traveling by yourself," he grumbled.

"Susan made it here all by herself. Besides, it couldn't be any worse that what we've already been through."

Jared made a rude sound. "That's supposed to convince me?"

"I don't have to convince you of anything," Alaina said, with a toss of her head. "As I've told you over and over again, you aren't my father or my husband."

"Thank God for that!" he said with feeling.

"My sentiments exactly." She turned on her heel and marched to the door. Then she paused and turned slowly back to face him. "Jared," she said softly. "Thank you for everything you did for me. I wouldn't be here if not for you."

"My pleasure."

Her gaze flew to his face. A warm glow in the deep brown eyes told her the words evoked the same memories for him as they did for her. Alaina's attention shifted as Susan moved slightly. It was impossible to miss the possessive way her hand still rested on Jared's chest, and he didn't seem to mind a bit. With a sudden knot in her throat, Alaina turned and walked out the door.

CHAPTER TWENTY-TWO

"This is Fort Bridger," the young man said, jumping down from his wagon and coming around to help Alaina. He seemed oblivious to the spectacular sunset that painted the sky over his right shoulder as he gazed up at her in adoration.

Alaina looked around in surprise. She'd fully expected to see a wooden stockade built around picturesque log buildings as protection against the warring Plains Indians. Not only was there no stockade, most of the buildings were either whitewashed rock, or clapboard. Fort Bridger looked more like a town than a fort.

"The sutler's store is over there. They'll know how to find your Pa." The young man sighed regretfully. "I'd like to stay and help, but my Ma's expecting me home for supper."

"I wouldn't think of delaying you any longer," Alaina told him with a grateful smile. "I'm already beholden to you. If it hadn't been for you, I'd have had to wait until the morning stage came out."

"Glad I could help." He blushed with pleasure as he climbed back up on the wagon seat. "Reckon I'd best be on my way."

"Thank you for bringing me here. I know you had to go out of your way."

"My pleasure." He touched the brim of his hat and drove away.

Alaina winced at his choice of words. It was the
same phrase Jared had used. The last thing she needed
right now was a reminder of Jared and his assumption
that she was headed to Laramie City. It wasn't like she'd
lied to him. She just hadn't corrected Susan's assertion
that she was going to help Angel.

That she'd ignored Angel's difficulties made her feel
guilty enough. But if she'd gone to help her godmother,
Jared would have figured out some way to keep her
from Cameron Price. This way, the deed would be done
long before Jared had a chance to interfere.

A tremor of nervousness skittered down her spine
as she started toward the sutler's store. For the first time,
it occurred to her that Cameron Price might not be
thrilled to see her. Though he obviously knew he had a
daughter, he'd never made any attempt to contact her.
What did she know about him after all, except that Jared
and her mother both thought he was a despicable cad?
Even Angel had been less than enthusiastic about him.
That Susan liked him was more of a strike against him
than a recommendation.

"Miss Ellinson?" The unexpected masculine voice
broke through her reverie and brought her head around
in surprise. A vaguely familiar officer was striding
toward her with a look of complete astonishment on his
face.

"It *is* you!" he said in stark amazement. "I could
hardly credit my eyes."

With a sudden jolt, Alaina realized it was the
Lieutenant from the train trip West. "Lieutenant
Kirkpatrick," she said with relief. Here was someone
who could help her locate Cameron Price.

"Are you here with your aunt and uncle?"

"No. I came by myself. I'm looking for someone. Maybe you could help me find him."

"I haven't been here long enough to know many people, but I can try. What's his name?"

"Cameron Price."

Lieutenant Kirkpatrick looked startled. "Captain Price?"

"Oh, you know him?"

"Yes," he said faintly. "As a matter of fact, he lives just across the hall from me in the bachelor officer quarters, but I'm not sure..."

"It's all right. We're related."

"You are?" He looked at her closely for a moment then nodded. "Come to think of it, you do resemble him."

"Can you tell me where he is?"

"Probably in his quarters, over on the other side of the parade ground." Kirkpatrick gave her a doubtful look. "I don't know if visiting him alone is such a good idea, even if you are related to him. If I weren't on duty, I'd escort you myself."

"I appreciate your concern, but I'll be fine. Just tell me how to get there."

As he reluctantly pointed out one of the few log buildings, Alaina had a moment of doubt. Even Sean Kirkpatrick was skeptical about her visiting Cameron Price alone. She was aware of his worried frown as he watched her walk all the way across the parade ground.

Her throat felt dry and a thousand butterflies danced in her stomach as she paused in front of the white picket fence to gaze at the bachelor officer's quarters. Though the sun had just set, it was nearly nine o'clock, far too late to be calling on a perfect stranger.

What if he had already gone to bed?

Then she'd wake him up, Alaina thought as she squared her shoulders and marched up the boardwalk to the door. After all she'd been through to get here, nothing was going to stop her! A flicker of movement in the window caught her eye and she heard male laughter. Well, at least she wouldn't be getting him out of bed.

With her heart pulsing in her throat, she knocked on the door and waited. Several minutes passed with no answer, so she knocked again, louder this time. Still no answer. Gritting her teeth, Alaina lifted her fist and pounded on the door.

There was a pause in the voices inside, then the sound of a door opening. A moment later, the outside door swung open and she found herself face to face with a middle-aged, balding soldier. She blinked in surprise. He was not at all what she imagined.

"Well, well, what do we have here?" he said with a knowing smile. "I'll wager you're here to see Captain Price."

"Yes, I am. Is he here?"

"Sure is, but I don't think he was expecting you."

"He didn't know I was coming."

"Ah, well somehow I don't think he'll mind. Come in, come in."

When Alaina followed him inside, she could see why they hadn't heard her knock. A long hall ran the length of the building with an apartment on either side. Cameron Price must live on one side and Lieutenant Kirkpatrick on the other.

"Someone here to see you, Captain," the man called through an open door on the left side of the hall. Then he smiled at Alaina and gestured for her to go first.

She saw Cameron Price the minute she stepped over the threshold. In an odd kind of way, it was like looking at an older, vaguely distorted, male version of herself. Even sprawled in a chair, with a semi-bored expression on his face, he dominated the room. One look at the sun-bronzed skin, well-muscled body and beautiful blue eyes and Alaina had a pretty good idea why Susan liked him so much.

Despite a touch of gray at his temples and a few extra lines and creases, Cameron Price was an extremely handsome man. Though she knew he had to be at least forty, Alaina had never seen anyone who carried his age so well. The laugh lines around his mouth and deep grooves in his cheeks only added to his masculine beauty.

He watched her over the rim of the glass as he lifted his drink to his lips. Alaina's anxiety increased by leaps and bounds as the bizarre nature of her position suddenly occurred to her. What did a person say to a father she had never met? 'Hello, I'm your long-lost daughter?' What if he didn't believe her?

"Well, gentlemen," Cameron said, lowering his drink, "what do you say we call it a night?"

For the first time Alaina noticed the cards and poker chips scattered among the glasses on the table. She'd interrupted a poker game, and judging from the pile of chips in front of Cameron Price, a lucrative one. He wouldn't thank her for that.

His eyes never left her face as his guests gathered their belongings and filed out amid murmurs of 'lucky devil' and 'must be the elusive laundress.'

"I had about given up hope that you'd ever come," he said, setting his drink on the table and rising languidly to his feet as the door closed behind the last of the card players.

Alaina's eyes widened in surprise. "You know who I am?"

"How could I forget a face like yours?"

So he noticed the amazing resemblance too. "I'm sorry about your game. I should have let you know I was coming."

"It doesn't matter," he said with a slow sensual smile. "The important thing is that you're finally here. I've been waiting for you all week."

Alaina frowned as he walked around the table. Something wasn't right here. She took an involuntary step back as he approached. "I think you've mistaken me for someone else. I'm not who you think I am."

"Oh? Who do I think you are?"

"I...I don't know." She took another step away from him and found the wall at her back. "But my name is Alaina Ellinson."

"Alaina." His voice was husky as he took her coat and the small bundle of clothes from her. "A beautiful name for a beautiful woman," he said, dropping them on a chair.

"No, you don't understand," she said frantically. "My mother is Becky Ellinson."

"That explains it of course." He traced her cheek with the back of his hand. "Your mother sent you. How refreshing. Most mothers warn their daughters against me."

Panic rose in her throat as he leaned forward and brushed his lips against her forehead. She put her hands against his chest and shoved. "No, please. You knew my mother in South Pass City. Don't you remember Becky?"

"South Pass City?" Cameron pulled back and stared down at her with a look of dawning horror. "You mean Becky White?"

"That was her name before she got married."

"Jesus!" He stepped away as though he'd been burned. "Then you're..."

"I'm your daughter."

Cameron stared at her for a full minute, then turned and walked to the dresser. He jerked open the top drawer and took out a pair of glasses. "Damned eyes," he muttered, hooking the bows behind his ears. "Don't work worth spit anymore."

As he turned toward her again, he suddenly looked every year of his age. The wire frames seemed to accentuate silver threads in his hair and the thick glass distorted his eyes until he looked almost owlish. She could see why he chose not to wear them.

Alaina shrank against the wall as he walked toward her again, but this time there was nothing lover-like in the way he touched her. He took her chin in his hand and turned her head this way and that as he studied her face.

"My daughter." His voice was filled with wonder. "You're all grown up."

"I...yes, I guess I am."

Cameron gazed at her a bit longer, then turned away. "I think I need a drink." He sat down and poured a generous amount of whiskey into his glass. "Join me?"

"No, thank you." Alaina searched her mind for something to fill the awkward pause. "I wasn't sure you'd believe I was your daughter."

He gave a humorless laugh. "A blind man could tell I'm your father. Well, maybe not a blind man," he said with a rueful smile, as he removed his glasses and stuck them in his pocket. "Why did your mother send you to me after all this time?"

"Mama didn't send me. I came on my own."

"Why?"

"I just wanted to meet you. Mama tried to stop me, but I came anyway."

Cameron grinned. "A little impetuous, are you?"

"A little. It gets me in trouble all the time."

He chuckled. "Looks aren't the only thing that you inherited from me, then." His smile faded as he stared down into his drink. "Did your mother marry the big Swede?"

"He's Norwegian, but yes she did."

"And did he make her happy?"

Alaina felt a pang of sympathy, but she couldn't lie to him. "Yes."

"I figured as much," Cameron said, swirling the whiskey in his glass. "He saved my life, you know."

"He did?"

"A bunch of renegade half-breeds held me prisoner in a box canyon. He came in alone, cut me loose and practically carried me out of there in broad daylight. It was the bravest thing I've ever seen anyone do, and he didn't even know who I was." Cameron stared pensively into his drink. "I've often wondered if he'd have bothered if he had."

"I don't think it would have mattered to him one way or the other." Alaina said. "He was the only one who didn't try to stop me from coming to find you."

Cameron raised an eyebrow in surprise. "He didn't?"

"He said I had the right to know my real father."

"A father," Cameron said, as though savoring the words. "You know, that's something I never thought I'd have a chance to be. I can hardly wait to introduce you to the Colonel and his wife."

"Then you don't mind that I came?"

"Mind? Of course, not. What man could resist showing off such a beautiful daughter? Besides, think of what we'll look like together."

"Look like?"

"I see you haven't thought it through." He set his drink down and rose from the chair. "Come here, I'll show you what I mean."

Alaina regarded the palm he held toward her suspiciously. Though he seemed completely harmless now, she wasn't quite sure she trusted him.

"I promise I'll behave myself," he assured her as he gestured toward the door into the other room. "I just want to show you the mirror."

Cautiously she moved forward and put her hand in his. Cameron flashed her a smile that would have melted the coldest heart, and pulled her through the door. It was obviously his bedroom, but there was indeed a large mirror on the wall next to the wardrobe. He stood behind her and pointed into the glass. "Look at that," he said in satisfaction. "We'll turn heads everywhere we go."

Alaina had to admit they did look good together. Her soft feminine features were the perfect foil for his rugged masculinity, especially since they looked so much alike. "It's amazing how much I resemble you."

"Yes, but you have your mother's smile," he said wistfully. He reached up and touched the heavy braid that circled her head. "And her hair. I never knew anyone with hair as beautiful as your mother's."

Alaina frowned. "My mother has dark hair."

"I know, but yours is thick and soft like hers. I always felt as if I were running my hands through a cloud of silk." He smiled. "You know, even as a baby you were like both of us all mixed up together into a new little person."

Alaina blinked in surprise. "You remember me?"

"How could I forget? You were the most beautiful baby I'd ever seen, and you were mine. Fathering you was the best thing I ever did." His mouth twisted ruefully. "And the worst."

"The worst?"

"Your mother was barely sixteen when I met her. I knew better than to get involved with someone of her tender years, but she was so beautiful I couldn't resist." He sighed. "When I finally got around to asking her to marry me she turned me down flat, and I guess I don't blame her. I probably wouldn't have made her a very good husband. She wanted a little cottage with a picket fence and a dozen children."

"Our house isn't exactly a cottage, and I only have five brothers and a sister, but Papa did build her a picket fence."

Cameron gave a crack of laughter. "There, I knew I wasn't the man for her. Good lord, seven children! As young as she is, she could have all twelve before she's done."

"Then you don't mind that she married Papa?"

"I was pretty heart-broken at the time, but I suppose it was for the best." He regarded her critically in the mirror. "Now, what are we going to do with you?"

"Do with me?"

"We'll have to find a place for you to stay while you're here. The Citizen Hotel will do for tonight, and I'll call in a few favors tomorrow. Meanwhile, we need to think of a convincing story about where you've been all this time."

"Can't we just tell people the truth?"

"What, that I never got around to marrying your mother, and you're my illegitimate daughter?"

"No, I guess not." Alaina frowned as she followed him back into the other room. "But what will we tell them?"

He took his uniform jacket off the hook near the door and put it on. "Don't worry. I'll think of something. Come on," he said, picking up her belongings, "let's go before it gets any later."

Alaina's head was whirling as they walked across the parade ground. Not only was Cameron Price glad to see her, he was thrilled with the idea of presenting her to his friends. She could hardly wait until Jared arrived. It was going to be immensely satisfying to say I told you so.

CHAPTER TWENTY-THREE

"**A**ngel said Lord and Lady Roxham are planning to come for the wedding, so we need to set a date soon," Susan said. "It will take them several months to get here from England. What do you think about Christmas time?"

There was no answer from Jared who lay in bed with his eyes closed.

"Are you awake?" Susan asked, peering at his face. After a moment, she sighed and pulled the blankets up around him. "Good night, Jared. Sleep well," she whispered. She tucked him in like a small child, then blew out the lantern and tiptoed out of the room.

The minute the door closed behind her, Jared opened one eye a crack to make sure she was really gone. "Thank God!" He threw back the covers and got out of bed. "This place is like a damn oven!" He stalked to the window and jerked it open. Then he stripped off his cotton nightshirt, wadded it into a ball and threw it across the room. "I wonder if she thinks she can sweat the sickness out of me," he grumbled, crawling back into bed. With the sheet pulled up to his waist, he laced his hands behind his head and lay back against the pillows with a sigh of relief.

The last eight days had been one irritation after another, not the least of which was Alaina's defection at the beginning. For the hundredth time, he reminded himself she'd gone to help Angel, and he was just being selfish. Still, after a week of putting up with Susan's inept attempts to take care of him, he was having a hard time convincing himself Angel's need was greater than his.

At least he knew where Alaina was for once. A smile flickered across his face as he thought of how neatly everything had worked out. There was enough snow in the high country that the survey crew probably wouldn't go out for a while yet, so he still had time to convince Alaina she was on a fool's errand. He seriously doubted she'd given up her notion of finding Cameron Price, but at least now Angel would be there to help.

First, though, he had to get Susan to Fort Bridger. He'd managed to avoid discussing the wedding so far, but she wouldn't be held off for long. There had to be a way to keep her at bay until he found out if Alaina was pregnant. Then suddenly he knew. Escape. If he wasn't around, she couldn't ask. The fever was gone and all his sores were healing. Maybe it was time to go.

The train for Evanston pulled out just before noon. If they left tomorrow, he could deliver Susan to her parents by evening and be back on the train the next morning. The more he thought about it, the more the idea appealed to him. For the first time, Jared agreed with Susan that it was a pity the train by-passed the fort and went on to Evanston. Even in the best of conditions, it took an hour to backtrack to the fort. Traveling with Susan was never the best of conditions. Still, even with Susan and all her luggage to transport to Fort Bridger, he could be in Laramie City by the day after tomorrow.

The thought of seeing Alaina again filled him with an unexpected feeling of anticipation. After eight days of Susan's vapid chatter, even a fight would be a welcome diversion. That brought him up short. Since when had he preferred Alaina's company to Susan's? *Since Susan had been thrown into a situation she was ill-equipped to handle,* he thought with some guilt. You really couldn't expect much from a woman who had trouble doing her hair without a maid. In her world, Susan could hold her own with the best of them, but with simpler, housewifery things she was lost. His mother was the same way.

At least Susan was always a lady, which was more than he could say for Alaina. Part of it was the difference between eighteen and twenty-two, and part of it was the expensive finishing school Susan had gone to. Mostly, though, the difference between the two women came down to their personalities. Until his illness, Susan had a calming effect on him. Alaina did just the opposite. He never knew from one minute to the next what she was going to do. Often as not, what started as a perfectly normal conversation wound up as a fight. Life with her would be total chaos.

Of course, they didn't fight all the time, he thought with a smile. Their passion was, if anything, more explosive than their disagreements. As he closed his eyes and drifted toward sleep, it was the memory of Bright Eyes asleep in the crook of his arm, and Alaina snuggled against the curve of his body that flitted through his mind. Funny how often he thought of them that way.

The next morning, he was shaved, dressed and on his way to the train depot before Susan even opened her eyes. By the time she'd completed her morning toilet, he had made all the necessary arrangements for their trip, eaten breakfast, and was headed back to the hotel.

She was standing outside his door with her hand on the doorknob when he rounded the corner at the top of the stairs.

"Jared! What on earth are you doing out of bed?"

"Making arrangements so we can leave this morning."

"Leave? Are you sure that's a good idea?"

He shrugged. "I've been up and about for several hours, and I feel just fine."

"I don't know. This seems a little foolhardy to me."

Jared raised an eyebrow. "I'd think you'd be anxious to get home. Besides, I'll go crazy if I spend another day in that bed. Can you be ready to go by eleven-thirty?"

"Jared! That's only three hours away. How do you expect me to get packed in such a short time without my maid?"

He forced himself to give her a placating smile. "I know it's asking a lot, but I already bought the tickets. Think how pleased your mother will be to have you home again."

"I suppose," she said doubtfully. "I guess I'd better go get started."

"I'll get you some breakfast."

She gave him a distracted smile. "Thank you, darling. I'll do my best to be ready."

Jared felt a flash of annoyance as she went back to her room. She acted as if he was asking the impossible. Three hours to pack ought to be more than enough for anyone!

Despite her misgivings, Susan was ready to go at the appointed time and was even in a fairly good mood. Though he had to hire a wagon and a driver to transport her luggage to the station, Jared felt like he had gotten off lucky.

As he escorted her down the stairs, Jared couldn't help but remember his trek across the Snowy Range with Alaina. It was a good thing Susan hadn't been along. Instead of one small cradleboard, he would have been expected to drag two trunks and a dozen bandboxes. Traveling light was not something she understood.

"What in the world are you smirking about?" Susan demanded as they stepped out into the street.

"I was just thinking how nice it was to be back on my feet again. What's going on at the station? It looks like the army has invaded."

"It appears to be a whole company," Susan said, shading her eyes. "Are those prisoners?"

"Looks like your father sent troops out after the renegades Alaina and I ran into up in the Snowys."

Susan glanced up at him in surprise. "I didn't realize it was that serious. You made it sound like it was of little consequence."

"Did I?" Jared had to struggle to keep the sarcasm out of his tone. Susan had made it very plain she wasn't interested once she discovered that he and Alaina had been at odds most of the time. He'd tried to tell her about the trip over the mountain more than once, but she'd given a delicate shudder and told him it wasn't a proper conversation for a delicately nurtured female like herself.

As they approached the station, a modicum of order began to appear in the chaos. Soldiers herded twenty to thirty prisoners onto a freight car. Their treatment was anything but gentle, with an occasional rifle butt making contact with a back or stomach. Jared experienced a flicker of sympathy until he remembered what they had done to Bright Eye's parents. Suddenly, he felt like taking a few jabs himself.

"Jared! Oh, thank heavens." Brandy darted out of the crowd and hurried toward him with the cradleboard secured to her back.

Jared's eyes widened in startled surprise. "Brandy, what are you doing here?"

"Oh, Jared, you've got to help Adam. He's been arrested."

He stared down at her in disbelief. "What?"

"The Captain arrested him day before yesterday."

"That doesn't make sense. Whiskey Jug Johnson has always been a good friend to the army. Surely they know he'd never be in cahoots with scum like the renegades."

"That isn't why they arrested him."

"No?"

"It has to do with me. Some soldiers came to the cabin." She looked away. "I don't know if they treat all unprotected women that way, or if they thought I was with the renegades."

Jared swore under his breath. "Did they hurt you?"

"No, but only because Adam came before they had a chance to. He disposed of all five of them without much trouble."

"Uh oh, he didn't kill anybody, did he?"

"No, but they all look pretty bad and a couple of them have broken bones. They told the captain it was an unprovoked attack."

"And he believed them?"

Brandy gave him a bleak look. "It was our word against theirs."

"Where's Whiskey Jug now?"

"In with all the other prisoners."

"What! They'll know he had something to do with the army coming to the Snowys this time of year."

"And they'll kill him," Brandy said tearfully. "I know. That's why you have to help him."

"Where's this captain now? I'll see if I can talk some sense into his head."

"I don't know. The last I saw him...wait, there he is now coming out of the depot."

"Why it's Captain Price," Susan said.

"Oh, great," Jared muttered.

"You know him?" Brandy asked hopefully.

"Oh, I know him all right, but I'm not sure that will work to Whiskey Jug's advantage."

Susan tossed her head angrily. "I don't know why you persist in maligning Captain Price. He's a good officer. I'm sure he'll set things to rights."

"I guess there's only one way to find out isn't there? I'll be right back."

"Jared," Susan said repressively. "You're forgetting your manners."

He gave her a blank look? "What manners?"

"Aren't you going to escort me to the train?"

"I don't have time for that right now. You'll be safe enough here until I get back."

Susan was horrified. "You want me to wait here alone?"

"You won't be alone. Susan Prescott meet Brandy Johnson. Now if you'll excuse me, I have urgent business with your friend Captain Price."

Susan glared after him as he walked away. "Sometimes I'd like to throttle that man."

"Have you known Jared long?" Brandy asked

politely.

"He's my fiancé."

Brandy's eyes widened. "Your fiancé! But I thought...uh...I didn't realize Jared was betrothed."

"Oh yes, for several months now. We haven't actually set the wedding date yet, though we're hoping for Christmas. His family will need time to make arrangements to come, especially his sister Lady Roxham. She and her husband will be coming from England, you know," Susan said with an air of condescension.

"Uh...no, Jared never talked about his family." *Not to mention a fiancée*, Brandy thought to herself. She wondered if Alaina and Susan knew about each other. For that matter, where was Alaina? One look at Susan's profile was enough to convince her it was probably better not to ask.

"You needn't worry about your husband," Susan was saying. "In spite of Jared's opinion to the contrary, Captain Price is a very fair man. I'm sure he'll set it all to rights."

Since she'd experienced the Captain's fairness first hand, Brandy didn't bother to comment. Though he'd gone out of his way for her, even sending someone to find her a dress to replace her bloodied buckskins, he had treated Adam unfairly from the beginning.

Brandy watched the interaction between Jared and the Captain. Though Price seemed to be listening, it was impossible to tell what impact Jared's words were having on him. She couldn't shake the feeling that she knew the Captain from somewhere, and yet the features weren't quite right. For some reason, the odd sensation was even more intense now that she saw him with Jared.

How very peculiar.

A small whimper drew her attention away from the two men. "Oh dear, Erika's awake. I was hoping she'd sleep awhile longer." Brandy reached into her bag, pulled out a bottle of milk, and handed it to Susan. "Would you mind holding this for a minute while I get my baby?"

Susan had little choice but to do as Brandy asked while the other woman shrugged the cradleboard off her shoulders.

"That baby is an Indian!" Susan said.

"Half Indian," Brandy corrected. "And both halves are very hungry. Could I have her bottle now?"

Susan couldn't get rid of the bottle fast enough. "I didn't realize you were married to an Indian," she said accusingly.

"I'm not. Adam's as white as you are. Brandy smiled sweetly as she stuck the bottle in Erika's mouth. "Her Indian heritage comes from her mother's side."

An uneasy silence fell between the two women as Brandy fed the baby, and they waited for Jared to return. Several of the soldiers glanced their way but didn't try to approach them. Even so, they were both relieved when Jared rejoined them.

"What did he say?" Brandy asked anxiously.

"That I'll have to convince Colonel Prescott when we get to Fort Bridger."

"He didn't believe you?"

Jared shook his head. "Said it was out of his hands. Once an arrest is made, only the fort commander can let a prisoner go."

"Do you know the commander?"

"He's my future father-in-law."

Brandy glanced uneasily at Susan. "I see."

"I did manage to convince him to put Whiskey Jug in a separate car." Jared reached into his pocket. "I bought you a ticket. I'll find the three of you a seat then go check on Whiskey Jug."

There was room in the first passenger car he tried. He stepped back off the train and nodded to the two women. "There are some empty seats about halfway back."

Brandy smiled at him as he helped her up the steps into the car. "I don't know how to thank you, Jared. Adam and I will be forever in your debt."

"That's what friends are for. Besides, Whiskey Jug saved my hide not too long ago."

"I guess he did at that," she said with another smile as she climbed the steps and disappeared into the car.

"Do you expect me to travel with an Indian?" Susan asked in a low voice.

Jared blinked in surprise. "Bright Eyes?"

"I don't care what you call her, she's a heathen." Susan gave a delicate shudder. "I can't believe you'd actually endanger me this way."

"For God's sake, Susan, she's a baby! What do you think she's going to do, scalp you?"

"I'm not talking about the baby, I mean her mother."

"Her mother's dead, killed by whites," he said flatly. "Brandy's a cousin and has lily-white bloodlines. As long as you keep a civil tongue in your head, you're in no danger from her."

"But she said..."

"Look, Susan, I really don't have time for this right now. If you want to go to Fort Bridger today, get on the damn train. Otherwise go back to the hotel, and I'll arrange to have someone come after you tomorrow."

Susan stiffened but apparently thought better of saying anything else. Without another word, she lifted her skirts and stepped up onto the steps at the back of the car. Jared didn't even wait to make sure she made it inside before he left.

Susan knew she had blundered badly. His agitation was apparent in every step he took as he strode down the length of the train. She bit her lip. It wasn't the first time in the last few days she'd had the impression he was slipping away from her. Since there had never actually been a formal announcement of their betrothal, he could still cry off. She couldn't allow that to happen. Somehow, she needed to bind him to her so tightly he wouldn't even consider straying. The question was how?

This would take even more careful planning than getting him to propose. Susan squared her shoulders. She wasn't descended from a long line of high ranking military men for nothing. Clever strategy and the Prescott name were nearly synonymous. Though she didn't have a plan yet, Jared Brady would not escape!

CHAPTER TWENTY-FOUR

"**W**hiskey Jug?" Jared slid back the door of the boxcar and peered inside. "Are you in here?"

There was a scuffling sound from the front of the car. "Jared? What the hell are you doing here?"

"Returning a favor." Jared swung up into the car and squinted into the darkness. "Brandy seemed to think you could use some help."

"Is she all right?"

"Appears to be," Jared shook his head as his eyes began to adjust. Even in the dim light he could see lumps and bruises on his friend's face. "Which is more than I can say for you. Must have been some fight."

Whiskey Jug snorted. "Not really. There were only five of them. I've beat more than twice that number in a brawl when I was dead drunk." He touched a cut on his forehead. "Most of this happened after I was arrested."

"Guess they didn't like what you did to their comrades in arms."

"Guess not."

"The Captain in charge thinks you might be one of the renegades."

Whiskey Jug made a derisive sound. "Then he has a damn short memory. I led him to their camp. He's just mad because I roughed up some of his men a bit."

"I don't suppose you could have shown a little restraint."

"None of them are dead, are they?"

"No."

"If I'd gotten there five minutes later, they would have raped Brandy." He looked up at Jared. "And your Captain would have five corpses on his hands."

"Instead he's got three men who had to be carried down the mountain on stretchers and two others that will be out of commission for quite awhile." Jared sighed. "Am I right in assuming the black eye Captain Price is sporting was your doing too?"

"Probably. He definitely didn't like the havoc I was creating in his troops. Hit me with the butt of his rifle." Whiskey Jug rubbed his jaw. "Dropped me like a rock. Just wait until I get my hand on the son of a bitch."

"You might try to be a little more conciliatory toward him, at least until we get to Fort Bridger."

"Why should I?"

Jared gave an exasperated sigh. "Because as far as he's concerned right now, hanging would be too good for you. Besides, he did bring Brandy and the baby along."

"He couldn't very well leave them alone on the mountain."

Jared raised an eyebrow. "Couldn't he?"

"All right," Whiskey Jug conceded after a long moment. "So, he didn't have to bring them along. That doesn't mean I have to like him."

"Nobody's asking you to. Just don't antagonize him any more. Once I get you to Fort Bridger I have a chance of getting you off. Colonel Prescott is reasonably open-minded, but Cameron Price has a good deal of influence with him."

Whiskey Jug's jaw tightened belligerently. "So, I'm just supposed to forget what that scum tried to do to

Brandy?"

"No, but sometimes you have to work through the powers that be instead of taking things into your own hands. I'm not entirely without influence myself, and I'll make sure they pay for what they did. Colonel Prescott won't let them off easy, I promise you. In the meantime, I want you to keep your mouth shut and your temper under control." Jared held up his hand before the other man could say anything. "Look, just do it for Brandy, all right? She needs you in one piece."

"All right," Whiskey Jug grumbled after a moment. "I promise not to do anything to make Price any madder."

"Good," Jared said. "Just try to remember that. I'd better go. I don't want to leave the women alone for too long with all these soldiers around."

He got clear to the door of the boxcar before Whiskey Jug spoke. "Thanks," he said gruffly.

"Don't mention it. Just make sure all my hard work doesn't go for nothing."

A young private stepped forward to shut the door after Jared jumped down from the car. The sound of metal grating on metal followed him as he walked along the train to the passenger section. The dark lonely boxcar wasn't the greatest way to travel, but at least Whiskey Jug would be safe there.

He reached the passenger car just as the train began to move. For a moment, he considered letting the train pull out of the station without him. The trip to Evanston and then on to Fort Bridger was going to be anything but pleasant especially if Susan felt threatened by the presence of a real, live Indian. The way she was acting you'd think Bright Eyes was a full grown brave dressed in feathers and war paint instead of a harmless little baby. With a deep sigh, he grabbed the railing and pulled himself on board before the train picked up too much speed.

The trip was even worse than he'd anticipated, but not because Susan was difficult to deal with. It was Brandy. Ever since he'd told her Alaina was in Laramie City, her disapproval had wrapped itself around him like a suffocating blanket. The way she looked at him made him feel guilty as hell and caused him to do some deep soul searching.

Maybe Alaina *had* earned the right to meet her father. He could broach the subject to her when he got back to Laramie City. A slight smile crossed his lips as he thought of her reaction when he volunteered to escort her to Fort Bridger.

A herd of buffalo blocked the track for the better part of an hour, delaying their arrival in Evanston until it was too late to head out to the fort. Cameron Price offered to let them camp outside town with the army, but Jared declined. Luckily, he was able to get three rooms at the hotel so Brandy and Susan didn't have to share.

His luck held clear until the next morning. They missed the stage out to the fort because it left too early for Susan. Jared managed to find a two-seated spring wagon to transport the two women, Bright Eyes, and Susan's trunks.

Unfortunately, by the time they got started, the army was already on the move and in front of them. They wound up following them all the way to Fort Bridger. With Susan's complaints about the dust and

Brandy's accusing eyes boring into his back, Jared wished he'd left them all in Evanston. When the buildings of Fort Bridger finally came into view late that afternoon, no one was happier to see them than Jared Brady.

"I really wish you had gotten ahead of the column, Jared," Susan said holding her scented handkerchief in front of her nose.

"Eating the dust of two dozen horse soldiers and three prisoner transports isn't exactly my idea of a good time either," Jared grumbled. "But by the time I got all your baggage loaded, we didn't have much choice."

Susan was instantly contrite. "Oh, darling, I didn't mean to sound like I blamed you. I just meant it's unfortunate we've had to follow the soldiers into Fort Bridger."

Jared didn't even bother to answer. Susan had been on her best behavior since they'd left Hannah, but he was out of charity with her. Maybe if he hadn't seen her recoil when he'd offered to hold Bright Eyes on the train, or if her sweetness had extended to Brandy, he might have felt differently. As it was, he could hardly wait to dump her and her mountain of baggage on her parent's doorstep.

Women! There was no dealing with them. But they were the least of his worries right now. All day he'd wrestled with the best way to argue Whiskey Jug's case. If the mountain man had been the slightest bit remorseful, Cameron Price might have viewed the case more leniently. As it was, Price was more likely to make Whiskey Jug pay for his attitude.

Even from here, Jared could see Captain Price at the head of his troops. He looked every inch the conquering hero he was. There were those who might have thought the Captain should have sent his second in command on the train with the prisoners and stayed behind with the main company of his men. There was no way Cameron would allow a mere Lieutenant to have the triumphal entrance into the fort. After all, he and his men had single-handedly captured an entire army of insurrection, and Cameron Price wasn't the type to give up a moment of the glory that was due him.

At least they'd been spared his presence for most of the trip. Other than a brief hello to Susan soon after they'd gotten underway and inviting them to camp with the army last night, he'd stayed away. For that, Jared was doubly grateful. Alaina's resemblance to her natural father had been unexpectedly unnerving. He wondered how he'd missed it before.

"Oh look," Susan said suddenly. "Everyone has turned out to meet us."

"Turned out for a peek at the prisoners, you mean. Captain Price no doubt sent someone ahead to tell them we were coming."

Susan patted her hair into place. "I imagine you're right. He's such a considerate man."

"Isn't he though?" Jared said with heavy sarcasm. "I think I'll see if I can pull out around the crowd."

"That's all right, darling. I really don't mind being jostled a bit for...Good heaven's Jared, look!"

Expecting some sort of hazard, Jared tightened his hands on the reins and turned his startled gaze to the left At first, he saw only the crowd who stood watching the prisoners with avid curiosity. Certainly nothing there for Susan to be alarmed about. Then he caught a flicker of blue out of the corner of his eye and turned slightly. The air seemed to freeze in his chest as he saw the familiar profile. Alaina! Not safely tucked away in Laramie City with Angel like she was supposed to be, but here in Fort Bridger where he had expressly forbidden her to go.

"Well, well, well," said Brandy from the back seat. "Looks like Alaina had a mind of her own, after all."

Susan was practically bristling with indignation. "That girl needs to be taught a lesson. Jared, where are you going? You can't leave me here alone… "

Jared ignored both of them as he tied the reins to the brake lever and jumped out of the wagon. He never took his eyes of his quarry as he covered the distance between them with long, angry strides. He didn't know which he wanted to do worse, take her over his knee and paddle her backside, or pull her into his arms and kiss her senseless.

Alaina was nearly all the way across the parade ground when an achingly familiar voice stopped her dead in her tracks.

"Alaina!"

She whirled around with her heart pounding in her throat, and unconcealed delight shining from her eyes. "Jared, you're well!"

"With no thanks to you," he grumbled. "I might have died for all you cared."

Alaina grinned as she drank in the sight of him. "From the chicken pox? I doubt it. Besides, I left you in capable hands," she said, stifling the urge to throw herself into his arms and smother his face with kisses.

"Susan will be the first to tell you she doesn't know one end of a sick room from the other. You said you were going to Laramie City," he said accusingly.

"No, I didn't. Susan did. It's not my fault you both

jumped to the wrong conclusion."

"You certainly didn't make any attempt to tell us any differently though, did you?"

She gave him an innocent look. "I didn't think you'd want me to contradict her. Anyway, neither of you really gave me a chance to say much of anything."

Jared made a disgusted noise. "As though that ever stopped you from making your opinion known. Frankly, I think you delight in flying in the face of authority."

"I think for myself and follow my conscience, that's all. I can't help it if you and I don't see things quite the same way."

"Don't see things the same way? Now that's an understatement if I ever heard —"

"Hello, princess," said a smooth male voice behind them.

"Uncle Cameron!" Alaina exclaimed spinning back around as Cameron swung down from his horse. "Oh, no, what happened to your eye?"

He touched his shiner. "Just a slight disagreement with a prisoner," he said with a shrug. "I saw you over here and thought I'd take a minute to say hello. I see you've met our government surveyor."

"Oh, Jared and I are old friends." Alaina could barely contain her laughter as Cameron Price dropped a fatherly kiss on her forehead. Either Jared had forgotten Cameron while he'd been reprimanding her, or he hadn't realized she'd made contact with her father yet. Whatever the reason, the look on his face was priceless. He reminded her of a beached carp. She smiled up at her father. "I see you had a successful trip."

"We did indeed. Thanks to a tip from your friend Jared, we caught them unaware and were able to take care of the problem before they gained any strength."

"Any idea what they were up to?" Jared asked with an effort.

Cameron shook his head. "Not really, but I do know it wasn't anything good. We found a Gatlin gun and enough rifles to start a small war."

Jared let out a low whistle. "Open revolt, do you think?"

"Either that or they were planning on going after a big gold shipment somewhere. We'll find out once we have a chance to interrogate the leaders." He focused on the parade ground behind them. "Here's Colonel Prescott now. He'll want a full report."

Alaina smiled up at him. "Oh that reminds me, Mrs. Prescott told me she's expecting you for dinner tonight. Everyone will want to hear how you captured the outlaws."

"Tell her I'll be delighted to come. Thanks for coming down to meet me. Sorry I can't escort you home."

"That's all right," Alaina said. "I'm sure Jared won't mind. I need to talk to him anyway."

Cameron remounted his horse and grinned down at Jared. "I don't suppose adding one more to your entourage will matter at that."

"No, probably not," Jared said with a long-suffering look. "But I do need to have word with Colonel Prescott first."

"I'll tell him." Cameron touched his fingers to the brim of his hat. "Good-bye, Princess. I'll see you later at dinner."

"Bye." Alaina waved enthusiastically as he rode away.

"I can't believe you let him kiss you like that," Jared muttered.

"What are you talking about?"

"I'm talking about the way he had his lips all over your face. Seems pretty odd from someone you just met."

"There's nothing the least bit *odd* about it. He's my father and proud of it."

"Sure, that's why you call him Uncle instead of Father."

"That was my idea," Alaina confessed. "It seemed the easiest thing to do. Cameron pointed out that we couldn't very well advertise the fact that he and my mother weren't married."

"And one lie is as good as another, right?"

"Oh, for pity's sake, Jared. I'm not going to stand here defending myself to you so you may just as well give it up and go talk to Colonel Prescott."

"I can't. He's still busy with your *father*."

"What do you need to talk to him about anyway?"

"Whiskey Jug got himself arrested."

"He what?"

Jared sighed. "It's a long story. Why don't you get Brandy to tell you?"

"Brandy!" Alaina said, brightening. "Where is she?"

"Over there in that wagon next the parade ground.
"

"Why didn't you say so?"

"I don't know," he said sarcastically. "I guess I was overwhelmed by your enthusiastic welcome."

"There she is. Oh, Jared, she has Bright Eyes with her!"

"Don't let me keep you," he called after her as she

hurried away.

Alaina grinned as she skirted the parade ground and headed toward the wagon. Jared wasn't exactly pleased with her, but apparently his week with the delectable Susan hadn't been a bed of roses either. Her grin broadened as she approached the wagon and saw Susan's expression. Her nemesis looked ready to chew nails. Better and better.

"Alaina," Brandy cried. "Am I ever glad to see you!"

"I'm glad to see you too," she said, climbing into the wagon. "Oh, Bright Eyes, I swear you've grown since I saw you last."

"How can you tell with her all swaddled up in the cradle board?" Brandy asked with a chuckle.

Alaina grinned. "I don't know, I just can. Hello, Susan. Nice to see you again."

"Yes, and such a surprise," Susan returned acidly.

"Strange, that's almost exactly what Jared said." Alaina exchanged a conspiratorial look with Brandy behind Susan's back. Then she sobered. "Jared also said Whiskey Jug had been arrested. What in the world happened?"

Brandy's smile disappeared as her face settled into a troubled frown. "It started several days after you left. Adam saw the army coming up the mountain just the way he and Jared had figured. He went out to lead them to the renegade camp. Adam was gone for several days, but I didn't worry because he said that might happen."

Alaina nodded. "He and Jared talked about that when he took us down off the mountain. They figured it was better if you didn't get involved. Not all soldiers are reliable."

"I wish they had told me that," Brandy said with

feeling. "If I had known it, none of this would have happened. Anyway, one morning five soldiers showed up at the cabin. I thought Adam had sent them so I let them in. Th...they grabbed at my clothes and tried to kiss me. Oh, Alaina it was horrible!"

"I can't believe any of my father's men would do such a thing," Susan said stiffly from the front seat. "You must have done something to provoke it."

"I provoked it by being a woman," Brandy retorted.

Alaina frowned. "Whiskey Jug arrived in the middle of it?"

"Yes, and he was magnificent! He put all five out of commission with hardly a scratch himself. Unfortunately, the rest of the army showed up about then, and Adam was arrested on the spot."

"Surely you explained what happened."

"I tried, but nobody paid any attention to me." Brandy sighed. "Adam was...a bit difficult."

"Oh, no. What did he do?"

"He tried to fight the whole troop. I don't even know how many he hit before they finally got him stopped. By then Captain Price was so angry, he didn't care what the truth was."

"Captain Price!" Alaina exclaimed, "but he's my...relative," she finished with a glance at Susan.

Brandy looked surprised. "He's the one?"

"How dare you claim any sort of relationship with Captain Price?" Susan asked, switching around and glaring at her indignantly.

"I'm not claiming anything," Alaina said calmly. "I'm just stating facts. If you have eyes in your head, you'll see I'm telling the truth. We look enough alike to be father and daughter."

"Of course," Brandy murmured. "That's why I kept thinking he looked familiar."

Susan turned back around and stared stonily ahead. "I won't believe it until he tells me himself!"

"Suit yourself," Alaina said with a shrug. It was just as well Susan had turned around. The sight of Brandy sticking her tongue out at her would probably have given her an apoplexy.

CHAPTER TWENTY-FIVE

"**D**id you find out where they're keeping Adam already?" Brandy asked anxiously.

Alaina nodded. "At the guardhouse. You can visit him now if you want to."

"Of course, I want to. It will only take me a minute to get Erika ready."

Alaina followed Brandy back inside the room at the Citizen Hotel. "You won't be able to stay more than a few minutes. I'm sorry, but it was the best I could do."

"I'm grateful for any time at all. How did you manage it? I mean we've been at Fort Bridger less than an hour."

"Through my friend Sean. He told the sergeant to give you some time with your husband."

Brandy glanced up from diapering Erika. "Sean?"

"He's a nice Lieutenant that I met on the train out here." She traced the edge of the bureau with her finger with feigned nonchalance. "Jared hated him on sight."

"Is he young and good-looking by any chance?"

Alaina grinned. "Very."

"Ah ha," Brandy said, as she scooped the baby up in her arms. "Jared's jealous!"

Alaina's grin faded. "Not hardly. You have to love someone to be jealous. All I've ever been to Jared Brady is an irritation."

"Are you sure about that?"

"Positive." Alaina followed Brandy out the door and

shut it behind them. "You came all the way from Hanna with him. Didn't he seem different to you?"

Brandy paused at the head of the stairs and looked back over her shoulder. "I guess he did at that. He was...I don't know...more authoritative I guess."

"That's the real Jared Brady," Alaina said gloomily.

"What's wrong with that? I was very impressed with the way he handled everything, including that fiancée of his." She gave Alaina a sidelong glance as she started down the stairs. "I must say she was something of a surprise. Neither you or Jared ever thought to mention her."

"I can hardly wait to see what happens when she finds out I've been staying with her parents."

Brandy blinked. "How did that happen?"

"They did it as a favor to my father," Alaina said. "I told them I'd met their daughter and how beautiful I thought she was."

"But you never thought to mention how well the two of you get along?"

Alaina grinned. "It must have slipped my mind." Her smile faded. "Anyway, Susan is a sore subject between Jared and I. He thinks she's the epitome of what every woman should be, while I think she's a self-centered, calculating little...you get the general idea."

"After spending most of the day with her, I tend to agree with you. I can't imagine what Jared sees in her."

"Jared Brady was born to wealth and position. There's a part of him that thrives on power. Susan's the perfect woman for *that* Jared."

"What about the other Jared; the one that's brave and honorable, the one that brought you and Erika safely across the mountain?" Brandy asked as they

walked out the door and into the street. "Are you going
to step aside and let her have him or are you going to
give her a run for her money?"

"I couldn't even begin to compete. She's wealthy
and sophisticated. I'll bet she'd even know how to set up
an elaborate dinner for all of his rich friends and
relatives."

"And you wouldn't?"

"I might be able to cook it, as long as I didn't have to
do anything too fancy. But there's no way I could be the
hostess." Alaina sighed. "And he's never relaxed around
me."

Brandy smiled slightly. "That isn't necessarily all
bad. Relaxed could develop into bored, you know. I
don't think you bore Jared."

"No, he's too busy being infuriated. He and I never
see eye to eye about anything."

"Still, he is jealous, and that's a good sign."

"It isn't jealousy, it's spite. He's done everything in
his power to keep me away from my father, and for no
good reason that I can see."

"Maybe he's afraid you'll get hurt," Brandy said
cautiously. "You really don't know Cameron Price very
well yet."

"I know him well enough to know that I like him,
and that he likes me. I can't figure out why Mama didn't
marry him."

"There's probably more to the story than you know.
At least you're getting to spend some time with him."

"And I'm sure Jared Brady will have something
rude to say about that."

"Why? I mean, he isn't a relative, and he's betrothed
to another woman. Seems to me it's none of his business

what you do."

"That's never stopped him," Alaina grumbled. "He's been even worse since he decided I should marry him."

Brandy stopped stalk still in the middle of the road and stared at her. "He asked you to marry him?"

"No, he told me I had to because...uh...because of the week we spent together on the mountain."

"You mean he feels obligated after he made love to you?" Brandy asked softly.

Alaina blushed to the roots of her hair and looked away. "Whatever gave you an idea like that?"

"Adam told me about how he found the two of you. Oh, don't look like that. I probably would have figured it out anyway. I've never seen a woman more in love in my life."

Alaina started to deny it, but the disbelieving look on Brandy's face stopped her midprotest. "All right, so I did fall for him. A fat lot of good it does me."

Brandy was pensive as they skirted the last set of white washed buildings and headed down the road toward the guardhouse. "He proposed, didn't he?"

"Yes, but only because he thought he had to." Alaina kicked at a stone. "I don't want him that way."

"Maybe he'd rather marry you than Susan. Any man with sense would."

Alaina sighed. "I'd never be sure it wasn't simply a matter of honor with him."

"What if he's in love with you too? You'd be throwing away his happiness as well as your own. Seems kind of unfair for you to make a decision without taking what he wants into account."

"I hadn't thought of that."

"There must be some way to find out what he really feels."

"You're right." Alaina looked thoughtful. "All I have to do is figure out how."

The opportunity to talk was lost as they climbed the two steps of the guardhouse, crossed a small porch and went inside. The sergeant in charge sat in a small office just inside the door. He looked up from a pile of papers on the desk. "Yes?"

"We're here to see my husband, Whiskey Jug Johnson," Brandy said.

The sergeant frowned. "Can't do that."

"But Lieutenant Kirkpatrick told me he'd set it up," Alaina protested.

"That he did," the sergeant said, scratching his nose. "But Johnson already has someone with him. Can't let you in until he leaves."

"I don't mind waiting," Brandy said with a stubborn tilt to her chin.

"This ain't a fittin' place for women and children."

"Would you rather we waited outside?" Brandy asked scornfully.

The sergeant shifted uncomfortably. "It might be best."

"Just be sure you let us know when his visitor leaves," Alaina said, as Brandy turned on her heel and walked out the door.

"Do think this is just a ploy to get rid of me?" Brandy asked when Alaina joined her.

"I don't know," Alaina said indignantly, "but if somebody doesn't come through that door in the next ten minutes, I'm going to go find my father. That sergeant will be sorry he was ever born!" She sat on the top step with a thump.

Brandy gave her a troubled look. "I don't know if that's such a good idea. Cameron Price would be more likely to lock Adam up and throw away the key than let me in to see him."

"Nonsense. My father would never—"

"Sergeant O'Rourke said you were out here," said a familiar voice behind them.

Alaina's heart jerked in her chest. Jared! She willed her heart to stop racing like a run-away locomotive. Why oh why did he make her feel this way?

"You were the one with Adam?" Brandy said in surprise.

"I had to find out exactly what happened." Jared sighed heavily. "If his attitude doesn't improve, I don't stand a chance in hell of getting him off. As if things weren't bad enough, I can't get Colonel Prescott to set the board of inquiry yet. The longer we wait the worse, Whiskey Jug gets. He's about as conciliatory as a piece of granite."

"And as friendly as a grizzly, I'll wager," Brandy said, handing Erika to Alaina. "Well, we'll just see about that!" She straightened her jacket and marched into the guardhouse, closing the door with a decisive snap behind her.

Alaina and Jared exchanged a look. "Whiskey Jug doesn't stand a chance," he said.

"I almost feel sorry for him."

"Don't," Jared said with feeling. "He deserves everything she says to him, and more. I was tempted to black both his eyes myself. Instead, I bit my tongue and walked away."

"Because he's your friend, or because you were

smart enough not to try anything that stupid?" Alaina asked, grinning up at him.

He returned her grin as he sat down beside her. "My mother didn't raise any fools. I hope Brandy can talk some sense into his head."

"If anyone can, it's Brandy. As far as he's concerned, the sun rises and sets over her."

Jared looked at the baby with a quizzical look on his face. "Is it just me or has Bright Eyes grown since we saw her last?"

Alaina giggled. "That's what I said too, but Brandy thought I was crazy."

"I don't know, she seems bigger to me." Jared touched the baby's cheek, and she responded by grabbing his finger.

Alaina chuckled. "Uh oh, you're stuck now. Once she grabs hold, you can't pry her off."

"I wasn't planning on going anywhere," he said with a slight smile. "You and I haven't had a chance to do more than exchange insults since I got here."

"That's about all we ever do anyway."

"I can remember a few times we found other things to do," he said softly.

Alaina's gaze flew to Jared's face. The warm expression she saw there made her mouth go dry and set her heart pounding. Maybe Brandy's speculation wasn't so ridiculous after all. Suddenly, she knew how to find out how he truly felt.

His gaze caressed her face. "It's time we got things settled between us, Alaina."

"I'm not pregnant," she blurted out. The words hung between them like invisible shards of glass. An endless moment passed and then another until Alaina blushed and looked away.

He pulled his finger from the baby's grasp, cupped Alaina's chin in his hand and gently turned her toward him again. "I don't believe you."

"Well, it's true." Alaina face turned an even darker hue. "My mother told me all about how a woman knows if she's pregnant," she lied, "and I'm not."

Jared looked doubtful. "You're certain?"

"Positive." She pulled her chin out of his hand and looked down at Bright Eyes in keen embarrassment. "You see, no permanent damage was done."

A feeling more like disappointment than relief swept Jared as he searched her averted profile. "What if you're mistaken?"

"Pretty hard to make a mistake like that." She forced a smile. "You're free to marry whomever you want."

"You're forgetting, I took your innocence."

"And *you're* forgetting, I was as much to blame for that as you were."

"Nevertheless, the decent thing to do..."

"Oh, for pity's sake, Jared. I release you from any obligation. Now forget about doing the decent thing and follow your heart."

A wave of irritation washed through him. She spoke as though his choice was an obvious one. How did she know what his heart wanted when he wasn't sure himself? When he'd first seen her today, he could have sworn he saw a flicker of something warm and welcoming in her eyes; something he responded to in spite of himself. If their meeting hadn't been so public, it would have started with a kiss. Now here she was, avoiding his gaze as though she found him repugnant.

Jared glanced away in frustration and saw a vaguely

familiar officer walking toward them. With a start, he recognized the young Lieutenant from the train. "What the devil is he doing here?" he growled.

Alaina looked up in surprise. "Oh, you mean Sean?" she asked as she caught sight of him. "He's stationed here. Isn't that a coincidence?"

"A damned unfortunate one."

Alaina ignored his remark. "I was surprised at first too, but it turned out to be a lucky chance. My father asked him to show me around while he was gone."

"I'll bet he's wondering how both Cameron and I can be your uncles," Jared said sarcastically.

"I told him I only said that because you made me mad." Alaina grinned. "He thought I was justified."

"I'll just bet he did," Jared muttered, but Alaina was too busy telling the handsome young Lieutenant how they had found Bright Eyes on the mountain to notice. From their animated conversation, it was obvious the two were fast friends, and that Kirkpatrick was responsible for Brandy's visit to the jail.

Jared watched them with a jaundiced eye while Alaina ignored him completely and lavished sparkling looks and bright smiles on Kirkpatrick. Apparently, she found the young Lieutenant more to her taste.

With a mumbled excuse about needing to unpack, Jared rose to his feet and left without a backward glance. He had better things to do than waste his time on an ungrateful child who had no more sense than to throw his marriage proposal back in his face.

Only Sean Kirkpatrick and Bright Eyes saw Alaina's wistful expression as Jared walked away.

Jared was in the middle of washing up in his room a scant fifteen minutes later when a knock sounded at the door. "It's getting so a man can't have five minutes to himself," he grumbled as he wiped the soap from his eyes. "Who is it?"

"Private Dobbs, Sir. I have a message for you."

Startled, Jared raised his head and stared at the door for a moment before reaching for a towel. "Just a minute." Private Dobbs was the striker assigned to serve Colonel Prescott and his family. Maybe the Colonel had relented and decided the date of Whiskey Jug's inquiry. Jared opened the door with a hopeful look on his face.

"I was told to wait for an answer," the young private said, handing Jared a folded square of pink velum.

Jared frowned as he looked down at the unfamiliar feminine script. This hadn't come from the Colonel, nor from Susan. That left only Mrs. Prescott. He unfolded the paper and read the few lines with a sinking feeling in his middle. Though it was written in the politest of terms, the note amounted to a summons from Susan's mother. She alluded to a matter of grave importance that needed to be discussed without delay.

He pulled his watch out of his pocket and made a face. If he were to arrive when Mrs. Prescott demanded, he would have to leave immediately. For a moment, Jared considered putting Susan's mother off until dinner, but then realized it might work against Whiskey Jug. Mrs. Prescott wielded a great deal of influence with her husband. "Tell Mrs. Prescott I'll be there as soon as I get dressed."

Jared shut the door behind the young private and dropped the note on the dresser with a sigh. Would this day never end? It had been one disaster after another. He took his time buttoning his shirt and putting on his coat before he headed out the door.

The walk to Prescott's imposing two-story house went by all too fast. Before he knew it, Private Dobbs was answering the door and showing him into the parlor. The scene that greeted him was enough to make the bravest man flinch. Susan sat on the settee, sobbing into a soggy handkerchief, and the glare Mrs. Prescott directed at him could have frosted a fire. Even more ominous was the embarrassed look of apology on Colonel Prescott's face. Jared wondered what in the world he'd done.

"Thank you for coming so quickly, Jared," Mrs. Prescott said imperiously. "Please have a seat."

Jared glanced at the chair she'd indicated. The straight-backed nightmare was the only unpadded chair in the room and set halfway between Susan and her father. Refusing to give the old harridan such a tactical advantage, he chose a velvet-covered armchair across the room. "You said we had a matter of some urgency to discuss?"

"I want to know exactly what your intentions are toward my daughter."

"Intentions?"

"Don't play the idiot with me," she snapped. "You've ruined an innocent young girl, and I want to know if you're going to make it right by marrying her."

Jared felt the color drain from his face. *How in God's name had the woman found out about Alaina?*

"Now Millicent," Colonel Prescott put in gently. "I wouldn't say Susan is ruined exactly, and he has promised to marry her after all."

"Of course, she's ruined. Any time a girl of her tender years is compromised there's no hope of a good marriage if it becomes known."

"I never touched your daughter," Jared protested as a sense of unreality washed over him.

"Perhaps not, but she touched you."

Jared's mind whirled in confusion. "Surely you don't think your daughter seduced me."

"Don't be ridiculous."

"Then what in the blue blazes are you talking about?"

Mrs. Prescott bristled. "I'll thank you to keep a civil tongue in your head, young man."

"For pity's sake, Millicent, just tell the boy what bee you've got in your bonnet," Colonel Prescott said in exasperation. "He hasn't got a clue. "

"I'm referring to the time my daughter spent taking care of you during your recent illness."

Jared frowned. "But you knew she was there. She sent you a wire." He glanced at Susan. "Didn't she?"

"Oh, Jared," Susan cried flying across the room and sinking gracefully at his feet. "It's all my fault. It never occurred to me to tell Mama that Phoebe wasn't with me."

"So?"

"So the two of you were unchaperoned for over a week," Mrs. Prescott said imperiously. "I shudder to think of the indelicate tasks she was called upon to perform."

"Nothing the least bit unlady-like I assure you," Jared said dryly. "She held my hand, brought me meals and made sure every square inch of my skin was covered with blankets at all times."

"The fact remains that she spent a week in your company without benefit of a chaperone. You can hardly expect me to overlook it."

Jared wondered why not. She certainly would if it suited her purpose to do so.

"I'm sorry, Jared," Susan said softly. "I didn't mean for this to happen."

Jared looked down at her soft gray eyes awash with tears and felt his anger melt away like snowflakes on a hot griddle. She was as much a victim here as he was. "It's all right, Susan, I never thought about us being alone either."

Colonel Prescott cleared his throat. "Since you're planning to get married anyhow, I can't see that it's much of a problem," he said gruffly. "Once the date is set I'm sure any gossip will die a natural death."

Against the genteel backdrop of her mother's opulent parlor, it was easy for Jared to remember why he wanted to marry Susan. Here, at least, was a woman who appreciated him. Susan Prescott was everything he'd ever wanted in a wife. She was well bred, educated, breathtakingly beautiful, and her melting looks were for him, not some trumped up young Lieutenant who had no more sense than to intrude on a private conversation.

"We were thinking about Christmas time," he heard himself saying. "But we can't be sure until we find out if my sister Shannon and her husband can be here."

He was rewarded by a dazzling smile from his fiancée. "Oh, Jared, I told Mama you'd come through."

"I think perhaps some sort of a party to officially announce your engagement would be appropriate," Mrs. Prescott said with satisfaction. "It won't be as lavish as if we were back home in New York, but I think we can manage something respectable."

Once that was done there would be no backing out for either of them without a major scandal. Though

Susan's distress had seemed completely real, Jared couldn't shake the feeling that he had just been very skillfully manipulated.

CHAPTER TWENTY-SIX

Alaina let herself in the front door of Colonel Prescott's house and moved quietly down the hallway. Thanks to Cameron Price, Mrs. Prescott had welcomed her with open arms and had been the most gracious of hostesses. She couldn't help wondering how long that would last now that Susan was home. There was no doubt in her mind that she would be leaving soon.

As she passed the open door of the parlor, she glanced inside and immediately wished she hadn't. Susan sat on the floor in a graceful pool of silken skirts, gazing adoringly up at the man seated on a chair next to her. Though his back was to the door, there was no mistaking who held her hand and touched the side of her face so lovingly. Jared.

"Ah, Alaina," said Mrs. Prescott. "Come join us. There's no need for you to skulk in the hall."

"I didn't want to intrude," she said, standing hesitantly in the doorway.

"Nonsense. You're like one of the family."

Susan gave her a welcoming smile. "Oh, yes, Elaine. Do come in. You'll want to hear our news."

"News?" Alaina asked cautiously. She had the sinking feeling she wasn't going to like it, whatever it was. Susan was too eager to share it with her.

"Jared and I just set the date for our wedding," Susan said brightly.

The floor rocked beneath Alaina's feet and the room

whirled about her. She willed herself to stay upright and managed a small, "Oh?" Jared must have come straight here the minute she'd told him she wasn't pregnant. So much for Brandy's theory.

"We won't be married until Christmas." Susan was saying. "But I do hope you'll still be here for the party."

"Party?" Alaina wondered if she was going to be sick right there on Mrs. Prescott's expensive floral rug.

Susan gave Jared a melting smile. "Yes, at the end of the week. Jared wanted to make our betrothal official before his survey crew has to go out for the summer."

"How nice. Congratulations to you both." Alaina felt as though her face was cracking as she forced her lips to smile. She knew Jared had turned to look at her, but she couldn't bring herself to meet his eyes. "I hope you'll forgive me, but I have to run. I have several errands I need to do before dinner."

Mrs. Prescott gave her a benevolent look. "That reminds me, Alaina dear. Dinner will be a bit more festive than usual tonight so I had Elise put a dinner dress in your room. I knew you'd want to help us celebrate."

"I...yes, of course. Thank you." With that, Alaina turned and fled before she disgraced herself. Blindly, she ran up the stairs and into the room she'd been given for the duration of her stay. She resisted the urge to slam the door knowing they'd hear it downstairs and realize she was upset. That was the last thing she wanted.

Alaina closed the door softly and leaned back against it, the tears she refused to shed lodged in her throat in a huge lump that threatened to choke her. For the first time, she realized in some secret part of her heart she hadn't really thought Jared would choose Susan over her. Once the engagement was officially announced, it could only be ended if Susan decided to call the wedding off. There was about as much chance of that as there was of man ever learning to fly.

Dispiritedly, Alaina wandered over to the bed and picked up the dress she was to wear to dinner. Her heart sank. It was obviously one of Susan's. The deep autumn gold would be beautiful with Susan's auburn hair, and she'd delight in the fussy ribbons and bows. It was just the sort of dress Alaina hated, with an over-abundance of lace flounces layered all the way down the skirt and a large tablier draped apron-like across the front. Worst of all, it was designed to wear with a large bustle, the kind Goudy's magazine referred to as a platter shelf. It was going to look stupid with none at all.

She dropped the garment back on the bed with a sigh. Susan had probably searched her wardrobe for the dress that would look the very worst on Alaina. Not that it mattered much anyway. Alaina didn't really feel much like going down to dinner. If it weren't for disappointing Cameron, she'd develop a splitting headache and stay in her room. Of course, playing right into Susan's hands like that went against the grain, too.

Alaina wandered over to the window and stared out over officer's row toward her father's quarters. Susan had clearly stacked the deck even though she already held the winning hand. Suddenly, Alaina couldn't stand the thought of her having it all her own way. With a determined air, she turned back to the dress.

After studying the garment with an objective eye, she decided it really wasn't as bad as she originally thought. Underneath all the ribbons and lace, the lines were good. There wasn't anything she could do about the color, but it might be quite flattering if she could tone it down a bit.

It only took a second to retrieve the small sewing kit Mrs. Prescott had loaned her to mend a rip in her coat and return to the bed. As she picked up the scissors, she felt a stab from her conscience. She really had no right to savage Susan's dress this way. On the other hand, Susan would have never lent it to her if she'd had any intention of ever wearing it again. According to Phoebe, the beautiful blue dressing gown had wound up in the trash. Alaina resolutely picked up one of the many ribbons that trailed down from the tablier. It would serve Susan right. After all, she was the one who had drawn the battle lines, and everyone knew all was fair in love and war.

Alaina's distress began to fade as she worked. Every snip of the scissors was like a poke directed at Susan and the malicious glee the other woman had taken in the little scene she had just enacted downstairs. By the time most of the ribbons lay on the bed in a golden heap, the lump in Alaina's throat had dissolved, and the anguish had faded to a dull throbbing ache in the vicinity of her heart. With luck, that would eventually disappear too.

She had been working nearly an hour when a knock sounded at the door. Alaina looked up in surprise. "Yes?"

"Madam sent me to...oh my," Elise, Mrs. Prescott's personal maid, stopped in the doorway and stared at the pile of discarded ribbon and lace on the bed.

Suddenly Alaina felt like a marauding vandal. "I'm too tall and thin for all of this," she stammered. "I'd look like a clown if I wore it the way it was."

"That is very true," Elise said in her flowing French accent. "But where did you get this dress?"

Alaina raised her brows in surprise. "Didn't you leave it?"

"No, no, no. The color is wrong for you. Someone has played a trick. Madam and I chose a rose-pink silk...." Elise broke off abruptly, as though she had said too much already. With a Gaelic shrug, she closed the door and dropped the bustle she was carrying on the bed. "But it is too late for that. You have already done much to fix the damage. Put it on, and we will see what else might be accomplished."

Alaina didn't know what to think. In the past, Elise had always appeared to look down her aristocratic nose at Alaina's limited wardrobe and common beginnings. Why would she suddenly want to help?

"Come now," Elise said, as Alaina hesitated. "I do not have all night. Madam wanted me to see if you needed anything before I went to Mademoiselle Susan's room, and that one will not be kept waiting for long. Stand up and I will undo your buttons."

Alaina did as she was instructed, but her curiosity got the best of her as Elise efficiently removed the blue dress and fastened the modest dimity bustle around her waist and hips. "I don't understand why you're doing this for me, Elise."

"I'm not doing it for you," Elise said, pulling the gold gown down over Alaina's head and doing up the long row of buttons on the back. "You are Madam Prescott's protégé. As such, your appearance reflects on me. I can not have you looking like something from a nightmare."

Alaina smoothed the fabric down over her hips. "I did the best I could with this. Do you think it will look all right?" she asked anxiously.

"Mademoiselle has an eye for fashion and a talent with the needle."

"Then you don't mind what I did to Susan's dress."

"Non, I don't mind." The shadow of a smile crossed her lips. "But I do not think Mademoiselle Susan will be pleased."

"Oh, dear." Alaina bit her lip. "I was sure she never wanted to wear it again."

Elise gave a little tinkling laugh. "That is not why she will be angry. You will be beautiful even though this is not a good dress for you. She sacrifices one of her favorites for nothing."

Alaina grinned in spite of herself. "Susan really liked this then?"

"Oh, assuredly." Elise picked up a packet of pins from the bureau. "Too much she loves ribbons and lace. Now we must fit this to your shape. You are taller, but not so large here and here," she said pointing to Alaina's bust and waist. "A square of that lace in the front will hide the fact that your breasts do not quite fill it."

Alaina grimaced. "Don't remind me."

"We are lucky this is a smaller bustle." Elise grabbed a handful of material at the back of the dress. "There will be enough extra here to make it cover your ankles."

With a dozen pins and a few deft tucks, Elise soon had the dress fitted to Alaina's trim figure as though it had been made for her. Then she stood back with one hand on her hip and the other tapping her lip as she gazed at Alaina critically.

"Is it going to be all right?" Alaina asked anxiously.

Elise was silent for a long moment then gave a decisive nod. "You have snatched victory from the jaws of defeat. In the rose silk you would have rivaled her for beauty. You will not outshine her now, but neither will you fade into the wallpaper."

"I don't know how to thank you," Alaina said with heartfelt gratitude as Elise unbuttoned the back of her dress.

"It amuses me to observe such skirmishes, but both sides must be even for the game to be interesting. Now I must go to Mademoiselle Susan and make sure she does not overdo her toilette in an effort to impress that oh so handsome kinsman of yours."

Alaina's eyes widened in surprise. "Cameron Price? Surely you're mistaken. Why, she's twenty years younger than he is and betrothed to another man, to boot."

"Perhaps you are right." Elise gave her an enigmatic smile as she walked to the door. "It is not something you have time to worry about, though. You will have to hurry to finish the sewing before dinner time."

Alaina nodded. "I know, but at least I have a chance of getting it done. I can't thank you enough."

Elise waved her thanks away. "It was nothing. Will you want me to do your hair?"

"Oh, no, I'm used to doing it myself. Mrs. Prescott and Susan will need you far worse than I."

"No doubt that is so. Bon Appetit."

Alaina smiled as the door shut. She wondered if Elise truly had been motivated out of a desire to make this evening's dinner party more interesting or if her stiff exterior hid a kind heart. Still, the thought of Susan being manipulated for someone else's entertainment was highly amusing.

It didn't take long to put the finishing touches on the dress, but it took considerable effort to put it on again and do the buttons up the back by herself. By the time she was finished, she felt as though someone had tried to rip her arms out of the sockets. No wonder Susan was almost helpless without her maid.

The sun had already set when Alaina sat down to do her hair. There wasn't time for an elaborate hairdo, not that she knew how to do anything like that anyway. She settled for pulling it all into a knot on top of her head and framing her face with small short curls. Then she stood up and looked at herself in the mirror.

The dress was nearly the same color as her hair and gave her skin a slightly sallow cast. Still, it was by far the most beautiful garment she'd ever worn and the overall effect was one of stylish elegance.

As she stood there staring at herself in the mirror, the door opened behind her, and Elise came in wearing a smug expression.

"Good, you have not left to go downstairs yet. Madam thought perhaps you might want to take an evening stroll with your uncle after dinner and would need a light wrap." She draped a long piece of blue silk around Alaina's shoulders, tucked it through the space at her elbows, and let the rest flow down over the skirt of the dress. "Ah, perfection," she said with a smile.

"It's beautiful." Alaina stared at her reflection in wonder. Suddenly, roses bloomed in her cheeks and her eyes were vivid blue. "I'm not sure I've ever seen blue and gold together, though," she said doubtfully.

"Not here in the territory, perhaps," Elise said with a dismissive shrug. "But it is all the rage in Europe. Now it is time for you to go downstairs. The guests are beginning to arrive. There are some who have to make an entrance, but you, I think, do not like to cause a fuss."

"No, I don't." With one last glance at her reflection, Alaina adjusted the blue wrap and turned toward the door. "Wish me luck Elise."

"You have no need of luck. Hold your head high and know you are beautiful. None will dispute it."

It was excellent advice, Alaina knew, and might mean the difference between surviving the evening and crumbling. Filled with brittle confidence, she left the safety of her room.

Mrs. Prescott and another vaguely familiar woman were standing in the hallway below as Alaina started down the stairs. She was half way down when Mrs. Prescott caught sight of her.

"Alaina, my dear, we were just talking about you," she said pleasantly. "You remember Sybil Goodrich don't you?"

"Yes, of course." Alaina smiled as she joined the other two. As soon as she heard the name she remembered. Sybil Goodrich was one of the first people Cameron had introduced her to. Her husband was a Major and second in command at the fort. "How are you?"

"I'm fine." She smiled warmly. "Actually, I'm feeling rather proud of myself."

"Oh?"

"You see, my husband is leaving on patrol in the morning, and I do get so lonely when he's gone. Millicent was telling me what a joy you've been, and it gave me a splendid idea." She fairly beamed at Alaina. "Why don't you come stay with me and keep me company while he's gone? Just think of the fun we'll have."

It was all Alaina could do to keep a straight face.

Mrs. Prescott hadn't wasted anytime figuring out a way to get rid of her unwanted guest, probably at her daughter's request. "I'm really very flattered," she murmured. "But Mrs. Prescott has been so kind. I hate to seem ungrateful..."

"Nonsense." Mrs. Prescott said with a deprecating wave of her hand. "We've selfishly kept you long enough. Don't give it another thought."

"All right then," Alaina said. "I'd be delighted to come stay with you, Mrs. Goodrich."

"Good, it's settled then." Mrs. Prescott smiled benevolently. "I'll have your things sent right over."

"You're too kind," Alaina murmured.

"Not at all. Having you around will do Sybil a world of good." She patted Alaina's cheek then hurried off to greet a new arrival.

Sybil clasped Alaina's hands enthusiastically. "I just know we're going to be great friends. Your uncle is a particular favorite of my husband's, you know."

"Then Uncle Cameron will be pleased."

"Oh, yes, I'm sure he will. He and my husband have served together several different places over the years, so we've known him simply forever." Sybil cocked her head to the side. "You know, it's strange. I don't remember him ever mentioning a niece."

"That's because discussing one's family is a fast way to become a dead bore," said a smooth masculine voice behind them.

"Good heaven's, Cameron, I didn't hear you come in," Sybil said a little breathlessly.

"I just got here. Hello my dear." He leaned down and gave Alaina a kiss on the cheek.

"Hello, Uncle Cameron."

Sybil frowned as she caught sight of Cameron's black eye in the dim light of the hall. "Good heaven's, Cameron, what happened to your eye?"

"It got in the way of a fist," he said with a shrug.

"I heard you captured a whole gang of outlaws."

"And some of them weren't too wild about the idea," he said, touching the bruised skin tenderly. "So tell me, what were you two lovely ladies chatting about when I so rudely interrupted you?"

"Your niece has just agreed to come stay with me for a while," Sybil said warmly. "I do hope you'll feel free to drop by for a visit any time."

"I'd enjoy that."

Alaina frowned slightly, aware of an undercurrent between the other two, one she didn't quite understand. Of course, they had been friends for a long time. The thought was lost in a swirl of apprehension as Sybil sailed through the parlor door and Cameron took his daughter's arm.

"Shall we go in?" he asked.

"I...I guess so."

"What's the matter?"

"I've never been to a formal dinner party before."

"Nervous?"

"A little. Silly, isn't it?"

"A woman is always nervous at her first dinner party." He patted her hand as he led her through the door. "Just relax, and you'll be fine."

"Good advice, but pretty hard to carry out."

Cameron leaned down. "Not if you imagine everyone else is walking around in their underwear," he whispered in her ear. "Just think of the armor Mrs. Prescott must be wearing under that dress."

Alaina's gaze flew to his face in shocked surprise. He gave her an audacious wink and nodded his head toward their hostess.

Mrs. Prescott's full figure was swathed in a tasteful gown of brocade and crepon. Alaina hadn't thought a thing about it before, but suddenly the rigid corseting and huge bustle were all she could see. She covered her mouth to stifle the giggles that erupted.

"There, you see? That's much better isn't it?"

"I'm not so sure. I'm afraid I'll be laughing at the wrong times all evening."

"All the better. Everyone will wonder what's so funny. Now, Alonna, take a deep breath and put a smile on that lovely face. We are about to take this room by storm." Cameron smiled urbanely as they walked through the door arm in arm.

Alaina's smile faltered slightly when he mispronounced her name, but she forced it back an instant later when she realized they were the center of attention. It was just as Cameron had predicted the night she arrived. Heads turned and admiring looks followed their progress.

As they stopped to chat with Colonel Prescott, a prickly feeling started between Alaina's shoulder blades, a kind of awareness that made her vaguely uncomfortable. It gradually increased until she could no longer stand it. Turning with seeming nonchalance, she scanned the room behind them.

A heartbeat later she found herself staring straight into the smoldering brown eyes and scowling countenance of Jared Brady.

CHAPTER TWENTY-SEVEN

Alaina couldn't tear her eyes away from Jared's accusing glare. Embarrassment and self-consciousness twisted through her, wreaking havoc on her poise and destroying her hard-won confidence.

Alaina wallowed in her inadequacies for a moment and then stiffened her spine. How dare he judge her and find her lacking? Determined to put him in his place, she concentrated on imagining him in his underwear as she had everyone else.

It was a big mistake. The picture that popped into her head was anything but laughable. She didn't need to guess what Jared looked like without his clothes. She knew. The memory of her hands wandering all over that beautifully muscled body sent a rush of warmth through her. As the image of their bodies intertwined darted through her mind, Alaina felt her face go hot, and she turned away in mortification.

For the next few minutes she pretended to be engrossed in Cameron's conversation with the Colonel, but her entire concentration focused on the man behind her, in spite of her wishes to the contrary.

Finally, she couldn't stand it any longer and decided to sneak a peek. Surely, his attention would be elsewhere by now so she could relax. Unobtrusively, Alaina looked back over her shoulder.

He hadn't moved; not one inch. Nor had the scowl on his face changed. If anything, it was more pronounced. This time Alaina felt a flash of irritation. What in the world had she done now? Not that he had any right to stand there and glare at her like that anyway.

Impulsively, Alaina wrinkled her nose at him and crossed her eyes.

Since all the other guests were otherwise occupied, Jared was the only one to see Alaina's grimace. For an instant, he was startled, then a reluctant grin tugged at the corner of his mouth. *Little wretch.* Only Alaina would do something so outrageous in polite company. But then, she hadn't been taught the social intricacies from the cradle the way his sisters had. Even though she looked every inch the society debutante tonight, she was still very much the little country girl.

Though Jared was completely unmoved by the stunning picture Cameron and Alaina made together, he couldn't deny the joy that hit him when he looked up and saw her standing in the doorway. Nor could he explain the emotion that ripped through him when she laughed with real pleasure at something Cameron whispered in her ear. It felt a lot like jealousy, but that was absurd. The problem was, it rankled to see her in the clutches of the biggest womanizer at the fort, even if he was her father. It was natural to feel that way; a lot had passed between them. Of course, she'd made it plain it meant nothing to her.

A movement at the door drew his attention. Susan paused in the doorway, as though surprised that everyone was there before her. She made a show of searching the room, ostensibly looking for someone. Every man there preened a little under her regard until she finally located Jared. With a smile calculated to break the heart of every male it wasn't aimed at, she started toward him. It was all so predictable it was almost humorous.

She was a vision in green satin, floating across the floor with the grace and beauty of a queen. Instead of the flash of pride he usually felt, Jared found himself wondering if he had a lifetime of such entrances to look forward to.

"Hello, darling," she said, gliding up to him. "I'm sorry I'm late."

Jared knew he was supposed to make some inane remark at this point, assuring her that he'd be willing to wait much longer, but suddenly he didn't want to play the game. "I thought that was the point," he said.

Susan's smile faltered for an instant then came back as brightly as ever. "Of course, it is," she said archly, "but you're supposed to pretend you don't know it. Well, what do you think? Was I worth waiting for?"

"Of course, you're stunning as always."

"You don't sound very pleased about it."

Jared sighed. "I'm sorry, Susan. I'm afraid I'm not very good company tonight. Too much on my mind, I guess."

She was instantly concerned. "What's wrong?"

"I just wish your father would set a date for the board of inquiry for Whiskey Jug Johnson."

"Well, why don't we go talk to him right now?"

Jared looked at her in astonishment. "You don't mind mixing business with pleasure?"

"If I'm going to be your wife, I'll have to get used to it. Besides, I know how important your friend is to you."

Jared was pleasantly surprised as she took his arm and led him across the room to her father. This was a side of Susan he'd never seen. Maybe he'd misjudged her.

By the time they reached Susan's father, Major Goodrich and Sybil had already joined the group and were involved in animated conversation. Cameron Price broke off in the middle of a sentence when they arrived.

"Ah, Miss Prescott," Cameron said, gallantly kissing Susan's hand. "You're so lovely you put the rest of us to shame."

"Why thank you, Captain Price, I...Oh!" Susan said in shock as she finally got her first good look at Alaina.

Alaina smiled sweetly. "I never thanked you for the loan of this dress."

"What did you do to it?" Susan hissed.

"Oh, just a few little alterations here and there. I hope you don't mind."

Susan suddenly remembered they were not alone and pasted a smile on her face. "I must say that's a very interesting color combination. I don't believe I've seen blue and gold together before."

"It's all the rage in Europe."

"Is it? How...surprising." Susan pulled herself together with an effort and very pointedly turned her attention to Cameron. "I'm so glad you could make it for dinner tonight, Captain. I'm just dying to hear how you captured all those outlaws."

"All in good time, my dear," said Colonel Prescott. "I think your mother wants us all to go in to dinner now."

With murmurs of assent, all the guests moved into the dining room. Jared was seated between Susan and Sybil Goodrich, with Alaina and Cameron directly across the table. It could prove to be a very long evening.

"I just can't get over how much you two look alike," Sybil said to Cameron as Private Dobbs brought in the first course. "It's really quite amazing. Are you her mother's brother or her father's?"

"We're related through her father," Cameron said smoothly, "though I was quite close to her mother at one time, too."

"You and your brother must be dead ringers for each other," said Major Goodrich.

"Practically twins," Jared murmured. "It's nearly impossible to tell them apart." Alaina glared at him across the table, but Cameron appeared completely unconcerned by the gibe. "As a matter of fact, we do. Of course, almost everyone in my family has hair and eyes like mine."

"Well, Alaina could easily pass as your daughter," Colonel Prescott put in. "In fact, if I didn't know better, I'd think that's exactly what she was."

Cameron looked at Alaina and smiled. "I couldn't be any prouder of her if she were my own daughter. I just wish we'd known each other sooner."

Jared gritted his teeth as Alaina blushed and gave her father a tremulous smile. It was enough to make a man sick.

"I want to hear about your latest adventure," Susan said with an avid expression on her face. It didn't take a genius to figure out why the conversation wasn't to her taste. "Do tell us how you captured the renegades."

"I'm not sure it's a suitable dinner conversation."

Mrs. Prescott gave a dismissive wave of her hand. "Perhaps not, but I'm sure all of us are dying to know what happened."

The other guests were quick to add their entreaties,

and Cameron was soon persuaded to tell his tale. Jared listened with a cynical ear. He knew it had taken a great deal of the amazing strategy Cameron Price was well known for, but he doubted the man had been quite as heroic as the tale made him appear. He was a good story teller; Jared had to give him that. His audience was on the edge of their chairs, barely aware of the courses that came and went or the food they consumed.

Cameron had talked his way clear through two courses, when Jared noticed Alaina watching her father with a strange expression. A touch of doubt, perhaps even a bit of disappointment shadowed her face. Maybe she was finally starting to see Cameron Price for what he was. Instead of gloating and giving her a richly deserved 'I told you so,' Jared found himself wanting to take her in his arms and soothe away her disillusionment.

"But, Captain Price," Sybil was saying. "You still haven't told us how you got your black eye."

"From tangling with a man the size of a mountain," he told her ruefully. "He was mowing my men down like a logger felling trees. He got one good punch in on me before I took him out."

"You hit him in the jaw with a rifle butt," Alaina said accusingly.

Cameron shrugged. "It was necessary. The man went berserk for no reason."

"I wouldn't call his wife being raped by five soldiers no reason."

Mrs. Prescott stiffened. "Really, Alaina. There's no need to use such vulgar language."

"I'm sorry, but I don't know what else to call it."

"I think you've been misinformed, my dear," Cameron said condescendingly. "No one was raped."

"Only because Whiskey Jug Johnson got there first and stopped them. I saw his wife's bruises myself."

"If she was injured, it was because they were involved with the outlaws, and she resisted arrest."

Alaina's mouth dropped open. "Involved with the outlaws! That's an outright lie and you know it."

"I know nothing of the sort. It seems rather odd she and her husband had no trouble with the renegades, if you ask me."

"The outlaws didn't know they were there," Alaina said.

"Oh, come now, Alaina. How could they not know?"

Jared glanced at the faces around the table. Susan had the self-satisfied look of a cat who had just finished a bowl of cream. The rest were all staring at Alaina with the same indignant expression. The little fool didn't even realize she was committing social suicide by challenging their hero.

"Because Whiskey Jug made sure they didn't know his cabin was there," Jared heard himself say. He was aware of six pairs of accusing eyes turning from Alaina to him. "He knows that mountain like the back of his hand; he's spent his life up there. If he doesn't want to be found, he won't be."

"I found him," Cameron pointed out.

"He found you, Captain. We'd discussed it at length the week before. Whiskey Jug figured on keeping track of the outlaws until you arrived so there'd be less chance of them taking you by surprise. If he'd been in cahoots with the outlaws, he could have set up an ambush anywhere along the trail, and you wouldn't have suspected a thing until it was too late."

Alaina nodded. "Whiskey Jug Johnson knew Jared was going to send a message to the fort when he took us down to Saratoga. If he hadn't rescued us, Jared and I would have wandered around until either the renegades caught us or we starved to death. Either way, we wouldn't have survived to tell the army the outlaws were up there."

Though he had said nothing, Colonel Prescott had been following the conversation closely. "Did you know about any of this, Captain Price?" he asked finally.

"Only that Brady had seen what looked like a small army assembling up in the Snowys."

"Perhaps we'd better set Whiskey Jug Johnson's board of inquiry for tomorrow and get this all straightened out. I'll expect everyone concerned in my office at ten o'clock sharp."

"Thank you, Colonel," Jared said with heart-felt relief.

"I do believe it's time to make your announcement now, dear," Mrs. Prescott said with a meaningful look at Susan.

Jared had the impression that Colonel Prescott rose to his feet a trifle reluctantly, but he smiled benignly at his guests. "Mrs. Prescott and I wanted all of you to be the first to share our happy news. Jared Brady has asked our daughter to be his wife and Susan has accepted him."

A delighted babble of excited felicitations broke out as everyone hastened to congratulate the happy couple. In the midst of it all, Jared happened to glance across the table. Alaina appeared anything but happy as she stared at her plate. Cameron seemed to be taking her to task, probably for challenging him in front of everyone.

Jared's stomach twisted painfully as she looked up and gave him a tremulous smile before turning to Cameron and murmuring something. Whatever she said must have placated her father because he patted her hand and smiled approvingly.

As though he felt Jared's gaze upon him, Cameron sent a blinding smile across the table to Susan. "I'd like to propose a toast," he said, raising his glass. "To our own sweet little Susan and the luckiest man at Fort Bridger. May you have a long and happy life together."

Amid the clinking glasses, Jared was aware of only two things, Susan's simpering acceptance of Cameron's compliment for both of them and the bleak expression on Alaina's face.

The rest of the evening passed with a carnival air, but it seemed endless to Jared. At last, Major Goodrich pleaded an early departure in the morning, and left with his wife. Sybil assured Alaina the guest room would be ready when she arrived if Cameron wouldn't mind escorting her. Jared was relieved when the party finally ended.

During the flurry of good-byes, Jared slipped out the door, down the hall and outside. He paused for a moment and breathed deeply of the clear night air. It felt wonderful after the cloying atmosphere of the dinner party. He had just started across the porch when the door opened behind him.

"Jared, wait."

Jared swallowed a sigh and turned back to his fiancée. "What is it Susan?"

She gave him a hurt look. "You weren't going to leave without saying good night, were you?"

"It's been a long day, Susan, and you were busy. If

326

you'll remember I just spent the last week in bed with the chicken pox."

"I'm sorry, Jared," she said, stepping closer and rubbing the bare skin of her upper arms. "It's just that we haven't had any time together today."

He gazed down at her for a moment, then gave her a rueful smile. "I guess I should be apologizing to you. Can you forgive me?"

"I don't know," she said, playing with the button in the middle of his shirt. "We're officially betrothed, and you haven't even kissed me yet."

Jared put his finger under her chin and tipped her face up. "That's easily taken care of," he murmured, lowering his mouth to hers. Her lips were soft and she tasted faintly of the wine they'd had for dinner; not an unpleasant combination. A small sound came from her throat as she put her arms around his neck and melted against him. Jared had just teased her lips apart when the door opened and Cameron walked out with Alaina on his arm.

"Oh!" The shock in Alaina's voice was unmistakable and worked on Jared like a blast of cold air. He pulled back with a jerk.

"There you are, Brady," Cameron said, as smoothly as though couples kissing in the shadows were an everyday occurrence. "Colonel Prescott said to tell you he wants a word with you."

"Tonight?"

Cameron was clearly amused. "If possible, however I don't suppose he'll mind if you finish up here first. Come along, Princess, we're obviously in the way."

Jared ground his teeth as they crossed the porch and walked down the stairs. For some reason, he was more embarrassed to be caught kissing his fiancée than he had been when Whiskey Jug had discovered him naked in Alaina's arms. "We'd better go in, Susan," he said.

"Oh, just a few more minutes."

"I don't want to keep your father waiting. He probably wants to talk about tomorrow's board of inquiry."

"What about me?" she said, pouting.

"It's been a long day for you too. I wouldn't want you to have dark circles under your eyes from lack of sleep."

Her fingers flew to her face as though she could already feel the ravages of a sleepless night. "Oh, goodness. Do you think I might?"

"Not if you go to bed right now." He kissed her forehead. "Don't worry, we're going to have plenty of time together."

Susan didn't argue as he led her back inside. In fact, she seemed reluctant to let him see her face in the faint light of the hall as she bid him good night and hurried upstairs. Jared watched her go with a slight smile on his face. Susan's predictability was refreshing after never knowing what Alaina was going to do from one minute till the next.

Private Dobbs appeared from the back of the house. "Colonel Prescott is in the library, Mr. Brady."

"Thank you. I'll show myself in."

Colonel Prescott greeted him with an affable smile. "I'm glad to see I caught you before you left. Join me in a brandy?"

"All right," Jared said cautiously. He seated himself on one of the overstuffed leather chairs as his host poured the drinks. "I assume you wished to talk to me about Whiskey Jug Johnson's Board of Inquiry?"

The Colonel handed him a glass. "In a manner of speaking. Actually, I'm more interested in your part in all this."

"What do you mean?"

Prescott opened a humidor on the desk. "Cigar?"

"No, thanks, I don't smoke."

"Pity. A brandy and a good cigar are two of the great pleasures in life." He frowned as he selected a cigar for himself. "How is it you came to be up in the Snowy Range this time of year with a young woman like Alaina?"

"It's a long story."

"I thought it might be." Prescott lit his cigar and settled into the other chair. "My wife says curiosity is my besetting sin, and I find myself most curious about this."

Jared thought longingly of his bed. "I suppose I should start at the beginning. You see, Alaina is my sister's god daughter." For the next three quarters of an hour Jared talked. Colonel Prescott asked a question now and then, but for the most part he sat quietly and listened. His glass was empty and his cigar reduced to ashes by the time Jared was finished.

"It sounds like the two of you had quite an adventure," he observed.

"I guess you could call it that. Frankly, it was an experience I don't care to repeat."

"No, I suppose not." Prescott got up and walked to the sideboard. "More brandy?" he asked, pouring himself another glass.

"I think I'll pass, if you don't mind. I'm really rather tired."

"Of course. I won't keep you from your bed any

longer. I appreciate the insight you've given me into the Whiskey Jug Johnson situation. Captain Price is a good man but tends to be somewhat impetuous. It looks like this time he jumped to the wrong conclusion entirely."

"I'm relieved to hear you say that, sir." Jared put his empty glass on the table and rose to his feet. "Whiskey Jug Johnson has always been a friend to the army. I'd hate to see him punished for that. Well, I'm for bed. Thanks for the drink. "

Colonel Prescott gave him a troubled glance. "It would seem to me that my daughter was not the only one you compromised."

Jared felt himself darken. "No, sir, she wasn't."

"And what do you intend to do about Alaina? You can't very well marry both of them."

"I'm aware of my responsibility. I told Alaina that if our escapade became known, her reputation wouldn't be worth a plug nickel," Jared said stiffly, "However, she refused to consider marriage. She insisted I should follow my heart."

"I see. She seems a most unselfish young lady."

"She's obstinate as a pig."

Colonel Prescott chuckled. "And fully as impetuous as her uncle. I doubt marriage to her would be restful."

"Not hardly. I find myself feeling sorry for her husband."

"Perhaps." The Colonel stared pensively down into his glass. "You know, my father told me a man should always look at a woman's mother before he considers marriage. I found that to be sound advice."

"Why is that?"

Colonel Prescott smiled. "Because every woman turns into her mother eventually."

"That's an interesting theory." In his mind's eye, he saw Milicent Prescott, a leader of whatever society she was in, beautiful and sophisticated. On the other side was the image of Becky Ellinson surrounded by children and smiling up at the man she loved with her whole heart and soul.

"I suspect Alaina's right. It is best if you follow your heart."

"I plan to." But Jared couldn't help wondering just what it was that his heart wanted him to do.

CHAPTER TWENTY-EIGHT

"I wonder how long a board of inquiry takes," Alaina said, settling herself on the steps outside the fort headquarters.

Brandy glared at the door. "I don't know, but I can't believe they threw us out just because we're women!"

"I don't suppose they would have listened to us anyway. No one seemed inclined to believe me last night at dinner when I told them what really happened to you. In fact, Cameron took me to task for it."

Brandy adjusted Erika in her arms and sat down. "For telling the truth?"

"I don't think he cared much one way or the other about that. He was upset because I dared to contradict him in front of everyone. I apologized and promised faithfully never to do it again. At least Colonel Prescott listened to Jared. I think things might go all right. Whiskey Jug could get off after all."

"If the man will keep a civil tongue in his head." Brandy sighed. "I threatened him within an inch of his life yesterday, but I'm not sure it did much good."

"Men!"

Brandy grinned. "Isn't that the truth? Speaking of which, how did things go with Jared last night?"

"For Susan, things went just great," she said gloomily. "They announced their engagement last night."

"But he's in love with you!"

"Wishful thinking, Brandy. After I released him from all obligation, he went straight to her. Susan was all a flutter when I got home yesterday afternoon."

"I wouldn't trust that viper as far as I could throw her. Maybe she lied."

"Jared was right there with her. Besides, you should have seen the way he was kissing her last night."

Brandy was shocked. "He kissed her right in front of everybody?"

"No, it was out on the porch after dinner, but they had to have known people were going to come outside." Alaina propped her elbow on her knee and leaned her chin against her hand. "As far as he's concerned, I was just an irritation that he finally got rid of."

"What about what happened between you?"

"What about it? It obviously meant less than nothing to Jared. All he cared about was that I wasn't pregnant. As soon as I told him that, he was off to Susan like a shot."

Brandy frowned. "Are you sure you aren't?"

"No."

"Then why on earth did you tell him that?"

"It seemed like a good way to be sure if I was really his choice," Alaina said unhappily. "And now I know."

"But what if you find out you're pregnant?"

"I don't know. I guess I'll worry about that if it happens."

"Isn't that kind of asking for trouble?"

Alaina shrugged. "The way I figure it, either I am or I'm not. If I'm not, I'd spend all that time worrying for nothing. Even if I am, all the worry in the world wouldn't change it. Besides, Jared's already chosen Susan. I told you before, I don't want him if he has to be forced to marry me."

Brandy frowned. "I hope you don't live to regret this."

"I rarely regret anything," Alaina said with a grin. "My mother says it's one of my worst faults. So, do you want to hear about the party last night or not?"

"Of course, I do. Somehow I can't believe you let it all go Susan's way."

"No not exactly." Alaina grinned mischievously. "You see there was this dress..."

The time passed quickly as Alaina warmed to her story. They giggled together over Susan's dramatic entrance, her reaction to the dress, and even Mrs. Prescott's ingenious method of getting Alaina out of her house. They were still discussing Sybil's surprising offer when the door opened behind them and heavy booted footsteps sounded on the wooden porch. As one, they twisted around to see who it was.

Alaina's heart sank when she saw Jared and Cameron. Where was Whiskey Jug?

Brandy was already on her feet with Erika held close to her breast as though to protect her when the two men reached them. "Adam?" she asked with a quaver in her voice.

"Has been completely exonerated of all charges," Jared told her with a smile. "Well, except for assault on U.S. army personnel, and the Colonel decided he's already served enough time for that."

"Then where is he?"

"Colonel Prescott kept him a few minutes. I don't know why, but I'm sure it's nothing to worry about."

"It seems I owe you an apology, Mrs....uh .... Johnson," Cameron said stiffly. "An officer has to make snap decisions based on the information at hand. I reacted to the situation as I saw it. Seems I was mistaken about what had come before, and I'm sorry."

"I tried to tell you what your men did but you wouldn't listen."

He shifted uncomfortably. "Yes, well, you have to remember I didn't know a thing about you, and they were my men. At any rate, I apologize, and I hope you and your husband will be my guests at dinner tonight."

"I don't know..."

At that moment, the door burst open and Whiskey Jug crossed the porch with three long strides. Without so much as a glance at anyone else he swept Brandy into his arms and kissed her soundly. He didn't come up for air until Erika made her presence known with an irritated squawk.

"Adam!" Brandy said a little breathlessly as he set her back on her feet. "For heaven's sake try for a little decorum."

"I've been as meek as a lamb for the last two and a half hours," he said, ignoring Jared who went into a fit of coughing. "And I haven't been able to kiss my wife outside of jail in too damn long!"

"What did the Colonel have to say?" Jared asked.

"Not much. He just wanted to tell me how much the army has appreciated all my help in the past and hopes I'll continue to do so."

Brandy winced. "Oh, no, please tell me you didn't hit him."

"Hell no! What would I go and do a fool thing like that for?"

Brandy rolled her eyes. "You tell me."

"You get the damnedest notions sometimes,"

Whiskey Jug said, with a shake of his head. "I'd best get you back up the mountain again before you get into trouble."

Since he leaned down and kissed her even more fervently than before, Brandy didn't have a chance to utter the protest he obviously knew was coming. By the time he was finished, her bemused expression clearly indicated she'd forgotten what she'd intended to say.

"Let's go home, sweetling," he murmured.

She blinked in confusion. "Now?"

"Sure, why not?" He stepped to the edge of the covered porch and peered up at the sun. "It's not even noon yet. We ought to be able to get to Evanston in time to catch the train east and be in Hanna by dark." He frowned suddenly and glanced over his shoulder at Brandy. "Unless you want to stay."

"No, I'm quite ready to leave, thank you." Brandy turned to Cameron with a smile that almost managed to look regretful. "As you can see, Captain Price, we won't be able to join you this evening."

Whiskey Jug's frown turned to a glare. "Join him for what?"

"Captain Price invited us to dinner this evening. I was about to give him our regrets when you arrived."

Cameron seemed unperturbed by Whiskey Jug's glowering countenance. "It's my way of apologizing for our little misunderstanding. Besides, I thought the ladies might enjoy an evening together before you leave."

Whiskey Jug snorted. "A misunderstanding, was it?"

"Now, Adam, he's apologized, after all," Brandy began, her voice tinged with alarm. "There's no need to—"

"I accept your apology, Price," Whiskey Jug said, ignoring his wife, "and thank you for your invitation, but we've been gone too long as it is. We have to be getting home."

"Maybe some other time," Cameron murmured.

"Say, Jared, do you think you could get us to Evanston in time to catch the train to Hanna?" Whiskey Jug asked.

"I think I can manage it without too much difficulty. I'll see if I can borrow a wagon."

"Oh, Alaina, why don't you come with us," Brandy said. "It may be the last chance we'll get to see each other."

"Well..." Alaina wasn't certain whether the time with Brandy would be worth the ride back alone with Jared. Then she glanced at Brandy's hopeful expression and the baby in her arms. Of course it was.

"Actually, I think it's a good idea," Cameron put in.

Alaina stared at him in surprise. "You do?"

"With Susan Prescott's party coming up, I'm sure you'll be wanting to do some shopping. The sutler here at the fort doesn't carry much in the way of female fripperies."

"But I—"

Cameron glanced at Jared. "How long before you leave?"

"I don't know. At least half an hour, I'd think."

"She'll be there." Cameron offered his arm to his daughter. "Come along, Alonna. Let's go find Sybil and see if she can go with you."

"It's pronounced Alaina," she said in exasperation.

"Oh, right. I've never figured out why your mother gave you such an outlandish name anyway."

"It's my grandmother's name," Alaina said stiffly.

"Ah. Well, that explains it, I guess," he said, dismissing the entire subject with a wave of his hand. "Now about this shopping trip. I'd take you myself but Colonel Prescott wants to start questioning the prisoners this afternoon. We'll be tied up for several days with that."

"I don't need to go shopping."

"Of course you do." He gave her a shrewd look. "I'll wager that dress last night wasn't yours."

"No, it was one of Susan's, but..."

"I knew it," he said with satisfaction. "The color was all wrong."

"What does that have to do with me going to Evanston?"

"Nothing really, except it made me realize you don't have any clothes except for that," he said, nodding at her blue dress. "They won't have anything fancy enough for the party, of course, but Sybil can help us there. You can probably find a couple of nice dresses for every day."

"I don't have much money and what I do have, I'll need to get home."

"What are fathers for if not to give their daughters pin money," Cameron said pulling a roll of bills out of his pocket. He peeled off several and folded them into her hand. "That should be enough to get what you need. No arguments," he said when she started to protest. "I want to show the world what a beautiful daughter I have. I can't do that unless you're well dressed. Besides, you don't want your beaus to lose interest."

Alaina gave him a blank look. "I don't have any beaus."

"Of course you do," Cameron said with pride. "I've

had any number of young fellows come to me asking if they could court you. I warned most of them off."

"Without asking me?" Alaina asked, bristling.

He shrugged. "They were enlisted men. I gave young Kirkpatrick my permission, of course, and Lieutenant Jenkins."

"What if I fell in love with an enlisted man?"

"Only officers will do for my daughter. Oh good, here's Sybil."

Alaina frowned as Cameron hailed Sybil, and they continued down the street toward her. She wondered suddenly if his interest in her had more to do with the power he could wield over her potential beaus, and how well she complimented his masculine good looks than any real personal feeling he had for her. The next instant, she rejected the thought as unworthy. He'd been thrown into fatherhood with no warning. If he fumbled occasionally, it was because he didn't know any better.

Much to Cameron's disappointment, Sybil wasn't able to accompany his daughter, but he still insisted the trip was necessary. When Alaina pointed out she'd be coming back unchaperoned in late afternoon with Jared, he just laughed.

"As I recall, you spent a great deal of time alone with him on the mountain. Surely you don't think he'd try to take advantage of you."

"No, it's just that we fight all the time."

Cameron chuckled. "Then you're perfectly safe with him, wouldn't you say, Sybil?"

"Completely. Besides, Jared Brady is a gentleman. Let's take a quick peek at my ball gowns to see if one is suitable for you to wear to Susan's party. You may need to buy some ribbon or lace."

"I don't want to go to Susan's party. Besides, if I'm going to Evanston, we don't have time for all this. Jared said we'd be leaving in half an hour."

"Nonsense. They'll wait for you. What do you think Cameron? Should we...?"

So it was that Alaina arrived at the Citizen Hotel fifteen minutes late with a long list of things to buy and a short temper. She was just in time to hear Jared threaten to leave without her if she didn't show up soon.

"No such luck," she snapped. "You're stuck with me whether you like it or not."

Jared rolled his eyes. "Oh great, you're in one of your moods. This trip should be fun."

Alaina ignored him as Cameron helped her into the back of the surrey, and she settled herself next to Brandy and Erika. "Sorry, I'm late, Brandy. I hope we can still make it in time."

"I don't think it will be a problem," Whiskey Jug said from the front seat. "We have plenty of time. Besides, I have a feeling Jared isn't one to let the grass grow under his wheels."

Jared didn't bother to answer as he slapped the reins on the backs of the team and the carriage started with a jerk. Alaina stared at his unyielding profile for a moment then turned to Brandy with a determined air. So what if Jared Brady had his nose out of joint. As she reached out to take Erika, she vowed to have a good time today even if it killed her. She'd worry about the trip back with his royal grumpiness when the time came.

CHAPTER TWENTY-NINE

"Oh, Brandy, I'm going to miss you so much," Alaina said, tearfully hugging her friend as the train pulled into the station.

"I know, I'll miss you too, but Adam's right, we've been gone too long. Our horses are safe in the Hanna livery stable, but it will be a miracle if bears or wolves or even Indians haven't found the goat by now."

"Oh dear, I hadn't thought of that."

"A goat is a small price to pay to have Adam back and his name cleared. Uh-oh," she murmured. "What's the matter now?"

"Don't be a jackass," Jared was saying. "Take the money and be done with it."

Whiskey Jug glared down at his friend belligerently. "I don't take charity from any man."

"And I keep telling you it isn't charity. It's a loan. You'll play hell getting home with no money in your pocket."

"With the price of pelts, I'd never be able to pay it back."

"I'm in no hurry. For God sake, Whiskey Jug, I won't even miss it."

"Jared, how would you like a buffalo skin?" Brandy asked joining the two men.

"A buffalo skin?"

"All tanned out and in prime condition. It's the softest, warmest blanket you'll ever find."

"Brandy—" Whiskey Jug said warningly.

"Adam, I love you dearly, but you haven't got the business sense of a mosquito. Hush now, and let me take care of this." Brandy patted his cheek then looked up at Jared expectantly. "What do you say, Jared? You and your surveying crew will be coming back to the mountains soon. Nights get pretty cold up there."

"Hmm, come to think of it, I do need a good bedroll. How much do you want for it?"

She took the money from his hand. "This ought to just about cover it."

"You know." He pulled out several more bills. "My fiancée has been wanting a pair of doeskin moccasins."

Brandy nodded as she accepted the money. "Adam makes the best moccasins in the world. I'm sure she'll be thrilled with them."

"Maybe I better get her a pair of mittens to go with them," he said, reaching into his purse again.

"An excellent idea," Brandy said with a grin. "Of course you'll want them lined with fur. It's well worth the extra—"

"All right you two, that's enough," Whiskey Jug said with a growl.

Jared handed Brandy the last of his cash. "You know, I never did give you two a wedding present. Here, take this and rent the bridal suite at the Saratoga hotel."

This time Brandy protested. "Oh, Jared, I don't think—"

"Consider it a favor to us," Alaina said. "We owe the clerk there, and this is an excellent way to pay him back."

"The Saratoga hotel." Whiskey Jug said with a sudden grin. "You know, that ain't such a bad idea."

"All Aboard!" The conductor's call caused a flurry of activity on the platform as everyone gathered their belongings. Another round of hugs, a hard meaningful handshake between the two men, and then they were gone.

"What do you suppose caused Whiskey Jug 's change of heart?" Alaina asked as the train pulled out of the station.

"I don't know, but it sure was unexpected."

"It must have had something to do with the bridal suite, but I can't imagine...oh my goodness!" Alaina put her hand over her mouth and turned sparkling eyes to Jared.

"What is it?"

"Do you remember what the clerk said when you told him you were a friend of Whiskey Jug's?"

"That the owner knew him too."

"Right, and that *she* would insist on the best for Whiskey Jug Johnson's friends."

"Good Lord!" They stared at each other for a long moment then simultaneously burst into laughter.

"I almost feel sorry for the owner," Alaina said between giggles. "Brandy will make mincemeat out of her."

"I don't know, Whiskey Jug seemed pretty pleased to me. Maybe he's been trying to warn her off, and she isn't one to take gentle hints."

"Oh, wouldn't I love to be a fly on the wall to watch what happens!"

They grinned at each other for a long moment, then Jared glanced away. "I suppose we'd better get your shopping out of the way so we can get back to the fort before dark."

"I'm finished."

His head swiveled back toward her in surprise. "Are you serious?"

"Brandy and I did it while you and Whiskey Jug were making all the arrangements for their trip."

"But you had less than an hour."

Alaina shrugged. "We found everything at the mercantile. It doesn't take long to make up your mind when there isn't a whole lot to choose from."

"You only went to one store?"

"I didn't see any point in looking elsewhere when it was all there. I'm really not all that fond of shopping."

"A woman who isn't fond of shopping," he murmured in fascination. "I didn't think that was possible."

"Don't worry. I'm sure Susan's more normal."

Jared sighed gustily. "That's the understatement of the century. She lives to shop."

Alaina studied an imaginary spot on her skirt. "I was surprised to hear she wanted a pair of moccasins."

"Not nearly as surprised as she would be."

"You can bet Whiskey Jug will have them done next time you see him, and the mittens too."

"They won't go to waste. You forget I have four sisters, any one of whom would be thrilled with moccasins and mittens."

"Even the one who's married to an English lord?"

"Especially Shannon." Jared said with a grin. "I'm not sure it gets cold enough in England for a pair of fur-lined, doe-skin mittens. But knowing her, she'd wait until it snowed, then use them to pelt her husband with snowballs."

Alaina laughed. "She sounds like my kind of

aristocrat."

"She is. In fact, you two would be dangerous together." His smile faded to a frown and his gaze turned introspective. "I'm afraid she and Susan will be a big disappointment to each other."

Alaina knew he was talking more to himself than to her. There seemed little she could say that wouldn't sound catty, so she changed the subject. "Was there anything you needed in town before we leave?"

"No."

"Then we may as well go."

"I guess so."

It was as if the mention of Susan had put a pall over them. Their good moods disappeared like a wisp of smoke, and they both became quiet and withdrawn. On the way to town they'd been able to ignore each other by concentrating on their companions. Now it was impossible. The sultry afternoon air was oppressive and the silence stretched between them taut as a bow string. They were within a few miles of the fort when Jared finally spoke.

"Are you enjoying your stay at Fort Bridger?" he asked.

"Oh yes, everyone has been very kind, especially Susan's parents."

Jared raised a brow. "Even her mother?"

"Mrs. Prescott has gone out of her way to be a gracious hostess since the day I got here."

"I suppose next you'll be trying to tell me you've enjoyed trying to carry on a conversation with her too."

"Well, she is a bit overpowering."

Jared gave a crack of laughter. "Try overbearing."

"Maybe you just rub her the wrong way."

"I do that, all right."

"I'm sure she just wants to make sure you're the man for Susan. Mothers tend to get overly protective when their daughter's happiness is involved." As she said the words, Alaina had a sudden image of her mother angrily denouncing Cameron Price and all he stood for. For the first time, she had an inkling what caused her mother's uncharacteristic outburst. Whatever had passed between them, Cameron had obviously hurt her mother badly. "That's why Mama didn't want me to meet him," she said with wonder.

"Who?"

"Cameron. She was afraid I'd get hurt. It never occurred to her he'd be different with me."

"Are you sure he is?"

"If he'd treated Mama the way he treats me, she would have married him."

"He treats you like a pretty little doll he can drag around and show off. I'll bet he doesn't even know your favorite color is blue, or that you have a sweet tooth."

Alaina glanced at him in surprise. "How did you..." Then she shook her head. "So what? None of that is important."

"The point is, he hasn't taken the time to get to know you."

"We haven't spent that much time together. He had to leave the morning after I got here."

"He can't even remember your name!"

"Neither can Susan, but you don't think any less of her!"

"She knows your name," Jared said defensively.

"She's called me Elaine since the day we met. If it isn't a mistake then she's doing it intentionally to put me in my place."

"There you go again, maligning Susan for no good reason."

"You started it by attacking my father."

"I'm just trying to protect you."

"I don't want or need your protection!" she snarled at him. "When are you going to get that through your head?"

"Maybe when you stop bumbling into one scrape after another. It would take a far better man than I am to keep you out of trouble. I feel sorry for the man unlucky enough to marry you."

"Jared."

Jared glanced at her, surprised by the odd sound in her voice. Her face reflected wide-eyed consternation as she stared at him. "Look, Alaina," he began apologetically. "I didn't mean—"

"Jared," she said urgently. "I don't like the look of those rain clouds! "

He turned and looked at the dark clouds roiling in the sky to the south. "Those aren't rain clouds, Alaina. That's hail."

"They're not like any hail clouds I've ever seen," she said doubtfully. "They're the wrong color."

"Trust me, I've been out in enough bad weather here in Wyoming to recognize the signs. We'd better take cover," he said, scanning the hills around them. Not so much as a single scraggly tree offered sanctuary from the storm. The fort and safety lay a good three miles ahead to the east.

"I think there's a small building along the road here somewhere," Alaina said nervously. "Do you think we could make it there?"

Jared frowned. As he recalled, the old dilapidated shed was about halfway to the fort, but for the life of him he couldn't remember if it still had a roof or not. He glanced at the rapidly approaching storm as he slapped the reins on the rumps of the horses. "We'll try for it."

Alaina stared at the clouds as though they were terrifying creatures after blood. "Oh, Jared, please hurry!"

As they raced toward the dubious shelter, Jared was vitally aware of Alaina's mounting panic. It was way out of proportion for the danger they were in. It was also very peculiar considering the other emergencies she'd kept her head through. By the time the shed came into sight, she was gripping his arm in white-knuckled fear.

"Can't you make them go any faster?"

"We're almost there, Alaina. Don't worry, we'll be all right." He had the distinct impression she hadn't heard him as she stared at the approaching storm.

The wind was whipping around them with frightening intensity when they finally reached their destination. The first bolt of lightning hit just as they scrambled out of the surrey. The blinding flash was followed almost immediately by a clap of thunder so loud it drowned out the scream of the horses.

Jared swore as the horses took off at a dead run leaving him and Alaina in the middle of the road in the sudden downpour. Alaina whimpered as the lightning struck again. He scooped her up in his arms and headed toward the dubious protection of the shed as the thunder rolled around them. Her arms tightened around his neck in a strangle hold as the hiss of hail pounded toward them.

Jared had a lot of muscle from packing his surveying

equipment over all kinds of terrain, but Alaina was no feather-weight, and her rigidity made her difficult to carry. "Loosen up," he panted. "You're stiff as a board." Alaina only squeezed harder.

Though the shed still had most of a roof and four more or less solid walls, it was so rickety Jared couldn't help wondering if it would hold up to the storm. The first hailstones were pelting them when he finally staggered through the door. He made his way to the far corner and collapsed onto a pile of surprisingly clean straw. At the other end of the building hailstones the size of small eggs were falling through the holes in the roof and past the window.

"It's all right, Alaina," he said untying the strings of her wet bonnet and tossing it aside. He could barely hear the sound of his own voice over the noise of the hail pounding over their heads, but she seemed to take comfort in his closeness. Jared leaned back against the wall and cradled her with his lips close to her ear. "We're safe now."

Since another ear-splitting clap of thunder punctuated his words, they did little to reassure her. She just burrowed deeper into his embrace. "I hate thunder and lightning."

"So I noticed."

"One of my uncles was struck by lightning when I was just a little girl. It was awful."

"It can't get us in here," Jared said, soothingly as he rubbed her back. Later he was never able to remember quite when he started dropping soft little kisses against her hair, or even when she relaxed and tipped her face up toward him. All he knew was that suddenly she was kissing him, hungrily and without restraint. Resistance was the farthest thing from his mind as she pushed him back onto the bed of straw, and he lost himself in her honeyed kisses.

Alaina squirmed against him trying to get even closer as she sought escape from the demons that haunted her. The sound of the storm receded from her consciousness, driven away by the fires his fingers ignited along her body and the way his mouth branded her with his passion. She matched him touch for touch, taking all he gave and demanding more.

With a deep groan, he rolled her to the side and trailed kisses down her neck. As his hand followed the curve of her rib cage to her breast, Alaina reached for the buttons on his shirt. A multitude of sensations crashed in on her, overwhelming her with their intensity. The pounding of his heart and the smooth muscular contours beneath her fingers mingled with an incredible feeling of rightness as he took possession of her, body and soul.

Alaina was barely aware of the front of her dress parting until she felt the soft kisses against her breast. She threaded her fingers through his hair as the sweet warmth of his mouth enveloped her. An emotion grew inside her, swelling to the point of bursting as the devastating waves of desire thundered through her. "I love you," she whispered arching into the intoxicating caress of his mouth.

His lips stilled. "What?"

"I didn't say anything," she murmured in a bemused voice. Until that moment she hadn't realized she'd said it aloud.

He lifted his head and stared down at her. "Yes, you did."

"I don't...Oh no!" Her eyes widened in consternation as a horrible roaring like a thousand freight trains suddenly filled the room.

Jared's head jerked toward the door. "Jesus, what's that?"

"We have to get out of here," she said, struggling out from under him.

"Why? What's going on?"

She grabbed his hand and started pulling him toward the door before he even gained his feet. "Hurry up. We'll be safer outside."

"Alaina, what's happening?" He yelled above the roar that grew louder by the second.

Raw terror showed in her face as she pointed toward the southwest. "That!"

Jared glanced over his shoulder. His mouth fell open in horrified wonder. A tornado was bearing down on them with the speed of a buffalo stampede.

CHAPTER THIRTY

"Come on, Jared," Alaina yelled tugging on his hand. "We've got to get to that gully over there." Water stood an inch deep in some places and was slushy with hailstones. Their feet slipped and slid in the muck as they ran, but panic spurred them on. Luckily, the gully wasn't far, and they dived into it when they arrived.

"We need to be down in the bottom," she yelled.

"It isn't safe."

"What?" Alaina strained forward to hear what he said over the roar of the approaching tornado.

Jared shook his head and pointed to the water already rushing through the gully. "There's going to be a flash flood," he yelled, cupping his hands around his mouth. He peeked up over the edge of the gully then grabbed Alaina and pushed her down onto the muddy bank. A moment later he was draping his larger body over hers, trying to give her a little extra protection.

Then the tornado was hurtling by them with nightmare winds and screeching like a thousand demons. Jared's ears popped painfully from the change in pressure. Seconds went by, minutes, a lifetime, and then it was over. As quickly as it had begun, the noise was gone.

Jared twisted around and peered over his shoulder just in time to see the last of the funnel disappear back into the cloud. Even as he slumped in relief, the sound of running water burst upon his consciousness. He looked down at the new menace. The water in the gully was already lapping at his boots and the level was rising fast. "Come on, Alaina, we've got to get out of here."

"What?"

"We've got to move," he said, dragging her up the muddy embankment. "It's a gully washer."

Moments later they were standing safely at the top. Alaina watched in amazement as the gully filled to the top with rushing water. "Where did it all come from?"

"The rain and hail. All the water is running down off the hills."

"We don't have gully washers at home," she said. "I guess I shouldn't have panicked that way. We were probably safer where we were."

"Good Lord," Jared said suddenly. "The shed!"

Alaina looked back over her shoulder and gasped in dismay. Bits and pieces of splintered wood lay scattered about the prairie, all that remained of the shed except a bare spot in the prairie grass to show where it had stood.

They stared at each other in stunned disbelief. "Do you realize how many close calls we've had in the last half hour?" Alaina asked in a shaken voice.

"Way too many."

Alaina's gaze dropped to the broad expanse of bare chest that showed through his open shirt. Her face darkened with embarrassment as her fingers went to her own buttons.

"Here," he said softly, "let me do that."

He gently pushed her hands aside and began doing up her buttons. It occurred to her that she really ought to be doing the same for him, but a streak of mud across his chest and stomach stopped her. "You're kind of a mess, you know," she said, tracing it with gentle fingers.

"Somebody dragged me out of a nice dry shed and forced me into a muddy gulch."

"Imagine that," Alaina said, making a tsking noise.

"You know, you aren't exactly tidy yourself."

Alaina glanced down at the mud all over the front of her dress and made a face. "The way those horses took off, my new clothes are probably half way to kingdom come by now. I don't suppose you have a handkerchief I could borrow."

"Anything to help a lady in distress." He pulled a handkerchief out of his back pocket and presented it to her with a flourish.

"Thanks," Alaina said, bending to dip it in a puddle of water next to her foot. "Though I'm not sure how much good it will do. "

Jared jumped as the icy wet rag made contact with his bare stomach. "Holy Hell!" he yelped. "What are you doing?"

"I'd think it was obvious," she said, wiping away the worst of the mud on his stomach and chest.

"Right, you're using my own handkerchief as a weapon against me."

Alaina giggled. "What a baby. Afraid of a little water."

"A little water! In case you missed it, that water was ice ten minutes ago."

"Papa always said cold water would put hair on your chest." Alaina dipped the rag in the water again and went after the mud on his neck and face.

"I don't need any more hair on my chest," he grumbled. "Are you about finished?"

"I've done as much as I can." She stepped back and surveyed him critically. "It's not great but at least you can button your shirt now."

"And now it's my turn to clean you up," he said with an exaggerated waggle of his eyebrows.

Alaina took several quick steps backward. "I don't think so."

"What's the matter, Alaina?" he asked as he stalked her. "Don't you trust me?"

"Not particularly."

"Afraid I'll get even?"

Alaina grinned. "Nope."

He looked surprised. "Why not?"

"Because you'll have to catch me first," she tossed back over her shoulder as she lifted her skirts and started running.

Jared never even considered how far beneath his dignity it was to chase her across the prairie. Within a short distance he began to gain on her, and she started to dodge in and out among the mud puddles, trying to escape her inevitable capture. They were both laughing when she reached the top of a small rise and stopped abruptly.

"Ha, I've got you now," he gloated, grabbing her from behind. Instead of the squeals and giggles he expected, she stood perfectly still and stared off toward the southwest.

"Oh no," she whispered.

Before them lay the path left by the tornado marked by uprooted sagebrush and flattened grass. At the far end lay the fort. Even from where they stood they could see the destruction.

"It went through the enlisted men's barracks," Jared murmured in horrified wonder.

"Oh, Jared, what if they were all inside because of

the hail storm?"

They looked at each other in dismay.

"They'll need our help," Alaina said in a shaky voice as she started down the hill. "Come on, people are bleeding to death while we stand here talking." She set off with such single-minded determination that Jared found himself hurrying to keep up.

"Look, Alaina, we're a good mile and a half away. If you keep up that pace you'll never make it."

She looked at him with troubled eyes. "What if we're too late?"

"Too late for what? If they have everything taken care of by the time we get there, they didn't need us anyway. If not, they'll want us as fresh as possible. You won't be able to do anybody any good if you're worn out when you arrive."

"I guess you're right." She looked away as he buttoned his shirt. Only a very loose woman would enjoy looking at a man's half naked body as much as she liked looking at Jared's. Who was she fooling? When she was around him, she *was* a loose woman. She sneaked another peek and was ashamed of the flash of disappointment she felt as the last button slid through its buttonhole. She would do well to remember that he belonged to Susan by choice.

"Looks like I've compromised you again," he said with a slight smile.

Alaina's heart jerked painfully. It was as though he'd read her mind. "Don't be ridiculous. Nothing's changed."

"It hasn't? Then how do you explain what happened back there in the shed?"

"What do you mean?" she asked cautiously.

"You tell me you don't want to marry me, but you melt in my arms like butter on a hot roll."

"I was scared."

"And that's all it was?"

"What else could it be?"

"I don't know, you tell me." He grabbed her arm and whirled her around to face him. "You said you loved me, Alaina."

"Did I?"

"Damn it, Alaina, don't play games with me."

"Look, if I said it, which I don't remember doing, it was in the heat of the moment and doesn't mean a thing. All we ever do is fight with each other, Jared. How could that be love?"

"We don't fight *all* the time," he said softly. "In fact, passion seems to flare up between us on a regular basis."

Alaina wanted to scream *'Because I love you and I lose control around you!'* but she knew what his reaction would be. He'd start insisting she marry him again. Not because he loved her but because he still felt obligated. She'd rather not have him at all than to have him on those terms. "Think about it, Jared; that only happens when we're scared or upset," she said, pulling out of his grasp and continuing down the road.

He fell in beside her. "Do you expect me to believe it's all a reaction to fear?"

"Have you ever been through a tornado or chased by renegades with any other woman?"

"No, of course not."

"Then how do you know you wouldn't react the same way?"

Jared looked nonplused for a moment and she pressed her advantage. "Do you fight with Susan?"

"No, but I don't see—"

"Don't you? Without something threatening us, that's all we do when we're together. I couldn't be happy that way, and I don't think you could either."

"That's the most ridiculous—"

"Jared, look," she said, grabbing his arm "the surrey."

She was running down the hill before he had a chance to answer. He watched her for a moment with a disgusted look on his face, then, with a shake of his head, followed her.

The surrey was securely wedged between two boulders that bordered the road. The team were still hitched up but were hopelessly tangled in the traces.

"How do you suppose they got stuck like that?" Alaina asked as Jared joined her next to the trapped wagon.

"They probably got spooked by a clap of thunder, shied off the road and ran through here. It's a miracle they aren't hurt."

"Can you get them out?"

"It may take a little patience," Jared said. "But it shouldn't be all that difficult."

"Can I help?"

Jared looked at the situation critically. "I doubt it," he said finally. "There's only enough room for one person. A second would just be in the way."

Alaina glanced toward the fort, then looked at the surrey doubtfully. "Are you sure?"

"Yes, why?"

"Because if you don't need me, I'm going to go on ahead to the fort."

"I'll probably have this rig out before you get

halfway there."

"Then you can pick me up on your way," she said resolutely. "If not, I won't lose any more time."

"Oh for the love of...Fine, walk to the moon if you want," he said in exasperation. "If nothing else, it will keep you out of trouble."

Alaina bit her lip. How was it everything she did made him mad? "Here's your handkerchief," she said, handing it to him.

"It's too wet to put in my pocket," he said, turning away. "You'd best get started if you're going to walk."

Alaina's eyes stung as she stared at the soggy, mud-stained square of fabric in her hand. What a stupid thing to do. Susan would know better than to return a gentleman's handkerchief without laundering it first. Maybe that was why Jared preferred Susan. She knew the proper way of doing things and didn't tumble from one scrape to another.

Alaina swallowed hard. Jared was ignoring her completely as he talked soothingly to the terrified horses. Maybe she shouldn't have been so adamant about walking. With a heavy heart, she turned toward the fort.

"Stick to the road. There's less chance of getting caught in a flood that way," Jared said. "And watch your feet. Snakes are unpredictable after a storm."

"No kidding," she snapped.

Their gazes met and held. Alaina was the first to break contact. "I'll see you at the fort."

"Take care," he said softly, as she walked away.

Alaina stopped at the first puddle she came to and scrubbed away the worst of the dirt on her dress. Her sense of urgency returned and amplified as she got closer to the fort. Her difficulties with Jared were forgotten in the horror of the destruction that lay before her.

The damage was even worse than it had appeared from a distance. The tornado apparently touched down just beyond officer's row, and ripped through the enlisted men's barracks on the southwestern corner of the compound. It had crossed the parade ground where it uprooted the flagpole, and tore the roof off the guardhouse before destroying a second barracks. The remaining four barracks had suffered a variety of damage including broken windows and gaping holes in some of the roofs.

The ground in front of the barracks looked like a battle zone. Dozens of injured men lay or sat on the ground. The number steadily increased as others limped out of the wreckage supported by rescue workers or were carried out on makeshift stretchers. It only took Alaina a moment to identify the post surgeon. He barked orders to half a dozen men as he worked frantically to patch the worst of the injuries.

She carefully made her way through the injured to his side. "Can I help?"

He glanced up at her then went back to work on a broken arm. "Oh, God not another one!"

Alaina blinked in surprise. "I beg your pardon?"

"Look, I appreciate your desire to help, but I don't have time to deal with another female that faints at the sight of blood."

"But—"

"Why don't you go on over to Mrs. Prescott's? You can help by rolling bandages with the rest of them. Somebody bring me a splint," he yelled over his shoulder. It was obvious he'd immediately dismissed Alaina from his mind, as he handed the young private a bottle of whiskey and a chunk of smooth wood. "I'm going to set your arm now, son. Take a couple of good swigs, then bite down on this block."

Alaina looked around until her gaze lit on a pile of broken boards that had been shaped into splints. She grabbed a short one, picked up a handful of bandages and hurried back just as the young private screamed in agony. The sound was muffled by the piece of wood in his mouth but was no less bone chilling.

"You did just fine," the doctor murmured gruffly as he reached for the splint, "the worst is over."

Alaina anticipated every order before the doctor barked it out and had what he required at hand almost before he knew he needed it. It wasn't until he was finished and she reached over and took the piece of wood from the soldier that the doctor realized who his assistant had been.

"You're very brave," she said, as she wiped the sweat from the private's forehead and gave him another drink of the raw whiskey. "Just rest now."

The private gave her a shaky smile and closed his eyes.

"Damn, I wish we hadn't run out of laudanum," the doctor muttered. He gave Alaina a long look from beneath his bushy eyebrows as he moved on to the next patient. "It appears I misjudged you, young lady."

"I used to help my grandmother. She was the local midwife and doubled as a healer when the doctor was out of town."

"She taught you well. Simkins, get me another bottle of whiskey," he yelled.

"Then you'll let me help you?"

"Nope. I don't need you near as bad as my colleague over on the other side of the parade ground. We put all of our most experienced men over here since that's where the worst injuries are. Dr. Corbett is making do with officers and the walking wounded. He could use a good nurse."

"Where will I find him?"

"In the middle of all the activity I expect. Tell him Dr. Stone sent you, that way you won't have to prove yourself again. Sorry I can't spare anyone to take you."

"Don't worry, I'll find him."

The doctor gave her an approving nod then frowned down at his next patient who had a large splinter of wood sticking nearly all the way through his leg. "Where the hell is that whiskey, Simkins?"

Alaina found Dr. Corbett with no trouble. Even from the back she could tell he was considerably younger than Dr. Stone. And tall. He was bent over a patient, but she could tell he was far above average height. "Dr. Corbett, Dr. Stone sent me to....oh my!"

At the sound of her voice, the doctor straightened and Alaina saw the patient he'd been working on. Her father. Cameron sat with his eyes closed and a thick bandage around his head. "You're hurt!" she blurted out.

Cameron's eyes popped opened. "Princess! Thank God you're safe. I was afraid you and Brady might have run into trouble out there."

"Nothing we couldn't handle. What happened to you?"

"A roof caved in on him while he was pulling people out of the wreckage," Dr. Corbett said, as he finished adjusting Cameron's bandage. "He'll be fine. You said you had a message from Dr. Stone?"

"He sent me to help you. Said you could use a nurse."

"The hell you will," Cameron cut in before the doctor had a chance to answer. "If you want to help, you can go roll bandages with the other ladies."

"I'll be of more use here."

"You'll just be in the way here."

Alaina straightened to her full height and glared at her father. "Dr. Stone told me to come help Dr. Corbett." "Alonna..." he said warningly.

"Frankly, Captain, I could use some help," the young doctor put in. "If Dr. Stone sent her that's plenty good enough for me."

"Then you'll let me help?"

"Gladly."

Completely ignoring her father, Alaina rolled up her sleeves. "All right then, Doctor, where would you like me to start?"

CHAPTER THIRTY-ONE

"**A**re you sure that's the last of them?" Alaina asked as Dr. Corbett packed his instruments back into his bag.

"According to Dr. Stone it is. We've managed to patch up everybody who needed it, including the prisoners." He ran his hand through his hair wearily. "I'm not sure I could handle any more just now anyway."

"Me either. Maybe I shouldn't have been so quick to insist I could help." What a nice face he had, she thought as she watched him. He was not handsome by any means, but pleasant. A faint sprinkling of freckles across his nose and a shock of unruly brown hair gave him a boyish quality that was hard to resist. All through the night, the warmth in the sherry colored eyes and a business-like attitude reassured the dozens of men they'd worked on. They liked Dr. Corbett, and so did she.

He smiled at her. "Thank God you were here. I couldn't have done it without you, Alaina. Good grief, is that the sun coming up?"

Alaina turned to look at a delicate pink line along the eastern horizon. "I believe it is."

"You two look like you could use some good hot coffee." Sean Kirkpatrick said, as he arrived with a steaming pot and a dozen tin cups. "It was a long night."

"For you too," Alaina pointed out as he handed her a cup. "I lost track of all the different things you've done for us, and now you're delivering coffee."

Sean shrugged. "I help out where I can. They'll be around with something to eat in a few minutes. Maybe I'll come join you for breakfast."

Alaina gave him a warm smile. "I'd like that."

Ben Corbett watched the handsome young lieutenant walk away with a speculative look in his eye. "Is there something between you and Kirkpatrick?"

Alaina looked up in surprise. "Sean? He's a friend."

"That's all?"

Alaina frowned. "Dr. Corbett..."

"All right, so he's none of my business," he said sitting down next to her. "By the way, my name is Ben, remember? We decided to put Miss Ellinson and Dr. Corbett behind us hours ago." He sighed tiredly as he leaned back against the building and stretched his long legs out in front of him. "Do you know, I wasn't supposed to report for duty until tomorrow?"

"Really?"

"I'm Dr. Stone's replacement. This is supposed to be his last day. I came two days early so I could get my bearings." He smiled as he took a sip of coffee. "Kind of ironic, isn't it?"

Alaina shook her head. "More like lucky, for all those poor soldiers anyway. One doctor couldn't have done it all."

"There you are!" Jared said, as he came around the corner of the building. "I've been looking for you." He glanced at Ben and frowned. "I spent most of the night helping the doctor. I figured I'd find you with him."

"You did. This is Dr. Corbett. Ben, I'd like you to meet Jared Brady."

"Nice to meet you, Dr. Corbett," Jared said. His

words were pleasant but his expression was anything but.

"Likewise." Ben stuck out his hand. "You must be another friend of Alaina's," he said with a grin.

Jared shook the proffered hand. "Another?"

"Lieutenant Kirkpatrick was just here."

Jared raised an eyebrow and Alaina blushed to the roots of her hair. "He was delivering coffee," she said, then was immediately irritated that she'd explained anything to him. "Were you looking for me for some reason in particular?"

"I took your things to Major Goodrich's house."

Alaina gave him a blank look. "My things?"

"You went shopping yesterday, remember? Sybil said you hadn't been home yet when I dropped everything off."

"No, I went straight to Dr. Stone, and he sent me here. Did you think I got lost on the way?"

"The thought crossed my mind. Dr. Stone said he'd sent all of the feather-headed females to Milicent Prescott, but she said she hadn't seen hide nor hair of you," he admitted with a slight smile. "I guess I should have known he wouldn't classify you with all the others."

"Good heavens, was that a compliment I just heard?"

"I suppose it was at that."

"I guess I was right about walking to the fort, since you didn't pick me up before I got here," she couldn't help adding. "I assume it took you longer to get the horses untangled than you thought it was going to."

"In a manner of speaking. One of them had a broken leg."

"Oh, no! Then I should have stayed to help after all."

Jared shook his head. "There wasn't anything you could have done. Besides, they did need you here."

"I'll resist the urge to say I told you so, though I did, you know."

A sound suspiciously like a muffled laugh that changed to a cough momentarily drew Jared's attention to the doctor again. "We need to talk, Alaina," he said with a glare at the other man. "...privately."

"We've already done that, Jared. Nothing has changed in the last twelve hours. Besides, I'm too tired to fight with you now."

"Why do you always assume I want to fight with you?" he asked irritably.

"I don't think you *want* to, it just happens."

"I see Lieutenant Kirkpatrick is returning with breakfast," Ben said with a hint of amusement in his voice. "Would you care to join us, Brady?"

Jared glowered for a moment then shook his head. "No, Colonel Prescott is expecting me. I'll find you later when you have time to talk, Alaina."

"That man doesn't know how to take no for an answer," Alaina said in exasperation as he walked away.

"Maybe because you lack conviction when you say it."

Alaina gave him a sharp look, but he was already greeting Lieutenant Kirkpatrick with an affable smile.

Jared's unreasonable attitude and Dr. Corbett's cryptic words were soon forgotten as Sean arrived with the food, and the three of them sat down to eat. Alaina enjoyed the company of the two men, though there seemed to be an inexplicable undercurrent between them. It probably had something to do with the long, difficult night they had just been through.

"I suppose it's time to start our rounds," she said, as she licked the jam from her fingers.

"Nope," Ben said.

"But the patients need to be checked."

"I know, but you're exhausted. It's time for you to go to bed. Doctor's orders," he added with a smile.

"You can't do it by yourself."

"Lieutenant Kirkpatrick can help me with the ones who can't wait. Then I'm going to get some shut-eye myself. Come on, I'll escort you home."

"No need for that. You're tired yourself," Sean put in. "I'll take her."

"I don't mind."

"I insist." The two men eyed each other belligerently for a moment then Ben grinned. "Well, Alaina, looks like you have two escorts." He stood up and offered her his arm. "Shall we go?"

It was rather fun walking home arm in arm with two attractive men who bantered back and forth trying to make her laugh. A huge depression in the center of the parade ground had filled with all the water from the surrounding area. When Alaina remarked that it looked like a lake, the two men immediately attempted to name it.

The names became progressively more ridiculous as they tried to outdo each other. Their exhaustion contributed to the degree of hilarity, and all three were nearly helpless with laughter by the time they reached the far side of the parade ground. The trio rounded the corner of the shattered barracks and ran smack into Jared Brady.

"Well, I'm glad to see someone found something to

laugh about," he said sourly.

Alaina gave him a sunny smile. "It's good for what ails you, Jared. Maybe you should try it."

"Maybe I would if I could find anything humorous."

"Uh-oh, your interview with the Colonel didn't go well?"

"It went fine. I'm just tired. I'd think you would be too."

"We're in the process of taking her home now," Sean said. "She'll be tucked into bed and sound asleep before you can say Lake Pig Wallow."

That set the three of them off again. Jared made a disgusted sound and walked away. "Bye, Jared," Alaina called after him merrily. "Sleep tight."

"You know, Kirkpatrick, I believe we put our friend's nose out of joint," Ben said.

Sean grinned. "He was a little green-eyed wasn't he?"

"If you think he was jealous, you're wrong." Alaina made a face. "He just doesn't like it when I don't do what he wants." Unaware of the look Sean and Ben exchanged over her head, she sighed. "He can spoil my good mood faster than anyone I know, but I'm not going to give him that kind of power today. Lake Pig Wallow, you say? How about Lake Mud-in-the-Face?"

The bantering resumed, and they reached Major Goodrich's in short order. Alaina bid her escorts good bye. She let herself in the front door and crept quietly up the stairs. It was all she could do to remove her clothes before she fell into her bed dressed in her underwear. She was asleep almost before her head hit the pillow.

It seemed like her eyes had barely closed when Sybil was shaking her shoulder. "Alaina, wake up."

"W...what?" Alaina stared up at her groggily. "What's wrong?"

"The dressmaker is here to alter my dress for you."

Alaina groaned and closed her eyes again. "I don't care."

"I know you were out late last night, but she's in great demand, and this is the time she had for us."

"Go away." Alaina buried her head under the pillow. "Leave me alone."

There was a moment of silence, then the sound of footsteps crossing the floor, and the door closing. Alaina sighed in relief and drifted back to sleep.

The next thing she knew, strong hands were pulling her from the bed. "Come on my girl. This is no time to be a slug-a-bed. Sergeant Brown's wife is here to fit your dress for Susan's party."

Alaina opened her eyes and stared at Cameron Price in astonishment. "What are you doing here?"

"Your uncle was kind enough to come upstairs and give me a hand," Sybil said, holding out a dressing gown. "Come on now, be a good girl and get up. You're keeping Mrs. Brown waiting."

"But I don't understand why it's so important. Surely Susan isn't still planning on having her party."

Cameron looked surprised. "Why wouldn't she?"

"Well, because of the tornado....all those men..." Alaina trailed off as she saw the incredulous expression on Sybil's face.

"Surely you don't think Susan was planning to invite enlisted men!" Sybil said in horrified accents.

"No, I thought....well....that she'd want to wait until things were back to normal, I guess."

"Even if she wanted to, she doesn't have time for

that," Sybil said, pulling the sleeve of the dressing gown up over Alaina's left arm. "Colonel Prescott is sending the survey crew out any day. Susan couldn't very well have an engagement party without the groom!"

Alaina's stomach plummeted. "Jared's leaving?"

"They figure it will be early next week at the latest." Sybil pulled Alaina's right arm through the other sleeve and adjusted the dressing gown around her shoulders. "There, you're all ready for Mrs. Brown."

"This is completely unnecessary. I'm not going to Susan's party."

"Of course you are," Sybil said. "I'll run and get Mrs. Brown."

Cameron leaned back against the door frame and crossed his arms as he watched her adjust the dressing gown. The bandage Ben had put on the afternoon before gave him a dashing heroic look, but his daughter was unimpressed.

"You know Sybil is going to a great deal of effort for you," he said as she crossed the room.

"And it's completely unnecessary. I really don't want to go to Susan's party. I'm going to be too busy helping Dr. Corbett." Alaina opened the armoire and peered inside. "Where in the world are my clothes?"

"You're planning to continue working with the doctor?"

Alaina looked at her father in surprise. "Of course I am. Dr. Stone is leaving tomorrow and Ben will need help."

"Colonel Prescott can assign men to help him. People will be able to overlook what you did last night, but if you continue, they won't."

She stared at him. "They'll be able to overlook me

helping injured men?"

"Certainly. They might even see it as a good thing as long as you don't overdo it."

"Dr. Stone said he had all kinds of women volunteering to help."

"And they did, by rolling bandages and fixing sandwiches."

"You mean none of them went so far as to get their hands dirty," Alaina said sarcastically.

"Mrs. Brown's waiting in the parlor," Sybil said as she came back into the room carrying a pink ball gown.

Alaina forced the muscles in her jaws to relax. "Where is my blue dress?"

"I had it burned."

"You burned my dress?" Alaina cried. She felt as though a giant fist were squeezing her heart.

Sybil's eyes widened in alarm. "I...it was covered with blood. I didn't think you'd care."

"You could have asked!"

"Don't you think you're over-reacting?" Cameron said sardonically. "It was just a dress."

"It was special to me," Alaina said, swallowing against the sudden lump in her throat. The last representation of her memorable night with Jared was gone, burned to ashes like an insignificant rag.

"I'm s...sorry, Alaina," Sybil said tearfully. "It was so filthy I didn't think it would ever come clean again."

Reminding herself that Sybil hadn't meant any harm, Alaina took a deep breath. "Jared said he brought you the clothes I bought yesterday?"

"Why, yes. I put them—"

"...some place safe," Cameron finished for her. "And she'll give them to you just as soon as Mrs. Brown finishes."

"That's despicable," Alaina snarled.

Cameron shrugged. "Call it what you want. Mrs. Brown and Sybil are going out of their way for you. The least you can do is cooperate."

Against her will, Alaina realized he was right. Sybil was merely trying to do what she thought was best. She deserved better from her guest. With a final glare at Cameron, she pulled the redressing gown tighter around her middle and marched out of the room.

"I don't think she'll give you any more trouble, Sybil," Alaina heard him say. "And it's time I got back to work."

"Will I see you later?" Sybil asked anxiously.

"Of course." Alaina could almost see the bone-melting smile her father bestowed on Sybil Goodrich. Not for the first time, she wondered about the relationship between them.

Mrs. Brown turned out to be a nervous little woman who fluttered around Alaina like a frightened sparrow. She chattered as she tucked and pinned until Alaina had to bite her tongue. "There," she said finally as she drove home the last pin. "This won't take too long. I'll probably have a few minutes to work right after the picnic today. I might even be able to finish it then."

"What picnic?" Alaina asked in surprise.

"Why, the one Mrs. Prescott is organizing. Miss Susan came up with the idea of the whole fort having a picnic out on the parade ground. Everyone's quite excited."

"Where did Susan come up with that idea? Somehow a picnic doesn't seem quite her style."

"She thought of it last night while we were rolling

bandages," Sybil said. "We were talking about the enlisted men's mess hall that had been damaged and how they would probably have to eat outside for a few days. Someone said it might be fun as long as the weather was nice, and Susan suggested we join them for lunch today."

"Eat with the enlisted men?" Alaina pretended to be aghast by such a thought. "Why, what can Susan be thinking?"

"Well, I don't suppose we'll actually be eating *with* them," Sybil said cautiously. "Uh...Why don't I run and get your clothes now?"

"Thank you. I'd appreciate that."

When Sybil left, Mrs. Brown smiled and patted Alaina's hand. "Don't you worry, Miss Ellinson. You'll be perfectly safe at the picnic. My husband told me they're singing your praises down at the barracks. Why, you're practically a legend already."

"That's probably because I'm common folk just like they are."

"Oh my no, it has nothing to do with that. They're calling you an angel of mercy."

Alaina found she was nearly as uncomfortable with that as she was with Cameron Price's attitude. Didn't anybody in this place understand the rules of common decency she'd been raised with?

As Mrs. Brown carefully removed the ball gown, Alaina glanced at the clock on the mantel. Eleven-thirty. There was little point in going back to bed. She was wide awake now. Ben would probably be getting ready to start his rounds soon if he hadn't already. She slipped into her dressing gown, thanked Mrs. Brown for her time, and excused herself.

Sybil had deposited the packages in Alaina's bedroom and disappeared. Alaina felt a jab from her conscience. She'd have to do something to make up for her churlishness later.

Alaina was slightly dismayed when she put on her new dress. The color and style were perfect for her, but it was a little tighter than she liked and hugged her bosom like a second skin. She ran a quick brush through her hair, and pulled it back into a practical knot on the back of her head. At least her father would be pleased. It was just the sort of flamboyant outfit he preferred.

Unbidden, Jared's words popped into her head. Did Cameron see her only as a pretty doll he could show off? He was more concerned about her dress for Susan's party than the horrors she'd seen the night before or any ill effects she might have suffered from going through a tornado. Suddenly she missed her papa, with his simple values and big comforting bear hugs. He would have been proud of her work with the wounded soldiers and would have understood her reluctance to attend Susan's party when so many were hurt. For the first time, doubt crept into her staunch support of her natural father.

"There she is, the Angel of Fort Bridger."

Jared looked up from the nail he was pounding in surprise. Since when did Fort Bridger have an angel? He followed the corporal's gaze and nearly dropped his hammer. It was Alaina, and she did look heavenly in her new dress. Even from this distance he could see the enticing way the garment clung to her figure. He stared at her in mute appreciation as she moved among the men helping Dr. Corbett change a dressing here, and giving smiling words of comfort there. There weren't more than a handful of women at the fort who cared about the injured men, and no one had spent so much time catering to their needs.

"Damn nice girl, too," put in the sergeant who was working with them to repair one of the damaged barracks.

And the one who's stolen my heart, Jared thought with a private smile. 'I love you.' Those three little words had cut through all his confusion and uncertainty with the power of a lightning strike. He hadn't realized until that moment how badly he'd wanted to hear them, or that he felt the same about her. Alaina could tell him it was just runaway passion until she turned blue in the face; he knew better.

"A man could easily fancy himself in love with her," the corporal murmured in awe.

"Not unless he wanted to tangle with her uncle," said Sergeant Tyre. "Captain Price let it be known he only considers officers as proper suitors. You don't qualify."

Jared turned to look at the man in surprise. "Suitors?"

"Word is Price is holding out for the highest rank, but he's got a sharp eye to the future and who's the most likely to help his career. Bets heavily favor Kirkpatrick now, but that will change as soon as Silverton gets back from the field. I figure he'll have a slight edge even with Kirkpatrick's head start."

"Silverton!" Jared exclaimed, revolted. "The man is a womanizing drunkard and fifteen years older than she is."

"True, but his father is a general and his grandfather

is a senator." The sergeant shook his head. "I think Price is barking up the wrong tree there, though. I can't see a general doing a favor for his daughter-in-law's uncle."

But he might for her father, Jared thought with a sick feeling. The idea of Alaina's future happiness being sacrificed on the altar of Cameron Price's ambitions was more than he could stand. She was so blind to her father's faults she'd never suspect a thing until she found herself married to someone as disgusting as Samuel Silverton. Without another word, he dropped the hammer into his bucket of nails and set off down the row of barracks toward her.

By the time he reached Dr. Corbett, Alaina had disappeared around the far corner, probably headed off on some errand or other. Jared strode past the surprised doctor and rounded the corner behind her. At least she was alone for once. "Alaina..."

She glanced back over her shoulder and made a face. "Just what I need," she mumbled as he caught up with her. "The last thing I want to do right now is to tangle with you. I thought you were going to bed."

"I thought you were, too."

"I did, but I couldn't resist the temptation to make tongues wag," she said sarcastically. "I suppose you're here to take me to task for working with Dr. Corbett too."

"Should I?"

"No, but when has that ever stopped you or anybody else for that matter? I'm sick and tired of everyone telling me what's proper and what isn't."

"Maybe if you stopped to think a little once in awhile, you wouldn't give tongues so much to wag about."

"What's that supposed to mean?"

"That's what happens when you do things like waltz across the parade ground at the crack of dawn, arm-in-arm with two men and flirting shamelessly with both of them."

"Flirting...!"

"It's bad enough that you've been carrying on with Kirkpatrick, now you've added this Corbett fellow and Sam Silverton as well." Even to Jared's own ears he sounded like a jealous fool.

"I haven't been carrying on with anybody," Alaina said vehemently. "And I don't even know Sam Silverton!"

Jared gazed at her flushed, angry countenance in consternation. This wasn't what he intended, and it certainly wasn't the way to tell her how much he loved her. Maybe if he showed her...Without even finishing the thought, he pulled her into his arms and kissed her passionately.

Alaina went rigid for a moment then pulled back her arm and slapped him as hard as she could. "You're despicable!" she hissed, her eyes filling with tears. "I hate you." She spun away from him and stalked out onto the parade ground.

"Alaina, wait," he called. She kept on walking, apparently oblivious to the crowd that had gathered for the picnic. With a muttered curse, he started after her. *Stupid, stupid, stupid,* he thought, fingering his fiery cheek. His exhaustion and inability to think clearly were responsible for the sheer idiocy of his actions. God help him if he couldn't fix the damage.

In her agitation, Alaina moved quickly, but Jared's long strides soon closed the distance between them. He reached out and grabbed her shoulder to stop her headlong flight. "Alaina....," he began.

"Don't touch me!" With the speed of a striking snake, she doubled her hand into a fist and slammed it into his midsection. While he was still gasping for breath she hooked her foot around his ankle and jerked his feet out from under him. "I'm not your little whore that you can take advantage of any time you want, Jared Brady," she snarled, glaring down at him where he lay on the ground gasping like a landed fish. "I'll thank you to keep your distance in the future!"

With that, she whirled and continued her march across the parade ground. Unfortunately, in her anger she paid little attention to the path of her flight.

"Elaine, what on earth? Have you run mad?"

Alaina's jaw clenched painfully as she looked up and saw her nemesis holding court in the middle of the parade ground. Susan was beautiful in brilliant yellow. Her dress was a masterpiece of ruffles and flounces that draped gracefully over a huge bustle while the tight bodice showed her voluptuous figure to perfection. Instead of a hat, she sported a matching parasol to protect her fair skin from the harsh Wyoming sun. She looked like a delectable daffodil against the green backdrop of the parade ground. Her expression was anything but sunny as she looked at Alaina with a scandalized stare.

"I just gave your fiancé a long overdue lesson," Alaina said.

"Really, Elaine, your behavior is reprehensible!"

"Oh, Suzy, you have no idea just how reprehensible my behavior can be," Alaina said with a sweet smile.

With that, she gave Susan a hard shove backward, right into the muddy depths of Lake Pig Wallow.

CHAPTER THIRTY-TWO

"Holy buckets of catfish, did you see that?" Sean Kirkpatrick asked in awe as he contemplated the destruction in Alaina's wake.

Dr. Corbett nodded. "From the beginning."

"What in the world set her off?"

"Brady kissed her," the doctor said tersely.

The Lieutenant blinked in surprise. "And she did that to him?" he asked, nodding toward the crumpled man on the ground.

"No, first she slapped him...hard. She didn't flatten him until he followed her and tried it again. Obviously an act of self-defense."

"Obviously. And Miss Prescott said something provoking I'm sure." Sean gave the other man an enigmatic look. "Alaina could probably use a strong shoulder to cry on right about now."

A silent message passed between the two. Kirkpatrick reached into his pocket and pulled out a coin. "Heads or tails, Corbett?"

"Tails."

They watched as the silver coin turned over and over in the air, until Kirkpatrick deftly caught it and slapped in onto the back of his hand. "Heads!" he said with satisfaction.

The doctor gave a slight smile. "Ah well, your friendship with the lady is of longer duration. Just be sure she knows she isn't alone here."

"You can count on it, Doctor," Kirkpatrick said, sticking the coin back in his pocket.

"In the meantime, I plan to pay Mr. Brady a visit."

"Don't be too gentle with him."

"I don't plan to be."

The lieutenant smiled grimly. "Good."

Ben watched as the other man skirted the crowd gathered around a muddy, disheveled Susan and strode purposefully after Alaina. With a resigned sigh, the doctor walked over to Jared Brady who had just picked himself up off the ground.

"Are you all right?" he asked.

"I think so, though I wasn't sure for awhile there."

"Any pain?" Dr. Corbett asked probing the area below Jared's ribs.

"No. Look, Doc, I appreciate your concern, but I have to catch up with Alaina," he said searching the crowd. "I'm fine, really I am."

"Good. Probably just got the air knocked out of you." Corbett straightened. "You know, Brady, this kind of goes against the grain with me since I'm really not a fighter." He shook his head regretfully. "On the other hand, I have an overdeveloped sense of right and wrong, and there doesn't seem to be anyone else around to see justice done."

"What the hell are you talking about?"

Jared never even saw the punch coming. In spite of his aversion to fighting, Ben Corbett had spent much of his youth in a boxing ring and hadn't lost his touch. A single right hook to the jaw and Jared Brady hit the ground like a pole-axed steer.

Ben gazed down at the unconscious man as he rubbed his stinging knuckles. "Don't guess you'll be catching up with Alaina, after all."

The dappled shadows beneath the small stand of aspens closed around Alaina in welcome solitude. Disillusionment swirled around in her like an angry cloud. How could she have ever fancied herself in love with Jared Brady? He was selfish and inconsiderate, the perfect match for Susan. They were both completely oblivious to the rest of the world except as it related to them.

Alaina angrily dashed away a tear that trickled out of the corner of her eye. She wouldn't cry over him; he wasn't worth it. Her head jerked up suddenly and her heart began pounding in fear as the leaves rustled and a tall figure blocked out the light at the entrance of the tiny grove. She'd been foolish to come here alone.

"Alaina? Are you in there?"

"Sean?"

"Right....ouch..." he swore under his breath as he made his way toward her through the intertwining branches. At last he plopped down on the log beside her. "This place is dangerous getting into." He reached over and wiped away another tear. "Are you all right?" he asked softly.

Alaina was unable to speak for the large knot in her throat. The gentle concern in Sean's expression crumbled her last defense, and she felt her lower lip quiver alarmingly.

"Oh, sweetheart, it's going to be all right," he said, gently pulling her into his arms.

His use of Jared's pet name for her brought the tears in earnest, and she sobbed out her anguish against his solid chest. How she longed for the safety of home and the wholehearted support of her parents. They'd have backed her in the coming battle with Susan even though they wouldn't have approved of the scene she'd just caused.

At last the tears ran out and she sat up with a shaky smile. "I'm sorry, Sean. I hate bawling like a baby."

"I don't mind," he said, handing her his handkerchief.

"If you're smart you'll stay as far away from me as possible," she said wiping her eyes. "I'm about to become a pariah. In case you missed it, I just dumped the darling of the fort into a giant mud puddle."

His smile flashed in the dim light. "I'm sure there were more than a few who were pleased to see Miss Prescott get her come-uppance."

Alaina grinned in spite of herself. "It *was* rather satisfying," she admitted. Then she sighed. "I have a feeling we haven't heard the last of it, though."

"No, probably not, but you have as many friends as she does here, maybe more after last night. Everyone is calling you the Angel of Fort Bridger. "

"Not everyone," she said gloomily. "There seems to be a lot of people here that think helping Dr. Corbett made me unacceptable."

"No one who matters," Sean said indignantly. "Any fool who feels that way isn't worth your time."

"But they do matter to my father." Alaina said, looking down at her hands.

Sean frowned in confusion. "Your father? But surely your uncle is the one who —"

"Cameron Price isn't my uncle," she said quietly. "He's my natural father." Alaina glanced up and found

Sean staring at her in thunderstruck silence. "Now I've shocked you as well."

"Good lord."

"My mother was married when I was born so I'm legitimate, technically anyway."

"That shouldn't matter one way or the other," he said staunchly.

Alaina smiled and touched his cheek. "You're a good friend, Sean."

He raised her chin with his finger. "I want to be more than that to you," he said in a husky voice.

Alaina closed her eyes as his lips descended on hers. She kissed him back, waiting for the explosion of passion she'd come to expect. Sean's kiss was softly sweet and very pleasant, but it moved her not at all. When it ended, she felt only a vague sense of relief.

Sean's disappointment was obvious on his face as he gazed down at her. "I was hoping I was wrong," he said with a sigh. "Does Brady have any idea how lucky he is?"

Alaina didn't even pretend to misunderstand him. "He couldn't care less."

"Are you sure?"

Alaina looked down at her hands. "He's betrothed to the oh-so-beautiful and sophisticated Miss Prescott, isn't he? She's his choice, plain and simple."

"Then the man's a fool!" Sean's mouth twisted ruefully. "I'm tempted to ask you to marry me anyway. You might come to love me eventually."

"And cheat some woman out of her happy ever after?" Alaina said with a smile. "I think not. You're every woman's dream, you know."

He brushed her hair back from her face. "Not quite

every woman's, it would seem."

"I only wish I'd met you first."

"Me too. I guess it wasn't meant to be," he said philosophically. "What now?"

Alaina sighed. "I'm not going anywhere for a while. There's no way I'm going to face all those people."

"I would have never figured you for a coward."

"Well, I am, at least when it comes to polite society. I don't even want to think about what Susan's going to do to me. What I'd really like to do is take a nap. I didn't get much sleep this morning."

"You can't very well do that here."

Alaina glanced around. The ground was damp from the torrential rains of the day before, and there was nowhere else to stretch out. "I probably could," she said doubtfully, "but it wouldn't be very comfortable."

"I know a way to get to Major Goodrich's house without crossing the parade ground."

"You do?"

"I can't promise we won't see anyone, but it will be less conspicuous at least."

"Oh, Sean, you are a lifesaver," she said gratefully.

"That's me." He rose to his feet then held his hand out to her. "Shall we go?"

Their route took them behind the blacksmith's shop and the fuel storehouse. Then they cut between the laundress' quarters and the bakery, before following a line of trees right up to Major Goodrich's back door.

With a furtive glance toward the parade ground, Alaina scooted across the open ground in back of the house and up onto the porch.

Sean watched her with amusement. "You're really serious about not running into anyone, aren't you?"

"I think I'd rather face the renegades. They were less bloodthirsty." She paused with her hand on the door knob and gazed up at him. "Thank you, Sean. I really appreciate what you did for me."

"I wish I could do more," he said softly. "I wish—"

"Shhh, don't say it." She put her fingers against his lips. "You deserve a woman who loves you with her whole heart."

"The way you love Jared?"

Alaina looked away. "I'm sorry, Sean."

"Don't be. My sister always says the joy of falling in love is worth the pain of falling out. Besides, if you ever change your mind, I'll be right here as your friend. In the meantime, you've got a big brother to protect you from all the razor-tongued harpies out there." He brushed his lips across her forehead. "Sleep tight."

Alaina smiled at the image of him as her big brother. "I will."

She watched as he strode around the side of the house. Why hadn't she fallen in love with Sean? He wasn't irritated by everything she did the way Jared was. More importantly, he wasn't in love with another woman. Maybe if she'd come straight to Fort Bridger instead of going across the mountain with Jared things would have been different. One thing was for sure, being in love with Jared Brady wasn't a joy. It would be a pleasure to put him behind her. As the idea occurred to her, her heart seemed to twist in her chest.

Alaina turned the knob and went inside. She could hear Sybil's cook humming in the kitchen, but there were no other signs of life in the house. Good. Some explanation would have to be given to Sybil, as well as an apology to Susan. Alaina was more than happy to put both unpleasant tasks off until later. She had one foot on the stairs when the front door burst open behind her.

"Alonna!"

Cameron's voice halted her in her tracks and made her stomach clench painfully. Her heart sank as she turned to look at him. The expression on his face was thunderous.

"I suppose you want an explanation," she said, biting her lip.

"I'm more interested in apologies than excuses."

Alaina's eyes widened in surprise. "You don't care *why* I did it?"

"It's not as important as repairing the damage you did. I just came from Prescott's where Susan is still suffering from strong hysterics."

"Why am I not surprised?" she muttered.

"Do you blame her?"

"It was only a little mud," Alaina said. "She'll survive."

"That isn't the point."

"What is?"

Cameron's face turned an alarming shade of red. "Her father is the fort commander. He has almost complete control over my career."

Alaina's mouth fell open in surprise. "Surely you don't think my actions will have any effect on your career."

"Of course it will. Everything you do reflects directly on me."

"That's why you insisted on the new clothes and the fitting for the party dress," she said with dawning comprehension.

"It's imperative that you look your best, especially

at Susan's party. The entire fort will be there." He gave her a severe look. "And there won't be any repetition of this afternoon's display."

"Don't worry, I'm sure there won't be any mud around. Besides, I fully intend to apologize to Susan. That should soothe her ruffled feathers."

"And Brady?"

"What about him?"

"I hope you plan on apologizing to him too."

"I'll do no such thing," Alaina said indignantly. "He insulted me."

"So you hit him?"

She blushed and looked away in embarrassment. "H...he also kissed me against my will."

"That's no reason to cause such a ruckus."

Alaina's gaze flew to his face in shock. "Didn't you hear what I said? Jared Brady called me names, accused me of all sorts of indiscretions, and then manhandled me! All I did was teach him to keep his hands to himself."

"You could have done it in a less public place. Everybody who is anybody saw you sucker punch him. They also saw the new doctor lay him out again after you left."

"Ben hit him?" she asked in surprise.

"Knocked him cold. Now everyone is speculating what there is between you and the doctor."

"There's *nothing* between us except friendship. All Ben did was defend my honor the way any of my brothers or cousins would have. I don't understand why you're angry with me. Jared is the one at fault." Her eyes suddenly narrowed. "It's Susan isn't it? She's the one who said I was going to tarnish your reputation."

Cameron looked slightly uncomfortable. "She may have mentioned it."

"Yes, I'll just bet she did. She sure didn't waste any time getting even," Alaina said angrily. "Well, you've made your point and hers. Now if you'll excuse me, I'm going to go upstairs and get some sleep. If you had left me there this morning, none of this would have happened!"

With that, she pivoted on her heel and stomped up the stairs. At the top she turned and glared down at him. "And for your information, my name is not Alonna. It's Alaina; uh...la...nu. I'll thank you to remember it in the future." She stalked into her room and slammed the door.

Feeling battle-scarred and betrayed, she curled up into a tight little ball on her bed. How Cameron Price had allowed himself to be manipulated by that scheming little hussy was beyond comprehension.

For the second time that day the image of her parents rose in her mind. If she'd been at home, Papa would have been there to offer comfort and let her sob out her woes in his protective embrace instead of blaming everything on her. He wouldn't have approved of her behavior and probably would have expected her to apologize to Susan, but he'd have soothed and comforted his daughter first. Then he'd have gone out and given Jared Brady the thrashing he deserved.

For once, she wished the tears would come. Maybe they would release the anguish of her shattered dreams and blind disillusionment. Jared Brady was a selfish snake and Cameron Price was a conceited peacock. How wrongly she had judged them both.

Cameron Price was as self-centered as he was

handsome. Though he had been enamored with the idea of being a father, the novelty was wearing thin. The reality of it obviously wasn't what he'd expected. At last she was beginning to have a glimmering of why her mother had chosen the kind and gentle Garrick Ellinson over the more handsome and charming Cameron Price.

Still, he had welcomed her with open arms and given as much of himself as he had to give. He couldn't be blamed for having no idea how to deal with a daughter he'd never known.

As for Jared Brady, she had simply expected too much. Jared had never given her any reason to think he would fall in love with her. It was the foolish hope of a star-struck girl. She was wiser now, a woman instead of a child, one who recognized defeat and knew when to walk away.

Gradually the knot of anguish dissolved and was replaced by peaceful acceptance. As sleep overtook her, the germ of an idea jelled and became a full-blown conviction. It was time for her to leave Fort Bridger.

CHAPTER THIRTY-THREE

"**I** wish you could have stayed longer." Sybil sighed as she watched Alaina stuff her nightgown into a borrowed satchel in the early light of dawn. "We could have had such fun."

Alaina smiled. "I would have enjoyed it, too. You've been so kind to me."

"I was glad to have you. Your uncle and I are old friends, you know." Sybil blushed and pulled her dressing gown tighter around her middle. "Well, I guess you'd better go. Your young men are waiting downstairs in the parlor."

Alaina paused at the door. "My young men? I'm traveling with Dr. Stone!"

"All I know is what my servant said. Probably misspoke. It's not surprising at this ungodly hour. Why do you suppose Dr. Stone wants to leave so early?"

"He plans to catch the morning train. If we don't leave by six o'clock we'll have to wait until this afternoon." She gave her hostess an impulsive hug. "Thank you for everything."

"You're welcome. Have a good trip." Sybil watched from the top of the stairs as Alaina descended.

Alaina turned and waved at the entrance of the parlor, then stepped through the door. She came to a halt just inside the door and blinked in surprise. Sean and Ben sat in overstuffed chairs on either side of the fireplace. "What are you doing here?" she asked in surprise.

Sean rose to his feet. "We've come to escort you to Dr. Stone."

"I need to stop and say good-bye to my...uncle first," Alaina said.

Ben smiled. "We have a good half an hour before Dr. Stone wants to leave. Plenty of time."

But Alaina was staring at Sean. One eye was so black and blue it was nearly swollen shut.

"What happened to you?"

He darkened slightly. "I...ran into something."

"It looks terrible."

"You should have seen it yesterday," Ben said cheerfully. "Don't worry, he'll recover." He took her satchel in one hand and offered her his arm. "Shall we go?"

When they got outside, Sean took her other arm. "Are you sure you want to do this?" he asked as they started down Officer's Row. "This thing with Susan will die down soon enough. I think most people secretly admire you for your courage."

Alaina made a face. "For losing my temper, you mean? I'm not particularly proud of the way I acted yesterday."

"I heard you apologized for it."

"I'm afraid the apology made her as angry as pushing her into the mud puddle." Alaina grinned. "She had to accept it and pretend to put it all behind her, you see. That wasn't what she had in mind at all."

Ben frowned. "So why are you leaving if you don't have to worry about Susan?"

"It has nothing to do with Susan." Alaina sighed. "It's time to go home. I've been gone longer than I intended."

"And there's nothing we can do to change your mind?"

"No." She smiled up at them. "But it's sweet of you to ask."

"There are your uncle's quarters. Do you want us to come in with you?"

"No." She glanced uncertainly at the windows. No sign of life was visible beyond their glazed surface. "Do you think he's awake yet?"

Sean pulled out his pocket watch. "Should be. Muster is in thirty minutes."

"We'll wait here until you get back," Ben said, as the lieutenant opened the outside door for her.

Alaina nodded and gave them a fleeting smile before stepping inside to knock on her father's door.

"Come in," came the muffled voice from within.

Alaina wiped her hand nervously on her skirt, then opened the door and walked inside. Cameron sat at the table eating breakfast and reading what appeared to be a lengthy report. He didn't even look up as she walked in. "Just hang my jacket on the hook. I'll pick it up on the way out."

"It's me," she said quietly.

Cameron's head jerked up. "Alaina!"

Her lips twisted ironically. At least he finally got her name right.

"Sit down and join me for breakfast," he said with a smile. "I'll call Private Tubbs and tell him to bring another plate."

"No thanks. I just came to say good-bye."

"Good-bye! What for?"

"I think it's time I went home."

Cameron stared at her for a long moment. Then he laid his glasses on the table, before rising to his feet and pacing to the window. "I've done a lot of thinking about what I said to you yesterday."

"Oh?"

"I was wrong about you helping the doctor. You saved lives out there. As for the rest of it, I over-reacted, and I'm sorry."

Alaina was startled. She hadn't expected an apology, and didn't think it came easily. "I guess I did, too."

"Not according to Lieutenant Kirkpatrick," he said, turning to look at her.

Alaina frowned. "What are you talking about?"

"The big fight he had with Jared Brady yesterday."

"They fought?"

"You didn't know about it?"

"No." Alaina frowned. "Are you saying they fought over me?"

Cameron looked slightly disconcerted. "Uh...no. I don't really know what it was about. It probably didn't have anything to do with you. At any rate, it will all blow over soon enough."

"So everyone keeps saying," Alaina said sardonically, "just before they tell me something else I should be embarrassed about. "

"There's no reason for you to leave. Even Susan will have forgotten it in a day or two. "

Alaina sighed. "I'm not leaving because of Susan. I've accomplished what I came for, and it's time to go."

Cameron raised his brows. "And what was that?"

"I wanted to meet my father," she said softly. "And make up for what my mother put you through eighteen years ago."

"What your mother put *me* through!" Cameron stared at her in blank astonishment. "What are you talking about?"

"She turned her back on you for another man," Alaina said uncertainly. "Didn't she?"

"Not exactly." Cameron laughed humorlessly. "It was more like she gave me what I deserved, though I'll admit I didn't think so at the time."

"Mama didn't leave you for Papa?"

"No. She had the good sense to walk away and never look back."

Alaina frowned in confusion. "I don't understand."

"No, I don't suppose you do. If I'd had a lick of sense, I would have left her alone." Cameron ran his fingers through his hair roughly. "I joined the army at the end of the War Between the States then came out West to fight the Indians. I made Captain at the ripe old age of twenty and won the Medal of Honor when I was twenty-one. By the time I met your mother, I was used to getting whatever I wanted. Not only was she beautiful, she was the most sweetly giving person I'd ever met in my life. I'm ashamed to say I took far more than I had any right to."

"Then you didn't love her?" Alaina asked in a small voice.

Cameron exhaled sharply. "God yes I loved her! I spent weeks feeling sorry for myself after she left. Then I realized how miserable your mother would have been as an army wife, especially during the Indian Wars of the '70's. She'd have never come close to that picket fence with me. I probably wouldn't even have stayed faithful to her."

"How can you be sure?"

"Because I know myself," he said ruefully. "Don't waste your pity on me. It was through my own foolishness that I lost her. I didn't realize what I had until it was too late."

"You still love her," Alaina said in wonder. "I knew it."

"In a way I suppose I do, or at least my memory of her. There's never been another to match my Becky, and I don't think there ever will be." He smiled crookedly. "But if I'd married her, we'd have made each other thoroughly miserable. Look, it's all ancient history now, and better left buried."

Alaina looked away. "Everyone said I shouldn't come. Maybe they were right."

"No!" he said sharply. "They were dead wrong. Damn it, Alaina, you're my daughter, my own flesh and blood. You can't know what that means to me."

"It's meant a great deal of trouble, I'm afraid."

"Only because I don't know the proper way of being a father. I'm a soldier," he said. "I've spent my whole life destroying. You're the only worthwhile thing I ever created." He smiled tenderly. "You're the best of your mother and the best of me all rolled into one. The hardest part of having you here is not being able to tell the world you're my daughter. I'm so proud of you, I want to shout it to the skies."

"You expect me to believe you've enjoyed the last two days?"

Cameron grinned as he walked to his dresser and took something out. "Not particularly, but then I'm afraid your impetuous nature is one of the traits you inherited from me, along with that streak of independence. Yours caused you to push Susan Prescott into the mud." He held up a medal dangling from a red, white and blue ribbon. "Mine earned me this."

Alaina gazed at it curiously as he put it in her hand. The medal consisted of a bronze star suspended from the talons of an eagle and depicted a woman with a shield. "What is it?"

"My Medal of Honor. I earned it by sheer stupidity."

"Stupidity?"

"I volunteered for a suicide mission and, in the process, managed to rescue an entire company of men who were pinned down by the enemy. It wasn't heroism; it was idiocy. Only a fool would have done what I did. I didn't stop to think about it; I never do."

"But that's not the only time you've been a hero. I've heard story after story about your bravery."

"Oh, they're true enough, but I'm no hero. To be honest, I'm not even particularly brave; just a man who acts before he stops to consider the consequences." He touched her face. "That and my looks are all I've ever given you."

"What about all the money you left with Papa?"

Cameron frowned. "What money?"

"The money you gave him when you left South Pass City."

Cameron shook his head. "I never even saw them after your mother turned me down. They were gone before I even realized they were leaving. Whatever gave you that idea anyway?"

"I don't know. It doesn't matter." But it did matter. The money had been from Papa all along. It was just one more example of the unselfishness of Garrick Ellinson. "Maybe you've just never had the chance to give me anything."

"I never made the effort," he corrected as he folded her fingers around the medal. "I'm rather selfish, you see, and have more than my share of conceit. That's why I want you to have this. You bring out a part of me I'd forgotten even existed. I've been more honest with you in the last ten minutes than I was with your mother the whole time I knew her."

"I...I don't know what to say."

"Say thank you, Uncle Cameron." He smiled. "I'm not much good at showing it, but I do love you. I have since the first time I ever saw you as a bright-eyed baby with your mother's smile."

Impulsively, Alaina stood on her tiptoes and kissed him on the cheek. "Thank you, Father. I'll treasure it."

"Father," he murmured. "I kind of like the sound of that."

Alaina looked down at the medal in her hand. "I wish I had something to give you to remember me."

"You don't have to. I'll think of you every time I look in the mirror. No man could have a better daughter." He pulled her into his arms and gave her a big bear hug. "You'd better go now. Your two young men are waiting rather impatiently outside. I saw them through the window."

Alaina gazed up at him through a sheen of moisture. "I'll write."

"I think I'd like that," Cameron said with a smile. "Who knows, I might even get around to writing back."

Unable to speak, she turned to go. She was clear to the door when his voice stopped her once more.

"If you ever need me, I'll be here," he said softly. "Don't hesitate to ask."

Alaina nodded wordlessly and walked down the hall to the outside door.

"Here she is now." Ben stuck his watch back in his vest pocket. "We'll have to hurry if you're going to catch Dr. Stone. Everything all right?"

Alaina nodded. "He gave me this." She held up the medal.

Sean gave a low whistle. "That's a Medal of Honor! It's the most prestigious award in the army. Very few have ever been given. You must mean a great deal to him."

"That's what he said." She looked up at him. "He also told me you fought with Jared yesterday."

"We had words."

Ben chuckled. "Hard knuckled words. Don't worry, Jared wasn't hurt much worse than the good lieutenant here. He'll have some aches and pains for a while, but there's no permanent damage."

"It really wasn't necessary for either of you to defend me that way," Alaina said, "but I do appreciate it."

"What are friends for?" Sean said with a grin.

"Looks like Dr. Stone is ready to go," she said, as they rounded the corner by the commissary. "You've both been so wonderful, I hate to say good-bye."

"Then don't," Ben said promptly. "We'd rather you stayed."

"You're sweet, but I've already stayed too long."

"If you two scalawags are finished filling this young lady's head with nonsense, it's time we got going." Dr. Stone said in his gruff voice.

"I'm ready," Alaina said with a smile then kissed both Ben and Sean on the cheek. "Thank you for being such good friends."

They loaded her satchel then helped her into the wagon. Alaina surreptitiously scanned the area, searching for a last glimpse of Jared, but he was nowhere to be seen. Her last sight of Fort Bridger was Sean and Ben standing side-by-side watching her leave.

Sean and Ben were soon forgotten as her mind turned to the mystery surrounding her birth. Cameron's revelations had only served to muddy the waters. She wanted to know the whole story; to understand what had happened between Becky Ellinson and the two men who loved her all those years ago. Maybe Angel could be persuaded to share what she knew.

But it was the image of Jared Brady and the anguished realization that she was never going to see him again that haunted her as the wagon rolled down the dusty road.

CHAPTER THIRTY-FOUR

Alaina arrived unannounced at Angel's house, but her godmother welcomed her with open arms.

"I'm sorry I wasn't here to help you with the children and Ox when they were sick," Alaina said, as she emerged from Angel's rose-scented hug.

Angel waved her apology away. "They were all pretty much recovered by the time you knew they were sick."

"So everyone is better?"

They were right as rain three days after Susan left."

"I wasn't sure you'd want to see me after all the trouble I caused last time," Alaina said, not quite meeting her Godmother's eye.

"Well, of course I want to see you. We never did get a chance to visit. Besides, from what I gather your leaving was as much my brother's fault as yours, probably more, knowing him. There are times when he reminds me very much of our father." She gave Alaina a sidelong glance as she led her into the parlor. "How is my baby brother anyway? I take it he survived his bout of chicken pox."

"Jared was fine yesterday when I last saw him."

"You didn't tell him good-bye when you left this morning?"

Alaina shrugged. "I doubt he was awake yet. We left at first light."

"And how is Susan?" Angel asked with seeming

nonchalance.

"Probably still a little out of sorts." Alaina permitted herself a small smile. "She fell into a mud puddle yesterday."

Angel's eyebrows rose a fraction. "Really? How...clumsy of her."

"Yes, it was." Alaina's smile faded. "But I'm sure she'll snap out of it soon enough. Her parents are throwing a big party tomorrow night to announce her engagement to Jared." She was vaguely surprised by the twist of pain the words caused. Would she ever be able to think of him without wanting to burst into tears?

"You decided not to stay for the party?"

"No. It's time for me to go home."

"I see," Angel said in a voice that made it sound as though she saw a great deal indeed.

Alaina gave her a sharp look, but Angel's expression was bland. "It's a good thing you came today."

"Oh?"

"Ox has business in Chicago next week. So he thought he might take a little side trip to see your parents. If you're ready to go home, then we might as well pack up the children and go with him. I've been wanting to visit your mother."

"Mama and Papa would love that. When would we leave?"

"Tomorrow." Angel smiled. "That is if you don't mind leaving so soon."

"No, I've done everything in Wyoming I came to do."

"You found Cameron, then?"

Alaina nodded. "At first I couldn't understand why Mama picked Papa over him."

Angel gave a wry smile. "But once you got to know him you figured it out, right?"

"Kind of, but I still don't know what happened. If Cameron loved her as much as he said, how did Papa come into the picture? Did he fall in love with her and somehow manage to woo her away?"

Angel gave an unlady-like snort. "Not likely. Your mother practically had to beat Garrick over the head to get him to admit he loved her."

"Then Mama fell for Papa while she was with Cameron? None of this makes any sense, Angel. The more I learn, the more confused I become."

Angel sighed. "And you want me to straighten it all out for you, I suppose."

"You're the only one who can. Mama won't. Cameron told me she gave him what he deserved but wouldn't say why. Papa...well..."

"...Papa doesn't say anything," Angel finished for her.

"Only that I had a right to know my real father."

Angel gazed at her silently for a moment then shook her head. "It beats me how I always wind up being the one who straightens out this mess. I had to do the same thing with your parents eighteen years ago."

"Then you'll tell me everything?"

"As much as I know. Did Becky ever tell you about her father?"

"Only that he died and left her with nothing but a day's wages and an old tent."

"Which were all gone soon enough in a mining town like South Pass City. She sold everything she owned and was on the verge of starvation when Garrick pulled her out of a flooded creek. I never knew how she got there or how he managed to save her, but she was bedraggled and half-dead when he brought her to me in the middle of the night. By the next morning they'd decided to get married."

"Then he was in love with her?"

"To my knowledge they'd never laid eyes on each other before that night." Angel said dispassionately. "He married her because she was alone and pregnant and had run out of options."

"Where was Cameron?"

"Long gone. He seduced your mother and then left one night without a word. To be fair, I don't think he had any idea you were on the way."

"Would he have stayed if he had?"

"It's hard saying. I do know it was his duties in the army that called him away. At any rate, your mother and Garrick settled down in a little cabin at the edge of town. Their marriage wasn't without its bumps, but I think they were well pleased with the bargain they'd made. You were born early that winter in the middle of a blizzard."

"In a storm so bad they couldn't send for the doctor, so Papa delivered me himself," Alaina said. "That's one story they have told me."

Angel smiled. "I'm not surprised. I think it was a pretty harrowing experience for both of them. Anyway, that's when Becky realized she was in love with him, though it took Garrick a lot longer to wake up."

"But I don't understand. How did Cameron come into it if they were married and in love? You said he wasn't even around."

Angel pursed her lips. "That's the really strange part. Ox was a bullwhacker at the time that brought freight into South Pass City. There was an accident and he broke his right arm. Garrick felt responsible, so he insisted on driving Ox's circuit with him to save the business."

"But that must have taken weeks!" Alaina exclaimed.

"Three to be exact. Garrick found someone to run his blacksmith shop while he was gone. Becky was not best pleased with him. I think they had words before he left, but I'm certain he had every intention of coming home to her at the end of the circuit."

"You mean he didn't?"

"Not exactly. The afternoon before they got back to South Pass City, Ox and Garrick stumbled onto a camp of outlaws. They would probably have left well enough alone except there was a captive. They couldn't abide the thought of leaving him there, so Garrick came up with an elaborate rescue plan."

"Cameron," Alaina murmured. "He told me Papa saved his life."

"He did, but it wasn't until later he realized who he'd saved. That's when things started to get complicated. You see Garrick wasn't really married to your mother."

"What?"

"Garrick used a fake surname when they took their vows. He figured the time would come when she wanted out of their marriage of convenience. When Cameron showed up wanting to marry Becky, Garrick thought the time had come, so he told her the truth about their marriage."

"But by that time she'd fallen in love with Papa and didn't want to marry Cameron anymore," Alaina said in wonder.

"Precisely. Of course, your mother thought Garrick wanted his freedom so she pretended to go along with Cameron's courtship for a while; too darn long in my opinion, not that anyone asked me."

"In the end she chose Papa."

"Of course she did, just as anybody with half a brain would. Cameron is nice to look at and could charm the queen out of her bloomers, but there's no substance to him. Garrick is as solid as they come."

"I found that out the hard way." Alaina looked down at her hands. "Do you think Papa will ever forgive me?"

"If I know Garrick Ellinson, he already has. Family is important to him."

"But I'm not really his daughter."

Angel made a rude sound. "His blood may not run in your veins, but I never saw any man love a baby more than he did you. Besides, it's only your perception that's changed; he's always known you weren't his natural daughter. Has he ever treated you any differently than the others?"

"No."

"There, you see? As far as he's concerned, you're his. It only takes an act of lust to beget a child. Being a father takes a whole lot more. Garrick Ellinson has been a father to you in every way that matters since the day you were born."

Alaina thought of Angel's words a great deal over the next few days. There was plenty of time for contemplation during the trip to Minnesota. All that had happened kept revolving in her head like a giant pinwheel. Her mother's situation had not been so different from her own, after all. By the time they arrived she had reached two monumental decisions. One was that she was strong enough to relegate Jared Brady to her past the same way her mother had Cameron Price. No matter how much she loved him or how badly it hurt, she would forget him as completely as Becky had forgotten Cameron.

The other became a driving force that grew stronger the closer they came to home. By the time they had all stepped off the stagecoach, it was nearly unbearable.

"Alaina!"

She hardly had time to see who had called her name before her feet left the ground. "Sven, put me down," she cried as he lifted her high and swung her around in his arms.

"I've missed you," he said with a big grin. "No one to tease."

"And I haven't had anyone's ears to box. Thanks for getting me up here where I can reach them," she said, laughing down at him.

"Must be some relation of Garrick's," she heard Ox say to Angel as Sven set her back on her feet with an expression of mock fear. "Nobody else is that big."

"Sven, do you think you could arrange some sort of transportation out to the house?" Alaina asked.

"Ja. I'm just now getting off work. I'll drive you all out myself."

"Thanks, Sven, you're the best of cousins," Alaina said. "Tell Mama I'll be along shortly."

"You aren't going with us?" Angel asked in surprise.

"Not just yet. There's something I have to do first."

An odd combination of anticipation and nervousness assailed her as she walked down the familiar street toward the blacksmith shop. Over and over she practiced the speech she had planned. It was the perfect blend of apology and adult independence.

Almost before she realized it, she was there. As she stood in the doorway of the smithy, the essence of the place overwhelmed her. The acrid smell of the forge and the rhythmic pounding of the hammer swirled around her like an old friend. From out of nowhere came a blast of homesickness so intense it nearly buckled her knees.

As if he felt her presence, Garrick looked up from his work. Uncertainty showed on his face as they stared at each other; her last words hung between them like invisible shards of glass. Alaina opened her mouth to reassure him, but all her carefully rehearsed phrases fled from her mind like autumn leaves before the wind. From deep inside came a single word so fraught with emotion that it felt as though it was being ripped from her. "*Papa!*"

Then she was running across the cinder floor straight into his outstretched arms.

CHAPTER THIRTY-FIVE

"Sand along the grain of the wood, Alaina." Garrick moved her hand up and down along the board. "That's it. See how much smoother it is?"

"Look how it brings out the lines in the wood. This is going to be really pretty when we get done," Alaina said. Garrick's woodworking hobby held little interest for her as she was growing up. In the four months since she'd been home she'd changed her mind.

"Ja, all it takes is good wood and a little elbow grease. When you get it all sanded down we'll oil it."

"Papa!" A voice called from the door of the barn.

"In the wood shop, Lars," Garrick called out.

A moment later, Alaina's younger brother appeared in the doorway slightly out of breath. "There's someone here to see you."

"Who is it?"

"I don't know, but Mama says you're to come up to the house right away."

"I'll be up in a minute."

"No, Papa, she said right now. It's really important."

Garrick looked surprised then rose to his feet. "I guess I'd better go see what has Mama all excited. Don't forget to bank the fire when you leave, Alaina."

"All right, Papa." She glanced at her brother as Garrick walked through the barn and disappeared outside. "Have you chopped Mama's wood yet?"

"Do I have to?"

"If you want fresh bread you'd better. Tomorrow is baking day."

"How come you don't have to do anything?"

"I helped Mama with laundry all morning. Besides, I'm going to take care of Taffy for Papa."

"You aren't my boss."

"No, but I can still take you down and sit on you. Now scoot!"

Lars gave her a disgruntled look, then hunched his shoulders and left the barn.

Alaina watched him go then turned back to the woodshop with a sigh. She'd come home from Wyoming and slipped right back into her old life as though nothing had changed. Yet, some things would never be the same.

She ran her hand along the smooth wood once more then carefully banked the fire in the little pot-bellied stove. By now she'd expected to be completely over Jared Brady, to have him fade into the back of her mind like the fond memory he should have become. It hadn't happened that way. If anything, her pain was worse than before.

In a gesture that had become a habit, she reached into her pocket and pulled out Jared's handkerchief. There were still faint mud stains on the cloth and the edges were beginning to fray, but it was her most prized possession; the last tangible piece of him she had, at least for now. She closed her eyes and rubbed it against her cheek. With the wedding only a few weeks away, final preparations would surely be underway. Jared's sister and brother-in-law would be arriving from England any day now, and Susan was no doubt in her element.

With an irritated sigh, Alaina stuffed the handkerchief back into her pocket. She had better things to do than torture herself this way. She gave the horse, Taffy, a generous armload of hay then put on her coat and pulled it closed against the bite of the Minnesota winter before she walked through the barn to get water.

As she crossed the barnyard to the well, she glanced at the unfamiliar horse tied to the hitching rack in front of the house and frowned. It had been ridden hard. The last thing it should be doing was standing in the cold like that. On the other hand, her father's visitor was obviously in a hurry and might not appreciate coming out and finding his horse gone. She stood there for a moment trying to decide what to do then shrugged. Walking the few feet to the barn wouldn't slow him down enough to worry about, and it might save his horse from taking a chill.

"Lars," she called. "When Papa's visitor comes out, tell him his horse is in the barn."

"Do it yourself."

"Fine, I will, and while I'm doing that you can feed and water both horses."

"All right," he said with ill-grace, "you win. I'll tell him."

"Thanks, Lars, I knew I could count on you," she murmured sarcastically. It only took a few minutes to lead the stranger's horse into the barn and give it an armload of hay. A few lazy snowflakes were beginning to drift down as she went to the well to draw the water. Papa had told her to get one of the boys to do any heavy lifting for her, but Lars was being difficult and none of the others were around. She settled for filling the bucket only part way and making several trips. By the time she'd carried enough water for both horses the snow was coming down steadily and a ten minute job had already taken her over half an hour.

It was time to go in and help Mama fix supper, but she found herself reluctant to leave the serenity of the barn. Her brothers would all be finishing up their chores and trooping inside. Usually the noisy household didn't bother her, but tonight the solitude of the barn appealed to her for some reason. What she needed was an excuse to stay for a few minutes. Her gaze lit on the stranger's horse, and she smiled. Since the owner hadn't appeared again, chances were good that he'd be staying for dinner. If that were the case, the animal needed to be tended to. Mama might even approve of her thoughtfulness.

"Too bad I can't take your saddle off," she murmured soothingly as she rubbed its neck. "I'll bet you could use a good rubdown. I can't imagine what your owner was thinking of to leave you standing out in the cold like that."

"I had other things on my mind," said a deep voice behind her.

Alaina whirled around. Her heart jumped to her throat and her stomach twisted in the strangest way as she stared at the achingly familiar figure in the doorway. "Jared?" she whispered.

"What are you doing here?"

"I had some business to discuss with Garrick."

"Oh." She turned back to the horse. "Are you staying the night?" she asked, trying to sound nonchalant.

"That depends."

"On what?"

"On you." He came into the barn and stood where she could just see him out of the corner of her eye. "Do you want me to stay?"

She never wanted anything so badly in her life. "Sure, why not? You can tell me how everyone at the fort is doing."

"That's the only reason?"

"What other reason could I have?"

"It seems to me that you and I have some unfinished business."

Alaina knew a moment of panic then forced herself to be calm. Papa wouldn't have betrayed her. Besides, he had no way of knowing that Jared was the one..."Not that I remember," she said cautiously.

"Then you have a poor memory. I spent the most of the last day you were at the fort trying to talk to you. When I wasn't being beat to a pulp by those self-appointed watchdogs of yours, that is."

"Ben and Sean thought they were protecting me."

Jared snorted. "It seems to me you did a pretty good job of protecting yourself."

"When you have as many brothers and cousins as I do, you learn how to make an impression."

"I was afraid you and Sven would be married by now."

"He asked me, but I turned him down."

"I thought the two of you had an understanding."

"I said we'd discussed marriage." Alaina smiled slightly to herself. "Of course, that was before Priscilla Drake moved to town. My cousin is what you might call smitten."

"And you don't mind?"

"No, I found I wasn't really in love with him after all," she said without raising her eyes from the horse. "Why don't you take this saddle off so I can give her a decent brushing?"

"Does that mean you want me to stay?"

Alaina shrugged. "You wouldn't get very far in this snow. Besides, Mama probably already has an extra place set for dinner."

Jared gave a frustrated sigh. "I'll take that for a yes."

She stepped back so he could get close enough to remove the saddle. Instead, he reached into his saddle bag and pulled out a bulky package.

"This is for you," he said, then turned his attention to the saddle.

Alaina stared down at the bundle in her hand. "What is it?"

"Why don't you open it and find out?" he said, as he threw the stirrup over the horn and started to undo the latigo strap that held the cinch tight.

Curiously, she untied the rawhide string. "The moccasins and mittens Whiskey Jug made for Susan," she gasped in surprise as the bundle fell open.

"The moccasins and mittens I had him make for my fiancée," he corrected. "If you'll notice, they're the wrong size for Susan." Jared threw the saddle over an empty saddle horse. "Whiskey Jug said he figured I'd come to my senses eventually and realize I was engaged to the wrong woman."

Alaina's breath caught in her throat. "And did you?"

"I think I'd known it for a long time," he said, "but it kind of hit me between the eyes during a hail storm." He reached out and traced her cheek with the back of his fingers. "Three little words wrecked more havoc on me than the tornado."

"What three words?" Her voice was barely discernible as she gazed up at him in rapt wonder.

"I love you," he murmured against her lips.

Alaina's breath escaped in a soft whoosh as his mouth caressed hers with gentle insistence. There was never any thought of resistance, in fact she didn't think at all, just reacted. The mittens and moccasins dropped to the floor forgotten, and her hands slid up his arms to his neck. She opened to him like a flower to the summer sunshine as their mouths molded together in glad recognition.

At last, Jared ended it by planting lingering little kisses against her lips as though he couldn't quite bring himself to break contact. "Would you say either of us is in the slightest danger right now?" he whispered watching her tenderly.

After a moment she opened her eyes and gazed up at him with a bemused look. "Danger?"

"Are you frightened?"

"No."

"And you melted in my arms anyway. So much for your excuses. What's between us isn't caused by fear," he said, running the pad of his thumb across her lips. "Aren't you curious about my business with your father?"

"A little."

"I came to ask for his daughter's hand in marriage." Jared pushed her hair back from her face. "He didn't seem particularly surprised."

Alaina tried to control the wild beating of her heart. Could it be that he really *wanted* to marry her? "What about Susan?"

"Susan decided we wouldn't suit." Jared smiled slightly. "I think it may have had something to do with the hunting trip I invited her to go on."

Alaina's mouth fell open. "Susan, hunting?"

"Drastic times call for drastic measures. I suspect Mrs. Prescott had an inkling of the way the wind was blowing last summer. She canceled the engagement party, and the Colonel sent me off to the mountains with the surveying crew before I had a chance to break it off and come after you. While I was gone, Susan and her mother made sure everyone in the fort knew we were engaged. By the time I got back the first of November, our betrothal was as solid as a brick wall."

"So you took Susan hunting?"

"I didn't have to. The threat of it was enough to send her running." He sighed dramatically. "I have a feeling her heart was given elsewhere by then anyway. I'd been gone for nearly four months. You can't expect someone to stay in love in the face of those kind of odds."

Alaina suddenly became extremely interested in the top button of his shirt. "I did," she murmured, staring intently at the mother of pearl circle.

There was a moment of silence then he tipped her chin up with his finger. "You did what?" he asked searching her face hopefully.

"I stayed in love with you. I thought it would fade, but it hasn't. When I saw you in that door..."

"She was right, then," he said, closing his eyes in relief.

"Who?"

"Brandy. She said you were madly in love with me."

"I tried to make it go away." She began twisting the button on his shirt nervously. "I did everything I could to forget you."

He smiled and rested his forehead against hers. "I spent most of May trying to convince myself you irritated the hell out of me. By the time I got to Fort

Bridger in June, I was going crazy searching for a way to force you to marry me. In July, Brandy told me what an idiot I was and said all I had to do was confess that I couldn't live without you."

"You can't?"

"No." Jared grinned. "The way I see it, marrying me is the least you can do. After all, you spent an entire day with Ben Corbett saving the lives of men you didn't even know."

"What did Papa tell you when you asked him for permission to marry me?" she asked in a small voice.

"That it was up to you."

"I love you Jared," she whispered. "I don't want to spend the rest of my life without you either."

She felt the tautness leave his body. "Thank God," he murmured.

Their lips met and locked in the darkness.

"Just what do you two think you're doing out there?" Alaina and Jared jerked apart and froze as her mother's voice came through the thickening snow outside.

There was a long pause. "Aw, Mama," said a young male voice just outside the door. "We weren't doin' nothin' bad."

"We just wanted to meet Alaina's beau."

"There will be plenty of time for that later. You're not going to make much of an impression sneaking around spying on them are you?"

"But, Mama, Alaina won't care."

"That's all you know about it," Becky said. "The last thing she wants right now is an audience. Now get in there and wash up for supper."

"Heck!" Lars grumbled. "It was just gettin' to the

good part."

"How are we going to know who won the bet if we have to leave now?"

"I don't know. Maybe we can sneak back out later..." The voices gradually faded away until the sound of the front door closing cut them off completely.

Jared chuckled. "My future brothers-in-law, I take it."

"They aren't going to live long enough to be your brothers-in-law," she muttered.

"It sort of reminds me of the things Shannon and I used to do to Ox and Angel," he said. "By the way, Garrick told me to be sure and ask you to show me the furniture project he's helping you with."

Alaina thanked heaven for the darkness of the barn as she felt herself blushing to the roots of her hair. She bent down to scoop up the mittens and moccasins to hide her embarrassment. "It isn't finished yet."

"Your father said that. He also said not to take no for an answer."

"All right," she said finally. "It's in the woodshop."

Alaina could almost feel his curious stare as she led him through the barn to Garrick's shop in the back. It only took a moment to find the matches and light the lantern. "It's over there on the bench," she said, as she carefully adjusted the wick and put the glass chimney back in place.

Alaina heard him walk across the tiny room to look. She swallowed hard and waited. An eternity passed. At last she couldn't stand it any longer and turned around.

"It looks like the pieces of a cradle," he said finally.

Alaina closed her eyes against the astonishment on his face. "It is."

A heartbeat later he had crossed the room, and she felt his hand moving over her coat, feeling the rounded flesh beneath its concealing bulk.

"My God, you said you were sure!"

"I lied," she said, opening her eyes. "Brandy told me I shouldn't, but it was the only way I could think of to find out whether you wanted me or Susan." She gazed up at him miserably. "Thirty minutes later you and Susan were officially engaged."

"I thought you didn't want me so I tried to convince myself it was her I loved."

"Really?" Alaina saw the truth of it on his face and felt a little of the ice around her heart thaw. "We've been a pair of fools haven't we?"

"You're going to have my baby." His face was filled with wonder as his hand went back to her stomach. "I'm surprised Garrick didn't come after me with a shot gun."

"He would have if I hadn't been so stubborn and had told him who to go after."

"Why didn't you let me know as soon as you found out?"

"You were out on the surveying crew. I figured by the time you got back to the fort, it would be too late. You were planning to get married in December."

"Looks like I still am," he said with a wicked grin. "There's no way you'll wiggle out of this once I fess up to your parents. They'll drag us both to the altar. No wonder Garrick was so pleased to see me!"

"What about your family?"

"As a matter of fact, they're all waiting on pins and needles to see if I'll be successful in my suit. I can have them all gathered in one place within a week, including Shannon and Robbie. What about yours?"

"They're all here." She shrugged. "Except Cameron of course, and I don't suppose Mama would be best pleased to see him."

Jared chuckled. "Maybe we should have a double wedding."

"What?"

"I told you Susan had given her heart elsewhere," he said. "What I didn't tell you is that she's going to be your new stepmother."

"My new..." Alaina's eyes widened. "Susan and Cameron? But he's old enough to be her father," she said incredulously.

"Maybe, but I think she's always had a partiality for him."

Alaina was thoughtful for a moment then nodded slowly. Elise had said as much the night of the dinner party. Suddenly she began to grin. "What a perfect match!" she said. "They were made for each other. Why, the wedding alone will be enough to dazzle the mind."

"Susan and her mother were already deep into the planning stage when I left. I wouldn't be surprised if Susan and Cameron are married before we are."

Alaina started to giggle, and he blinked in surprise. "What's so funny?"

"Oh, Jared, I just realized, in about four months Susan's going to be a grandmother!"

"Good Lord!"

"Can you imagine how pleased she'll be?"

Jared grinned. "You're going to pay Susan back for every mean thing she ever did to you without lifting a finger. When do you plan to let them know about the blessed event?"

"There's no hurry. Good manners dictate that I

invite them to the christening of their first grandchild. That should be plenty early enough."

"It also won't give Susan any time to prepare if Cameron decides to brag about being a grandpa."

Alaina sighed in satisfaction. "There is a God in heaven."

Jared laughed. "I think I'm glad you're on my side." He lifted her chin with the crook of his finger and gazed down at her. "You still haven't given me my answer."

"You haven't asked me yet."

"Will you marry me, or do I just carry you off to the woods? We could build a lean-to and wait for Garrick to hunt us down so he can force me to do right by you."

Alaina looked thoughtful. "You know, that does have possibilities. The way it's snowing, Papa might not find us for days." She sighed dramatically. "But Mama already has dinner on the table and won't appreciate the delay. So, I suppose I'd better say yes."

"I knew I liked your mother." He traced the line of her jaw with his knuckles.

"We'd probably better go in to dinner while the food's still hot," she said regretfully. "You must be hungry after your long trip."

"Starved," Jared murmured as he undid her hair and let it fall around her shoulders. He gave a soft groan as he ran his fingers through the soft silken mass. "All I've been able to think about for months is the taste of wild honey." He lowered his head to hers. "I'm afraid your mother's good home cooking will be stone cold by the time we get there."

And it was.

ABOUT THE AUTHOR

Carolyn Lampman has won several industry awards for her previous novels, including the National Reader's Choice Award and the Coeur Du Bois Heart of Romance award. She was also a finalist for RWA's coveted RITA and the EPPIE. Carolyn lives in a small town in Wyoming with her husband, a Welsh Corgi, and a herd of grandchildren who come and go.

Made in the USA
Middletown, DE
17 August 2023

36866960R00239